I0524340

Where Have all the Young Girls Gone?

Vicki Wootton

Published by
Stargate Publishing
Vancouver, Canada

Where Have all the Young Girls Gone?

ISBN: Print: 978-1-989149-07-2
Copyright © by Vicki Wootton, August 2018
Revised edition 2016

All rights reserved. No part of this book may be reproduced or transmitted in any form or by any means, electronic or mechanical, including photocopying, recording, or by any information storage or retrieval system, without permission in writing from the copyright owner.

This is a work of fiction. Names, characters, incidents, and some places are products of the author's imagination and are used fictitiously, and any resemblance to any actual person, living or dead, or events are entirely coincidental.

Cover photo © Patrice Dufour of Vancouver, used with permission
Photo of girl's face © Marek Bernat, used with permission.

Other works by author

Speculative Fiction novels
Fatal Harvest 2002,
Forbidden World, 2006, revised 2015
Reluctant Warriors, 2008, revised 2017
At War with Terror (2013),

Fantasy
The Children of Light Trilogy (The Whisperer) 2016-
2018
Aisling's Revelation 2018

Reference
Names of the World. 2008

Blog: https://vwrite.online/

JULIA

Chapter One

"The worldwide decline in female births is already causing a noticeable decrease in world population," Doctor Simon Livingston of the Social Sciences Department at the University of British Columbia stated at the World Congress on Population in Sidney, Australia last week. Doctor Livingston continued, "Across the world, the average male/female birth ratio is now 5:1", which means that five male babies are born for every female.

This trend was first noticed in Vancouver in 2012 when hospitals reported boy babies outnumbered girl babies five to four. It has taken a mere 28 years to reach the current ratio. There is room for guarded optimism, however; the rate of decline has leveled off slightly over the past five years. Scientists in many fields continue to speculate on the reason for this crisis, but no one yet has come up with the cause, or suggested a viable solution.

Report in the Vancouver Globe, August 2040

Aldina Finisterra stopped playing the piano in the middle of Lennon and McCartney's Eleanor Rigby, breaking her husband Raymond's concentration. He looked at her, eyebrows raised.

"Sorry," she said. She put both hands behind her hips and straightened her back.

"What's wrong, love?"

"Nothing. Just a little twinge." She leaned forward and adjusted the score. "Let's try again from beginning of the chorus."

Members of a string quartet, Raymond and Aldina were rehearsing Raymond's new arrangement of the Revolver Suite for an impending festival celebrating the centenary of John Lennon's birth. They were rehearsing at home by themselves because of Aldina's advanced pregnancy.

Aldina was a big woman, tall and robust, with warm grey eyes, straw-colored hair, and the complexion of someone who spends a lot of time out of doors. She was wearing a pale blue coatdress of lightweight cotton.

Raymond leaned his cello against the piano and went over to her. "Has she decided to come finally?" The baby was already a week overdue.

"This could be it," Aldina replied. "Trust her to announce her arrival in the middle of a rehearsal." She put her hands on the keyboard. "Come on, Ray, let's at least finish Eleanor."

They continued to play for a few more minutes, but their concentration was off and they finally gave up.

"Maybe that's what we should call her," Raymond said as he closed the lid of his cello case. "Eleanor."

"No, it doesn't do anything for me." Aldina put the cover down over the piano keys and stood up. "I've got a better idea, how about Julia, after John Lennon's mother? It's a pretty name."

"Nice, and appropriate," Raymond replied. "And she'll even have a Lennon-McCartney song all her own." He put his arm around her shoulder and walked her out of the room.

"Are you ready to go to the clinic?"

"Not yet. There's plenty of time, if the boys are anything to go by. Let's have some lunch first. I hope you remembered to plug the car in; I'd hate to have the battery die on us halfway there."

"Of course I did, but I'll check anyway to ease your mind."

Their three sons, John, Paul, and David, had gone to stay with their maternal grandmother in Chilliwack until the baby was born and Raymond was on leave from his day job as a landscaper with the city parks board.

About four hours after the first twinge, Raymond unplugged the car and drove Aldina to the Arbutus Park Health Cooperative, a family health clinic in Kitsilano, where the baby would be born.

The clinic was a full city-block of converted townhouses. The site of the Arbutus Park Co-op had been purchased five years earlier. Plummeting housing prices tied to the population decline made such projects much easier to finance. It was jointly owned by the co-op members—mostly healthcare recipients— and the group of gay healthcare practitioners that ran it. The staff included just about every field of healthcare professional from lab technicians to surgeons. Some of the townhouses had been joined together to form larger units, and the insides of most of them had been gutted and fitted for a variety of purposes. Parts of central courtyard had been glassed over and turned into atria, which, with plants in containers and casual seating, provided a pleasant area for convalescents and patients waiting for treatment.

Many low-risk births and minor surgical procedures took place in small clinics run as co-ops. They had a warmer, homier atmosphere than hospitals, which contributed to the clients' comfort and reduced anxiety. They also had the advantage of being able to provide healthcare at cost.

Raymond parked the car in the parking area under the buildings. He helped Aldina in her struggle to get out and followed her up the stairs that led to the central atrium. They went straight to the cluster of units that housed the maternity unit.

Aldina had chosen to have a water birth. When she reached the third stage of labor, the midwife, Jeff, and his assistant helped her down into the warm pool, which was about three meters in diameter. Both Jeff and Sam, the nurse, climbed into the pool with her, wearing white shorts. Raymond sat on the edge with his legs dangling in the water, supporting Aldina's head.

Julia made her appearance at seven fourteen p.m., although, as Jeff noted, her black hair had been in evidence for several minutes ahead of the rest of her.

"Here she is, Alda," Jeff said, handing her the towel wrapped infant. "A perfect little girl."

As often happened when a girl was born, there was a reporter waiting for them when they left the delivery suite. Raymond groaned.

"Be thankful there's only one," Jeff murmured, patting Aldina's arm. "Let him take a picture, then I'll get rid of him."

"How are you feeling, Ms Finisterra?" the reporter asked.

"Tired," she replied.

"Mind if I get a picture of the baby for the Vancouver Globe?"

"If you must, but make it quick. My wife needs to rest."

"What are you going to call her?"

"Julia." Raymond and Aldina replied simultaneously.

As soon as the reporter had snapped a picture, Raymond pushed Aldina's recliner through a door and nudged it shut, leaving Jeff to answer questions."

When her brothers came home from Chilliwack on Julia's third day, they watched their mother's every move as she tended the baby, fascinated by the little girl. At first, they took an inordinate amount of interest in the novelty of their baby sister, but their natural exuberance took over after a few days and they started going out again with their friends, relating all they had learned about this mysterious creature, the girl.

During her toddling years, Julia was both protected by her brothers and exploited when they subjected her to undignified exhibitions of her female attributes for their friends.

However, she took the curiosity of the boys in her stride, soon learning that these events would usually be rewarded by some sort of treat. She seemed to know instinctively it would be inappropriate to tell their parents. It wasn't that she was a pushover; she soon came to realize that she could usually turn the situation to her advantage. In addition, she was quite capable of digging her heels in when things didn't go her way.

It started when she was two. She was playing in the sand box, shoveling sand into one of David's toy trucks, when her second oldest brother John joined her, accompanied by his friend Victor.

"Hey, Julia, want an ice cream?" John asked. He was a sturdy six-year-old with reddish brown hair and blue eyes.

She looked up from her pile of dirt. "I-cweam." She dropped the spade and stood up, looking at her brother expectantly.

"Yeah, but first I want you to do something for me." He took her hand and led her into the shrubbery at the end of the garden, then kneeling down in front of her, undid her diaper.

His friend, Vic crowded behind him, looking over his shoulder. "I can't see anything," he complained. "Make her lie down."

"Why don't you lie down so I can put your diaper back on? Then we can go get some ice cream," John said.

Once the diaper was back in place, John picked her up. "Good girl."

"I cweam," she replied.

Julia was an attractive child with creamy skin, thick dark hair, and soulful brown eyes. She got her coloring from her father, and she had inherited her mother's inner strength.

Julia started school when she was four. There were twenty-two boys in her class and eight girls, which was about average ratio in that particular school. Although she attended public school, Julia was never allowed to go anywhere without an escort for protection. It had been apparent for years that girls and women had to be safeguarded, not only from unwanted attention, but also from the threat of abduction and assault.

Chapter Two

First boy: "I bet you don't know what's over that wall."
Second boy: "I do so... What?"
First boy: "It's the girls' school."
Second boy: "Wow! Have you ever met a girl?"
First boy: "Uh, uh. My brother has, though."

Overheard conversation

What's wrong, Farida?" Julia asked her friend. Farida had been moody and downcast for several days, sometimes lashing out at Julia for no apparent reason. This time, she responded by bursting into tears. She sobbed for a few moments, her shoulders heaving, while Julia comforted her by patting her back. Finally, she stopped and looked at Julia, her eyes still swimming in tears.

"My father's going sell me," she announced.

"What?" Eleven year-old Julia was horrified. She'd heard of things like that happening in far-away places, but not in Canada. "Are you serious? People can't sell people, not even their fathers."

"Well he is," Farida asserted.

"Who's he selling you to?"

"Some rich guy at the temple. He's some sort of big shot there. My mom says he's got about a zillion sons and he's trying to find wives for them. He wants me to marry the oldest."

"Ugh, yuk! You're not serious. You aren't old enough to get married."

"But it's true," Farida insisted.

"When?"

"I don't know. Soon, though."

Julia was beginning to believe Farida. After she considered it for a moment, the idea began to take on a certain glamour.

"Do you have to go live with him, when you're married?"

"Of course."

"Will you have to ... you know ... like, sleep with him?" Julia squirmed uncomfortably at the idea.

"Not 'til I'm old enough."

"When will that be?" Julia didn't know whether to feel sorry for her friend or envy her. It sounded so grown-up.

"My mom said when my periods start."

"God, that's awful. How old is this guy? What's he like?"

"He's about nineteen. I haven't met him. I hope he's not a fat little man like his father."

"God, that's so old." Julia sat, pensive, for a moment, trying to put herself in Farida's place. The idea gave her a shivery feeling. She couldn't imagine marrying someone she had never met, but assumed it was customary in Farida's culture.

"I'll run away," Farida said miserably, but without much conviction.

"You can't do that," Julia replied, "Where would you go?"

"I don't know. I'll think of something."

"What are you two whispering about?" Julia's youngest brother, David, was coming across the lawn from the house.

"Hey, guess what?" Julia jumped excitedly. "Farida's ..."

"Don't tell anybody," Farida interrupted. "It's a secret."

Since the public schools had separated boys from girls when she was six, Julia attended an all-girls school in a converted mansion on a quiet street in the Shaughnessy area. The school had about a hundred students. The only thing that distinguished it from its neighbors was the high brick wall that surrounded it, and the armed guard inside the gate. The girls were all delivered to and picked up from school in motor vehicles. No one walked.

"I saw him," Farida said offhandedly the following Monday at school. She told Julia about the events that had taken place the previous Saturday

"What's he like?"

"He's okay, I guess, for somebody so old. At least he's not fat, and he's taller than his father." Farida sighed.

"Did he say anything to you?"

"Are you kidding? All he and his brothers did was stare at me, as if I was some sort of dog they were buying. I was so embarrassed."

"God," was all Julia could think of in response. She thought for a moment then asked, "Is he good looking?"

"I guess."

Her mind didn't dwell on Farida's problem for long. When she got home that afternoon, she felt a strange atmosphere in the house. Both her parents were home, which was unusual in itself at that time of day. Their friend and fellow musician, Antoine LaSalle was also there. The three grownups were in the sitting room, her parents side-by-side on the sofa, Antoine sitting on the adjacent love seat.

"Come in, Julia. We've got something to tell you."

Julia walked a little way into the room and looked at the three faces, trying to gauge whether or not it was good news. Her father looked as if he was trying to put on a good face. Her mother looked happy, but a little worried, while Antoine, who was about ten years younger than her father was—which made him eight years younger that Aldina—looked happy and nervous.

"What is it?" Julia asked. She went over to her father and leaned against his knees.

He patted her shoulder. "Your mother's getting married again," he said.

"But how can she?" Julia protested, feeling as if the ground had opened up under her. She looked up at his face. "What about you, Daddy?"

"It's all right, angel. We can both be married to her." He looked over at Antoine.

Julia turned and followed his gaze. Antoine smiled at her and nodded his head. He had a dimple when he smiled.

She had to admit he was handsome with his shaggy, ear-length brown hair and blue eyes.

It was her mother's turn to comment. "You see, dear, there aren't enough women for all the men in the world, and Antoine is a good friend of both of us." She looked at both men in turn. "Oh dear, I'm not saying this very well, am I?"

"It's all right, Alda," her father said. "What Mommy means is she still loves me, and she loves Antoine as well, so we're all going to live together."

"But where will he sleep?" Julia asked, fearful that she might have to give up her room and move in with David.

"That's another thing we wanted to tell you," Mother replied. "We're going to move to a bigger house." She smiled at Antoine.

Julia sat on the couch between her parents and thought about this for a while. Her mind was in turmoil, trying to assess the effect all these changes would have on her. She had too many questions and couldn't decide which had priority. Finally, she sighed and looked up at her mother. "Can I be a bridesmaid?"

***

Farida Khalsa stared down at her hands. Earlier that morning, her mother and grandmother had carefully painted the backs of both hands with intricate traceries of kohl. She looked at her hands because they had told her she must not raise her eyes during the ceremony. Gold jewelry weighed heavily on her shoulders and wrists. She was wearing a bright pink langha, the traditional long tunic, over matching pants with purple and gold-embroidered bands around the ankles. She had wanted to wear red, the traditional color for weddings, but her mother said it was too strong for a little girl. Still it was a pretty garment. A gossamer-light pink veil, embroidered with gold thread, covered her head and draped over her shoulders. Her gaze, kept low, moved around to where her mother and grandmother were standing with the groom's mother and two grandmothers. Most of the women present were her mother's age or older; there was no one Farida's age at all.

She remembered her grandmother's wedding pictures. There had been many girls her grandmother's age, friends, sisters, cousins.

The men started singing the hymn, "*Kita loria kam so Hari pai akhia*", seeking the blessing of God on the ceremony.

She heard her father's soft voice say, "It's time, child."

Her four brothers stepped into place on either side of her. Farida was aware of a group of men approaching the front of the temple where she was standing. One of them, she knew, was her bridegroom, but she didn't dare look at him.

She had been introduced to Sarap Gurdwara Singh briefly a few weeks earlier when the final arrangements had been made for the marriage. She had been awed by the tall, slender young man who seemed impossibly old to be marrying someone as young as she was. He was nineteen; she was eleven. However, perhaps he had no more choice than she had. It was an arrangement agreed upon between their fathers.

Farida's mother had wept when she told her daughter about the impending union. "We have no choice, child; Dada's business will fail if he doesn't get the money. Think about your brothers; what will they do if the business goes under?"

"But what will I do? Will I still be able to study? Where will I live?"

This question brought fresh tears to her mother's eyes. She hugged the little girl. "You'll have to go and live with your husband's family, darling, but Dada has asked them to let you use one of their terminals to keep up with your schoolwork."

"Will I have to sleep with him, like you and Dada?"

"Not right away. Later, when you get older. For the time being, you'll be like a daughter in the family." She sniffed and squeezed Farida very hard. "You're so precious, little Farida."

The Priest started to intone a hymn from the Guru Granth, the Sikh Holy Scripture. Her father took her hand and placed in it the end of a silk scarf, then he moved away from her towards one of the nearby men—Sarap, she realized. Keeping her head down, she glanced through her lashes and saw her father give the other end of the scarf to him, then back away with his palms pressed together. Sarap held onto the scarf.

She had been through several rehearsals of the ceremony with her brother Raj standing in for the groom, so she knew what to do next. She and the groom made obeisance to the Guru Granth, and then he draped the scarf over his shoulder, still holding the end, and turned his back to her. The chanting turned to singing and they started to walk around the canopied Guru Granth. Her brothers walked beside her.

She became dazed as the long ceremony proceeded, alternating between chanting and singing of hymns, more circling, and then sitting cross-legged on the floor to listen to admonitions from the priest. At last, everyone stood up for the final Ardas.

When it was over, they were served the sanctified pudding, and then everyone moved into another room for the wedding feast.

***

Julia stood on the sunny lawn beside her father, holding a spray of flowers. Aldina was between Raymond and Antoine facing the minister. It was the first time Julia could remember seeing her mother in a dress. In truth, she couldn't remember the last time she had worn one herself. Aldina's dress was ankle-length crêpe in deep teal decorated with tiny lavender floral sprays. Julia had chosen a cream colored, high-waisted gown trimmed with dark green.

The three brothers stood behind their parents, John and David in dark blue suits with matching high-necked shirts, Paul in a white high-buttoned jacket and pants, his hair freshly shampooed and sweeping in glossy waves over his shoulders.

The ceremony was being held at the home of Antoine's parents. Most of the guests, not surprisingly, were men and boys. Aside from Antoine's mother, Adele, the only other females were Antoine's cousin Gabrielle, her two-year-old daughter Charm, and Aldina's friend Spencer.

The minister opened a leather-bound bible and began to read from a sheet of paper held on the pages.

"We are gathered together in the company of family and friends to celebrate this day the union of Antoine Louis LaSalle with Aldina Marie Finisterra and Raymond Charles English."

He turned to Antoine. "Do you, Antoine, promise to honor, cherish and respect Aldina and Raymond for as long as the union shall last?"

"I do."

"Do you vow to value and protect the children of Aldina and Raymond as if they were your own?"

"I do."

The minister smiled at John, Paul, David, and Julia in turn. "Although this is not part of the ceremony, I would like to add that I hope you young people will welcome Antoine into your family with kindness and respect, and come to regard him as a second father."

Julia nodded earnestly, although she wasn't sure about the father part.

"Good."

Antoine took the ring Raymond was holding and placed it on Aldina's finger, and then she handed her bouquet to Julia and put a matching ring on his. Antoine kissed Aldina and shook hands with Raymond.

After the exchange of vows, the guests began to socialize. Some—children in the lead—went to the marquee in the garden to help themselves to food and drinks from the buffet.

Julia gloried in the unaccustomed masculine attention—she rarely had the opportunity to meet boys socially—but she was soon brought down to earth when two older boys cornered her while she was searching for a lavatory.

One boy pulled her into a corner, pinning her arms behind her. "Let's see what you've got," other boy said, grabbing her skirt.

"No!" she shrieked at the top of her voice.

"Let her go, you stinking little creeps." John barged into the room.

"We were only playing," the boy whined, letting go of Julia's arms.

Julia ran to John who took her arm. "That was stupid to go wandering off alone," he said. "Where's your beeper?"

"I forgot to bring it."

John sighed and shook his head. "If your legs weren't screwed on, Julia, you'd be riding in a wheelchair."

He was still blocking the boys' escape. He turned to them. "If I see you even looking at her again—well you know she's got three big brothers and two fathers—so I'll leave it to your imagination what will happen."

Chapter Three

Geoffrey's twenty-first birthday gift was an hour with a female prostitute. For Geoffrey, a carpenter, this may be the only time in his life he makes love to a woman. Like many working men, Geoffrey will probably get most of his sexual gratification from girlfriends because the cost of female call girls will be out of his reach.

Even though the proportion of women choosing the oldest profession is higher than ever in history, there are still far too few to accommodate the male population. This gives these women a unique opportunity, not only to command high fees for their services, but also to occupy prestigious positions in society.

"I can pick my clients," twenty-five-year-old Sharley stated in our interview. "And I can choose when I want to work." Sharley admitted to an average income of twenty thousand dollars per month. Sharley lives in a prestigious townhouse complex on the North Shore and entertains some of the leading members of the government and diplomatic community.

Excerpt from article in Trend magazine, July 2051.

After Aldina's marriage to Antoine, the couple went away for a weekend at Harrison Hot Springs. They tried not to make a big deal of the event, hoping that everything would settle into place with as little stress as possible.

Raymond took the two youngest children, Julia and David, by boat up the Burrard Inlet to the top end of Indian Arm, where they went ashore and camped for the night.

The family moved to a larger house in Point Grey a few months after the wedding. It had five bedrooms upstairs and two in the basement, and a wonderful view of English Bay.

Julia had believed when she was younger that the Bay was named after her father. It was a big letdown to discover that it had received its name long before he was born. Another of life's little disappointments.

"It's hard to believe that forty years ago this house would have cost over two million," Raymond commented as he unlocked the front door.

"I know," Aldina replied. "My Gran told me that they paid two hundred thousand in 1980 for their little house on West Tenth, and now they'd be lucky to get twenty-five thousand."

The foyer and adjacent living room were two stories high. A staircase with graceful white banister, curved up around one corner to a gallery that faced the entrance and the stained glass window over the front door.

"You boys can have the basement," Raymond said. "There's a staircase at the back, off the kitchen."

John and David jostled each other racing for the kitchen. Paul, off in his own world, had disappeared around the side of the house.

"Where am I going to sleep?" Julia asked.

"Up here," her mother replied, starting up the stairs.

A short hallway with two doors on either side led back from the gallery. One of the doors stood open, revealing a bathroom. Aldina pushed open the door next to it.

"This will be your room." It was a small corner room with windows on two sides. The walls were painted a sickly yellow-green color.

"Ugh, I don't like that color," Julia cried. "It looks like pea soup.

"Don't worry, we'll have it fixed up for you," her father said from the doorway. "What color would you like?"

Julia didn't have to think for long. "Blue, like Mommy's necklace."

"That's turquoise," Aldina said. "I think that's a good choice. We can leave the woodwork white, though. Now, let's see the rest of the house."

They left Julia's room and went across the hall. This is Daddy's room," Aldina said pushing the door.

"But I thought... Aren't you and Daddy going to sleep in the same room?"

Raymond cleared his throat, but remained silent.

"Well you see, love, I have two husbands now and it wouldn't be fair to sleep with one of them all the time."

Julia frowned. "Couldn't they both sleep in your room?" she asked.

"I don't think that would work too well."

They walked back down the hall to the front of the house.

"It would get a bit crowded with all of us in the same room." Aldina went into the bedroom that opened off the gallery at the front of the house. "This is going to be my bedroom."

It was a big, airy room with two large windows overlooking the front garden and two smaller ones on the side. There was a doorway opening into a large dressing room and bathroom to the right of the door.

Julia looked around judiciously, and then turned to her parents. "It looks big enough to me. You could put one bed over there and another here..." She stopped when she saw them smiling at her and shaking their heads.

"Don't worry, sweetie, we'll work it out." Raymond said, putting his arm around her shoulder and drawing her out onto the gallery. "We can put my album covers along here," he added, nodding at the wall.

He was referring to his prized collection of twentieth century rock and roll record album covers, some of which were not only extremely rare, but also quite beautiful: Fleetwood Mac's *Then Play On*, the Beatles' *Rubber Soul*, and the Small Faces cover decorated with the *Ogden's Nut Gone Flake* label.

It took some adjusting, but Julia got used to her mother's new relationship. Such marriages were not officially legal, but plural partnerships were now a fact. It became a case of the law following recognized customs.

There were other alternatives for men, such as homosexuality. Boys were even encouraged to follow the gay lifestyle, but it is not something that can be forced; it just didn't appeal to many men. Some young men underwent sex-change operations and became "girlfriends". Hormone therapy for males was covered by the government medical insurance.

However, many young men, having no outlet for their sex drive and not having the resources to channel their feelings into constructive activities, turned to violence. Assaults on women and the men associated with them became commonplace. Riots and vandalism increased, in spite of government support of sports. Indeed, many sporting events ended in riots. In the spring of 2053, after a demolition derby in Surrey, twelve people were killed, including two of the contestants, and more than twenty were injured badly enough to require hospitalization.

Law enforcement officials were often just as frustrated as the rioters were and frequently chose not to use their pacifying equipment, but waded into the melees with batons flying, gratified by the opportunity to bust some heads.

***

"What are you doing, girl?"

Farida jumped. She hadn't heard her mother-in-law enter. "My history assignment," she replied.

"You spend too much time on that computer. From now on, you'll only use it after you've finished your work."

Tears filled Farida's eyes. She turned the terminal off and stood up meekly.

"There's a big pile of laundry to be folded," Sarap's mother said, "and when you've finished that, you can start preparing the vegetables for dinner. There's a lot of work with all these men; I can't do everything myself."

How did you manage before you got me to be your slave? Farida thought.

"Why can't they help with the work?" she said. Her brothers helped their mother sometimes.

Sarap's mother glared at her. "They are men. Housework is not for men to do."

Farida went down to the laundry room in the basement of the house. She was only allowed down there when the male family members were away at school or work. Apart from the laundry facilities and utility room, this was their domain, where they slept and had their recreation. Even Sarap, her husband, slept down here. Farida slept in a small room off the kitchen on the main floor. Her parents-in-law also had their suite on the main floor.

Sometimes, when the boys were at school and her mother-in-law busy, Farida would sneak into Sarap's room and look at his posters of biological specimens under electron microscopy. His room was always neat, bed made, his microscope and books neatly lined up on the desk beside trays of slides.

With a sigh, she opened the door of the industrial-size dryer and pulled out a pile of garments: men's shirts, men's pants, men's underwear, their socks and turban cloths, and at the bottom, an afterthought, her own nightgown.

Farida wasn't mistreated by her new family, not enough to complain about, and she could understand her mother-in-law's need for help with the big household; it just wasn't such a warm, loving home as her own had been.

She was allowed to go home, to what she thought of as her own house, after temple every week and stay for supper, then her father drove her back to her husband's house. She treasured those evenings, which somehow helped her get through the rest of the week.

Sarap talked to her sometimes, shyly asking her how things were going, what she was studying, but both were too introverted to talk about anything deeper. Farida always felt like a child when they were together. Sarap was studying bio-genetics at the University of British Columbia. She wanted to ask him to tell her about it, but was too timid.

She didn't like Sarap's second brother, Rajinder. He was smaller than Sarap, with thick eyebrows. Whenever they met, he'd give her a sly look, filled with innuendo, that made her skin crawl, and more than once, when they were forced to pass closely, he'd brushed against her body, keeping the contact longer than necessary. She tried to avoid Rajinder as much as possible.

The other five brothers, ranging in ages from seven to fifteen, varied in their attitude to her. The younger ones were somewhat in awe of her. She was probably one of the few girls they had ever met. The older three, teenagers in high school, teased her in a friendly way when no one was around, but were respectful when their parents or Sarap were present.

The brother with whom she got along best was ten year-old Keval. He was a thoughtful boy—some might call him dreamy—whose face would frequently light up with a bright smile as if he'd just had a wonderful revelation. She helped him with his homework and sometimes they played computer games together. Sarap's mother frowned when she saw them together, enjoying themselves, but she didn't interfere because Sarap seemed to approve.

Farida had been working all day, cleaning, ironing and preparing food for the upcoming festival. She was exhausted. She hadn't been able to get to her schoolwork at all and the year-end exams were starting the following week. Not only did she need to pass, she had to get good marks if she wanted to get into the fast track to university.

She gave her hair a few final, weary strokes and put the brush down, and then she climbed into bed and picked up the book reader. Before she had read more than a couple of lines, the words started to blur and shimmer through tears. She put the reader down and brushed her hand against the lamp to turn it off, then curled up and let herself go. Fearing someone would hear her sobs, she pulled the covers over her head. She was so homesick and anxious, wondering whether she would be able to finish her education.

The floor creaked and the room was illuminated by the door opening. Startled, Farida wiped her eyes and turned to face the light. She saw a tall slender figure silhouetted against the kitchen light.

"What's the matter, little butterfly? I was getting some water and I heard you crying." It was Sarap. He came over to the bed and sat on the edge.

"I-I'm just tired," Farida stammered. Her heart thumped in her chest. It was the first time he'd come to her bedroom.

Sarap put his arms around her and drew her onto his lap. She stiffened with fright, and then tried to relax. He was her husband, but she had hoped to have a few more years before 'that' started.

He must have sensed her reaction because he pressed her against his chest like a baby and began to smooth her hair. "Don't be afraid, little Farida; I'm not going to hurt you." His voice was soothing; the tone one would use to calm a child. "I'm sorry you're not happy. Tell me what's bothering you?"

She relaxed a little more. This was the way her father used to hold her when she was little. "Sarap," she said hesitantly, "Will I be able to go to university when I get older?"

He pulled back and looked at her face. "Is that what you want?"

"Yes. I want to be a scientist like you."

Sarap looked surprised. Perhaps this was the first time he had realized that this girl, his wife, was a person in her own right.

"Let me ask you something. Is there any other reason you'd like to be a scientist, apart from my interest in science?"

Farida moved off her husband's lap back onto the bed while she thought about the question. Dare she admit her secret fantasy of being the person who discovered the solution to the genetic mystery that plagued the world?

"I want to work on genetics to help find a way to make more girls. If ... I mean, the more people working on it, the better ... you know ... the chances of somebody discovering something."

"And you'd like to be that person." He smiled at her.

She nodded. "But I really would like to work with you." She thought for a moment, summoning the courage to ask. "Sarap, do you think I could borrow some of your books?"

"You really do want to study genetics. Of course you can borrow some books, love. I'd advise you to start with the biology, though. You will find it easier to follow. It's no good going onto the more advanced stuff before you learn the basics. I'll leave a few on the clothes dryer for you."

He stood up. "Now try to get some sleep. I'll see you in the morning." He pulled the covers over her and then bent and kissed her on the forehead. "Little wife," he whispered as he turned to leave.

She touched her face where he'd kissed her, aware of an unaccustomed warmth in her groin. He's really nice, she thought. Maybe it won't be so bad.

That night, she dreamed she was riding a horse and got the same feeling of warmth and sexual excitement where her body pressed against the saddle.

Chapter Four

"Go ahead, sir, you're on the air"

"Me?"

"That's right, sir. Now the subject this morning, as you know, is Ladyloves. How do you feel about them?"

"I think they're great."

"Do you have one yourself?"

"Well ... er ... yes."

"Good, good. Now, sir, tell me what you like best about—should I say her?"

"Yes. Well, for one thing, she's always there when I get home."

"Does she have a name?"

"Yes. I call her Marilyn."

"How does she affect your sex life?"

"Hmm. Well, it's good, like she feels so real, warm, and soft, but firm, you know.... And she moves and talks."

"What sort of things does she say?"

"Well, like, 'How was your day?'"

"Anything else?"

"Um ... things like, 'Oh, yes, baby,' when we're ... you know."

Excerpt from radio talk show transcript.

A small slender man arrived at the house one morning in a micro-utility vehicle. With his two assistants, he started to unload an assortment of tools and bring them into the rear entrance. All the activity aroused Julia's interest and she ran downstairs to find out what was happening.

"What are they going to do, Daddy?" Julia asked Raymond, who was in the kitchen showing house plans to the small man.

"Nothing you need worry about," he replied. "Just some renovations. Go back to your schoolwork and I'll tell you later."

Julia retreated to her room, not entirely reluctantly. The two younger men had been looking at her with embarrassing intensity. She sat for a moment in front of her screen, contemplating the feelings this attention had aroused in her.

That evening at dinner, Raymond explained the renovations. "We want to be sure you and your mother are safe." He glanced at Antoine who nodded his agreement. "With all the rioting and home invasions, we want to have a safe hiding place, just in case."

"But I thought the walls and lights were supposed to stop anyone getting in," David said.

The previous year, a three-meter high brick wall topped with razor wire had been built to enclose the property. Floodlights and alarms were installed around the house.

"I still think it's a good idea," Raymond said.

"They don't always put it on the news," Antoine added, "but the violence is getting worse. There've been two cases of girls snatched from their own homes in the past month. Last week there was a case of thugs breaking into the home of an eighty-two year old woman while her sons were away."

"What happened to them?" David wanted to know.

"What do you think?" Antoine replied. "The old lady didn't survive. The two girls are still in the hospital."

"How do you know all this if it's not in the news?" Paul asked.

"I'm in insurance. I see the claims."

A sick sensation grew in the pit of Julia's stomach. She didn't want to hear about these things. "I want to know about the hiding place."

"We're going to build a little room off the basement. There'll be access to it from concealed door in David's closet."

"Hey, that's *so* tight," David exclaimed. He'd just added a new adjective to his vocabulary. "Just like in a book."

"When did you ever read a book?" John teased. "You'll have to clean up your mess. We don't want to lose our womenfolk because they trip over your junk trying to get to the hideout."

The builder's name was Edgar Lance. He was a quiet, thoughtful man, a little older than Raymond and Aldina, with brown hair, warm brown eyes, and a neat beard. He often sang or whistled snatches of operatic arias as he worked. It soon became evident that he was becoming more than a contractor employed by her parents to do renovations. When his assistants left after their day's work, he often stayed behind. At first, they sat outside or in the living room, talking about music and drinking tea. Then he started joining them for dinner several times a week.

It came as no surprise when Aldina announced that she had grown very fond of Edgar and they were planning to invite him to join the family. Raymond and Antoine must have agreed because the following weekend, Edgar Lance moved in. There was no ceremony this time as there had been with Antoine. He got the small bedroom that opened off the gallery behind Raymond's room.

Edgar's soft voice and slow, studious movements made Julia feel comfortable in his company. She enjoyed walking around the garden with him discussing everything from the shortage of women to growing roses.

"Is my mother the first woman you've known?"

Edgar laughed. "No. I have a mother and a sister. My sister's a lot younger than I am. She was born of my mother's second marriage."

"No, I mean..."

"Oh, you mean man-woman stuff." He cleared his throat—a sign Julia had come to recognize as either embarrassment in grownups or reluctance to talk about something. "I don't know if I should tell you about this sort of thing."

"For goodness sake, Edgar, I'm thirteen. I have to learn some time." She flashed him a smile.

"Oh well, but if your parents get upset..."

"What makes you think I'll tell them?" By now, she was intrigued. This must be something spicy.

"Well, you know what a call-girl is?"

"Of course, it's a prostitute. Men who have had sex-change operations. But I thought they were called girl-friends."

"No, I mean women."

"You mean women sell themselves? Now?" She was amazed. It was something she knew was common in the past, when there was the same number of women as men, but nowadays.... Prostitution had always been treated as the very lowest occupation, condemned as criminal most of the time. How could women today be involved in something like that? They were supposed to be treated with respect, cherished and protected. "But I don't understand. How do they get into something like that?"

Before answering, Edgar brushed some leaves off the garden seat and sat down. Julia sat on the grass at his feet. "Various ways, I suppose. Some of them just rebel against their families. Some are induced into it by unscrupulous men, often their husbands or brothers."

This was another shock. She had believed that every family was dedicated to caring for girls and women, protecting them, as hers was. "Why would they want to do something like that?"

"Money," Edgar replied.

Yes, that made sense. She could imagine that rich men would pay a lot of money to do it with a real woman. But Edgar wasn't rich.

"Did you, you know, go to them many times?"

"Oh, no. Just a couple. The first one was a birthday present from my father when I turned nineteen. The second time, I won some money on the lottery and decided to treat myself."

"God." She cupped her chin in her hand. "How much do they charge?"

"Aren't you getting a little too interested? I'm not sure your parents would be pleased at my discussing this sort of thing with you."

"How else will I learn about life if people don't tell me? I never get to go out anywhere and the stuff on the net is mostly disgusting trash. How much?" she persisted.

"It varies, I suppose. I've heard of men paying as much as a thousand dollars for a whole night. Some older or less attractive women charge as little as two hundred."

"Are there a lot of them?"

"I don't think so. Maybe about fifty or so in the whole Vancouver area."

"Wow. They must be pretty busy. I bet they're rich, too."

"What are you two talking about so seriously?" Aldina appeared through the French windows of the living room.

"Nothing much," Edgar replied. "Just solving the problems of the world."

"Well, let me know what you've come up with." She reached them and sat next to Edgar, taking his hand in hers.

"Well, I've got to do some geometry," Julia said, rising to her feet.

**

At thirteen, Julia felt restless and uneasy much of the time, as if she were under constant scrutiny and everyone was waiting for something to happen. She started wearing boys' baggy shirts and pants to hide the developing femininity of her body and insisted on having her hair cut in the same style as her brothers, at least the two who had short hair.

She didn't see much of her two older brothers, John and Paul. They were both at university, John in his junior year at Simon Fraser, Paul a senior at UBC. She was much closer to David who was only two years older. He was the one who helped her with her lessons and taught her to play softball. David's friends were the only boys around her age she ever met more than once. Since the girls' school had closed, she hardly ever went anywhere. She only felt safe going out if she disguised herself as a boy and was accompanied by several adults.

There was a small park at the end of their street, just a stretch of grass with a baseball diamond and soccer pitch marked out. Julia loved to put on one of David's shirts and a pair of ragged jeans and go to the park for a game of softball. She became one of the boys for an hour or so. It was one of the few times she felt truly alive.

Lately, she had been binding a silk scarf around her developing breasts under her shirt, hoping to keep them from bouncing when she ran around the bases or jumped to catch the ball. She didn't want them to think of her as a girl. That would change everything. She wouldn't be able to play anymore and really let herself go. She knew she needed these interludes with David and his friends to let off steam and burn off some of the frustration of always being confined.

In spite of the enjoyment she got from the games and pretending to be a boy, Julia could not deny the feeling she got when she was close to one of the boys, and especially when she thought about him in her room at night. His name was Chandler, but they all called him Shandy. What it would be like to be alone with him, she wondered. What would he do? She had seen some of the porno videos her brothers watched and thought them disgusting and ridiculous. She couldn't imagine doing those sorts of things with anyone, even with Shandy. But to have him touch her.... She pictured his face, his light brown eyes and curly dark blond hair. His mouth. He had the sexiest mouth she had ever seen, wide sculpted lips, pinky beige and so soft-looking. Imagine him kissing her. She shivered and rolled onto her face.

Chapter Five

Home invasions on the rise

"It was the scariest thing that ever happened to me," Monica Callaghan told the Globe. *"We were woken up by something crashing against the front door, then we heard breaking glass from the back of the house. My son rushed into my room carrying one of the shotguns. He told me to get under the bed. We ... I suppose it won't hurt to tell you this; we've already installed new security measures ... we had a concealed space under the bed where a person can hide. I did as he told me. By this time, we could hear men's voices shouting, coming up the stairs, then I heard the blast of a firearm. It was so loud, it sounded like an explosion. Someone screamed then it sounded as if he was falling down the stairs. For a moment, I thought someone had shot my other son; I was terrified. But then I heard him call out to his brother, 'I got one of them!' After that, it was chaos, people shouting, gunshots, things breaking, police sirens. I was shaking so badly...."*

Ms Callaghan went on to describe how her sons chased the invaders from the house almost into the arms of the police, who arrived in time to arrest two of them. In addition, a young man is now in hospital recovering from a gunshot wound.

Excerpt from report in the Vancouver Globe

Julia woke with a start. It sounded as if dozens of people were shouting outside in the street. She saw reflections of orange light flickering on the ceiling. Still sleepy, she sat up and turned on the light to see what time it was. 1:32. She could hear men's voices banging doors from downstairs, inside the house.

She heard her father tell someone, "Go and wake your sister; tell her to come downstairs quickly."

"I'm up," she called just as David barged into the bedroom.

"Well hurry," her brother urged her. He was trembling, whether from fear or excitement, she couldn't tell; probably a bit of both. "Come on; you and Mom have to go down into the hole." *The hole* was what they called the hiding place under David's room."

"What's happening?" Julia asked as they ran down the stairs to the ground floor.

"I don't know; it sounds like a riot. Someone just climbed up on the wall next door and threw an incendiary into their bushes." Her father and mother were waiting for her in David's room. They'd already moved David's hockey equipment and his shoes out of the closet and would replace it once they were safely in their hiding place.

"Okay," her father said. "Now, you and your mother can go down. Good, you've bought a sweater, Julia; you might need it down there." Then he addressed both women: "You remember how to lock the door?"

"Of course; we've practiced enough."

"All right; off you go. We'll let you know when it's safe to come out."

***

Raymond went around the house, checking the various lookout posts. John, Paul, and David were spread around the upper floor, David at a window on the south side, John on the west—looking towards the front entrance gate, and Paul on the north. They were each holding a small gauge rifle and peering through the slats of Venetian blinds.

"How's it going?" Raymond asked John, looking over his shoulder.

The noise outside had increased considerably since Raymond first set up the lookouts. They could see the glow of flames outside the gate; whether they were burning torches or bonfires started on the road, it was hard to tell. The wall was too high for them to see anyone close to the house, but they could see rioters farther away up the street where they'd set fire to some trees.

A flaming torch flew over the wall and landed in the big monkey-puzzle tree in their front garden. The tree went up in flames and was almost destroyed by the time the vertical sprinklers came on. A head and arms appeared above the front gate. John fired at the man at the same time as someone on the ground floor. A howl of rage came from the target as he disappeared from view. The sound of approaching sirens animated the mob into a frenzy. They began to disperse in various directions, still shouting and jeering, but they didn't escape completely; a helicopter flew low over the running figures, spraying them with gas.

Raymond gave the signal for his wife and daughter to come up from their hiding place and everyone crowded into the dining room to answer questions from the police.

Raymond was particularly upset about the destruction of the tree. It had long been on the endangered species list and was close to extinction.

Chapter Six

"It would be unfair to arouse men's desires with seductive exhibitions of female flesh when there is no likelihood of follow-up or consummation," stated designer, Claudia van Fleet. "On the other hand, women should not be restricted from enjoying beaches and swimming pools, nor should they be encumbered with bulky, heat-trapping garments. I believe my new line offers a striking compromise."

Introduction to Claudia's beachwear design show,
March 2054

One day, David came to her room and sat on the edge of her bed. His dark hair fell over his eyes as he looked down at his hands clasped between his knees. Julia sat in the chair by her terminal, watching him curiously. He obviously had something he wanted to say, but was taking an awfully long time to get it out.

Finally, he looked up. "You know the guys we play softball with?"

"Yes, I know them," Julia replied.

"Hmm. How do you feel about them?"

"They're okay I guess." What was he so uncomfortable about?

David looked down again, shifting his position on the bed. "Is there any... I mean, do you like any of them more than, you know?

"God, David, why are you asking me this? What's wrong?"

"Nothing." He looked up quickly. "Nothing's wrong. It's just, one of the guys, you know, he sort of likes you."

Julia felt her face turning red and spun her chair around to hide it from him. Which one? Could it be ...? No that would be too much to hope for.

"Who?"

"Shan."

"Shandy?" her voice came out in a squeak. She could hardly believe it.

"Well," David repeated, "how do you... I mean do you like him?"

"Yes, he's all right."

"I mean that way."

"What way's that, David?"

"You know."

She turned back to face him. Now he had turned red.

"What if I do?"

"Well, he was wondering if he could come and see you."

"He's always coming here. Why do you need to ask me?"

"But that's just with me. He wants to see you."

"You mean alone?"

David nodded.

At last, she thought, it was going to happen. But what would happen, she hardly dared to guess. Her heart began to beat faster.

Julia was in a fever trying to decide how to act with Shandy, what to wear, what to say. After David left, she opened her closet and started to look through her clothes.

She had shorts, baggy pants, jeans, tight pants, knee britches, and leggings; then there were the tops, sheer blouses, knitted sweaters, cotton shirts, and tee shirts. She pulled out a pair of shorts and a sheer blouse. No. Much too obvious. Leggings. Yes, they would show off her legs. She threw a pair of dark green velvet leggings on the bed and began to scramble through the tops. She picked out a short cream top with beads. Julia threw off her clothes and put on the leggings and top, then she looked in the mirror, turning this way and that. No, they wouldn't do. The leggings made her bottom look too big and the top concealed the shape of her breasts.

She settled on a pair of jeans and a blue cotton shirt. She didn't want him to think she was trying to seduce him, or that she was frigid.

She heard the bell on the gate ring, and then David opening the front door. The plan was that he would take Shandy down to his room in the basement and she would go down and join them. She went down the stairs, her heart was thumping so hard, she could barely breathe. The house was unusually quiet. Where was everybody? She knew Raymond and Antoine were playing tonight, but where were her mother and Edgar? She went back up the stairs far enough to see the door to Aldina's room. There was a plastic owl hanging from the doorknob, the sign that she didn't want to be disturbed. Edgar was probably with her.

Julia and the two boys sat on the edge of David's bed and discussed the last softball game for a while, and then they fell silent. David turned on the entertainment screen and they pretended to watch it.

David cleared his throat and stood up. "I'm going to play a game in the rec room. If anybody comes, I'll yell something."

David's room opened off the recreation room, so he would be just outside. After the door was closed, Julia stood awkwardly just inside the door. Shandy picked up the TV tuner and changed the channel.

"Why don't you sit down? You'll be able to see better." Shandy swung his feet up onto the bed and scooted over to the other side where he made himself comfortable with pillows propped against the headboard. Julia perched on the edge of the bed. It was the only place from which the monitor could be seen.

"Do you like this show?" he asked.

"It's okay."

"Is there anything else you'd like to watch?"

"Maybe there's a movie," Julia suggested.

He finally found a channel showing a drama. A lot of men on horseback, wearing strange costumes and wielding heavy swords, clashed with another group of horsemen similarly attired, all the while emitting blood-chilling howls.

She felt him looking at her, but pretended not to notice, concentrating on the screen.

"Why don't you put your feet up and get comfortable?" He suggested.

Julia lifted her feet onto the bed and leaned against the headboard. *I can't believe this is happening,* she thought. I'm on a bed, alone with a boy, (man). He was so close; she imagined she could feel the heat from his body across the gap between them. She clasped her hands in her lap and gazed at the monitor, not understanding anything she saw. She felt him move. His hand slid across her thigh and touched hers. She uncurled her fingers and moved her hand into his and he squeezed it, and then drew it onto his thigh. She could feel the warmth of his leg through the cloth of his jeans.

They sat like that for a while, pretending to watch the drama on the screen. Suddenly, he let go of her hand and moved, rocking the bed.

"Julia, look at me."

She turned to face him. He was on his side leaning on one elbow. His beautiful mouth was partly open. He moved quickly, rolling over and pulling her down under him. Then his mouth was on hers, his fingers in her hair, holding her head. At first, she held her lips rigid, and then she allowed them to soften in response. It was the most blissful thing she had ever experienced.

"God, Julia." He pulled away, raised up on his hands, and looked down at her, and then he rolled to the side and started to unbutton her shirt.

"Hey, Edgar, how's it going?" David's voice, pitched louder than normal, broke the spell.

Julia quickly sat upright and buttoned her shirt, and then she slipped into her shoes and hurried to the closet. This was how they'd planned it if anyone came. While she hid in the closet, Shandy strolled casually into the recreation room. "How about another game?" he said. "The movie stinks."

***

In the summer of 2055, Raymond, Edgar, and Aldina took David and Julia to Saturna Island in the Gulf of Georgia for a vacation. They had borrowed a cottage from one of Edgar's friends for two weeks. It was a small island with less than fifty permanent residents, but there was plenty for the young people to do. They could swim from one of the narrow beaches, fish from the small dinghy that came with the cottage, windsurf, or simply lie on the beach and read. In the evening, they played games.

Julia and Aldina had new swimming costumes for the vacation. Aldina's was a navy two-piece suit with knee-length shorts and a short-sleeved top; Julia's was a little more daring: a short-legged, sleeveless one piece.

37

One morning, Julia was strolling along the beach in her swimsuit, picking up the occasional seashell and sand dollar, when she spotted a young man sitting back under the trees. He was engrossed in something he was working on, but she couldn't make out what it was. Curious and somewhat apprehensive, she moved closer. Julia thought she'd met everyone on the island in the week they'd been there, but she didn't recognize him.

Once he noticed her, he looked at her silently until she felt uncomfortable.

She stopped about ten meters away. "Hi," she said.

He squinted at her. "Hi."

He had long black hair and dark brown eyes. His skin was tanned to a rich reddish brown. She saw he was working on a piece of wood using a narrow pointed instrument.

"What are you carving?" she asked, approaching him to get a better view.

He held up a small carving of what appeared to be a fish, decorated with the swirls and circles that characterized native carvings.

"It's beautiful," she said, kneeling in the sand beside him. "Is it native?"

He nodded.

"Are you native?"

The man nodded again.

"Which Nation are you from?"

"Kwakiutl." The way he said it, it sounded like Kwogyool with soft consonants.

"Wow. My name's Julia; what's yours?"

"Gabriel."

"What a beautiful name! Do you live here?"

Gabriel shook his head. "Visiting."

God, he's so shy, she thought. He looked about eighteen. "How did you get here?"

"Canoe."

"You mean you paddled here? Where from? Where's your canoe?"

He nodded towards a place farther down the beach and she saw the curved point of the canoe protruding from the underbrush.

"Are you hungry?" she asked.

"A bit," he nodded.

Julia sat down and opened her bag. She took out a plastic container half full of mixed nuts and dried fruit and snapped off the lid. "Help yourself." She held it out to him.

He dropped his knife and took a handful. "Thanks."

"Here, have a drink." She handed him a bottle of water.

"So, where did you come from? In the canoe."

"Sidney."

"Is that where you live?"

"No. Port Hardy."

"Where's that?"

"North end of the Island," he replied, meaning Vancouver Island, which everyone just called the Island.

"Gabriel," she said, looking him in the eye. "There's nothing to be afraid of." Maybe it's something to do with her being a girl. "Are there many girls where you come from?"

"A few." He looked down at his carving, an unreadable expression on his face.

"Did something happen? With a girl?"

"Look, I don't want to talk about it. Okay?" he said sharply.

"I'm sorry." She tried to think of a way to get through to him. He was very attractive. Maybe if she told him something about herself.

"I'm from Vancouver. I have three brothers, but only one of them is here with us—my parents and me. My mother has three husbands, but one of them stayed in Vancouver. He couldn't get time off from work." She sensed that he had become tenser. "Would you like to come to our cottage and meet them?"

Speechless, he gathered his tools and put them in a small leather roll-up pack, then stood up. "I have to go." He brushed the sand off his legs and turned away.

"Wait, Gabriel. How long are you staying here?"

"I haven't decided," he replied.

"I'd like to see you again," she said, standing up herself. She took a step towards him. "Why don't you come back after supper and we can go for a swim. Or I'd love to have a ride in your canoe."

He turned and looked at her again. His time his eyes were warmer. "Maybe."

Julia met Gabriel every day for the next week. He had a small tent pitched deep in the bush near where his canoe was tied up. He gradually dropped his guardedness and relaxed. They went out in his canoe and he showed her how to catch a salmon with a hook and line. They swam together in the shallows with snorkels, examining the teeming underwater life. Sometimes they walked through the ancient forest where Julia saw speckled yellow slugs more than ten centimeters long.

"Where are you off to every day, all by yourself?" Aldina asked her.

"She's probably got a secret lover hidden away somewhere," David teased.

Julia felt her face heat up. "God, you're so crass, David. Is that all you can think about?" She had to think of something quickly. He was too close to the truth.

"Would you like to come with me?" she said. "You can help me look for rare plants." She had brought a botany text with her to the island and always carried it with her when she went out.

"No thanks, I've got better things to do with my time."

"Yes, I know. Like following Sophia Carter around like a love-sick puppy."

It was David's turn to blush. He scowled at her and left the room.

***

Julia and Gabriel had finished their swim and were coming out of the water onto the beach.

"Damn," Julia said. "I've forgotten to bring a towel."

Gabriel bent and picked up his towel from a clump of grass. "Here, you can borrow mine; I've got another in the tent."

"Thanks." Julia took the towel. "Let me dry your back first."

Before he could protest, she rubbed his back and arms, and was about to start on his legs when he gently pushed her hand away. "I'm fine."

Julia squinted at him, grinned, and wrapped the towel around herself.

As they strolled back through the woods to the tent, Julia noticed that Gabriel was keeping some distance between them. When they reached the tent, he reached through the flap and brought out another towel, which he draped around his shoulders, and then he sat cross-legged on the ground.

Julia sat a meter away, facing him, and rubbed her hair with the towel.

"I have to go home tomorrow," Gabriel announced.

"Why can't you stay longer?" she said.

"I have to be back in time for the Sockeye run, to help my dad."

"What's the Sockeye run?"

"It's when the salmon, the Fraser River Sockeye, start coming back to the Fraser to spawn. It'll start any day now. We have to do our harvesting while they're still running through the Johnstone Strait. My father and Uncle Gregory have a seine boat and me and my brothers have to help them."

"I wish you didn't have to go," she said. "I've had such a good time this summer."

"Me too," he said, staring at the ground.

"What time will you be leaving?" she asked.

"Sunrise, if I wake up that early."

"How long does it take you to get home?"

"A couple of days."

"You mean you can paddle all that way in two days?" she'd looked up Port Hardy on the map and knew it was at least five hundred kilometers away.

Gabriel smiled. "I cheated a bit. I'll paddle to the mainland, and then drive the rest of the way. I left my car in Sidney. I borrowed the canoe from my cousin."

"What made you come all the way down here by yourself?"

Gabriel ducked his head. "I needed some time alone to think."

"Did something happen in Port Hardy?"

He raised his head and looked at her. There was pain in his eyes. He nodded. "A girl, like you guessed the first day."

Julia waited to see if he would continue.

"We'd been dating about five months. She decided she liked my brother, Sebastian, better."

"I'm sorry," Julia said.

Gabriel shrugged. He stood up and started rubbing his legs with the towel.

Julia got to her feet and went closer to him. She scuffed the dirt with her toe, and then looked up at him. "Gabriel, will you kiss me?"

He looked startled. His eyes glowed warmly, his mouth curved into a faint smile. He stepped closer and held her upper arms, then leaned forward and kissed her gently on the mouth. When he pulled away, she put out her hand and caressed his chest. The skin was silky smooth and warm.

She looked into his eyes, and as if a signal had passed between them, they were in each other's arms. Julia wasn't sure whether she pushed him or he dragged her, but suddenly they were inside the tent, on the sleeping bag, tugging at their swimwear.

"Was that your first time?" Gabriel asked when they pulled apart. He kissed her nose and stroked her cheek with his finger.

Julia nodded.

He wrapped her in his arms. "I'm sorry, little one; I didn't want to hurt you."

"Oh, you didn't hurt me, Gabriel. It was the most beautiful thing that ever happened to me."

"Then why are you crying?"

"Because... You're going away and I don't know when I'll ever see you again."

She sat up and started to pull on her swimsuit, realizing this was the first time she had ever been naked in the presence of a man. It felt deliciously daring.

When they finally parted, she asked him for his telephone number. "I'll call you when I get home," she promised.

"I may not be there. I start U-Vic in September."

She never made the call, although she had the urge to many times. She never saw Gabriel again, but she would never forget him, her first love.

Chapter Seven

"So how do young women meet potential husbands?"

"Well, there are their brothers' friends."

"But isn't that a rather restricted range of choices?"

"I agree. Sometimes groups of parents arrange for their young people to meet and become acquainted at social gatherings. Then there are the dance clubs where kids get together—with adult chaperones, of course."

"Is it true that some parents accept financial compensation from the families of the men their daughters marry?"

"Regrettably, yes; but that is not as prevalent as rumors would suggest. Unless a young woman has a strong mother, she is sometimes exploited by male relatives."

"I understand that, even with the huge surplus of men, marriage is not the most popular option for young women."

"Correct. There are still a few employment opportunities open to women: designers, writers, even media stars—although that can be a bit risky unless they have constant protection. Some women opt for becoming courtesans. Many 'traditional' female professions such as nursing, teaching and clerical work are riskier for them."

Excerpt from radio interview with sociologist Donway Archer. August 2056

Raymond had been spending more and more time alone in his room. Julia often heard the sound of one of his beloved rock albums through the door when she passed.

One evening, she knocked on his door. "Can I come in, Dad?" she called.

She heard his chair creak and then the door opened, letting out the distinctive aroma of marijuana smoke. The only light in the room came from the floodlights outside, filtered through the closed Venetian blinds. For a moment, she thought she was seeing a stranger, he looked so gaunt. In the light from the hall, his hair seemed to have more grey in it.

Why didn't I notice before? she wondered.

"What are you doing, sitting in the dark?"

"It's the best way to listen to the music," Raymond replied. "I'll turn on a light. Come in." he opened the door a bit wider and went over to the bed and snapped on a small lamp.

Julia went in and perched on his desk chair.

"What's that you're listening to?"

"It's a group from the nineteen-sixties called *It's a Beautiful Day.*"

"I like it."

"Yes, they were quite innovative in their time. I believe they were the first rock group to use an electric violin as a lead instrument, but they didn't make many recordings, unfortunately."

"Not like The Rolling Stones, eh?"

"No, indeed. They were still going strong in the 2010s; Mick Jagger was a grandfather by then, but he still had the energy to put on a good show." He leaned forward with his hands together, forearms resting on his knees. "What can I do for you, love?"

45

"Nothing. I was just wondering how you were. I hardly ever see you anymore."

Raymond sighed and rubbed his face. "I know. I'm sorry. I haven't been feeling like company much lately."

"Is something wrong, Dad?"

The *Beautiful Day* disk ended and another one dropped into its place. Raymond listened for a moment. "Fleetwood Mac. They were great in the early days, before they went to America. After that, they got too commercial. Made a lot of money, but...." He shrugged.

"Are you depressed?" Julia persisted. She was taking psychology as one of her optional courses.

"I suppose I am a bit," Raymond conceded. He pulled his feet up on the bed and leaned back with his hands clasped behind his head.

"What's wrong, Daddy? Is it Mom and the other two?"

"Not really. They're all right." He sighed. "Things are not going too well in the parks. It's depressing to see the trees dying and not be able to do anything to save them."

"Why are they dying?" Julia asked.

"The weather. They're cold weather species; they can't survive this heat. The cedars in Stanley Park are finished; the Douglas firs are almost as bad. You'd think it was a logging camp these days with all the tree felling that's going on. All you can hear, all day long, is chain saws and logging trucks. There are hardly any evergreens left alive. It used to be the biggest stand of virgin forest within a city in North America."

"God," she replied. "What are they going to do?"

"We'll probably be planting southern pines, sycamores, eucalyptus, maybe even citrus, things that thrive in hot weather. If we don't make some changes soon, all it will be fit for is cactus."

Julia went over to the bed and knelt on the floor, resting her head against his leg. "I'm sorry, Dad. I wish I could do something to cheer you up." She accepted his explanation, even though it didn't ring true somehow.

He smoothed her hair. "You've cheered me up just being here." Raymond said. "How are things going with you?"

"Fine." Julia thought for a moment. "Dad, did you ever go on a date?"

Raymond sat up and swung his legs off the bed. "Anyone special in mind?" he asked.

"No it's just, you know, in all the old videos, people ... men and women ... go out together, by themselves. I was wondering, you know, what it was like."

"I see. Well, your mother and I used to go out a lot. We went to concerts and clubs; we played tennis and went for walks in the park." He stopped and listened to the music for a moment. "I don't know what to tell you. It was fun. It was exciting. I was always afraid she'd meet someone else and stop seeing me."

"But she didn't, did she?" Without waiting for an answer she continued, "Don't you think it's ironic that with all the men in the world, I'll never be able to go on a date?"

"It would be much too dangerous for you to be out alone with a boy, love."

"I know that, Dad, but still..."

"Is there anyone special you're interested in?"

"What chance do I get to meet boys? I'm always being watched and can't go out anywhere without a whole team of bodyguards."

Raymond laughed at her dramatization of the situation. "We just don't want anything to happen to you. What about the club dances?"

"They're okay, I guess, but it's always the same boys, picked by the hosts and parents. They're not very interesting and they're all the same—boring, trying too hard to impress."

"Well what sort of boy would you like to meet, someone like Paul?" He grinned

"That would be a bit too weird, but at least he's interesting, different."

"Well, we'll have to see what we can do, won't we?"

"What do you mean?"

"Maybe we could have a party and invite some friends of friends and relatives."

"Wow! That would be super-tight."

***

The party took place in November. True to his promise, Raymond, with the help of other members of the family, had rounded up twelve young men, and five other young women around Julia's age. Furniture was pushed back against the walls in the big living room to make room for dancing, and the buffet and tables in the dining room were loaded with food and drinks. Julia knew two of the girls. One was her cousin, Miriel, who was wearing a slinky floor-length, tight fitting dress of black satin with slits up to her thighs. Julia though it was a bit over the top. She had chosen to wear a knee-length blue velvet skirt with a long-sleeved blouse in darker blue, studded with crystal beads. She wore dark blue tights and silver sandals.

Julia had met Tallis, the daughter of one of Edgar's friends, a few times before. Tallis came dressed in a plum-colored outfit that resembled a leotard and tights that revealed her slender body almost to the bone.

Paul had brought one of his friends and the two of them, decked out in black robes with strings of beads and headbands, sat in a corner by the stairs with an old-fashioned hookah, passing the mouthpiece back and forth, as they watched the festivities. Occasionally one of them would make a remark and they would both dissolve into a fit of giggles. The girls ignored them.

The music was, of course, classic rock, interspersed with some modern *sling*. The young people found the old-fashioned music was quite as stimulating to dance to in contrast to the more sedate sling and the floor was constantly filled with swaying bodies.

Julia noticed him the moment he entered the room. He stood out from all the other young men. For one thing, he was dressed differently. He had on black, tight-fitting trousers with a pleated white shirt and a white jacket. Strangest of all, he wore a bow tie and a cummerbund. She had only seen such clothes in old videos, but the effect, to her, was stunning. His hair was black, ear-length, parted neatly at the side with a dark wing falling over his brow. When they were introduced by Edgar, she noticed his eyes were dark grey. He was taller than Edgar, but not quite as tall as Paul.

"Cornelius," she said when they were introduced. "That's a mouthful. Is that what everyone calls you?"

"My friends call me Neal," he replied, his mouth twitching as he suppressed a grin.

"What shall I call you?" Julia asked.

"That depends on whether we are friends, doesn't it?"

God, she thought. I wish. "Okay. Neal."

He smiled. "Want to dance?"

She nodded and they moved into the center of the room. Someone had just put on a sling recording; now they could dance together. Neal put his right hand around her waist and took her right hand in his left and they began to move to the music.

49

It was like a dream come true, dancing in the arms of an elegant, handsome stranger. *I'll remember this moment for the rest of my life, she thought. I'm so glad I wore this dress.* She knew instinctively he wouldn't be impressed by an obvious attempt to be seductive.

"I like your dress," he said, as if reading her mind. "You've got good taste, if you don't mind me saying so."

She didn't. She looked over his shoulder, blushing. "Thank you. I like your outfit too."

He squeezed her hand and pressed her closer to him.

After the dance was over, they went to the refreshment table and helped themselves to punch and some finger-food. "Let's go and sit on the stairs to eat this," he said.

She saw Paul smirk at them as they passed and responded with a haughty lift of her chin.

They sat on the stairs and watched the activity below. The music had livened up again. David was dancing with Tallis while several other young men hovered around them. Her mother and father were dancing together, showing the young folk how people used to dance a hundred years ago. She was embarrassed for them, but nobody else seemed to find it odd.

"Who's the girl with the silver hair in the red body suit?" Neal asked.

Julia felt a sting of jealousy. "Tallis Campbell," she replied. "Why?"

"Oh, nothing. I think I've seen her before somewhere."

"Do you think she's attractive?"

"In an obvious sort of way. I think she tries too hard. I'm not interested in her." He put down his plate and took her hand, then turned to face her. "Tell me about yourself."

"There's nothing much to tell. What do you do? Are you going to university?"

"I just graduated, last May. I work with father."

"My God, how old are you?" she blurted.

"Twenty-two. Since we're on the subject, how old are you?"

"Sixteen."

"Sweet sixteen and never been kissed." He smiled at her. "I bet that's not true, a pretty girl like you. You must have boys lining up at the gate."

She turned away and looked down at the dancers to hide her embarrassment. "Not really," she replied. "What do you and your father do?" she asked to get away from that subject.

"We have a marine salvage business."

"What does that, I mean, I don't know what...."

"It means, basically, that we pick stuff up out of the water, wrecked boats, lost equipment, things like that, the occasional body."

She turned quickly and looked at him to see if he was serious.

Seeing her eyes widen, he laughed. "Just kidding. Although we did drag up a body once. Somebody who fell or was dumped off a foreign freighter. That's another thing we find sometimes, freight dumped off ships."

"Why would they do that?"

"Sometimes, it's contraband they drop overboard for their contacts to retrieve. Other times, when the cargo has been damaged or, in the case of food, spoiled, they just dump it."

"What do you do with the stuff you salvage?"

"Sell what we can, recycle. Sometimes we work for the police or customs, and then we have to turn it over to them. But they pay us a good fee for our services."

He stood up. "I think we should go back down and circulate. Your father's been looking at us as if he's ready to bring out the shotgun."

"Don't pay any attention to him. I'm not a child." But she got up and followed him to join the rest of the party.

They each danced a few times with other guests, but towards the end of the evening, he found her again. He stood a short distance away and smiled at her, raising his eyebrows. She excused herself from the two boys she was talking to and followed him to the kitchen.

"Can I call you?" he asked. "I'd like to see you again."

"Yes," she said with a coolness that belied what she was feeling. She could barely breathe. She glanced down, wondering if the pounding of her heart could be seen through her blouse.

Neal put his arms out and pulled her to him. She turned her face up and found his lips on hers. After kissing her gently, he drew back. "I have to go, but I'll call you." He turned away before she could respond and almost collided with John who was standing in the doorway, scowling.

***

Aldina, Antoine, and Raymond were practicing in the music room when Neal called. Just seeing his face on the screen made Julia feel as if she was about to melt. As soon as the call was finished, she dashed downstairs.

"Can I go out tomorrow night with Neal?"

"What?" Raymond stopped playing abruptly and looked at Julia. "I don't think that would be a good idea, Jul. We hardly know him. How do we know ...?"

"Let her go," Aldina interrupted. "She's got to start living sometime. Besides, Edgar vouches for him; that's good enough for me."

Julia looked at her mother gratefully, really seeing her for the first time in a long while. It was amazing how little she seemed to have aged. Her face was smooth and unwrinkled apart from some lines at the corners of her eyes. There wasn't a strand of grey in her hair, although the style had changed from her former shoulder-length waves to a short cap-like cut. She didn't tower over Julia so much as she used to, and her waist had thickened a bit, even though she continued to be as active as always. She still wore the same Divas—the one-piece pantsuit, made famous by Diva, the media star of the twenties. Although Julia thought it a bit dated, she had to admit the style looked good her mother.

"Isn't he a bit old for her?" Raymond persisted.

"Only six years. What difference does that make? I like him."

Aldina raised her eyebrows and smiled. "Where was he planning to take you?"

"He mentioned the Pavilion."

"That sounds safe enough." Aldina said. "You're keeping very quiet, Antoine. What do you think?"

He smiled sheepishly and shrugged. "I don't see any harm."

"Thanks, Mom, Antoine.

"All right," Raymond conceded, "but only if one of the boys goes along with you."

"Oh, dad." She had hoped to be alone with Neal.

"I don't want anything to happen to you. You'll be much safer with two escorts."

Julia sighed. At least they were letting her go, and she had to admit, she wouldn't even have met Neal if her father had not thought of having a party.

Neal arrived at six in his Orca. Julia's heart began to race when she saw the car come through the gate. She looked in the hall mirror and decided gold high-heeled sandals were too dressy with her simple trousers and silk shirt, so she dashed back upstairs to her room and exchanged them for black ballerina slippers. She also took off the turquoise bracelet and replaced it with a plain gold chain.

When she came downstairs, Neal, dressed in a high-necked shirt of black silk with matching pants, was sitting in the living room talking to Raymond. They stood up as she reached the bottom step.

"Where's David?" she asked.

"I'm coming." David sauntered in from the kitchen.

"At least you're wearing something respectable for a change," she said, relieved that he had put on a sweater and long pants instead of his usual cut-offs and down-at-heel sandals.

David grimaced at her. "Shall we go?"

"Take care of her, and don't stay out too late." As David passed, his father handed him a cash card. "To help with the expenses, but don't go overboard."

Julia took her jacket from the banister and slipped it on.

She was breathless with excitement as the car drove through the gate and onto the street. Neal turned to look at her. "You look good," he said. "Yellow really suits you. How are you?"

"Fine," she said, aware of David in the seat behind her.

As they drove down the hill towards the city center, the whole of downtown Vancouver lay before them, its lights reflecting off the water of English Bay. The North Shore glittered and sparkled beyond the dark patch of Stanley Park and the Burrard Inlet. Julia had seldom been out at night and was amazed by the amount of traffic and the speed at which it moved. The night was filled with a cacophony of car horns, the high-pitched toots of cycles and the intermittent blasts of recorded music from passing vehicles. On Fourth Avenue, the tops of buildings were lit up with animated advertising. They crossed the Burrard

Street Bridge and turned right under the bridge into the West End. It seemed as if every motor vehicle in Vancouver had swarmed into this kilometer-square neighborhood to join the slow moving, noisy procession through the grid of narrow streets and apartment towers.

They made their leisurely way along Beach Avenue, Julia was amazed to see women in sparkling dresses lining the sidewalk, smiling and making hand signs at the passing traffic. Occasionally, a vehicle would stop and one of the women would climb in.

"I thought it was dangerous for women to be out at night without protection. What are they doing?"

David snorted.

"Don't worry about them, they can take care of themselves," Neal said with a laugh. "And they're not real women."

"Oh," Julia felt embarrassed at being so easily taken in. "You mean they're ...?"

"You got it. Girl-friends."

"God. I can't imagine doing something like that."

"You mean having the change?"

"Yes. And selling yourself that way."

He gave her an enigmatic look. "It's a matter of supply and demand. Damn." The traffic that had just picked up a bit of speed was brought to a halt by a traffic light. "They make a good living, but they burn out young. They're finished, used up by the time they're thirty. That's why they have to hustle while they can."

A face appeared in the passenger window, grotesque with red-rimmed eyes and tattoos, saliva running down his chin. He leered at Julia who cringed away. David put his hand out of the window and shoved the man, sending him backwards to land on his rear end.

"Get lost, roach."

"I didn't do nothin'," the man whined, getting slowly to his feet and staggering away.

The lights changed and they were moving again.

She looked over at the sparkling radiance of English Bay to where the freighters anchored offshore blazed with lights above their dancing reflections. As they entered Stanley Park, she saw the dead trees Raymond had told her about, a forest of dying evergreens, brittle and brown. The cedars, hemlocks, and firs had grown here in an ideal environment for countless centuries until the climate changes—twentieth century man's gift to nature and the future. A pile of logs stood next to a massive machine at the edge of the driveway. It's no wonder her father was depressed.

Lights blazed from the windows of the Pavilion. One of Vancouver's trendiest restaurants, it stood at the edge of a bluff overlooking the Burrard Inlet. Neal handed his ignition card to a valet at the door and ushered Julia inside. David followed them, hands in pockets.

"I've reserved a table by the window," Neal told them. "The view's fantastic."

Julia looked at the menu set discretely in the tabletop. "Salmon! I don't believe it. I thought only First Nations were allowed to catch salmon."

"They are allowed to sell some of it," Neal replied. "Would you like some?"

"But it's so expensive."

"Don't worry about that. Have you ever tasted Salmon?"

"Only from a can. We had some one Christmas. My grandma had saved it for years."

"Come on, try it. It's great with the asparagus salad."

"All right, I'd love to." She pressed the button next to the braised salmon and asparagus salad.

"What are you having, David?" Neal asked.

Julia sensed some tension between him and her brother. Neal was probably resentful that she'd brought a chaperone. She wasn't too happy about it herself but she'd made up her mind not to let it mar her enjoyment of the evening.

"I'm having steak." David pushed the menu button.

"God, David, how can you?"

"I'm paying for it," David retorted.

"But red meat, it's so..." Julia shuddered.

"I'm not asking you to eat it," her brother replied.

"What would you like to drink?" Neal jumped in before an argument could develop. "If you press the blue button, you'll get the drinks menu."

Julia looked at the beverage menu and frowned. "I don't even know what half this stuff is. What are you having?"

They were interrupted by a commotion at one of the other tables, a woman and three men shrieking at one another. Suddenly, the woman jumped up, overturning her chair, and darted through a door at the back of the room. The headwaiter went over to the table and spoke to the men who stood up and moved towards the door. One man stood there and waited for the woman while the other two went outside.

"I wonder what that was about," Julia said, embarrassed by the public scene.

"Oh it happens all the time. It's a sign of the stress everyone suffers. The woman is probably married to some or all of those guys. Things build up."

Julia could relate to that, except that in her household, flare-ups were rare. There were more likely to be silences and heavy atmospheres through which one trod carefully, or kept out of the way.

They finished eating, although Julia noticed that David hadn't been able to finish his steak. Julia decided to try one of the fancy coffees with liqueur, but didn't find it half as enjoyable as she'd imagined it would be. However, given the high price, she forced herself to finish it.

Neal leaned back in his chair and smiled at her. "What would you like to do now?" he asked.

"I don't know. What time is it?"

"Nine-thirty," David said. "I think we should go home."

Julia looked down at the table, disappointed. "Do we have to?" she asked Neal.

"Don't look so glum, we have time to go somewhere else if you want," Neal replied with a smile.

She returned his smile, relieved.

"Let's go. I've got an idea." He stood up and helped her on with her jacket. "It's time you saw a bit of the night life of this town. You too," he added to David.

After parking in an underground parkade off Georgia Street, they took an elevator to the top of one of the towers. The room, which filled the entire top floor, was surrounded on all side by glass. It seemed as if everything in the room was made of glass, even the floor, which was suspended over a sheet of rippling water. The room sparkled and shimmered with reflections from the candles that lit every table and the lights surrounding the tiny stage.

Julia was enthralled by everything, the seductive beat of the music, the glitter. The air that cycled through different fragrances, some, like jasmine, she recognized and other more exotic scents that she couldn't identify. Neal guided her with his hand on her back to a table by the wall that concealed the service area. They sat side by side on a padded bench covered in soft silver leather. David pulled out a chair and perched on the edge of it, scanning the room.

"What are you drinking, Dave?" Neal asked.

Julia tensed. She knew how much her brother disliked having his name abbreviated but, apart from a brief scowl, David let it pass.

"I'll have ale." He took out his father's cash card and laid it on the table. "Let me buy them."

He ordered drinks, a non-alcoholic for Julia and tequila for Neal.

"The next show should be starting soon," Neal said when they'd been served their drinks.

The music stopped and the dancers left the floor, then the lights around the stage brightened and three figures appeared from one side. They wore elaborate costumes sparkling with sequins and metallic beads, mesh stockings and high-heeled silver shoes. Hair piled up on their heads in elaborate coils, two were blondes and one was a brunette. Their faces were made up to exaggerate their features, deep purple lipstick, sparkles on their eyelids and cheeks, their eyes outlined heavily with kohl. Thick waists and narrow hips were the only indication they were not born female.

They performed to a frenzied Latin rhythm, singing the Spanish lyrics in throaty contralto voices and moving their hips to the beat.

Julia was speechless. She sipped her drink and absorbed everything.

After the applause had died down from the first number, the music started again, this time with a slower more sensuous rhythm. The three performers started into a sinuous dance with much suggestive swaying and thrusting of hips that brought whistles from the audience. As the beat picked up, they slowly stripped off their long gloves, one at a time, and threw them casually over their shoulders. The audience, mostly men, cheered enthusiastically and yelled "More, more! Take it all off!"

The music beat faster and the dancers, keeping time with their hips, unhooked their skirts and let them fall to the floor, then casually kicked them out of the way. They were left in short shorts, and brief jackets, their long legs emphasized by the mesh stockings. Slowly, they unbuttoned their little bolero jackets and peeled them back, revealing their small, pointed breasts. They let the jackets slide down their arms and drop on the floor. The audience went wild as the three dancers began to spin faster and faster, ending up in a split on the stage with their arms outstretched, smiling brazenly.

Bowing to the audience, the two blondes scooped up their garments and left the stage. The brunette picked up her bolero and put it back on, then began to sing, quite movingly, an old love song from the twenties.

Neal put his arm around Julia's shoulder and leaned close to her ear. "How do you like it?" he asked.

"They're so good," she replied, eyes gleaming in the candlelight. "How do they, you know, make themselves look so much like women?"

"Surgery and hormones, mostly."

"She's—should I call them she?" Neal nodded. "She's got such a lovely voice."

The other two singers returned and the group did a few more numbers. When the performance ended, Neal took Julia's hand. "I think I should be getting you home. It's almost eleven."

"Do we have to go?" she asked. "Can't we have just one dance?" This was what she had been waiting for, hoping for all evening, to be in his arms again.

Neal looked at David.

"All right, but just one. If I don't bring you home at a decent hour, your folks might not let me take you out again."

She was in his arms, feeling his heart beating through his shirt and breathing in his scent, hardly able to believe this was happening to her. His face pressed against her hair, then he moved slightly and she felt his breath in her ear. "Enjoying yourself, Julia?" he murmured.

"God, I wish we could do this forever."

"So do I." He kissed her ear. "But we really should go. I think David's getting a bit impatient, sitting there scowling at us."

Reluctantly, she let him lead her off the dance floor and waited while he retrieved their coats from the cloakroom.

"We'll have to do this again," Neal said in the elevator. He kissed her gently. David rolled his eyes and sighed.

Chapter Eight

Dear Dad:

We arrived in San Antonio, TX last night. They didn't tell us where we were going until an hour before we left, so I couldn't let you know any sooner. We're supposed to be helping pacify a rampaging group of militant fundamentalists. I don't know if you've seen anything on the news about it, but they've been bombing medical research facilities and killing anyone they think relates to genetics. I don't know what their reasoning is, but with crazies like these, it could be anything and they're armed to the teeth with military-grade weapons.

It's pretty hot here after six months in Siberia.

Part of an email message from a member of a NAMA.

Neal continued to court Julia for the next year, taking her out, and being invited to the house to share a meal and join in family activities. On one such occasion, they were having dinner at the big table in the dining room. For once, everyone was there, except Paul, although no one was surprised when he was absent. He seemed to live in a different world from everyone else.

A door slammed at the back of the house and footsteps clumped towards the dining room, then Paul appeared in the doorway. Aldina gasped. Everyone stopped eating and turned to stare at him open-mouthed. His hair was shorn off, gone were his robe and beads, replaced by a collarless blue shirt and khaki trousers.

Paul scowled at them. "Is something wrong?"

"Your hair..." Julia said.

"Yes, I've had it cut." Paul replied. He crossed to the sideboard and picked up a plate, which he piled with food, and then he sat down by his father.

"I've got an announcement to make," he said.

John rolled his eyes. David started eating again, but everyone else was waiting to find out what had caused such a radical change in Paul.

"I've decided to join NAMA."

Everybody spoke at once:

Aldina: "What's NAMA?"

John: "Are you out of your mind?"

Julia: "I thought you were a confirmed pacifist."

Raymond: "Let's discuss this, son."

David: "Tight!"

"I thought you'd say that," Paul replied calmly. Turning to his mother, he added, "NAMA is the North American Mercenary Association. They work on contract to governments all over the world. Join the mercs and see the world!"

"You can't be serious," Aldina pleaded. "You might get killed."

"I think it's fantastic. Where would you go?" David asked.

"There's plenty of wars to choose from and NAMA's involved in most of them." He was correct. There was the conflict in the Balkans that seemed to have been raging, on and off, for several hundred years; the Brazilian border disputes with Chile, Peru, and Bolivia each trying to claim the last few pieces of the Amazon rain forest; the usual conflicts in what was left of Africa and the Middle East; plus at least three wars in Southeast Asia.

"You mean they could be fighting on both sides?" Raymond asked.

"Theoretically, they could, but I'm sure there would be provisions for that type of conflict. It wouldn't be very profitable if they were killing their own employees."

"But why did you choose NAMA?" Julia asked. Her eldest brother could be a pain at times, but she still didn't want him to go away and possibly be injured or killed. "Why can't you join an expedition to the North Pole or something?"

Men's unfulfilled sexual tension had to have an outlet. Many men found relatively peaceful means to relieve the pressure that built up; they played competitive sports, climbed mountains, trekked through the arctic wilderness, or pitted themselves against great rivers and oceans. Currently, there were at least three expeditions pedaling across the Atlantic. Some created marvelous constructions—sometimes architectural wonders, other times beautiful abstractions built for their own sake. Sadly, the primitive instinct to battle still prevailed. One of the world's growth industries was mercenary operations, which saved many governments the expense of keeping standing armies. All they needed to do was contract a mercenary army when a conflict arose. There was always plenty of work for mercenaries.

"How do you expect me to pay for something like that? It's not cheap. None of those things is. Besides, this will give me a chance to see something of the world and get paid at the same time. The money's good and most of it— apart from a little spending money—goes straight into the bank."

"How long have you signed up for?" Raymond asked.

"The standard seven-year contract with a bonus option for extending it at the end of that time."

The discussion continued for the remainder of the meal, but Paul was not to be swayed. It ended up with Raymond in a rage and Aldina close to tears. Julia quietly suggested to Neal that they go outside for a while and sit in the garden.

After Paul left for the training camp, an atmosphere of gloom descended on the house. Julia began to spend more and more time away from home with Neal. He proposed to her at her seventeenth birthday party.

Chapter Nine

If the shortage of women is spoiling your party plans, we have the solution. Why not invite some of our specially trained young ladies as guests? Our girls are guaranteed to liven up your gathering with their sophistication and socials skills*. We have trained musicians, singers, and dancers. They are all skilled in the art of conversation and are good listeners with impeccable manners. Available for weddings,

graduations, birthdays, anniversaries, and other social events.
*All services are strictly platonic.

Text of ad appearing in several E-zines.

Weddings, being so rare, had become even more a cause for celebration than they were in historic times and lasted for several days. Julia's wedding started two days before the ceremony with a small music festival held in her honor in the Chan Center at UBC. The string quartet in which her parents and Antoine played were featured in the program, playing the Revolver Suite they'd been rehearsing the day she was born. Several other popular Vancouver musical ensembles added their talents to the event. Although the theatre was not filled, almost two hundred people attended the concert.

The following afternoon, a tea party was held in the garden of their home to introduce the couple to friends and well-wishers, and to display wedding gifts. After the garden party, Julia had the evening free. She was supposed to relax and build up her strength for the following day, but was too nervous and spent most of the time running up and down stairs checking on her wedding outfit and going over the lists she had pinned up everywhere.

"For goodness sake, Julia, sit down. You're making me nervous," Aldina said at one point. "Everything will be fine."

Julia perched on the edge of a chair, twisting her hands. "I can't help it," she said. "I'm sure we've forgotten something."

"You'd think you were the first person to ever get married," David said.

"Are you sure you've got everything ready?" she asked. "I don't want you holding everything up at the last minute because you can't find your shoes or something."

"God, Julia, lighten up."

Aldina stood up and held her hand out to Julia. "Come on; let me give you a massage. It'll relax you so you can get some sleep. You don't want to have bags under your eyes tomorrow."

An hour later, Julia lay in bed, trying to sleep. It was nine forty-five and still light outside. The window was open, letting in a warm, fragrant breeze. She could see her wedding gown, hanging on a hook on the wall. It was cream satin with a long narrow skirt and a little lace jacket. She had decided to wear a circlet of cream roses in her hair instead of the traditional veil.

This is probably the last time I'll sleep alone, she thought with a feeling of delicious anticipation. She stretched and yawned, then turned on her side and closed her eyes with a smile on her lips.

She went through the wedding in a dream. There were no problems, apart from Neal's father getting noisily drunk. She had only met Cyrus Gianakis once before. He was a bitter man, unforgiving of the wife who deserted him for a younger man several years earlier. He now put all his energy into his business, and spent his non-working hours drinking and brooding. He was rude and discourteous to several women at the reception, muttering that women are all alike, always scheming and deceiving. He treated Julia with barely concealed hostility, although he had been amiable enough before he started drinking. *In vino veritas?* she wondered.

One bright spot was seeing her friend, Farida, again—a very grown-up Farida, hanging onto to the arm of her handsome husband, Sarap. She looked spectacular in a short white dress that showed off her long shapely legs, and a nosegay of blue flowers pinned in her hair.

"You look great," Julia said. "Marriage must be good for you."

Farida's eyes glowed as she glanced at Sarap. "It's wonderful. I hope you'll be as happy as we are."

"What are you doing these days?"

"I start UBC in September. I'm so excited. Sarap just got his doctorate, so he might be one of my professors."

"She's a very smart young lady," Sarap said. "Did you know she is going to be the one to solve the female population crisis?" He put his arm around Farida's shoulder and pulled her close.

Farida blushed. "What are you doing," she asked, "besides getting married?"

"I'm studying design at Emily Carr." Julia looked around the room and saw Neal watching her with a slight frown on his face. "I'd better circulate. I'm so glad you came. I'll talk to you later."

Julia had the option of choosing the surname she would use after she was married, she decided on her mother's family name, Finisterra. "It's not that I don't like your name, Dad," she explained to her father when she made the decision. "It's just that Finisterra sounds nice, sort of musical. Julia Finisterra."

"What about your husband's name?"

"Julia Gianakis. No, it feels a bit weird."

For their honeymoon, Neal borrowed a friend's sailboat. They sailed among the Gulf Islands, anchoring in sheltered bays at night and just going where the mood took them. Raymond had been worried about pirates, but Neal assured him that that the boat was rigged to discourage anyone trying to board her. The entire rail around the vessel was electrified so that, at the push of switch, it could discharge enough volts that anyone trying to come over the side would receive a nasty jolt.

As it was, they saw very few people, mostly pleasure cruisers like themselves, and a few fishermen. The weather was very hot, as was to be expected in June, but the sea breezes helped them to keep relatively cool. When they came back to the city and settled in their own security apartment in the West End, Julia couldn't have been happier. Everything she had dreamed of had come true. She had married Prince Charming and believed she would live happily ever after.

Chapter Ten

Many married men find it difficult to handle the stress of being a husband. Most men are inclined to be conformists; they want to be part of the crowd, and being married, when so many of their friends and associates are not, sets them apart. It isn't that they're not accepted by their coworkers and friends, but they feel as if they're different somehow. Of course, they do face a certain amount of ribbing and suggestive comments from other men. This wears on them after a while. They also feel alienated by the envy of other men.

One of the causes of these [depressive] episodes is being different from other men, but I believe the major contributor to their psychological stress is the need for constant vigilance. They have something that other men covet, and they are terrified of losing it, so they must be super-vigilant, or at least they believe they must. Not only does this restrict their lifestyle, it causes tension between the couple. She must be sheltered and protected. He's afraid something might happen while he's away from home, so he calls her several times a day. When they go out together, he feels the same anxiety.

This constant vigilance puts a strain on both partners. The wife chafes at being under continuous observation and becomes resentful, feeling she is not trusted. Her anger drives her spouse's stress up another notch. It's like a constant feedback cycle.

Part of a speech given by Egon Markham, PH.D.
At a conference on The New Marriage, October 2057

It started when they had been married about six months. The Gianakis's business was not doing well and Neal had been showing signs of stress, either in morose silences or in brief flare-ups of anger. He was always remorseful and affectionate following one of his outbursts. Sometimes he would stay out after work and occasionally he came home drunk and angry, but she placated him by inviting him to bed. She felt the worst thing she could do would be to nag him about it. She was always on edge, trying not to do anything that would set him off.

This night she knew something was different. The door slammed, and then she heard a crash. She rushed into the entrance hall and saw him scrambling to his feet. The rug lay in a crumpled heap in the corner.

"Fucking piece of garbage," he yelled, picking up the rug. "Get rid of this shit." He threw the rug at her. "Burn it. If I ever see it again, I'll kill you."

Julia froze, terrified. She started to back away from the stranger in Neal's body.

"I'm talking to you, bitch." He started towards her, but bumped into a table, sending a vase crashing to the floor. "Now look what you've made me do."

He grabbed her arm in a painful grip. The smell of alcohol on his breath made her want to gag. She recalled something she'd heard about dealing with mad dogs: don't let them sense you're scared. She lowered her eyes so that he wouldn't be able to read the fear, but she couldn't hide her trembling. She stood, barely daring to breathe, horrified, waiting.

"I'm talking to you, bitch. Where's my dinner?"

She looked down at his hand on her arm. "It's ready, in the kitchen. I'll get it for you right away." Was her voice steady enough?

He let go of her and lurched into the living room. "And don't take all night. I'll eat it in here."

She hurried into the kitchen and put a plate of curried lamb into the microwave. When it was ready, she put it on a tray with a fork and napkin, and took it in to him. "Would you like some coffee?"

He took a forkful of curry and spat it out, spraying particles all over the carpet and coffee table. "What is this crap?" He picked up the plate and hauled it across the room where it smashed against the window. The plate disintegrated, but the window was unharmed, except for a greasy smear of food. "Why don't you learn how to cook like a proper wife?"

Julia couldn't believe he could look so nasty. His skin was blotchy red, his eyebrows drawn together, causing ugly creases in his forehead, and his mouth was curled in a surly snarl.

"I thought..." she began

"I don't care what you thought," he interrupted. He stood up and advanced towards her. "And while we're on the subject, why aren't you pregnant? I've been fucking you every night for six months. What's the matter with you? Are you using something?"

Tears sprang to her eyes. Is that all it was to him, fucking? She'd thought he was loving her. "I-no..."

"Get in the bedroom and get those clothes off." Neal snarled.

"But I've got to clean up..."

He struck so fast, she didn't have chance to duck. The punch landed on the side of her face, driving her head against the wall. Her ears buzzed, sparks flashed behind her eyes, and then she felt the pain, sharp and burning. He was still raving at her. "... in bed by the time I get there."

He staggered off to the bathroom and she heard water running. Dazed, Julia went to the bedroom and sat on the bed. What was happening? Was her dream of happiness just a juvenile fantasy? The thought sickened her. She was beginning to suspect he took after his father.

The toilet flushed and the bathroom door slammed back against the wall. Neal came into the room, undoing his shirt as he walked. "What? You're not ready? I thought I told you to get naked."

He lunged at her and tore her clothes off, not caring that he was destroying them. When he'd finished undressing her, he slapped her across the face again and threw her across the bed. He dropped his pants around his knees and fell on her.

He bit her neck and breasts savagely, while he plunged into her and pumped violently for about half a minute. Then he went limp. He pulled away with a groan and started towards the door, but his legs were tangled in his pants and he crashed to the floor. He pulled one leg free and rushed into the bathroom where she could hear him retching.

Julia moved to the far side of the bed and sat up. Trembling, she picked up her torn shirt and put it around her shoulders. She didn't know what to do to avoid any more blows.

A few minutes later, face pale and eyes glazed, he came back into the bedroom and fell facedown across the bed. He didn't even look at her. Within seconds, he was snoring.

Julia went to the bathroom and took a hot shower. She stood in front of the mirror, wrapped in a towel. There was a red lump on her cheek, turning black. Her left eye was swollen almost shut, the area around it turning purple. The bites on her neck glared angry red. She started to sob when she lowered the towel and saw the bite marks on her breasts.

After putting on a nightgown, Julia went to clean up the mess in the living room, and then she brought a blanket and pillow and made a bed on the sofa. She cried for a long time before she fell asleep.

Someone was shaking her shoulder. Where was she? She aroused slowly, and then a sharp pain in her neck brought back the events of the previous night. It was still dark outside; the room was illuminated by a glow from the bedroom.

"Baby, are you awake?" Neal. "Is it all right if I put on the light?"

Julia gave a non-committal grunt, which Neal took for assent. The lamp behind her came on, dazzling her.

"My God, sweetheart, what happened to you?" Neal put his arm under her shoulders and lifted her, then slid under her onto the sofa. He held her in his arms like a baby.

"Don't you remember?" she said.

Neal groaned. "Oh, God. I'm sorry, honey. Forgive me, please, baby. It'll, never happen again, I promise. You're everything in the world to me. I can't bear to see you hurt."

He started to cry. He squeezed her hard, rocking back and forth.

"You're hurting me, Neal," she said. The situation was so alien to her she was stunned. She hated to hear him sobbing like this; it broke her heart. Could she believe that he really did love her? Was it the drinking that had turned him into a monster? She began to feel a spark of hope.

"Do you really mean that, Neal?"

He shuddered and wiped his arm across his face. "Of course, baby. I love you so much. You're the best thing that ever happened to me." He buried his face in her hair. "God, how could I have been such an animal? I won't drink any more, I promise. You do still love me, don't you?"

"Yes, I love you," Julia replied flatly.

"Come on, let's go back to bed. It'll never happen again, I swear."

But it did. And worse. A few months later, Neal arrived home with another man. She heard them outside the door, giggling and shushing each other while Neal fiddled with the key card, trying to get it in the slot. Finally, the door opened and they fell inside. "I'm home," Neal shouted pointlessly. This brought on another fit of giggling. "I've brought you something."

The two men staggered into the living room where Julia had been working at her terminal.

"What'd I tell you?" Neal said to his friend. "Isn't she a sweetie?"

Julia watched them warily, wondering what sort of outrage he was planning this time. The man with Neal was a little older, maybe thirty. He wasn't bad looking in a rumpled sort of way, with thick, straw-colored hair and blue eyes. He was shorter and more sturdily built than Neal.

The man suppressed a smirk and approached her with his hand outstretched. "Rave, short for Raven. I was born with black hair, so that's what my mother called me," he babbled. "Pleasure to meet you, Julia. I've heard so much about you from old Neal, I feel I already know you. He's a very lucky man." He turned and winked at Neal who was leaning nonchalantly against the wall, watching.

Julia shook his hand apprehensively. "Nice to meet you, Rave." She looked over his shoulder and saw Neal smirking.

"Let me get you a drink," Neal said, making for the kitchen. "Sit down, relax."

He returned carrying three tumblers of clear liquid with floating ice cubes. "Here you go, lover, help you relax." He handed a glass to Julia.

She didn't want a drink, but she was afraid to refuse it. She took a little sip—it was gin—and set it down on the lamp table.

Neal sat beside her and put his hand on her knee. "Aren't you going to ask me about the present?" he said with a silly laugh.

"Okay, what is it?" she asked without much enthusiasm.

"Da-dah!" he sang. "There it is—a real live raven." He pointed at the other man who grinned back.

"I don't understand," Julia said. "What are you talking about?"

"I brought you a man. Thought you might like a little variety, like your ma."

Julia went cold. A sick feeling of dread swelled in the pit of her stomach. "It's a joke, right?" she stammered.

The grin on Neal's face was replaced by storm clouds. "It's not a joke," he snarled. "Rave's an old buddy of mine. I promised him a good time for his birthday and you're not going to spoil it. Are you?" he finished, grabbing her by both arms.

Julia looked past him and saw that Rave was no longer grinning. He looked both hurt and a little afraid.

"It's all right Neal," he said. "I thought you said she..."

"Shaddup!" Neal yelled. "I promised you a good time and this bitch is not going to spoil it for you."

He pulled Julia to her feet and ripped open her shirt, then he tugged at her bra until it was torn apart. "See, what'd I tell you?" he said, grinning at his friend. "Isn't she a beauty?"

Julia folded her arms across her chest, tears running down her face. "Please, Neal," she whimpered.

Rave stood up and sidled towards the front door. "Listen, man, I think I'll be going. Some other time, eh?"

Neal let go of Julia and rushed at Rave. "NO!" he screamed, grabbing the man's arm.

But Rave jerked free and opened the front door. "Catch you later. Thanks for the drink," he said as he disappeared into the hall.

Neal rushed at Julia and punched her in the face. He hit her so hard, she went sprawling backwards over the coffee table, landing with her head against the bookcase. He ran around the table, brushing aside the fallen plants, and started kicking her in the ribs as she lay stunned.

When Julia came to, the apartment was silent. She was alone, surrounded by a litter of broken plants and spilled soil. When she tried to draw a breath, a sharp pain shot through her chest. There was something wrong with her shoulder and she couldn't get up. The arm wouldn't support her and the pain was excruciating.

After several aborted attempts, Julia managed to sit up. Head spinning, she scooted along on her bottom until she could reach the cordless, which had been knocked off the table when she fell. She wiped the dirt off it on the carpet, and then rested for a moment to draw a few painful breaths.

She needed help, but she felt humiliated and afraid her family would find out what had happened, but whom else could she call? She didn't really have any close friends except Farida but she would feel much too embarrassed to have Farida find out. There was nobody she could trust with such an intimate matter. The only person that came to mind was Edgar. She had enjoyed his company and their many conversations and she felt they had a special bond. She punched in the number, praying her mother wouldn't answer.

"Speak to me." David's cocky style of answering the phone.

Julia used every gram of strength she had left to keep her voice steady. "David, is Edgar around?"

"Hey, Jul, are you all right?"

"Of course. I'm just winded. Is he there?"

"Been working out, eh? Yes, I'll get him."

Julia leaned back against the bookcase and closed her eyes. Please hurry.

"Julia?"

"Ed, can you come over?"

"Sure. Is something wrong?"

"Hurry," she sobbed and dropped the phone.

When Edgar arrived, he took one look at Julia and called an ambulance. "You need to be in a clinic," he told her.

Julia knew he was right. She could barely move without sharp stabs of pain. "Can't we go in your car?" she gasped.

"I wouldn't even dare move you until I know how badly you're hurt. It looks to me as if your shoulder might be dislocated."

Edgar swept a clean space on the carpet with his hand and sat down beside her. He didn't seem to know what to do with his hands after that. First, he reached out and touched her hair, then stroked her leg. Finally, he held her hand. "I wish they'd hurry," he said, glancing towards the window.

Before long, they heard the high-pitched whine of the approaching ambulance.

The ambulance took her to the Arbutus Park clinic in Kitsilano. Edgar was right; she did have a dislocated shoulder as well as a couple of broken ribs and numerous bruises. The medics gave her some painkillers and reset her shoulder. Edgar waited outside in the atrium while they patched her up. When the medics had finished, they allowed him back in.

"Is there somewhere safe she could stay until she's feeling better?" Doctor Golden asked Edgar.

"She could come home to her parents' house," Edgar replied.

"No," Julia said. "I don't want them to know."

"They're going to find out some time," Edgar replied.

"I'll leave you two to decide," the doctor said. "You need lots of rest, and think about what I said about counseling. Excuse me." He left, quietly closing the door.

"Look, Julia, you can't go back there. How long has this been going on, anyway?"

"Oh he has a few drinks sometimes and then he gets a little crazy. He's under a lot of stress. The business isn't doing too well."

"That's no excuse. In addition, it is his fault. You don't have to half kill someone just because everything isn't going your way. You can't go back there. He might succeed next time." Edgar paced down one side of the treatment table and up the other, using the only free space in the tiny room.

"It'll be all right, Edgar. He's always really nice afterwards and feels so bad about..." She realized what she had admitted and stopped.

"So this sort of thing has happened before. I was afraid of that. It's typical of the syndrome. Come on, I'm taking you home. And the doctor is right; you should go to a counselor. And don't blame yourself; it's not your fault. You need to keep that in mind."

Too drowsy and weak to protest any more, Julia allowed him to lead her to his car and drive her up the hill to their house in Point Grey. Edgar had called ahead to warn her parents that they were coming and it looked as if every light in the house was on when they arrived.

"God, you look as if you've been boxing with a bear," David said when her saw her. "I'll kill that bastard if I ever get my hands on him. I always felt there was something off kilter..."

"Leave her alone. She doesn't want to hear that sort of talk right now," Aldina said. "Let's get you to bed, sweetheart. You can sleep in Paul's room so you don't have to climb the stairs. Raymond, why don't you go and make her some hot *Ovaltine*?"

Neal called her the next day around noon. He looked dreadful on the monitor, pale and hollow-eyed, his dark hair stringy and tousled. Julia waited for him to speak first.

"Oh, baby, I'm sorry. God, I don't know what came over me. I acted crazy. I promise you, I'm going to get help. It's the booze. My old man..." He appealed to her with those heart-melting eyes.

Julia watched him silently.

"When are you coming home, lover? I miss you. Do you want me to come and get you this afternoon?"

"I don't think that would be a good idea," she replied breathlessly, trying to suppress a wince of pain whenever she inhaled.

His face turned ugly. "Why? Is your sanctimonious family trying to turn you against me? Well you're my wife and I want you home."

Oh, God, he's still drinking, she thought in despair. Where had her Prince Charming gone? What happened to the man she loved?

"Look, Neal," she said weakly, "I don't feel so good. I'll talk to you later." She pressed the button to disconnect.

He kept calling all afternoon, but she told her family she didn't feel like talking to him. He finally gave up when Raymond threatened to get a restraining order and place a ban on his number so his calls would be blocked.

A few days later, she went to see Kelly, the psychologist at the clinic. They talked for about forty minutes, until Julia began to get restless. Kelly looked at the clock.

"I guess you want to get going. Are you in pain?"

She nodded, "a little," and started to get up.

"Would you like something?"

"I've got my medication." Julia took out a pill container and popped a couple of painkillers in her mouth, washing them down with water.

"You mentioned something about not having many friends you can turn to," Kelly said as she stood up. "I have an idea. Someone I'd like you to meet."

Julia looked at him. "I don't understand."

"There's a woman I know. I'd like you to meet her. Is it all right if I ask her to call you?"

"I don't know," Julia replied. "Who is she?"

"Just a friend. You'd like her. She's very warm and she's only a bit older than you."

Julia's interest was stirred. What harm could it do? In addition, it would be a chance to get out of the house and meet someone new and who knows? They might become friends.

Julia received a call from the Kelly's friend the next day. From what she could see on the screen, the woman was in her mid-twenties. She had long blonde hair and wore a pale lavender shirt with a wide collar. "My name's Pascal Templeton. I promised Kelly I'd give you a call. I think I may be able to help."

Julia flushed, feeling uncomfortable. "What did he tell you about me?" she asked.

"Not much. Just that you needed a friend to talk to."

"I'm not that needy," Julia replied. "You don't have to go out of your way for me."

"No, you've got it wrong," Pascal said. "I'd *like* to meet you. I might need a friend too. And I know what you're feeling..."

"How can you possibly know how I feel?"

"I've been there, love." Pascal's expression was warm and friendly. "Shame? Blaming yourself for what happened? Depressed?"

"I thought anything you told to a therapist was confidential."

"Oh, he didn't go into specifics; he just said you had similar experiences to my own."

Julia nodded reluctantly. "What do you want to talk to me about?"

"I'd rather talk to you in person. Can you come to my place so we can talk without being interrupted?"

"Where do you live?" Julia was intrigued. Besides, she needed someone she could trust and confide in, although she still felt it was too premature to pin any hopes on a stranger.

"You know Kensington Gardens, the new development on the south side of False Creek?"

Julia knew it. For the past several years, the city and various contractors, in a burst of urban pride, had been razing the old run-down apartment buildings and seedy condominiums. The old site was being rejuvenated with spacious single-family houses in a park-like setting, complete with heavy security. It was being billed as a haven where women could live in safety, the ideal place to raise a family.

"Sure. When would you like me to come?"

"How about this afternoon? My kids will be in school until four."

Without telling her family where she was going, Julia called a Security cab. The Security Cab Company had been founded about fifteen years earlier when it became dangerous for unescorted women to travel outside their homes. The two-passenger vehicles had darkened bulletproof windows and the drivers were all armed. One of the conditions of employment was that the drivers were married, gay, or the fathers of daughters. The driver of Julia's cab stopped at the gatehouse of Kensington Walk and waited until she was safely inside the gate before driving off.

Julia's arm was still in a sling, but the pain in her shoulder and ribs was not as bad as it had been. The bruises on her face had faded enough for her to be able to conceal them with makeup.

Pascal had told her to turn right inside the gate. She could see the glitter of False Creek through the shady old trees that dotted the sweeping lawns. Several women were sitting at a table under one of the trees with some toddlers playing on the grass nearby. She followed a wide paved walk, bordered with palm trees, and circled a fountain. The houses were spaced about twenty meters apart, surrounded by individual flower gardens and shrubs. They were built in Retro-Moroccan style with thick white walls and flat roofs, although they all had individual designs. Some had greenhouses on the roofs. Number 14 had salmon and magenta bougainvillea growing on the walls that surrounded the garden.

The door opened before she could ring the bell. Pascal, in a one-piece trouser suit of peach crepe smiled warmly at Julia. "I was watching for you. Come in." She was almost as tall as Julia, but not so slender. With her large grey eyes, generous mouth and flawless complexion, she was a lovely woman.

Pascal led Julia through the tiled entrance hall into a small room at the back with French windows overlooking a private garden. In the middle of the lawn was a stone-rimmed pool with floating water lilies. The room was furnished all in white against pale yellow walls, with splashes of citrus colors on the sofas and chairs. Two walls were lined with shelves of books.

"This is beautiful," Julia said. "So peaceful."

"Sit down. I'll get you something to drink. Do you like cranberry juice?"

"Love it."

"Now, let's talk," Pascal said when they were both seated with their drinks. "First of all, I'll tell you a bit about myself. You wouldn't believe how common this story is." She stopped and sipped her juice. "You notice I didn't offer you anything alcoholic?"

Julia nodded.

"Never touch it. I've seen how it can destroy people. I was married to a man I thought was a prince, every woman's dream. Well, he turned out to have Beauty and the Beast all in one body."

Julia found herself hanging onto every word, astonished at how Pascal's story paralleled her own. She nodded.

"It would be an understatement to say he had a drinking problem. Anyway, to cut a long story short, after a broken arm, several cracked ribs and numerous black eyes, he was history."

"Neal has promised to get help," Julia said.

"You love him, right?"

Julia nodded, tears filling her eyes.

Pascal put her hand over Julia's and squeezed. "They all do. It doesn't work. Oh, Peter was so charming; he could talk the pants of a nun. I believed it when he told me he would get into treatment program. I *wanted* to believe him. I was crazy about the guy. He did enroll in a program for a while, but it didn't take much to set him back on the old track. He lost his job. This time he didn't just hurt me, He started in on the baby. I thought he was going to kill him. That's when I packed up and left." Pascal looked down at her hands, then back at Julia. "Do you mind if I ask you how old you are?"

"I'll be eighteen next month. We haven't even had our first wedding anniversary yet." She pulled out a tissue and wiped her eyes.

"You're young. You know, Julia, you have your whole life ahead of you. The first thing you need to do is take control of it yourself."

Julia nodded miserably.

"I know you don't want to hear this, but the sooner you call it quits with this guy, the better chance you have. What do you do? For a living, I mean."

"I'm still a student. I'm taking design at ECO, Emily Carr Online."

"Good for you. You'll have something to occupy yourself and take your mind off things."

"But I don't want to leave him. He's my husband and I still love him. If he gets help, I know we can make it work."

Pascal gave her a penetrating look. "It's not my place to tell you what to do, but may I make a suggestion?"

Julia nodded.

"Why not wait until he's been in a program for a while and see if it's working before you go back? If you go back to him now, while he's still angry, there's no knowing what might happen to you. And he needs an incentive to do something about his problem." Pascal said, wording it as tactfully as she could.

"I suppose you're right," Julia admitted reluctantly. "Did you get married again?" The house was obviously expensive and Julia wondered how Pascal could afford it. There were not many opportunities for women to have careers.

"Oh no. Once was enough."

"But how do you manage?"

Pascal stood up. "Let me show you the house."

She led Julia into a huge living room with Persian rugs on the floor, a real marble fireplace, a grand piano and harp in one corner. The wall overlooking the garden was all glass.

"It's so beautiful," Julia said.

"I'll show you the kitchen and nursery, and then we'll go upstairs."

They went through a large dining room with beautifully designed modern furniture and built-in cabinets into a large kitchen. All the appliances were concealed, giving the room a sleek, unified look. It was all white except for a blue tiled border on the walls, and a blue double sink. Even the floor was white—glossy polished marble.

"The children's rooms are back here." The nursery consisted of two sunny bedrooms opening off a playroom.

A curved white staircase led up to the second floor. "This is my private space," Pascal said as they rounded the top of the stairs. Julia gasped. The whole area was carpeted in white. On one side was a small sitting room with a mirrored bar, a sound system, a video and communications complex. It had low comfortable seats that looked as if you could sink right into them, and a small fireplace behind a glass screen. Opening off it on the garden side was the bedroom. It was huge with a big white bed in the middle—very feminine with lace-trimmed draperies hanging from a brass rail above the bed, and peach satin pillows. In one corner was a round step-down tub large enough for a whole family. Another room opened off the bedroom. It contained a massage table, some exercise equipment and a shower. French doors opened off the bedroom onto a roof garden over the kitchen.

"Like it?" Pascal asked proudly.

"God, yes. It's fantastic."

"Now I'll answer your question." Pascal sat down on a chaise longue and gestured Julia to a chair.

"What question?"

"I believe you wanted to know how I made my living."

"Oh, yes."

"In a very old and honored profession. I entertain men." She looked at Julia, waiting to see what her response would be.

"Oh." Julia was flabbergasted. She looked around again, searching for something to say. "But this is so, well feminine. I wouldn't have thought men would..."

Pascal laughed. "They love it this way. You have to understand men. They like to feel they have power over you. This," she waved her arm around, "It makes them feel they've penetrated your inner sanctum. What did you expect, red velvet and black leather?" She laughed again.

"I guess that makes sense."

"Not only that, it makes them feel safe. In a way, I make this a sanctuary for them, a place where they can relax and forget their troubles." She stood up. "Of course, they pay for it. Well."

Julia was genuinely intrigued. "But, I mean, what if the guy was ... well ... repulsive? I couldn't imagine..." She hesitated, seeing the amused gleam in Pascal's eyes.

"Oh, I'm very selective. There are plenty of men to choose from, believe me. Most of my clients are regulars. Actually, apart from the formality of fees, we're more like friends. I only consider clients who are recommended by people I know and trust. It's a very exclusive club." She chuckled.

"How many clients do you have?"

"I haven't counted them lately, but I'd estimate about sixty-five or seventy."

"How can you ... see so many?"

"Oh, some of them only call me once a year. Several live out of town, but with most, it's about once every four to six weeks. I only see one a day and I insist on having two nights off a week. I make a good living, as you can see."

"Would it be rude to ask how much ...?"

"You sound interested," Pascal said with a knowing smile.

"No, well..." Julia blushed. "It's just something I never knew much about."

"Come on, let's go downstairs," she said, linking her arm with Julia's. "It depends. If I really like the guy, and he doesn't have a lot of money, I'll charge him five hundred for an evening. Usually, though, it's a thousand to fifteen hundred."

"Wow." Julia did a quick mental calculation. Six to seven thousand a week, that's over twenty-four thousand a month. They reached the front hall. Julia looked at her watch.

"I think I should be going."

"Let me call you a cab, and then I have to go and meet the children."

"How many do you have?"

"Two. Nicky, he's ten, from my marriage, and Jessica. She's seven, the daughter of one of my special clients."

She went over to the com unit on the hall table and punched in the number of the cab company. When she replaced the receiver, she turned to Julia, taking her hand. "You know, Julia, you could have all this."

Julia was embarrassed. "But you're beautiful. I'm just a skinny...."

"Don't say that. Don't you know how attractive you are with all that dark hair and those lovely brown eyes? You could use a bit of padding, though," she added with a laugh. "You could have your cake and...." Pascal shrugged. "You know, you seem much more relaxed now. I want you to come again and have another chat. How about Friday? That's my next day off. Maybe we could go shopping."

Riding home in the cab, Julia had to admit she was feeling much better. Pascal did seem to have everything: a beautiful home, children—a daughter! and freedom. She thought about Neal and the man, Raven, he'd brought home and tried to make her.... God, it was so sordid. Compared to that, Pascal's life seemed elegant, classy. She had to give her marriage a chance. She owed Neal—and herself—in spite of everything. It wasn't easy to leave someone you loved.

Chapter Eleven

"Yes, Ron, what's on your mind today?"

"It's these sissy things they're teaching boys in school."

"Like what, sir?"

"You know, cleaning the house and cooking, stuff like that. Next thing you know, they'll be teaching them to sew."

"I take it you don't think boys need to know things like that?"

"Course they don't. That's women's work. I don't want my sons turned into sissies."

"Are you married, sir?"

"Of course I am."

"So, your wife takes care of the house and things like that?"

"Sure. It's her job."

"I see. How many sons do you have?"

"Four."

"How do you think they'll manage when they're grown up and on their own?"

"What do you mean?"

"Last time I checked, a man has a less than one chance in forty of getting married, to a woman. Sir...? I think we've lost him. Next caller."

Excerpt from radio talk show transcript, July 2057

When Julia arrived home, she found Paul there in his new military uniform. He looked a different person from the weird brother she had grown up with, immaculate in his zippered blouse of dark green and neat khaki trousers.

"Hey, what happened to you?" he said when she walked in with her arm in a sling.

"Hey, yourself. What are you doing here? You look great," she answered, sidestepping his question.

"He's going overseas," David said, sounding a bit envious.

"You are?" The thought scared her. "Where? When?"

"Come in the kitchen, Antoine's making some tea. Might as well get it over with while everybody's together, that way I won't have to listen to the protests more than once." He put his arm gently across her shoulder, but removed it when she winced. "Sorry."

"Who's going to protest?" David asked innocently.

"You know you'll miss me, kid."

When they were all settled around the table with their iced tea, Paul told them he would be leaving for Bolivia with a contingent of NAMA the following week.

"Lucky dog," was David's response.

"Is it dangerous?" Julia asked.

"I wish you weren't doing this. Promise you'll write every week, so I'll know you're all right," Aldina said. Her hands gripped her glass so tightly, her nails turned white.

"I still don't like it, son," Raymond said. "Just be careful."

There followed a stream of exhortations and reassurances until everyone ran out of things to say. Finally, Paul stood up and turned to Julia.

"Much as I enjoy being the center of attention, I think I'd like a quiet talk with my sister in the garden. Come on, kid."

"How could I refuse such a charming invitation," she said with a gaiety that belied her apprehension. This might be the last chance she would have to talk to him before he left and she had no idea how long he'd be gone. Surely, she could tolerate a little more advice or consolation, whichever he was planning to offer.

"You look really sharp in your uniform," she said when they were outside.

"Yeah," he said. "But what's happening with you? I heard a bit about it from Dad, but..."

"It's nothing," she replied. "Just, you know, drinking."

"You want me to have a talk to him?"

"No. Oh God no. We'll work it out. He's going to get in a program."

"Sure. You believe that. I'd like to wring his soddin' neck. You're not going back to him, are you?"

Julia lifted and raised her uninjured shoulder, the closest she could come to a shrug. She really didn't want to discuss this. "I'm going to wait and see what he does. If he sticks to the program, I guess I will. I mean if he makes the effort.... You know, he really feels bad about it. He just can't help himself sometimes. He's been under a lot of stress the last few months."

"You're just making excuses for the bastard." Paul spun around, looking up at the sky. "God, I wish I wasn't going away. I'd kill the sod if he ever hurt you again. I'll have a word with John. Maybe he can watch out for you."

"No," Julia cried. "I don't want..." She started to cry. It was all too much: the problems with Neal, Paul leaving, maybe to be wounded or even killed.

"I'm sorry," Paul said, patting her back. "Somebody's got to take care of you. We don't want anything to happen to our little sister."

"Nothing's going to happen." She sniffed and rubbed her nose with the back of her hand. "I'll be fine. It'll work out."

Julia moved back into her old room while Paul was staying. Neal called her every day, pleading with her to come home. He said he'd been going to AA meetings and wasn't drinking. She told him she'd like to wait a couple of weeks longer to see if he stuck to it, and if he did, she would come back.

"Couldn't we at least meet somewhere, maybe have dinner?" he begged one morning. "I miss you, baby. I love you so much, it's tearing me apart."

On the screen, he looked as if he was in genuine pain. Julia relented. "All right, but nothing fancy."

"How about one of those little Greek places on Fourth Avenue? That's about half way."

They discussed the details, agreeing to meet the following night. Julia was on edge the whole day, waiting until it was time to leave. She longed to see him and was afraid she wouldn't be strong enough to resist him.

Raymond drove her to the restaurant and waited to see her safely inside. Julia made him promise to come and pick her up in two hours. She didn't trust herself to leave, once she was with Neal.

He was sitting at an inside table, sipping something colorless from a tall glass. He put the glass down when he saw her and stood up. Her heart did a flip-flop. He was so handsome. She felt the old stirring of desire he always aroused. Her legs felt so weak, she wasn't sure she'd make it to the table.

Neal took her in his arms, nuzzling her neck, and murmured, "Oh, baby, you feel so good." He pulled out a chair for her, then sat down opposite. The candle on the table made his eyes glow when he looked at her. "How are you?" he asked

Julia squeezed her hands between her thighs under the table to stop them shaking. "I'm fine. Much better."

He looked down sheepishly. "You know I'm sorry, sweetheart." He brightened. "It's going really good with the recovery program. I understand more about what was happening to me and why I was doing those things. I feel so much better."

He did look healthy. His skin had good color, his eyes were bright, and the shadows that often underscored them had gone. His hair looked glossy and well groomed.

"You look great," she said. "Don't you think we should order something? I've only got a couple of hours." Set limits.

When they had ordered, he held her hands across the table and looked into her eyes. "I don't suppose I could talk you into coming home for a few hours. You could go back to your house afterwards if you want to. I'm so lonely and the bed is so big and empty without you."

Julia withdrew her hands from his grasp. It would be so easy to weaken. She wanted him as much as he wanted her. The arrival of their food gave her time to think about how to reply. She shook her head. "Let's stick to the agreement, okay?"

"I love you, Julia."

"I love you too."

After that, they picked at their food and talked about trivial matters. When Raymond arrived to take her home, Neal didn't go outside to speak to him.

Neal came to the house to pick her up ten days later, but waited for her at the gate. He was too embarrassed to confront her family.

"Welcome home, baby," he said, throwing open the apartment door.

To her amazement, the place was spotless. She was sure he would have forgotten to recharge the cleaning bots, or process the trash, but apparently, he'd handled everything like a pro. There were even fresh flowers on the table.

"Come and see what I've got for you?" He took her hand and pulled her to the bedroom.

A lovely gilt-framed antique mirror was hanging above the clothes press. It reflected another vase of flowers standing on top of the press.

"It's beautiful," she cried, throwing her arms around him. She kissed him. "Thank you, thank you, thank you."

"Anything to make you happy, my beauty. Every time you look in it, you'll see the girl I love." He picked her up and spun her around, then lost his balance and fell across the bed. "From right now, we're starting a new life." He rolled over with her still in his arms and kissed her.

One evening about a month later, Neal came home looking depressed, but he was sober. He dropped his notebook on a chair and flopped down on the sofa with a sigh.

"What's wrong?" Julia asked. "You look a bit down."

"The business. We lost another client today. The old man... Oh, shit, it's not his fault. There just isn't enough work to support us. We had to let Quinn go yesterday. The guy's been with us twelve years."

"Are you hungry?" Julia asked. "I've made your favorite, lasagna."

Neal sat down at the table while Julia got the hot dish out of the oven. She put it on a mat on the table and went back for the salad and garlic bread, then sat down opposite him.

Neal looked up from his plate. "We're going to be a bit short of money for a while."

"I wish I could help out. I'll have my degree next year, and then I'll be able to get some work, I hope."

"It's all right, baby, we'll manage. It's just as well you didn't get pregnant, though."

"Neal, there may be something I can do to help. I had a call today from an old friend."

He looked up warily. "Boy or girl?"

"Girl, of course, silly. You remember I told you about that girl at school who got married when she was eleven? She was at our wedding."

"The Hindu?"

"Sikh."

"Same thing."

"God, you're so ignorant sometimes."

"Whatever. Anyway, what's this got to do with our money problems?"

"I'm getting to that. She a science student at UBC. She was telling me about a program they have at University Hospital trying to find out how to increase the female birth rate. Her husband is one of the scientists. She says they are always looking for egg donors. They pay well for donations."

Neal put down his fork and looked at her. "What do you mean, egg donors?"

"You know, ova from fertile women."

"You've got to be kidding."

"You must have heard about it. I thought everybody knew about the research they're doing."

"How do they get these eggs?"

"Well, according to Farida, you have to take these fertility hormones for a while, and then when you're ready to ovulate, you go to the clinic and they harvest them."

"How?"

"I don't know, but I'm sure it's harmless."

"How can you be so sure?"

"I know Farida wouldn't recommend something that would hurt me."

"Ah, so this so-called friend is soliciting you for donations for her old man's experiments. Is that it?"

"No," Julia was surprised that he was so angry. "It wasn't like that. She just told me about it. She's a donor herself."

"What if it fucked up your chances of having a baby afterwards?"

"It doesn't. Farida just had a baby, that's what she was calling to tell me."

Neal picked up his fork again and resumed eating. He chewed for a moment, and then asked, "What do they do with these eggs?"

"They're trying various things, according to Farida. Manipulating the chromosomes to try to induce the development of females. They're even trying to make the egg develop without sperm, I think it's called parthenogenesis. If they did that, the baby would be an exact copy of the mother with only her genes. They fertilize some of them with sperm from men who have had daughters."

"What do they do with the fertilized—what do they call them, embryos?—that aren't female?"

"I didn't ask."

They ate in silence for a while, and then Julia asked, "Well, what do you think?"

"I don't know. Let me think about it. I don't think we're that desperate yet. What do they pay?"

"Do you want me to find out more about it? You know, just in case. Think of it as a contribution to science."

Neal shrugged. "It wouldn't do any harm to ask, I suppose. And find out if it would affect our love life. We don't want anything interfering with that."

For some reason, Neal's last statement offended her, making her feel like a sex object, but she chose not to comment on it.

Julia was happy again. A few months earlier, she hadn't dared to hope that it could happen. She still called Pascal every week, partly because she liked the woman, but also, she had to admit, to gloat a little. She had been right after all, in spite of Pascal's reservations. Her studies were going well and she received good marks in the December exams. There were only four more months to her degree.

They went to Julia's parents' house for Christmas. The family was less than enthusiastic about Neal being there, but they tried not to treat him like an outsider. After all, he was trying. He hadn't touched any alcohol since the summer.

In January, Julia went to University Hospital to make her contribution of ova. To her delight, Farida was there to meet her.

They hugged each other, and then stood back for a mutual inspection. They hadn't seen each other since Julia's wedding, but they'd kept in touch by email and telephone.

"You're looking good," Julia replied. "Motherhood must be good for you. How's the baby?"

"Oh, he's wonderful. He can sit up by himself now."

They chatted for a minute or two about babies, and then got down to business.

"First of all, take this medicine. It's a mild tranquilizer to help you relax." She handed Julia a medicine cup containing pale pink liquid.

"Will it hurt?"

"No. But some people tense up and make the procedure difficult. It's best if you're relaxed. Now, go into that cubicle and get undressed. Just the bottom; you can keep your top on. Wrap this sheet around you when you're ready and come with me."

When Julia was ready, Farida took her through a door into a brightly lighted room with a treatment table in the center. The room had cupboards around the walls and counters with trays of instruments and other equipment. A slim bearded man in a turban and green gown stood by the table.

"You remember my husband, Sarap," Farida said.

"Hello, Julia" he said in a warm baritone.

A nurse came into the room and helped Julia up onto the table. Farida walked to the door.

"Aren't you staying?" Julia asked.

"No. I have to get back to class." She smiled at Julia and left.

The procedure was not painful, just uncomfortable. Fortunately, it was soon over. The tranquilizer had worked so well, Julia had to rest for a while after she dressed. She was just beginning to think about moving when Farida came back. She'd changed her blue smock for street clothes.

"How are you feeling? A bit woozy, I bet."

"I'm all right now."

"Has the nurse taken your blood pressure?"

"Yes. About five minutes ago."

"Good, let's go and have lunch."

"Fantastic," Julia replied. She took Farida's arm and squeezed it. "It's really good to see you again. Where are we going?"

"There's a women's lunch room in the student union. Food's not all that special, but you're safe from harassment and it's cheap."

While they were eating, Julia asked the question that had been on her mind for a while. "Do you have many successful results in the program? I mean female embryos?" She had been assured that if one of her eggs was fertilized, she would be offered the opportunity of having it implanted in her own uterus and bearing the child herself.

"The ratio's not much better than the than in the general population."

"What is the ratio now, anyway?" Julia asked.

"It's about one in twenty."

"God, that's so low. I guess I don't stand much chance of having a daughter, do I?"

"You have as good a chance as anybody."

Julia picked at her salad for a moment, thinking. "Does that mean that one in twenty eggs produces a female embryo?"

"No, not that many. We harvest about fifteen to twenty eggs from each donor, but not all of them are viable and of those, only a few are successfully fertilized."

"I suppose some of them are used for the other experiments too."

Farida nodded. Her eyes lit up. "It's so exciting, being in on this work. We have some very talented scientists here. I just know we'll make a break-through before long. I can't wait to get my degree,"

"What are you working on now?" Julia asked.

"I'm a lowly technician in the genetics lab at the moment. That's where they do the genetic engineering. We're trying to remove the Y chromosome in fertilized eggs."

"What would that do?" Julia asked.

"Y chromosomes produce boys. Only sperm with the X chromosome produces a female blastocyst."

"What's that?"

"It's the fertilized ovum before cell division takes place."

Chapter Twelve

Female birthrate plummets

The number of female births worldwide has dropped to one in twenty-five, the International Committee on Population announced today.

"This is the average," Dr. Jonas Halpern emphasized. "The ratio differs in some areas. For example, in eastern Africa it is as low as one in forty-five, while in Scandinavian countries it's around one in twenty."

"The increased disparity leads to antagonism between the sexes," stated sociologist Georgia Burton. "It also makes organizations that employ women vulnerable."

Vancouver Globe, September 29, 2058

Julia received her Bachelor of Arts degree in April. Neal accompanied her to the college for the graduation ceremony and stood proudly with her family while she was presented with her diploma. There were five women graduates in her class and about thirty men.

After the ceremony, they went for lunch at a waterfront restaurant overlooking English Bay.

"All I need now is a few commissions," Julia said.

"That shouldn't be too difficult, not with your talent," Raymond said.

"Thanks for the compliment, Dad, but you have to get people to know you're there and what you can do. It's not easy, especially when you can't go around and talk to people and show them your portfolio in person."

"I know you're a designer," David said, "But what exactly do you design? Cars? Boats? Shoes?"

"No, silly, you have to be an engineer to design cars and boats. My field is graphic design. I do all sorts of things: stationery, cards, wrapping paper, even books, but I would like to specialize in fabric design."

"How do you go about getting clients?" Aldina asked.

"I've designed an Internet site to display my portfolio. I'll send out a bunch of sample designs to companies I'd like to work for, call a few people and hope for the best."

As Julia predicted, it wasn't easy to find work. The fact that she was a woman gave her a slight edge—the rareness factor—but after two months, Julia had only received one commission. That was to design some gift-wrap suitable for children. It hardly paid enough to cover her expenses, but she took it, hoping it would lead to more work or at least a referral or two.

Neal was becoming increasingly tense as his business slid downhill. He had a massive row with his father, accusing him of drinking away all the profits and driving clients away with his surly attitude. After that, he started staying home several days a week.

Julia felt as if she had to walk on eggs to avoid upsetting him, but she knew she had to say something about the situation. There was barely enough money in their account to pay the rent.

"Have you thought of getting out of it and trying something else?" she asked him one evening after dinner.

"Like what?"

"Well, you could start your own business."

"Yeah, sure. And what would I use for money? This kind of business needs expensive equipment."

"Do you think he would retire and leave you to run it? I know you could do well on your own; with your personality, you could soon get new customers."

Neal sighed. "I've been thinking about it. But he'll be hard to budge. He's already accusing me of trying to take over his business. And I'd have to support him. I just found out he's liquidated the pension fund."

The following morning, Neal left for work in a more hopeful mood and Julia relaxed a little. She waited all day, hoping he would call and tell her everything was being worked out, but as the hours ticked away, she became more and more apprehensive. He would call if there were good news. Six o'clock came around, then seven. She cleared the table and put his dinner in the refrigerator, then went back to her terminal and continued searching the Net for design opportunities.

She was startled awake at ten-thirty by something crashing against the front door. She sat up, disoriented, her heart racing. Another loud bang on the door brought her to her feet.

"Open this fucking door."

God, he'd wake all the neighbors. Frozen with fear, she rushed to the door and undid the latch. Neal tumbled into the apartment, his clothes torn and dirty, reeking of alcohol and vomit.

Silently, Julia bent to help him up but he brushed her off. "Get out of my way, bitch." He staggered into the living room, supporting himself on the wall, and slumped down on the sofa. "Get me some beer." He demanded.

"Neal, you know we don't have any," she replied, trying, but not quite succeeding, to control the tremor in her voice.

"Well get some."

"I think you've had enough, sweetheart. Why don't you let me make you some coffee?"

Neal lurched to his feet and came towards her, a look of such hatred and rage on his face, she barely recognized him. She backed away, aiming for the bathroom, but he was on her before she even reached the door. He punched her in the face, cracking her head against the corner of the door frame, then grabbed her shirtfront and began to pound her head against the wall, saying in a voice filled with venom, "I shouldn't have listened to you and your stupid suggestions. You're nothing but a brainless cunt. You can't get a job. Shit, you can't even get pregnant. I don't know why I ever married you, you skinny bitch. You…"

Julia didn't hear any more. She was unconscious.

She came to lying on the floor outside the bathroom. Her head felt as if it had been split open and she had a deep, grinding pain in her abdomen. The carpet was wet under her. At first, she thought it was blood, but then realized she had wet herself. She dragged herself up until she was sitting with her back against the wall. Pain shot through her head when she moved, and sparks swam around her. Suddenly, she knew she was going to vomit. She dragged herself painfully into the bathroom without trying to get up and reached the edge of the bathtub just in time to lean over and throw up. She wiped her chin on the bath mat and leaned back with her eyes closed.

The apartment was silent. He must have left again. The memory of the hateful words he'd spewed at her came back. Tears ran down her face. She moaned softly to herself, feeling utter despair.

Pain brought her back to the present. She couldn't understand why her abdomen hurt so much. She didn't remember him hitting her there. She wrapped her arms around her waist and tried to think of what to do next. A shushing noise rose and fell in her ears, like waves on the shore, with every stab of pain in her head. It was so hard to think.

She knew she had to get out of there; he might come back any minute and finish what he started. He could kill her. Filled with dread, Julia dragged herself to the bedroom where she'd left the portable phone. She found it and slowly pushed Pascal's speed-dial number. Pascal had made her promise that if ever anything like this happened again, she was to call her, no matter what time of the day or night. Julia didn't want her family to know. Not yet, anyway.

Pascal answered after three rings.

"Pascal." Julia's voice was slurred. She realized her lips were swollen. She touched them gingerly and found a crust of dried blood.

"Who is this?" Pascal asked warily.

"It's Julia."

Her name came out sounding like Chubia, but Pascal understood. "Julia. Has it happened again?"

"Umm," Julia replied. She was beginning to fade again.

"It sounds bad, girl. Hold on; I'll get help. Just hold on, sweetie."

Julia dropped the telephone and slumped against the bed. The next time she came around, she was in a lighted room, surrounded by friendly, concerned faces. The only person she recognized was Pascal, who was wearing a white medical gown over her clothes.

Julia was lying on a padded table, covered with a thin sheet.

One of the men in white said. "Can you tell me your name?"

"Julia."

"Good. Do you know what day it is?"

"Friday?"

"Uh huh. Do you know where you are?

She tried to shake her head gently. It hurt so much; she gasped and closed her eyes.

"You're at the hospital. Now, tell me where it hurts?"

Julia started to move her hands over her abdomen, but her left arm was held back by a tube attached to a needle stuck in the back of her hand.

"Yes, we've seen your abdomen. You have some very nasty internal bruising. It looks as if you've been kicked, but the baby hasn't been harmed."

This got Julia's attention. Her eyes flew open "Baby?" she said weakly.

"Yes. Didn't you know you were pregnant?"

She closed her eyes again, but couldn't trap the tears that spilled out. Pregnant! A week ago, she would have been overjoyed, but now....

The doctor wasn't going to give her time to think about it. "How does your head feel?" he asked.

She put her hand on her forehead and groaned. "Terrible."

"We're arranging for a scan. It'll only be a few minutes. You can talk to your friend until they're ready for you. The nurse will stay with you, as well." He signaled for the other medical staff to leave, then patted Pascal on the shoulder. "See you later, Pascal."

Pascal sat down on a stool by Julia. "Oh, sweetie," she said, taking Julia's hand. "This is terrible for you. Everything seemed to be working out so well. Is this the first time since ...?"

"Yes."

"And you're pregnant. I can't believe you didn't know. You can't be very far along."

"I guess I wasn't paying much attention. I've had other things on my mind." Pregnant. God! "How did they find out I was pregnant, anyway?" Julia's speech still had a lisp.

"I guess they gave you a pretty thorough examination. Especially after finding the bruises on your tummy. They used ultrasound."

"How long have I been here?"

Pascal looked at the watch that was set like a jewel in her finger ring. "Almost an hour. We thought you were never going to come around."

"What am I going to do, Pascal?"

"Don't worry about that now. We have to get you fixed up first. Khalil is afraid you might have a fractured skull."

"Khalil?"

"The doctor. His name's Khalil Yahya. He's a friend of mine. That's why I had the paramedics bring you here, to his clinic. He's good."

Dr. Yahya came back into the cubicle. He was a slender man of about forty-five, average height, with thick grey hair and moustache, and warm brown eyes. "We're ready to take you for the scan now," he said, putting his hand on Julia's shoulder. "It'll soon be over, and then you can have a nice sleep in a comfortable bed."

Julia's skull was not fractured, but she had some intra-cranial bruising. Julia stayed at the clinic for several and, in addition to Pascal, her mother and father visited her every day. When Julia introduced her parents to Pascal, they took to one another right away. Aldina seemed very impressed by Pascal's elegance. Neal was banned, of course. Not that he knew where she was. He'd tried a couple of times to pry her whereabouts out of David and Aldina who had answered the phone when he called, but they had hung up on him without speaking. days until she was out of danger, and then went back to her parent's home.

She was still trying to get used to the idea of being pregnant. She'd been married over a year, but didn't know if she wanted a baby at this point with her life in such turmoil. As soon as she was well enough, she went to the Arbutus clinic.

Robbie was her favorite doctor at the clinic. He was close to fifty and had long curly hair that he tied back when he was working. He always wore colorful floral shirts over tight-fitting white trousers, and sported a sparkling sapphire on the side of his nose. Legend was that he'd had affairs with nearly everyone on the staff at the clinic, but managed somehow to keep everyone on a friendly basis. Most of the younger men treated him like a father figure now that he was getting into middle age. If there was any friction among the staff, they managed to hide it from their patients. They reminded Julia of a big happy family.

After the exam and tests, Julia sat in a sling chair in Robbie's office and waited for the verdict. The white walls were decorated with brightly colored abstract and quirky surrealistic paintings.

"Well, you're definitely pregnant." Robbie said, turning from the monitor where he was going over the test results. "Have you thought about whether you want to continue the pregnancy, that is providing it's not a girl?"

It was against the law to abort female fetuses.

Julia shook her head. "I don't know." She sighed. "Everything's such a mess."

"I know you're in pretty bad shape right now, love, but you can't leave it too long if you want to terminate." He stood up and came to her side. "How about we determine the sex first, and then decide?"

When he put his arm around her shoulder, Julia had the urge to pillow her head against his well-padded body. It would be so comforting, so safe. She caught a whiff of herbal cologne with a touch of mint.

"All right. When could it be done?"

"How about tomorrow?" he went back to the terminal and pressed some buttons. "We could do it in the morning if you like. There's an opening at nine-thirty."

A week later, Julia came back to the clinic for the test results. She was bewildered by her reception; everyone she met looked at her with a friendly smile, as if she were some sort of celebrity. Robbie was in a particularly jovial mood as he ushered her into his office.

"Congratulations," he said.

"What's going on, Robbie?" Julia replied.

"It's a girl!"

"Oh, my God." Julia's heart skipped. She put her hand protectively on her abdomen.

"You've hit the jackpot, love. What is the ratio now? One in twenty-four?" Robbie was so elated he threw his arms around her and squeezed her hard. "We'll have to take *extra* good care of you now." He said as he released her. Then he looked serious. "And no more of this rough stuff. I know it's none of my business, so don't answer if you don't want to, but are you planning to go back to your husband?"

Julia shook her head. "I don't know," she replied dismally. "I'm so mixed up; I don't know what to do."

"I understand," Robbie said. "I want to recommend you come in and talk to Kelly once a week. He's our best counselor in matters like this. Maybe together, you'll be able to sort things out."

"You mean about having a baby?"

"Not entirely. I mean abusive relationships." Robbie sighed. "I don't know if you're aware of this, but there's a statute on the books that allows a concerned party to apply for what they call 'custody of the fetus'. What that means is that in the case of a female fetus, if a relative or medical professional believes there's a danger to the survival of the unborn fetus, he or she can apply to the court for the protective custody of the mother until the child is born."

Julia turned pale. "Oh my god, you wouldn't...."

Robbie held her hands between his warm palms. "Julia, love, that's the last thing I would want to do, but I wouldn't be surprised if your parents thought about it, if you go back to a potentially explosive situation. It's a miracle that kick in the guts didn't cause you to abort."

Julia recalled Neal's ugly invective the last time he'd beaten her. Was it possible he was revealing what he really felt about her? The memory made her squirm with shame. She puffed out a lengthy breath.

"I'm not sure I want to go back to him," she said. "He seems to be two different people and I don't know which one is real. I think he's the one that needs counseling."

"You are probably right," Robbie replied. "But that's something only he can decide."

"What about the baby? If I don't go back to him, will he be able to take her away from me. It is his daughter."

"Don't worry about that love. I'm sure there are plenty of people who would testify to his abuse. He wouldn't stand much of a chance. Besides, the courts always find in favor of the mother, unless she is truly unfit or incapable of taking care of the child."

Neal continued to call several times a week, sometimes charming and contrite, others, abusive and demanding. He wanted her to come back. Julia kept the news of her pregnancy to herself, sharing it only with her parents and Pascal. She dreaded what Neal's reaction would be when, if, he found out.

Julia felt the added stress of his constant barrage of calls, even when she didn't talk to him, and she began to sleep badly. She suffered from severe nausea and had little appetite. When she went for a checkup two weeks after discovering she was expecting a daughter, she had lost almost two kilograms. She was pale and listless.

"This won't do, love," Robbie said. "You've got to take better care of yourself, start to eat more."

"I know, Robbie, but I feel so sick all the time. Every time I eat something, it just comes right back up."

"It's probably the stress," Robbie replied. "I don't like to resort to drugs, but I'm going to prescribe something. It'll help reduce your anxiety and help you sleep better. Other than that, it would be a good idea if you could go away somewhere for a while. Is there anyone you could stay with?"

"I've got grandparents in Chilliwack. I suppose I could stay with them."

"Hmm; I'm not sure it would be very safe out there. There's been a lot of trouble with riots and attacks on women."

"They live in a gated community with good security" Julia said, although she was not too enthusiastic about the idea. She would be bored silly, staying with two old people, not being able to go out anywhere or have access to an up-to-date terminal. At least she would be away from Neal's constant harassment, in a healthy rural environment.

Julia decided to stay put in the end. The counseling sessions with Kelly were going well, once she'd overcome her initial reluctance to talk about her relationship with Neal and the shame it engendered in her.

"You have to believe, Julia, none of this is your fault," Kelly reiterated many times. "You're a good person and you've done nothing wrong, so there's no reason to blame yourself for what's happened."

"But I feel so stupid, being taken in by him."

At some point in one of their early sessions, Kelly had disclosed that he'd had an abusive, alcoholic father, reminding Julia of Neal's father. Kelly neither said anything derogatory about Neal, nor tried to blame him.

As a result of the counseling sessions, Julia decided to engage a lawyer. Her happy experience with the Gay Men's Family Clinic led her to a gay men's law cooperative. Somewhere in the back of her mind was the conviction that having a gay lawyer was almost the same as having a woman represent her.

She had to go to her old apartment in the West End to pick up her personal belongings. She took John and David with her for protection. By calling the apartment first, they found a time when Neal wasn't there. Julia still had the keys and she doubted Neal would have changed the locks. They arrived around 10:30 am and were out of there by 11:15. She didn't take the mirror Neal had bought for her after his first assault.

The sickness abated after a couple of months and Julia developed a healthy appetite. She continued to seek design contracts and even acquired a couple of new clients. She was excited about her prospects with one of these, although the work was not in the field she had planned to pursue. A small publisher wanted a design for a book cover. He'd been impressed by some of her designs on the Net and contacted her for this one assignment, but had hinted that there might be more in the future. Since the company also published music, there was the possibility she might be able to do disk covers as well.

She continued to visit Pascal once a week. Julia valued their friendship. She'd never been close to another woman before, apart from her mother, and found it refreshing to have someone with whom she could discuss anything without fear of being laughed at or rejected.

Pascal introduced Julia to one of her own favorite pastimes: shopping. Julia had never thought much about it before, being accustomed to ordering things online. She'd rarely been to a shopping mall, believing, like Aldina, that they were too much bother with all the security and a poor selection of merchandize from which to choose. However, Pascal showed her a new aspect of shopping at Granville Island, close to her False Creek home.

Thirty years earlier, the decaying buildings of the Granville Island Market had been torn down because of the rising sea level, and replaced by the Crystal Gallery, a sprawling glass and steel structure like a giant Victorian greenhouse. The Gallery catered primarily to women and when Julia went in with Pascal, she imagined that half the women in Vancouver must be there. She'd never seen so many women in one place before. There were a few men, of course, but women of all ages were in the majority.

"I can't believe you've never been here," Pascal said when she saw Julia's wide-eyed wonder.

"I always thought it was for rich people and never bothered. To tell the truth, I've never been too hung up on buying things. We've never really been able to afford anything but necessities."

They strolled along a central concourse paved in black and white marble with fountains every fifty meters amid clusters of potted palms. Both sides of the concourse were lined with shops and boutiques selling everything from lingerie to home furnishings. There were several coffee shops and restaurants with outside tables. Soothing baroque music played in the background and a soft breeze cooled the air, countering the heat of the sunlight that passed in through the polarized glass walls and ceilings.

"God, where do you start?" Julia asked when they reached the halfway point. She looked up at the mezzanine level above the concourse.

Pascal laughed. It was like taking a child to her first toyshop. "Well, what do you need the most?"

"I don't know. I doubt I could afford anything, anyway?"

"How about clothes?" She looked at Julia critically. "You're going to be bursting your seams pretty soon, the way you're filling out."

Julia allowed Pascal to drag her into a boutique where an elegant woman of about sixty was arranging a long gown on an acrylic manikin. Something else new to Julia. She'd never seen a woman working in a public place before.

"Hi, Kalienne," Pascal greeted her. "This is my friend, Julia. We just want to take a look around."

"Hello, Julia. Welcome." the woman said. "Go ahead. Enjoy." She went back to her task.

There weren't many garments on display in the boutique, but the dresses and suits on the manikins were all elegant and beautifully designed in harmonious colors and exquisite fabrics.

Julia spotted a short flared dress in a soft white fabric with fuchsia and gold flowers. "This is beautiful," she said. "Is it the only one they've got?"

"At the moment, yes," Pascal replied. "They only display models. If someone likes something, they have it made up for her. Mass-production in the fashion industry is outdated. Too much waste. Even when you order something on the net, it has to be specially made."

"So I guess you could have a different fabric if you wanted?"

"Yes. Come over here and see the swatches."

At the back of the shop, swatches of material hung from brass rods on the wall behind a glass table. Julia took down one of the bundles of fabric and went through the samples with professional interest. It was a good opportunity to see what sorts of designs were popular.

Kalienne came over. "Can I help you with anything?"

"I was wondering which of these fabrics are the most popular," Julia said.

Kalienne raised her eyebrows. It wasn't the sort of question she usually heard. "Have a seat," she replied.

They sat around the table while Kalienne went through the fabrics and pointed out some of the bestsellers.

"Thank you so much," Julia said. She stood up and went to the model with the dress, thinking she should buy something to repay the woman's courtesy. "I was wondering about this dress."

"It's lovely, isn't it?" Kalienne said, coming up beside her. "I think it would look very good on you. Do you want to try it on?"

"I'm not sure I could afford it," Julia said, blushing. "But—oh, why not?"

It was a little tight, but it made her feel so elegant and a little embarrassed about her plain cotton trouser suit.

"It was made for you," Pascal said. "Don't you agree, Kalienne?"

Kalienne nodded agreement.

"But, how much would it cost?"

"She's expecting a baby," Pascal said before the other woman could answer. "A girl!"

A meaningful glance passed between the two women.

"That's wonderful," Kalienne said. "Congratulations, dear. We offer a special discount for prospective mothers of girls. How does a hundred dollars sound?"

Julia had a suspicion that this special discount had only just been initiated and that somehow Pascal had a part in it, but what could she say? The price was about a fifth of what she had expected. She had just received the payment for one of her commissions, so she was feeling more financially secure, and besides, she had very few expenses, living at her parents' home.

"I think that's very generous. I want buy something else, at the regular price, to make up for it."

"There's no need for that," Kalienne replied. "You can always come back."

'No, I mean it. I'm growing out of all my clothes and need to buy some new stuff anyway."

She wandered around and chose a trouser suit with a long tunic top. She selected the fabrics and had her measurements taken by Kalienne, then she and Pascal returned to the mall.

"What was going on with you two in there?" Julia asked. "You were up to something. There's no way that dress could have been a hundred dollars. The fabric alone would cost that."

"Moi?" Pascal looked as innocent as a newborn lamb. "Nothing. Kalienne knows how to attract loyal customers. She knows you'll come back now, so in the long run, she'll profit by it. Besides, I spend a fortune there. She's an old friend of my mother's. I've known her forever." She grinned at Julia.

"I see," Julia said. "Well, I'm still grateful." She looked around. "Do you think we could sit down for a while and have something to eat?"

"Yes, of course. I forgot; you're eating for two now."

They sat at a table outside a coffee shop where Pascal sipped a cappuccino while watching Julia demolish a double serving of raspberry cheesecake and gulp down a large mug of hot chocolate topped with whipped cream.

"I want to buy you a present," Pascal said when Julia had finished. "Come on."

"You don't have to do that," Julia said. "Coming here with you is enough."

"Come on, girl, don't argue. Let me have some fun, okay?"

She took Julia up to the second level where there were more shops dedicated to home furnishing and decoration. Halfway down one side was a little place that specialized in baby furniture and accessories.

Julia was entranced. She darted from one item to another, picturing her own precious daughter in a nursery, surrounded by colorful accessories. She wondered where they would live and if there would be room for a nursery. If Julia stayed with her parents, the baby would have to sleep in her room.

"Over here," Pascal said, bringing Julia out of her reverie. She was standing by a row of bassinets and cradles.

"Oh, my God," Julia said, clasping her hands together. "They're adorable."

"How about this one?" She pointed to a white basket cradle trimmed with white lace ruffles and satin ribbons.

"It's beautiful," Julia cried.

"Yeah, it's my favorite. Come on." She grabbed Julia's arm and led her to the service terminal. "I'll take that one," she told the man.

"You can't buy me that. It's much too expensive," Julia exclaimed. "I thought you meant a little blanket or mobile or something."

"Are you trying to tell me what I can spend my own money on now?" Pascal said. She handed her debit card to the man at the counter. "We'd like to have it delivered, please.

Julia wondered what she'd done to deserve a friend like Pascal, and how she would ever be able repay all her kindness and support.

"I've got a favor to ask," Pascal said when they were outside. "How would you like to design some decorations for my daughter's room? She's outgrowing her old baby ones."

God, Julia thought, she's a mind reader too.

Chapter Thirteen

Girl-napping has risen to epidemic proportions in many African countries. In some central African nations, small armies roam the countryside, rounding up females of all ages, some as young as a few weeks old. The governments of these nations say there is little they can do to control this banditry; however, aid-workers report that many politicians may be actively involved, or at least benefiting from the situation.

"It seems odd that many of the most prominent citizens have wives and female slaves, while most average citizens have none," one aid worker told our reporter.

Vancouver Globe, November 20, 2058

Julia arrived home one afternoon in a cab and saw Neal's Orca parked at the gate. "Keep going," she urged the driver, but it was too late. Neal had his hand on the door handle.

The driver looked at her, waiting for instructions. She hesitated. Neal's face was almost touching the window.

"I know it's you, Julia. Come on out, I only want to talk to you. Please, baby."

Looking at his face outside the cab window, Julia realized she no longer felt either love or fear for him. "It's all right," she told the driver. Can you let the window down?"

The window slid open about ten centimeters and Julia spoke through the gap. "I've nothing to say to you, Neal. Would you please leave?" She pressed her shopping bag to her abdomen, not wanting Neal to see the burgeoning pregnancy.

"But honey..."

"I mean it, Neal. Go away and leave me alone. Get out of the way, we're going in now." She turned to the driver. "Drive through the gate," she said, pressing her remote control to open it.

Neal stood stubbornly in front of the gate, hands on hips.

"If you don't move, I'll have to ask the driver to remove you. He won't hesitate to use mace." She felt a bit guilty for putting the driver in this position, but it was part of his job, and she intended to give him a good tip.

"Bitch," Neal snarled, stepping to one side.

It was then that she decided to file for divorce. It was over. Some romance, she thought bitterly. She would be nineteen in two months. At least she'd have Catherine.

***

Following Catherine's birth, Julia began to feel hemmed in at home. She wanted her own place. However, she wasn't making enough money to be able to afford it.

One evening, she sat talking Pascal in front of the lighted fireplace. Outside, a thunderstorm was raging, emphasizing the coziness of Pascal's den. Catherine was sleeping in her cradle nearby, peaceful and sated, only a tuft of black hair visible out above the covers.

"Motherhood suits you," Pascal said. "You're looking much more relaxed that when I first met you."

"I am. It's such a relief to be free. I just wish I could find a way to earn more money so that I could get my own place."

"Have you thought of getting married again?" Pascal asked. "I'm sure there are plenty of men who would die for the chance."

"Not for a long time," Julia replied ruefully. "It scares me just to think about it."

"Not all men are like that, you know. I could introduce you to some very sweet guys. With money, too."

"I know." Julia reached over and touched Pascal's wrist. "You've been very good to me. I don't know how I'd have got through this without you."

"You've given me a lot too, Julia. All women need at least one close woman friend. But you didn't answer my question. Would you like me to introduce you to someone?"

"Not right now. Thanks Pascal, but with the baby and breast feeding, you know, it's too much."

"Maybe later," Pascal said. "I won't forget."

Julia gazed at the flames in the fireplace for a while, thinking, and then she turned to Pascal. "What's it like, your work?"

Pascal gave her a piercing look. "It can be fun. Sometimes it's a bit of a pain, especially when the guy's in a bad mood and I have to work hard at trying to make him relax. But it's rewarding."

"I mean ... you know ... the sex part."

"I knew that's what you were getting at. As I said before, I choose my clients; I mean I can refuse if there's something I don't like about a man. So it's not so bad. You get quite fond of the regulars, once you have them trained. They become part of your life, like old friends. And sometimes it can be exciting. The variety. I never allow anyone to stay the whole night. I don't want my kids to wake up and find some stranger in bed with their mother."

"What if you're not in the mood?"

"It's a job, love. In any job, you have to do your work to the best of your ability, whether you feel like it or not."

"You make it sound so perfect," Julia said.

"You should try it sometime," Pascal said with a grin. "It would solve a lot of your problems."

Chapter Fourteen

New traffic plans for downtown

In an effort to stem street violence, stretches of several major streets, including Broadway, Fourth Avenue, Georgia and Granville Streets, will be enclosed with glass roofs, a spokesman for the city planning department announced today. These streets will be turned into virtual tunnels, with controlled access and exits. Private vehicles and pedestrians will use the upper level and the lower level will be given over to public transit.

These new malls will be patrolled by security police day and night, and there will be frequent weapons checks to make the environments safe for women and children.

There are also plans to replace the old Granville Street Bridge with a sky tunnel, joining the shopping areas north and south of False Creek.

Plans and models of the projects are on view in the concourse of the Vancouver Public Library on West Georgia Street until January 31, 2061

Vancouver Globe, September 21, 2060

Ten months later, Pascal arranged a small dinner party for Julia; just herself, Damien, the father of Pascal's daughter, and a man called Arens Findlay. Findlay was about thirty-five. He was quite tall and slim with blond hair and grey-green eyes. His shyness made Julia feel less intimidated to be meeting him. She concentrated on trying to put him at ease and draw him out.

Around eleven, Julia was getting sleepy and said she was ready to go home.

"Why don't you drive her home?" Pascal said to Findlay.

"I'd love to," he replied.

Julia was impressed by Findlay's car. She'd never ridden in such luxury, nor ever expected to. It was one of the new hover model Jaguars, capable of running on the road or on a cushion of air a few centimeters above the ground. The two capacious side-by-side seats were upholstered in pale grey suede, matching the lining of interior. The control panel looked as if it were made of abalone shell, mottled iridescent greens and violets.

"Where do you live?" Findlay asked.

Julia told him and he pushed the starter, and then punched a few buttons to program the route. The vehicle hummed to life and started to move. It ran smoothly with a faint hum and deceptive speed. Findlay pushed another button and they were surrounded by soft music, something classical that Julia didn't recognize.

If it had been left to Findlay, there would have been complete silence all the way to Julia's house. He acted as if he hadn't spent much time in the company of women. Julia realized he was probably intimidated by her, so she tried to put him at ease by getting him to talk about himself.

"I know you're in property development," she said. That had been brought up at dinner. "But what exactly does that mean?"

"It just means we buy up old properties—buildings and land—and either renovate them or tear them down and replace them." He didn't look at her as he spoke.

"What sort of buildings?"

"Different kinds. Right now, we have a project on Davie Street; we've taken out the whole block between Jervis and Bute. And we're tearing down an old high school in New Westminster."

"What are you going to build in their place?"

"The Davie street block is going to be a CLE, Complete Living Environment. The New West site will have a smaller school and community park."

CLEs were becoming popular in the city. They combined housing with shops, Complete banking centers, restaurants, and recreation facilities, all safely protected behind tight security fences. Theoretically, you could live in one without ever needing to go outside the complex, if you worked from home.

"This is it," Julia said. It had taken hardly any time to reach her house.

The car stopped at the gate without so much as a twitch. Before opening the door, Findlay looked at her and said, "It was nice to meet you, Julia." He held out his hand to shake.

"Thank you, me too." she replied. She shook his hand, charmed by his shyness. "Thanks for driving me home."

"Julia?"

"Yes" she looked at him expectantly.

He hesitated for a moment, as if trying to find the right words, then said. "Good night. I'll wait until you're inside." He pushed the button to open the door.

Inside the house, Julia sighed and shook her head.

Next morning, Raymond knocked on her door and called out. "There's a call for you, Julia,".

"Thanks, dad, I'll take it in here."

Julia was trying to put some clean clothes on Catherine who was squirming and trying to get free to chase the new kitten.

"All right, you little poop," Julia said, putting her daughter on the floor. "But you're going to get scratched if you don't leave her alone."

Catherine chuckled and crawled off towards the little tabby that was playing with her discarded sock.

Julia pushed the activate button on the console and Pascal's face appeared on the screen.

"Good morning," she said. "You look as if you've just been through a wrestling match."

"Thanks," Julia replied, brushing a strand of hair off her face. "Right on the button. And as usual, my opponent got the better of me. I still don't understand how anyone that small can annihilate a 1.8-meter woman."

"Don't ask me to explain," Pascal said with a smile. "It's one of the mysteries of life."

"What's up?" Julia asked.

"Did you have a good time last night?"

"Wonderful. Sorry, I should have called to thank you."

"That's not why I'm calling. How did you like Arens?"

"He seems quite nice, but he's so shy. Trying to have a conversation with him is like pulling up dandelions."

"He's led a sheltered life. His mother left him when he was four and he was raised by his father and uncles. He hasn't had much experience with women."

"I kind of guessed that."

"Anyway," Pascal went on "Damian just called and he said Arens would like to see you again."

"What, you mean like go on a date?"

"Well, a little more formal than that." Pascal smiled wickedly. "You know what I mean?"

"Oh, God, Pascal. You mean like you and ...?" Julia flopped down in a chair, a strange pressure swelling in her chest. She couldn't lie to herself and say she hadn't thought of it, but now that she was actually confronting the issue, she was afraid.

Pascal nodded.

"But..., God..." Julia's lips twitched as she suppressed a smile.

"Julia, it's a perfectly honest, legal profession. There's no shame in it. You're a good-looking woman; you could do well for yourself. At least consider it. And I think Arens would be the perfect person to start with. He's young and presentable, and he's got bags of money." Pascal swept her hair back, a wistful look on her face, and then she smiled. "I'd love to have the opportunity of breaking him in myself, but it's you he's interested in."

"Pascal!" Julia couldn't help grinning at her outrageous friend. "It's impossible, though. I have nowhere to take him. Can you see me bringing him here with my family all around and Catherine sleeping in the corner?"

"You'll have to get your own place."

"How can I? I can't afford it."

"Couldn't you borrow some money from your family?"

"I suppose so." Julia paused. "But I don't even know if I want to do this."

"Oh, you do, I can tell. I know you well enough by now."

"Well you know more than I do. I'm still not sure."

Julia thought about little else after the conversation with Pascal. The idea of becoming a courtesan—the name Pascal preferred for her profession—was both scary and exciting. In spite of the fact that it had been legal for forty years, there was still a trace of the forbidden about it. How, for example, would she break it to her parents? What would their reaction be? Then she thought about the luxury of Pascal's house. It was so enticing.

"I'm such a wreck," Julia said "How could I get naked with anyone looking like this. I'm all flab since the baby."

Julia was sitting in Pascal's garden with her friend, sipping cranberry cocktail.

"You've lost some weight, too." Pascal could always be trusted to be honest.

"What can I do?"

"Well, basically, you've got good form; you just need firming up and rounding out more. I think you should go on a high protein diet and join a women's fitness club. Get some exercise."

After discussing Pascal's suggestion for a while, Julia had another question. "I wouldn't know what to do. I mean, suppose you've had dinner and you're back home. How do you get started with someone like Arens? I'm sure he's much too shy to make the first move himself. He'd probably be scared to death."

"Well, the first thing you've got to do is help him to relax. Take his jacket and sit him on the sofa. No bright lights. Soft music is good. Offer him a drink."

"But how do you get started if he doesn't?"

Pascal smiled. "There are ways. One way that always seems to work for me, if the man is timid, is to sit on the floor next to him and lean your arm on his thigh. Keep talking as if nothing is happening. Look up at him while you're talking. Start to run your finger slowly back and forth along the inside of his thigh, getting a little higher each time. It will drive him crazy."

Julia grinned. "I can imagine. If that won't get him, nothing will." Then she remembered how it had been with

Gabriel on Saturna Island; he also had been shy and she had been the one to initiate what happened.

"Another way is the old neck massage. If he seems tense, start to massage the muscles at back of his neck and shoulders; tell him you'd like to help him relax. After a while, ask him if you can take his shirt off so you can do it properly. Well ... you get the picture."

"I can't believe we're having this conversation," Julia laughed.

"Another thing," Pascal added. "With someone like Arens, with most men, really, it's best not to wear anything too obviously seductive or tarty. You know what I mean, no black leather and red garter belts, things like that. Don't wear things that are too tight or transparent, no plunging necklines. Most of the men who will be clients aren't looking for a whore. They want the kind of woman they would marry and take home to meet their mother. That's another thing; we'll have to get you a wardrobe."

"What will I do with Catherine?"

"You could leave her with your mother. You're lucky she lives here. Mine lives in Saskatchewan. I have to have a nanny to look after mine while I'm working."

Julia spent the next three months getting herself in shape. Reluctant to ask her parents for money, she had arranged, with Pascal's help, for a small loan from a trust company. "Think of it as an investment," Pascal told her. The president of the Trust was one of Pascal's *special friends.*

Julia rented a luxury two-bedroom apartment overlooking Queen Elizabeth Park and furnished it. She shopped with Pascal for new clothes, had her hair styled. She was ready to go into business and she was terrified.

"One final word of caution," Pascal said before Julia had her first 'date' with Arens. "If you are going to be serious about this business, don't fall in love."

"Don't worry," Julia replied, "I've been stung by the love bug once and I'm still aching from it." She would be twenty-one in two months.

***

"I think he's in love with me," Julia said to Pascal at their weekly get-together. She had entertained Arens twice now. She found him a pleasant companion, but she certainly didn't feel that way about him. "I don't know what to do."

"That's always a problem when it's their first time. You'll have to find a way to get him to back off a little. I suggest that next time he calls, you tell him you're busy."

"I don't want to scare him off, I need the money."

"We'll have to see if we can find you some more clients." She looked Julia up and down. "You're looking great, by the way."

"Thanks. I still think I'm too flat-chested, though." She looked at Pascal's ample bosom.

"You look fine to me, but you could always have augmentation, if you feel so strongly about it."

"I can't afford it."

"Things will pick up. It just takes a little time."

"I was wondering if I should advertise on the Net."

"Better not," Pascal replied. "You'd be inundated with weirdoes and it wouldn't really help. If you want to have a high-class business, you have to be discreet. I'll see what I can do to get the word out."

"Pascal, I'm glad Kelly introduced us; you're a good friend."

True to her word, Pascal provided Julia with another contact the following week. He was middle-aged Afro-Canadian who owned an electronics business. His name was Saxon King. He was a soft spoken, slender man with courtly manners who put her at ease immediately.

Before the year was out, she had six regular clients and a number of casual referrals from Pascal and her clients. The word was getting out in the more exclusive circles.

Chapter Fifteen

New penalties proposed for assaults against women

A new bill was introduced in parliament today by the Hon. Denton Keene, Reformation Party member for Regina South, proposing stiffer penalties for attacks against women.

"We need to make it clear to these hooligans that they cannot get away with their barbarous attacks against the fair sex," Mr. Keene, the father of an eighteen-year-old daughter, stated at a news conference in Ottawa this afternoon. "Although females are now a small minority in the population, it is up to all of us to protect, indeed, cherish them. Women are essential to the very survival of humanity and anything that threatens to harm our sisters, our wives, or our daughters, should be dealt with rapidly and with the utmost severity."

Mr. Keene's bill calls for a mandatory life sentence in cases of abduction, the death penalty for killing a woman or girl, and chemical castration for men guilty of rape.

Report in the Vancouver Globe, October 18, 2061

Julia?"

"My God, Dad, what is it?" Raymond's greying hair was unkempt and there was pain on his haggard face, underscored by the dark shadows around his eyes.

"Something terrible's happened," he said in a choked voice. "Your mother...."

Fear gripped Julia's heart. "Dad. She's not ...?"

"She's alive, but she's—it's quite serious."

"What happened?" Julia asked, dreading the answer. "Where is she?"

"She's in the University Hospital." He paused and rubbed his face with his hand. "She went out last night with Edgar. We waited for them to come home, but ... they were so late. Antoine and I were just about to go looking for them when the police called."

"Were they in an accident?" *For goodness sake, get to the point, Dad and stop keeping me in suspense.*

"No. they were attacked. It seems they stopped at the top of the hill to watch the sunset. This gang of ... gang dragged them out of the car. I knew we should have got ... it's too late now." He looked into the video monitor, face registering his helplessness.

"Will mother be all right? What about Edgar?"

"He was beaten pretty badly; broken ribs and fingers. Your mother will recover, but I ... They're monsters. I hope they all get wiped."

Her mind was already in gear. What to do with Catherine? ... order a cab. "I'm going out there."

Julia was glad to see Robbie at the hospital. He'd just finished talking to the doctors who had treated Aldina.

"Julia, I'm sorry." He hugged her.

"How bad is it? Dad was barely coherent on the phone."

"I haven't seen her yet, but they tell me she's badly battered. She put up quite a fight, but there were too many of them. It's the psychological damage I'm concerned about."

"You mean she was raped?"

Robbie nodded. "I'm afraid so."

Julia buried her face in her hands. "Oh, god." How can you face the idea of your own mother being raped? It's too horrible to contemplate. Tears squeezed through her closed lids. "Oh, Robbie, poor mother."

Robbie put his arm around her shoulders. "It's outrageous. Something's got to be done about this situation before everything falls apart."

Julia wiped her eyes. "Do you think they'll let me see her?"

"I was just going in. You can come with me if you like, but I must warn you, she'll probably look terrible."

With his arm still around her, Robbie led Julia down a blue-carpeted hallway, around a corner and through a glass-paneled door. Edgar was sitting on a chair beside a still form in the room's only bed. Afraid to look at her mother, Julia concentrated on Edgar for a moment. Both his eyes were blackened, his nose was red and swollen and seemed to be twisted sideways. A sling around his neck supported his hand with its splinted fingers. He tried to stand when they entered, but the effort caused a spasm of pain. He held his free arm against his ribs.

"Julia," he gasped in a hoarse, nasal voice. "I'm sorry. I tried..."

"It wasn't your fault, Edgar." Poor gentle Edgar. She tried to imagine him fighting the thugs who'd attacked them, trying to protect Aldina.

"They tied me up. I couldn't..." He trailed off, tears seeping through his swollen eyelids.

129

"I know, Edgar; no one's blaming you."

Robbie was at the head of the bed looking down at Aldina. Julia steeled herself to join him. She looked peaceful enough, lying there with her eyes closed. Her face was bruised and there was a patch of syntheskin on her forehead, covering a sutured gash. An intravenous line ran into the back of her left hand.

"She hasn't regained consciousness yet," Robbie informed her.

"Does she have a head injury?" Julia asked, alarmed.

"No. they scanned her. No broken bones. It's the shock. After severe trauma like this, some people retreat into themselves. She'll pull out of it eventually, but she'll need a lot of support."

"Poor mother." Julia took her mother's hand and stroked it. The large capable hand seemed shrunken and vulnerable.

Aldina moaned, but her eyes stayed shut.

"Can she hear us?" Julia asked.

"Probably," Robbie replied. "Anyway, talk to her. The sound of your voice will comfort her."

"Has dad seen her?" Julia asked.

"He was here all night," Edgar replied. "He just went home to get cleaned up. He's taking it very badly." Edgar paused to get his breath, and then continued, "I feel so guilty. If only..."

"The two most useless words in the language," Robbie said gently. "You did what you could, old man. It will do no one any good to keep on berating yourself."

As if to emphasize his words, Aldina groaned again and tightened her fingers on Julia's hand.

Aldina came out of the coma that evening, but was listless and withdrawn. She went home to the Point Grey house after two days. The bruises on her face and body disappeared, but the wound to her psyche did not heal so quickly. She didn't want to do anything or see anyone. She lost her appetite and slept badly. To Julia, her mother seemed to have aged twenty years overnight. She looked like a haggard, shrunken old woman, although she was only forty-eight. Kelly, the best trauma therapist at the Arbutus clinic, came to see her twice a week.

The only times Aldina brightened up was when she was with Catherine. The two-year-old had no concept of depression over things that had happened in the past. To her, everything was now, or right now, she wanted her granny to get her a cookie or glass of juice, or to push her on the swing. After a few minutes with Catherine, Aldina became animated, seemed to have more energy.

Raymond was depressed as well, his frustrated rage burrowing itself deep inside. He was gentle and solicitous with Aldina, playing her the music she loved in the hope of bringing her out of it. Edgar began staying away from the house for days on end, feeling responsible for what had happened and unable to face the family. Eventually, he packed his belongings and moved out, leaving Antoine and Raymond to cope with the sick woman.

David and John had already moved out and found places of their own. David was living in a group situation with three other men and a young woman. John at twenty-five was in his third homosexual relationship.

Julia found it depressing to go to the old house. All the light and life seemed to have gone out of it.

"Why don't you sell it and get a smaller place?" Julia suggested to Raymond during one visit.

"I've been thinking about it. I was waiting for your mother to get better. Right now all she'll say is 'do what you think best,' so I don't know how she feels about it. Andre agrees with the idea."

"I think you'd all be happier and safer in one of those new Habitats." She took his hand. "I worry about all of you, Dad. The violence is getting worse. It's not safe for anyone go out at night."

"What about you and Catherine? I worry about you as well."

"We don't go anywhere much," she replied. "And I always use Security Cabs."

Chapter Sixteen

61-10-18

Hi, Jul:

How's life treating you? Thought I'd drop you a line to let you know what's happening out here in the steamy Amazon.

That's right, the Amazon. We moved down to the jungle a week ago and made the most amazing discovery. We're a bit off the beaten track; the place doesn't even have a name, just map coordinates that I'm not allowed to tell anyone. Anyway, we were putt-putting up this little tributary to the back door of the universe when we came across this real primitive native tribe. I doubt if they'd seen or been seen by outsiders for centuries, if ever. They were quite friendly and welcomed us to their village, but here's the kicker: there were just as many women in the tribe as men. (Cute little ladies without so much as a feather to cover their bodies.) It seems that whatever is plaguing the rest of the world hasn't reached here yet.

It's a safe bet that once the outside world hears about them, they'll have to build an international airport to handle the traffic. It's a pity, because they're really nice people and very hospitable and gentle.

We moved on to a camp about fifty kilometers from the village the next day, but I'm sure we'll get a chance to keep track of what happens if they don't decide to move us again. You can never tell in this business. (Incidentally, I signed on again for two more years before the move.)

Take care and give hugs and kisses to my niece. By the way, how's Mother? She tries to sound cheerful in her letters, but I have a feeling she's covering up. Dad sounded a bit down in his last email.

Paul

PS This place really stinks. Millions of bugs and other creepy-crawlies and the air is so thick and steamy, you could stir it with a spoon. It's a big change from the mountains.

Julia! How are you?"

"Great. You're looking good, Farida." Julia continued, "The reason I'm calling is to tell you about something I heard from Paul—you remember my brother? It may have some bearing on your research, although you may have heard about this before."

"What is it?"

Julia told her about the tribe Paul's team had found in the Amazon.

Farida nodded. "Yes, that fits in with virus epidemic theory. If they were completely isolated, they would not be affected, although there's a very remote possibility they may have immunity. It's worth looking into. Thanks Julia, I'll pass it on to Sarap."

***

62-2-3

Hi, Jul:

Thanks for the Christmas presents. The pictures of you and Catherine are peak. She doesn't look much like our family, does she? Probably takes after him. I sort of suspected Mother was depressed. Is she still seeing a therapist?

My predictions about the native tribe weren't far off. It's amazing how quickly the word gets out. You didn't tell anyone, did you? Just kidding.

A team of scientists arrived here from the good old US of A last week accompanied by a bunch of officious Brazilian bureaucrats. If it hadn't been so tragic, it would be funny. Some of our guys were asked to accompany them, apparently to protect them from blowpipes and spears. These scientific flops tried to bribe the men in the tribe to give sperm samples by offering them some cheap gadgets—solar watches, penknives, magnifying glasses, stuff like that—but the old chief had a fit. He ranted at the scientists and the government officials for about half an hour— something about trying to steal their life force—then he said something to his people and everyone disappeared into the jungle.

So there were the chief and his ancient wife alone in the village with six frustrated scientific types and four Brazilians radioing like crazy back and forth for instructions.

They decided to retreat to our base and wait until the natives returned to the village, which they did the next day. In the end, the Brazilian government decided to round up the whole tribe and move them to a reserve near Manaus so that they would be accessible to anyone wanting to study them.

They wanted us to help, but the captain was so outraged, he threatened to call for UN support to stop them. The bureaucrats called in the Brazilian army and the deed was done before the UN could intervene.

I wonder what will happen to those poor people. Sounds like the sort of thing that happened in Canada two hundred years ago, taking Native children from their families and putting them in church schools.

We're moving again. I can't tell you where, but I'll try to write again soon.

Let me know if you hear anything about this Brazilian tribe. Love to you and Catherine.

Paul.

Julia got a sinking feeling when she saw Neal's face on the video screen. He was just as handsome as ever, but this failed to arouse any feeling in her. He looked a bit thinner and had several days' stubble on his face. "Hello, Neal. What do you want?"

He gave her the crooked smile that would have melted her heart at one time. "Aren't you even going to ask me how I'm doing?"

"How are you?" she asked mechanically. As if I care, she thought.

"Oh, you know, so-so."

"How's the business?"

"I'm into something else now. The old man screwed up once too often." He scowled, and then grinned again. "How's my daughter?"

An icy dagger pierced her. She swallowed and turned away from the monitor to hide her fear. "How ...? She's not your daughter."

"Come on, Julia. You can't fool me. I know when she was born. Unless you were screwing around even then. Although I doubt it. You were always a tight-ass. How come you held out on me?" He was building up a rage. He took a deep breath and spoke more calmly. "I want to see her."

"Well you can't." Julia retorted.

"You can't keep me from seeing my own daughter. I can get a court order."

"Just try," she snapped. "Goodbye, Neal." She hit the disconnect button.

She realized that sweat was trickling down her face, although she was quite cold.

***

"Are we ready?"

The legal panelist looked around the table. Neal, true to his threat, had forced the issue of access to his daughter. The all-man panel—made up of a social worker, a psychologist and an arbitrator—had listened to all the arguments and was about to present a decision. Julia and Neal sat facing the panel, separated from each other by their respective lawyers.

Julia clenched her hands under the table.

"I'll give you a brief summary of the decision now. You will each receive a complete copy to review with your counsels." The speaker, a social worker, was a chubby bald-headed man of around forty with the worried expression of someone who took these emotional disputes to heart. He looked at his notebook and cleared his throat.

"While sympathizing with the mother, Ms Finisterra, for her pain and suffering while married to the claimant, we have come to the conclusion that, given Mr. Gianakis's demonstrated efforts to control his substance abuse and his enrollment in a therapy program, we cannot legally deny him access to his biological daughter."

Julia gasped. The panelists looked at her sympathetically.

"We are satisfied that Mr. Gianakis has presented adequate proof that he has not used any mood-altering drugs or alcohol for the past eighteen months, and is undergoing therapy to deal with the underlying emotional and psychological problems, therefore, we do not consider him to be a threat to the safety of Catherine Finisterra. However, taking into consideration Ms Finisterra's concern that allowing the child to be left suddenly in the company of a complete stranger would be traumatic, it is our decision that the visits should be started gradually. For the first six months, Mr. Gianakis will be allowed two hours per week with his daughter, Catherine, and only while accompanied by a person the child knows and trusts."

Julia relaxed slightly. At least he wouldn't be taking her off somewhere alone.

"We'll leave it up to Ms Finisterra to decide who that person will be, however, we will expect to be advised as to his or her identity." He paused for a moment and glanced at Julia and Neal, then continued reading from his screen. "One of the most compelling reasons for allowing the child to spend time with her father is the benefit a little girl would derive from a healthy, loving bond with a close adult male relative, preferably a father."

She has my father and … Julia opened her mouth to protest, but her lawyer put his hand on her arm. "Not now," he murmured.

"Damn him," Julia said when they got outside. "Can we appeal?"

"It's not advisable," her lawyer, Abelard, replied. "The courts are too busy and they don't take too kindly to people wasting their time and questioning their decisions. Besides, it was a pretty fair decision."

Julia sighed. "I guess. If he starts anything, can we have it changed?"

"You mean like drinking? Yes, I'm sure the court would consider an appeal in such an event. Try it for a while and see how it goes. It might be good for Catherine. After all, it's her we are concerned about."

"I know," Julia admitted. She recalled Neal's seductive charm. Was she afraid of losing her child's affection to him?

"Have you thought about who should accompany her during the visits?"

"I'll have to think about it. Maybe David. I could ask him, anyway."

"I thought he hated Neal. Maybe that wouldn't be such a good idea. You wouldn't want to put her in the middle of something unpleasant."

"I guess you're right."

"What about your father?" Abelard suggested.

"I'll talk to him," Julia replied. At least Dad was more mature and would do his best to cover up his hostility.

***

"Where are you going to meet?" Julia asked.

"In the park," Raymond replied. "I thought we'd go to the conservatory. She's been there before, so it will be familiar, and it's close to home."

Julia knelt in front of her little girl and seated her sun hat more firmly in place. "Have a good time, sweetie." She kissed Catherine's pale cheek and stood up.

At three, Catherine was small for her age, slender and pale with hazel eyes and light brown hair. She was a quiet, thoughtful child who seemed quite content to play alone with her toys, or watch videos with Julia. While she enjoyed going out with her grandfather Raymond or Uncle David, she was always happy to get home. When in the company of other children, she tended to be withdrawn.

"Take care of her," Julia said to Raymond as they were going out the door, hoping she wasn't communicating too much of her anxiety to Catherine.

Julia had two hours to kill. To take her mind off the pending meeting of Catherine and Neal, she went into her studio, a converted bedroom where she worked on her fabric designs She looked critically at the half-finished sheet of silk stretched on the huge frame under the skylight, sighed, and picked up a red broad-point stylus.

Catherine

Chapter Seventeen

Setback in X-Virus Research

Drs. Christophe Letelier and Antonio Geraldo of the European Fertility Research Center in Basle, Switzerland announced today that they have verified that the so-called X-virus— believed to be the cause of the current drop in female births—is capable of mutating at an alarming rate. This does not bode well for hopes of discovering a way of combating the dangerous virus.

"Like the flu virus," Dr. Letelier stated, "it would require a new vaccine for every new mutation, which appears to occur every ten to fourteen months."

The good news is that the virus could mutate itself out of business—change to the point where it no longer affects the X chromosome.

Scientists have long known that the low female birthrate was caused by a deficiency of the X chromosome in sperm. In 2060, Russian researchers in Voronezh identified a virus that attacks the X chromosome and since then scientists throughout the world have been searching for a way of defeating it.

Vancouver Globe, October 19, 2061

Catherine liked going out with Grandpa. He was big and strong enough to protect her. Sometimes he was funny, especially when he played silly songs for her on his guitar. One time he'd smelled funny when he came to take her out, sort of sour, and Mommy had been mad with him and wouldn't let her go. They had a big fight and Catherine got scared and hid in her room, hugging her blue kitty. He never smelled like that again.

They were going to the park. It wasn't very far so they could walk. His hand was so big and warm, holding hers, but he walked too fast and she had to do little skipping steps to keep up. She liked the park. Sometimes, Uncle David took her to the playground and pushed her on the swings, but Mommy never took her there. She said there were too many bad men so she could only go if Grandpa or one of her uncles was with her.

They had to go up a big hill. She wished grandpa would carry her. She started to drag her feet.

Grandpa stopped. "Want me to carry you?" he asked.

Catherine nodded and held up her arms then he hoisted her up. She put her legs around his waist and looked over his shoulder. You could see everything from up here, the mountains, and all the big buildings downtown, just like from their windows at home.

A car was coming up the drive behind them. It was a little blue one with a man inside. She hoped he wasn't a bad man. The car slowed down when it got close and grandpa stopped and looked round. He nodded at the man in the car who rolled down his window.

"Want a lift?" the man asked.

"No," Grandpa said. "We'll meet you at the top."

"Hello, Catherine," the man said.

She buried her face in her grandfather's shoulder until the car was gone.

"Is he a bad man?" she asked.

"He's your father," Grandpa replied.

"He is?" This was a new idea to her. "Mommy said I haven't got a father."

At the top of the hill was a big round glass building. She'd been there once, but didn't remember very much except it was hot inside and there were lots of plants and birds. The man was waiting by the entrance. He must have left his car somewhere else because she couldn't see it.

Grandpa put her down and shook the man's hand. "Neal," he said. Then he turned to her. "Catherine, this is Neal. He's your ... father. We're going to look around the conservatory with him for a while. Say hello."

Grandpa sounded funny, as if he didn't like the man.

Instead of greeting the man, she hid behind grandpa's leg and peeked at him.

"Give her time," Grandpa said. "She's not used to strangers."

The man rubbed his hands together and turned away. "Let's go in," he said.

The whole dome was filled with trees and plants. It smelled funny but nice and warm. The air felt like the bathroom when her mother filled the bath with hot water and poured in some crystals.

Catherine saw a brightly colored bird flit from one tree to another. "What's that, Grandpa?"

The man was standing near her now. "It's called a macaw," he said. "Look down there, see the fish?"

Catherine looked where he was pointing and saw a pool surrounded by rocks and ferns with red and gold fish swimming in it. A frog jumped off a rock into the water, making ripples that spread out in rings. Catherine laughed.

She hadn't noticed it happening, but after a while, she realized the man was holding her hand and grandpa was walking behind them. Maybe he wasn't so bad after all.

"Grandpa said you're my father," she said, feeling unusually bold.

"That's right," the man replied. "I am." He stopped walking and squatted beside her. "I hope we'll be able to get to know each other better, would you like that?"

He seemed all right, he smelled nice, like soap, and he had nice eyes.

"I don't know," she replied.

The man smiled. "Had enough of this place?" he asked. "Maybe we could go for some ice cream, that's if it's all right with Grandpa."

Catherine turned away from the man and took her grandpa's hand. She looked up at him to see how he would respond.

"Fine," he said.

After eating their ice cream, the man wanted to pick her up, but she squirmed away and hid behind her grandfather. The man slammed the car door when he got in, then he honked the horn and waved to her. He was smiling, but she didn't know if he was mad or not.

She saw Mommy on the balcony when they got back. They waved to her and went inside. When the elevator arrived at the seventh floor, she was waiting out in the hall. She scooped Catherine up in her arms and kissed her.

"Did you have a good time, sweetie?"

"It was okay," Catherine replied.

"Come in and have some tea, Dad," Julia said as she ushered Catherine into the apartment. "What did you do today?" she asked her daughter.

"We saw a man," Catherine replied.

"Did you like him?"

"I don't know." Catherine glanced at her grandfather. "Grandpa said he's my father."

"He is."

She thought this made Mommy sad.

"How can he be my father?"

She saw a look pass between her mother and grandpa.

"I used to be married to him. It's like your grandpa and grandma. Grandpa's *my* father. That's why I call him dad."

"He is?" This was too strange for Catherine. She looked at grandpa, then back at Julia while she thought about it. "Do I have to call the man 'dad'?"

Her mother smiled. "Not if you don't want to, sweetie. Would you like to see him again?"

Catherine shrugged. "He bought me ice cream. He's got a blue car," she added. She knew about eight colors now, but she liked blue best, and then purple.

***

Sarap turned over on his back and sighed.

"What are you worrying about now?" Farida asked. She reached out in the dark and took his hand.

"My brothers. I think they resent me for being the only one who's married. I wish I could help them; I feel so sorry for them." He leaned over and kissed her. "I know what they're missing."

"I don't think they resent you at all. Well, maybe Rajinder, but Keval is much too nice to hold it against you."

"Dada was telling me Rajinder is thinking of going to India to find a bride."

"They have the same problem in India," Farida replied.

"I know, but there are men there who are more willing to sell their daughters to someone with enough money."

Farida felt a twinge of discomfort. This hit too close to home. She knew her father hadn't really sold her; he'd paid back the loan by now. She turned on her side facing Sarap, but didn't reply.

"How's your work with the ova going?" her husband asked.

Farida sighed. "Still no luck. We manage to get the eggs to divide all right, but after about eight cell divisions, they just stop. Another batch died this morning. We're going to try another tomorrow. How are you doing with the chromosomes?"

"We're going to start trying a new technique. That wretched virus is so insidious. I wish we knew where it came from. It's too damned specific to be an accident."

"You mean somebody created it? I wouldn't be surprised. There are plenty of cultures that value male children more than female. It's hard to believe that scientists would be a party to something so irresponsible, but given the fanaticism of some of their governments.... I hope it doesn't take as long to find a cure as it did with HIV; there'll be nobody left."

Neither spoke for a while, but just as Farida thought Sarap had fallen asleep, he turned over again and breathed deeply.

"Farida, love?"

"Hmm." She was almost asleep.

"How do you feel about Keval?"

"You know I like him. We've got along well since we were kids." She recalled the many times they had studied and played together after her marriage to Sarap. He was a gentle, thoughtful man, incapable of harming anyone. "I've always been sorry he couldn't find a wife."

"He's very fond of you, too."

"What brought this up?" she asked sleepily.

"I was wondering...."

"What?"

"Could you feel for him the way you feel about me? I mean...." He broke off, unable to put his thoughts into coherent form.

The shocking nature of what her husband was hinting brought Farida fully awake. "You mean, like being married?" Her heart lurched. However, she had to admit the thought appealed to her. She did love Keval, but she had believed it was as a brother. Now the idea had been brought up, she realized that maybe her feelings were more than platonic. "How would you feel about it?"

"To tell the truth, the idea scares the hell out of me," he put his arms around her and held her tight. "I'm so scared of losing you, my little wife, but he's my brother and I love him too. I keep telling myself that sharing my good fortune with someone I love would be a good thing, but...."

"Did he say anything to you about this?"

"No, but I've seen the way he looks at you. He obviously adores you and it's eating him up inside."

She buried her face against his chest and mumbled, "Holy truth, Sarap, I don't know what to say. I think I could live with the idea, but it's up to you. I don't want to hurt you."

He kissed the top of her head. "Let's get some sleep. We can talk about it another time, if you want to."

Keval visited them the following rest day. As was his custom, he came laden with gifts for everyone: a flowering plant for Farida, a toy for his nephew and a video for Sarap. Farida saw him looking wistfully at her son and her heart went out to him. If ever anyone deserved to have children, it was Keval. He was one of the rising stars of the video industry in Vancouver. His productions were starting to attract a worldwide audience, and he was a popular figure in the city's creative community, but it was obvious there was something missing in his life.

Keval had stopped wearing the traditional turban and had his hair cut shoulder length. Clean-shaven, in loose white trousers and yellow shirt, he looked remarkably handsome. When he turned his beautiful black eyes on her, a wave of warmth infused her. She saw the affection that Sarap had talked about in his glance.

She finally admitted what she had been hiding from herself for a long time: she would not object to having him as a partner, but how could she tell Sarap? Should she leave it up to him? After all, he had been the one to bring it up.

As they sipped their tea and nibbled on sweets, Farida wondered how they could broach the subject that had been on her mind since her bedtime conversation with Sarap a few nights earlier. Farida looked at Sarap, who was sitting on the floor with their six-year-old son. He felt her gaze and looked up, and then he looked at Keval. He got slowly to his feet.

"Let me help you take the dishes out," he said, starting to load empty cups and plates on the tray.

Taking his hint, Farida picked up the teapot and started towards the kitchen.

"Need a hand?" Keval offered.

"No, you stay with Ranjit; we'll be right back."

Sarap put the tray down on the kitchen counter and turned to Farida who was still holding the teapot. "What do you think?" he asked in a low voice.

"I don't know, Sarap. I don't want anything that will hurt you, or our marriage."

"But if I don't mind?"

How could he not mind? Farida thought to herself. She nodded.

"Shall I talk to him?"

Emotions churned in Farida: excitement, apprehension, hope, fear. She nodded again, incapable of saying the words. She put the teapot down carefully.

They returned to the sitting room hand in hand.

Sarap didn't bring the subject up with his brother that day, but discussed it with him at lunch a few days later.

***

The marriage ceremony was less formal than wedding of Sarap and Farida. They were not allowed to marry in the temple and made do with a civil ceremony, which Sarap's mother refused to attend.

Ranjit was delighted to have his uncle Keval living in the same house, but Farida was more apprehensive about the new situation. The love she felt for Sarap was deep and unshakable, but the thrill of a new romance was irresistible. The feelings she had believed were sisterly affection for Keval blossomed into passion, although guilt lingered in the background every moment.

Fortunately, both men worked long hours at their jobs and weren't home very much, and her own work kept her at the university for many hours during the day. She suspected that the two brothers had made a secret agreement that when one was home for an evening, the other would be away. When Keval was out of town filming for a few days, she could spend intimate evenings with Sarap, and conversely, when Sarap spent the night awaiting the outcome of an experiment, Keval would be home to keep her company.

Her happiness was not perfect, however. Her husband's parents, especially her mother-in-law, condemned the arrangement, saying in it was a sin against God.

"I took this girl into my home like a daughter," Mrs. Gurdwara Singh ranted on one visit. "And look how she repays me. She has betrayed one son and seduced the other into a life of sin. I hardly dare show my face in the temple."

Farida, in the kitchen making tea, could hear every word. She clenched her hands and struggled to keep back tears.

"Mother!" Sarap replied sharply. "I will not have you talk about my wife like that. It was not Farida's idea, anyway. If you insist on being so disagreeable, I will have to ask you not to come here again."

"Parmjeet, calm down, and stop exaggerating," his father said.

"Don't you want to see your sons happy?" Sarap continued. "At least Keval has a somewhat normal life with the chance to be a father. That's more than the other four have."

"If she does have another baby, how will you know who the father is?" his mother continued stubbornly.

"That's our business, mother."

Farida was glad Keval wasn't there. He was so sensitive; she hated to think how his mother's attitude would affect him.

"And how do you know she won't take up with somebody else?"

"Mother, that's enough. If you don't stop this minute, I'm going to ask you to leave."

"Don't worry, we're going. Come on, Gurdip, let's go. I know where I'm not welcome."

A wail of distress came from the bedroom. The angry voices had woken Ranjit. Farida rushed to his room at the back of the house, thankful of an excuse to get away. The front door slammed, and then Sarap joined her at their son's bedside.

"I'm sorry, love," he said, putting his arm around both of them.

"I'm sorry," she replied. "I should have known how they would feel."

"It's not your fault. They'll come around eventually. I wouldn't be surprised if she's a bit jealous."

Chapter Eighteen

Every man should have a wife
So he can lead a normal life.
Government procrastinates,
Doing zilch to find us mates

Demonstrators' chant.

Julia awoke with a start. It was still dark outside but a flickering reddish glow penetrated the window blinds.
Voices shouted back and forth, some angry, some sounding panicked.

She got out of bed and wrapped herself in a robe, then went to the window and opened the blind. It was the park. The trees were on fire, surrounded by darting figures. It wasn't clear whether they were trying to combat the blaze, or make it spread.

"Mother!"

Now Catherine was awake. She slept on the lower level in the room below Julia's since they'd moved to a larger apartment. The entire upper level was Julia's domain.

Julia ran down the stairs to her daughter's room. Catherine was standing at the window in her nightshirt, looking at the activity below. She turned when Julia entered. "Look, Mother, the park's on fire." Her eyes were big and round.

"Don't be frightened, sweetie," Julia said, placing a hand on her shoulder.

"I'm not scared," Catherine replied. "I know it can't get up here. Look, there are the fire trucks."

The firefighters converged on the scene from all directions, lights flashing and sirens whining. Two helicopters flew overhead, dispensing canisters of gas over the people on the ground, who were already scattering into the shadowy side streets.

A few days later Catherine gazed out of the window of the cab that was taking her to school, noticing an unusually large number of men on the street. She could feel the tension in the air. The fires last week had shaken her up in spite of her bravado at the time. The cab turned onto Cambie Street right into a mob milling around City Hall on the corner Twelfth Avenue. The driver tried to back up around the corner, but was blocked by a vehicle behind him.

Someone in the crowd yelled, "There's one." Several younger men broke away from the mob and converged on the cab, which was forced to a standstill.

Catherine knew they couldn't see her because of the darkened windows, but the look on their faces—a sort of cunning hunger—terrified her. They looked as if they wanted to devour her.

They began to pound on the outside of the cab and yell, "Let her out! Let her out!"

Several men began to rock the little vehicle and she was afraid it would turn over.

"Curl up on the floor," the driver said.

She obeyed without hesitation. It had been drilled into her that she should do as he instructed if they ever ran into trouble. She felt the driver move. She couldn't see what he did, but the men outside started to shriek in pain, and then the cab was moving again.

"You can get up now," the driver said. "They're gone."

When Catherine was back in her seat, he handed her a wrapped candy. "Here, eat this, it'll make you feel better."

She'd been given these candies before after stressful events such as a visit to the dentist and they always made her feel calmer, so she unwrapped it and put it in her mouth.

"I'll take you on to school, but I'll have to call your mother and see if she wants me to bring you home."

"What did you do?" she asked.

"Turned on the current," he said. "It electrifies the outside of the cab and gives them a shock."

"Cool," Catherine replied. She shuddered to think of what might have happened if it hadn't worked.

"You're going to have to have a home tutor," Julia told Catherine that evening. She was more shaken up by Catherine's narrow escape than she cared to admit.

"Oh, Mother." Catherine pouted. "I want to go to school. I never go anywhere else."

"It's too dangerous for you to go out alone. Besides, you'll be able to talk and play games with your friends on the Net."

"But that's not the same. Please don't make me stay home."

"They're talking about closing the girls' schools soon anyway. It's getting too dangerous having so many girls all in one place, even with guards."

Catherine continued to spend time with her father, but now, instead of going skating or boating, they were forced to spend their time together at his home or in one of the fortified shopping malls. She now saw him one day a week and sometimes even stayed overnight at his apartment.

Catherine enjoyed the visits, although Julia was still apprehensive. At least he hadn't tried to turn their daughter against her. She reciprocated by saying nothing derogatory about Neal in Catherine's presence.

Chapter Nineteen

63/07/21

Dear Jul:

Sorry to take so long answering your last email, but we've been taking part in a highly classified mission, installing electronic monitors in a mountainous region somewhere in South America.

I am now in charge of a monitoring team near the Peru-Bolivia border. See, your big brother's doing all right, after all. It's quite safe, so don't worry about me. We spend most of the time in a fortified bunker with our computers and scanning devices, analyzing information from the external monitors. It's the guys who have to go out on patrols that that have to be careful. Tell Mom and Dad I'll write as soon as I finish my next shift.

Gotta go—chow time.

Hugs and kisses to you and young Kate.

Paul.

When Julia saw her father's face on the screen, he seemed to have aged two decades. His grey-tinged skin sagged and his eyes were dull and lifeless.

"Dad? What's wrong?"

"We've had some bad news." He looked away from the viewer.

"Is it Mother?"

Raymond shook his head. "It's Paul. We just got news from NAMA headquarters in Tulsa."

"He's not been ... killed...?" A lump formed in Julia's chest pressing upwards, cutting off her breath and leaving behind a chilly hollow feeling.

"No." Raymond cleared his throat. "All they could tell us was that his unit encountered a group of rebels who dropped nerve gas on them. He's been moved to a hospital in Chile, but there's not much hope for recovery."

Julia pressed her fist against her teeth. Tears gushed from her eyes. "Oh, God," she moaned. "Oh God. Paul." She looked up at the monitor and saw her father's cheeks were wet too. "Is there anything we can do?"

He shook his head.

"How's Mother?"

"She collapsed when the news came. Robbie and Kelly are with her. I'll have to get back to her now."

"Dad, I'm so sorry." Julia wiped her eyes. "I'll be there as soon as I can get a cab."

Julia disconnected and punched in the number for Security Cabs. A recorded message responded: "Due to the current civil unrest, Security Cabs is now operating on a revised schedule. Our hours are now from 0600 to 1900. We sincerely regret any inconvenience this may cause and recommend clients use the Fly-by-Night Copter service, which accepts our client cards at par. The number for Fly-by-Night is 72-415-415."

"Oh, drat, I'd forgotten about that!" She jotted down the number and then looked in her appointment book for the number of the client she was expecting in an hour.

After clearing it with him, she went downstairs to explain to Catherine's tutor that she had to go out.

"I'm not sure how long I'll be gone," she said. "I don't know how late I'll be. Is that a problem?"

"It's all right, Julia dear, I'll stay. It's my day off tomorrow."

"Thanks, Elwyn."

Elwyn Close was a twenty-six-year-old gay man who regularly tutored and minded Catherine. Since she had stopped going to school, he came every evening to be with her while Julia was working. He had formerly been a schoolteacher, but now freelanced as a tutor to three girls who had to study at home. In the mornings, Catherine worked on her school assignments on a terminal linked to the Net, sometimes with help and encouragement from Julia. In the afternoons, they usually did something together, went visiting or shopping, then, after dinner and a rest, Catherine did lessons with Elwyn. He stayed with her until she was asleep.

After settling with Elwyn and explaining to Catherine why she had to go out, Julia called the copter, put on her warm winter cloak and took the elevator up to the roof.

There was a chill wind blowing. She wrapped the cloak more snuggly around her and looked towards the north for the flashing lights of the copter. The city lay in glittering islands of light among dark uninhabited zones. Off to the east, a fire flickered in one of the dark areas. Julia shivered. She looked back at the city core. Tiny beads of light moved along invisible strands joining some of the higher buildings—the new cable system, although cable was something of a misnomer, the spun silksteel threads that joined the towers were superfine, but as strong as spider's silk.

The copter appeared unexpectedly from her left, the wind having muffled the whine of its rotor, and landed gently on the roof pad. She climbed into the passenger seat and buckled herself in.

"Denman West Habitat," she told the pilot.

Julia's parents and Antoine had moved to this new habitat five years earlier. The complex replaced what had formerly been six blocks of apartment buildings between Nelson and Pendrell streets, bounded on the east and west by Denman Street and Stanley Park. Like all the newer habitats, it had a copter pad on the roof of the largest building.

When Julia arrived at the family condominium, Robbie met her in the hall. His hair and beard were completely grey now, his face was a map of lines, and his paunch was expanding. Julia realized for the first time Robbie was getting old.

"What a terrible thing," he said. "It's almost worse than if he'd been killed outright."

"I don't really understand," Julia replied. "What has happened to Paul? Is there any hope?"

Robbie shook his head mournfully. "What I can gather from the message your parents received, there isn't much." He took both her hands. "Come and sit down, I'll try to explain it."

Julia released her hands and removed her cloak. "I should be with mother."

"She's sleeping now. I had to give her a sedative so that she could get some rest." Robbie shook his head and rubbed the back of his neck. Julia knew he disliked sedating people. "She's going to need all her strength for what's to come."

Julia followed him into the solarium, a glassed-in room filled with plants and outdoor furniture. They sat on facing basket chairs. "What happened to Paul?" she asked.

"Well, as Raymond told you, it was a nerve-gas attack. They would all have been killed outright if they hadn't been wearing protective gear; as it was, only a small amount of the gas penetrated their masks."

"But what does it do?"

Robbie leaned forward, elbows on knees, hands clasped. "Once it gets in the bloodstream, it goes quickly to the brain and starts destroying neural tissue. In your brother's case, the destruction was incomplete."

"So how bad is it?"

"The toxins are quickly broken down by the body's defenses, so the damage was not serious enough to cause death. Other than that, all I know is that he's severely disabled."

"Oh, God. Is he coming back here?"

"Yes. They're transporting him from Santiago on Friday."

"Friday! That's the day after tomorrow."

Julia stood up. "I should go and talk to Dad and see mother," she said. "Thanks, Robbie."

Robbie accompanied Julia to Aldina's bedroom and nodded to Kelly. "We'll be on our way, then," he said. "Kelly will pop by tomorrow to see Aldina. Good night."

When they were gone, Julia looked at the scene in the softly lighted room. Raymond, who had been sitting on one side of the bed, rose and came over to her. She realized that their eyes were now level; he seemed to have shrunk since she'd last seen him.

"Oh, Dad," she said, moving into his arms.

He pressed her to him, one hand patting her back. Unable to choke back the tears, Julia sobbed. Catherine's face flashed in her mind when she thought about how Raymond must feel. He's lost a child, the most painful loss anyone could ever endure.

"It's pretty bad, huh?" she said finally, pulling away and wiping her eyes.

Raymond nodded and wiped the back of his hand over each eye. "Your mother..."

"I can't imagine..."

What can you say at such a time? Anything is inadequate or worse, trite. She looked at her mother's ravaged face, now eased by sleep. It's going to be awful for her when she wakes up, Julia thought.

"Is there anything I can do?" she asked. "Have you eaten?"

Antoine stood up. "I'll go and fix us something," he said.

On the following Saturday, Julia went to see Paul. He had arrived by air the previous evening and been transferred immediately to the University Hospital. The neurologist on duty explained Paul's condition and prospects to her before she went in to see him.

"I'm afraid the prognosis is not good," he said. "He has lost much of his motor function, and as far as we can tell, many of his cognitive processes."

"What does all that mean?" Julia asked.

"Basically, he is in a vegetative state, unable to move or respond to sensory stimuli."

"You mean he's in a coma." Julia wondered if they used the technical jargon because the facts were too painful for even medical people to face.

The doctor nodded. "I'm afraid so."

"Will he come out of it?"

The man stood up and smoothed his white coat. "It is not very probable. The brain scans reveal very little activity, and in spite of the advances in medical science, we have not yet found a way to regenerate neural tissue. Even if we could, everything he knew and all he'd learned throughout his life would be gone, language, skills, everything. I'm sorry." He turned towards the door. "Would you like to go in now?"

The neurologist led her to a softly lighted room with a row of glassed-in cubicles down one side. Outside the compartments, technicians sat in front of a row of monitors, studying the dials and video displays, occasionally turning a dial or tapping a few characters on a keyboard. Julia could see green-suited nurses working in some of the enclosures.

Paul was in the last cubicle. He was supported on padded slings in a stainless steel frame that oscillated slowly from side to side. His body was covered with a dark green sheet that concealed the attachment sites of the various tubes and wires connecting him to a low panel on the wall, and by extension, she assumed, to the monitors outside. He lay perfectly still, apart from the rocking of the bed, his eyes closed, skin still tanned from the tropics. He might have been dead. His head had been shaved. She wondered whether that had been by a medical team, or if he had chosen that style. It made him look very vulnerable.

"Will he be able to hear me if I talk to him?" she whispered.

"Probably not," the doctor replied, "but it wouldn't do any harm." He went out, leaving the door open.

Julia approached the bed and touched Paul's tanned fingers. She closed her eyes, but tears squeezed through the lids. "Paul." She stroked his face. "It's Julia."

There was not even a flicker of movement on the still features. The face looked peaceful and very young, but Paul wasn't there.

"I love you, big brother," she said. A tear dropped on his mouth when she bent to kiss his cheek. She wiped it off with her thumb. The respirator pumped a steady rhythm, breathing in and out for him.

This isn't life, she thought. *Why don't they let him go? What's the point?* Nevertheless, you cling to the faintest glimmer of hope. In any case, it wasn't her decision to make. What would I do if it were Catherine lying here? She wondered. That thought was unendurable and she quickly suppressed it.

***

Catherine had a lonely life. She had no opportunity to play outside or go anywhere with friends. She would have been terrified had anyone suggested such a thing. Sometimes, she was able to visit the home of a girl she had known at school. There were two girls she had befriended during the two years she had attended school: Leigh, a petite vivacious Filipina her own age; and a chubby, sullen older girl called Maddie. Catherine liked both girls for different reasons: Leigh because her temperament was the opposite of Catherine's own. Leigh, with her bubbly personality, was able to bring her out of herself and encourage her to have some light-hearted fun. Maddie, under the sullen exterior, had a wicked sense of humor. Catherine could empathize with her—to a certain extent, she understood the girl's dissatisfaction and feelings of inadequacy. Her mother was a youthful slender woman who had born five children with three different partners. Maddie, the only one with a weight problem, felt like the ugly duckling of the brood.

"Why can't I ever go to Maddie's?" Catherine pouted. She couldn't understand why her mother never let her go and play at her friend's house. She would have liked to see Maddie's brothers. There were no boys her age in her own family and she had no opportunity to meet any. She was curious.

"I'd rather have her here where I can keep an eye on you."

"But you let me go to Leigh's." All Leigh's brothers were grown up and had left home, except for the baby who was only three.

"That's different."

"I bet it's because of her brothers."

Julia gave her a peculiar look, making Catherine wonder if she had a reason for not wanting her to be exposed to older boys. Mother had three older brothers. What had they done? she wondered. Maybe Maddie could tell her something about having brothers.

"Boys are so disgusting." Maddie said with a grimace. "When I was little, they used to bring their friends to look at me."

"Look at you? Oh," she added when Maddie pointed to her lap.

"They leave me alone now, though," Maddie said with satisfaction. "I can clobber any one of them."

Julia was always anxious when Catherine went to stay at her father's, but sometimes she needed to have a day to herself. Neal now lived in a less secure apartment on the North Shore. It was not a family complex, being inhabited solely by men. Although Neal swore Catherine was perfectly safe, Julia was less confident.

Chapter Twenty

Then and now

How have people's lives changed in the last fifty years?

In 2023, at least half of all office workers were women, now they're mostly men.

Seventy-five percent of nurses were women; now it is very rare to find a female nurse in any public institution.

Fifty percent of medical doctors were women; it is currently one percent.

Female domestic workers now comprise about one-point-five percent of the occupation, and those only working in homes with at least one female family member.

Male prostitution was a rare underground occupation; now it is an accepted part of society.

The fashion industry has changed radically. With the decrease in female customers, clothing stores and ready-made women's clothes have disappeared and been replaced by sample boutiques, online, and in exclusive shopping centers. Now women choose the sample they want and order it to be made to their personal measurements and choice of fabrics.

With similar drops in the demand for female cosmetics, hygiene and other beauty products, these products now comprise less than five percent of the cosmetics industry.

And last, but not least, there has been an incredible increase in male violence.

Excerpt from a magazine article

Since entering adolescence, Catherine had become more curious about Julia's occupation, making Julia feel as if she was under constant scrutiny. It wasn't that she felt there was any shame in being a courtesan, but she wasn't sure she would want Catherine to follow her example. She recognized the ambiguity of the feeling, but assumed most mothers felt that way, whatever their occupation. They were reluctant to see the beloved child become involved with a man.

Julia made a good living as Pascal had predicted. They had moved to a house at False Creek, close to Pascal's home. It was centrally located and had many conveniences, shops, entertainment centers, and outdoor recreation facilities. Catherine had her own ground floor suite, and it was safer for her to leave the house by herself provided she didn't leave the compound.

Catherine had her fourteenth birthday party at her mother's and next day, went to spend a weekend with Neal. She was small and slender for her age, and in thick insulated pants and ski jacket, with her hair tucked up in knit cap, she could easily have passed for a boy. Neal was taking her skiing on Grouse Mountain. They had a picnic lunch packed in the back of the car and were ready to leave.

"Damn," Neal said. "I've forgotten the sun screen. Stay here and keep the doors locked; I'll be right back." As he turned away, she heard a click and all the locks were activated automatically.

Catherine remembered she'd left her mittens on the kitchen table. She looked at the control panel, trying to guess which buttons would unlock the door so she could follow him. It had to be L or D, something like that. There was one marked SL. Security Lock? When she pushed the button, the window in the roof slid back. Skylight? She kept pushing various buttons until she heard the locks snap open. She didn't notice the two men silently approaching the car until their shadow fell over her. Before she had chance to react, they grabbed her and were dragging her away. One of them clamped something soft over her mouth and nose. That was the last thing she was aware of until she came to, lying on a firm padded surface in a moving vehicle. She opened her eyes, but couldn't see anything; the compartment she was in was completely dark—no windows or even cracks to let in light. When she tried to move, she found her hands and feet secured with leather straps. Filled with terror, she could barely breathe. Whatever they'd used to knock, her out had left a nauseous taste. She gagged and swallowed saliva. Remembering how she'd dealt with nausea when she had a severe attack of influenza, she took some deep breaths.

The vehicle was jolting over a bumpy, unpaved track and splashed through slush of melted snow. She closed her eyes and did a mental inventory. No pain anywhere—apart from being tied up she was unharmed. *What are they going to do with me?* she wondered. It wasn't hard to guess. The news media were full of stories about girls being abducted. Usually, they were sold, but sometimes brutally raped and dumped, half-dead, where they may or may not be found in time to save their lives.

Catherine blinked to relieve the painful pressure behind her eyes, determined not to cry. I'm just a little girl, she thought, forgetting her frequent assertions that now she was fourteen, she should be treated like a grownup.

She thought of her mother. What would Julia do? She would surely be a lot braver than Catherine felt. She would look for the first chance to escape. Catherine tugged at the straps on her wrists. They were too tight for her to slip her hands through. The same with the ones around her ankles. The straps were anchored to metal rings set in the surface she was lying on and didn't allow much range of motion. She couldn't even reach her face to wipe her eyes. After a while, she gave up, and eventually dozed.

She was woken later by a door slamming and men's voices. The vehicle jolted as someone climbed out, then she heard the snick of a lock and a panel slid open at her feet. It was dark outside. Someone shone a light in her face, dazzling her.

"Help her out," a man ordered calmly.

One of the men climbed up beside her and unfastened the straps without saying a word. When he had them undone, he backed out and pulled her towards the opening by her ankles.

"Don't hurt her," the other man said. "The Reverend wants her in good condition."

"A virgin!" said another man with an unpleasant voice. He snickered.

"Be quiet, Zach," the original speaker said. He sounded older than the other two.

Catherine was relieved to hear that they didn't want her to be hurt, but the rest of the conversation did nothing to gain her confidence. She sat up when she reached the back edge and allowed the man who had untied her to help her climb down. She looked around her and saw no sign of any lights to indicate anyone lived in the area, although she could see the shadowy outline of a small building. The air was freezing, made worse by a cold breeze. A dog barked in the distance and was answered by an eerie howl from another direction. They must be out in the country.

"Damn coyotes," one of the men muttered.

"Where are you taking me?" Catherine ventured in a timid voice.

"You'll see," the older man replied. He seemed to be in charge. "Bring her inside."

The man who had untied her took her arm and gently drew her along after the leader towards the building. A door opened letting out a flood of warm light to illuminate the surroundings. There was not much to see, some bushes and a few trees, ground covered with clumps of dry grass surrounded by patches of snow. Twin tracks led up to the parked van in which they'd arrived. Once inside the building, which looked like an old farmhouse, Catherine was able to see her captors. The one she had pegged as the leader looked about Antoine's age, in his early fifties. He had thinning light brown hair and blue eyes, and was dressed the way she thought a farm worker might, in dark green one-piece overalls with a rough grey shirt and brown boots. The man who had untied her was dark and slim; the other was short and pudgy with long blond hair and an unpleasant, sneering expression.

The kitchen of the farmhouse was a spacious room with an old-fashioned cooking range and a boxy freestanding refrigerator with a noisy motor. The older man pulled out a chair from the wooden table.

"Sit down. I expect you're hungry. We'll get you some supper." He turned to the blond man. "Zach, you can warm up the food in the microwave. Tom, give her some milk to drink."

"Could I have some water?" she asked.

"All right, water."

Encouraged by the fact that they were not treating her badly, she asked, "When can I go home?"

Zach sniggered and the older man scowled at him. "You're going to a new home," he said.

Catherine burst into tears. "I don't want a new home. I want to go back to my mother," she sobbed.

"Your mother's the Whore of Babylon," Zach said. "You should praise the Lord we rescued you from her before she corrupted you as well.

"Watch your tongue, boy."

Catherine sobbed harder, covering her face with her hands. She flinched and opened her eyes when she felt a hand touch her shoulder.

"It'll be all right, child. We're not going to harm you," the older man said. He withdrew his hand.

"Who are you?" Catherine wanted to know.

"I'm Reverend Jesse Oregon; these two are members of our congregation. You'll be seeing a lot of us from now on."

The dark-haired man put a glass of water on the table in front of her.

"This here's Tom Singleton." He indicated the dark man, and then nodded towards the blonde-haired boy who was taking two plates out of the microwave. "And that's my son, Zach."

Catherine sniffed. Oregon tore off a strip of paper towels and handed it to her so that she could wipe her face. Zach put two more plates of food on the table and pulled out a chair for himself.

The other men sat down at the table. Before picking up their forks, they bent their heads and clasped their hands together while the Reverend Oregon started on a lengthy prayer. When it was finished, they all said 'Amen' and started to eat.

Catherine looked at her plate of chicken with mashed potatoes and gravy. The smell of it made her feel sick. She knew if she tried to eat it, she would throw up.

Oregon, seated across the table, saw she wasn't eating. "Come on, girl, eat your supper."

"I can't," she said in a soft voice.

"What's the matter?" Zach said nastily. "Not up to your standards?"

"I'm not hungry. I feel sick."

"You need to keep your strength up. We've a long trip ahead of us tomorrow. The Reverend won't be happy if we starve you."

"I'll eat it if she doesn't want it," Zach offered.

"You would, garbage-gut," Tom said softly.

It was the first time Catherine had heard him speak. He had a nice voice. She looked at him and saw his face had turned red. He was looking down at his plate.

"Is there anything else you'd like?" Oregon asked. "How about some apple pie?"

Catherine nodded. "Okay."

"Hey, not fair," Zach protested. "We have to clean our plates before we get dessert." He reached over and took Catherine's plate. "I'll clean it for her."

She picked at the pie, which had a hard crust, and managed to eat about half of the serving. After they had finished eating, Oregon led her out of the kitchen into a short hallway with doors along one side. He opened the door closest to the kitchen.

"This here's the bathroom. Get yourself cleaned up, and then I'll show you where you can sleep."

Oregon was waiting outside the door when she came out. He opened the next door down the hall and ushered her in. "There's a clean nightgown on the bed. Good night."

He closed door behind her and went back towards the kitchen.

***

"What do you mean, she's gone?" Julia shrieked. A wave of fear and panic surged through her.

"What I said: When I got back to the car, she was gone," Neal replied in exasperation.

"I can't believe you left her alone," Julia said.

"I was only gone a couple of minutes and I made sure the doors were locked."

"So how did they get her out?" Julia sighed, trying to stay calm. "Have you called the police?"

"Of course I have. I'm not stupid, Julia, in spite of what you think."

"I wouldn't say leaving a fourteen-year-old girl alone outside was exactly brilliant," she retorted. "What did they say?"

"She may have wandered off somewhere..."

"What?" Julia shouted, "Are they out of their minds?"

"Calm down, Julia. Getting worked up isn't going to help. That's not the only theory they're working on."

He could be so infuriating. Why shouldn't she be worked up? Didn't he realize that her innocent young daughter had disappeared? Who knows what was being done to her at this very moment? Julia tried to push that thought to the back of her mind. She raked her fingers through her hair and took a deep breath.

"So what else are they doing?"

"They're going around the neighborhood, asking people if they saw anything. And they're going to set up road blocks and search vehicles." She heard someone else talking in the background. "Listen, Julia, Detective Seriev wants to talk to you."

The face of a middle-aged blond man came into view on the monitor. "I'd just like to get some information from you Ms ..."

"Finisterra," Julia filled in for him.

"Mr. Gianakis has given me a description of your daughter, but maybe you could help fill in on a few gaps. Does she have any emotional or health problems?"

"What do you mean?" Julia asked.

"Well, is there anything that might make her behave in any way unusual?"

"No, of course not.

"What about behavior? Is she rebellious? Does she resent restrictions?"

Catherine? Julia would have laughed if it hadn't been so serious. "None," she replied. "She's a very quiet girl. She doesn't seem to mind not being able to go out and do the things normal...." Julia put her hand over her mouth. "I don't mean she's not normal; I was referring to the way girls have to live these days. That's not normal. Anyway, she seems content with her life. What are you getting at?"

"I'm just trying to cover all possibilities," the detective replied. He looked down and then back at the screen. "Have you seen any strangers in or near your home recently?"

"No. I mean I haven't noticed any. Do you think someone might have been watching us?"

"It's possible. We can get the videos from residential security and go through them to see if there's anyone that can't be accounted for, but it will take time."

"What do you think has happened to her? Has she been kidnapped?" Julia realized how melodramatic that sounded, but she had to bring it out in the open.

Detective Seriev's face had the bleak expression of someone who has seen every horror of which humans are capable. "It's possible. Much as I hate to admit it, the kidnapping of young women is becoming much more prevalent." He sighed. "I understand you entertain a number of clients in your home, Ms Finisterra."

Julia was surprised by the change of subject. "Yes. What does that have to do with Catherine's disappearance?"

"Nothing, I hope," Seriev replied. "But we have to consider every angle. I assume your clients are aware that you have a daughter?"

"Some of them, yes, but she doesn't come into contact with any of them. I keep my business completely separate from my family."

"I understand, but if she doesn't turn up, we'll have to interview them."

"But I've know most of them for years," Julia protested. "My business is based on trust on both sides. If I started revealing..." She stopped, realizing that Catherine was more important than any other consideration. "Of course," she said quietly.

"Right. I'd like to come over and look at her room, see the layout of the complex and so on," the detective said. "I could be there in fifteen minutes. Would that be convenient?"

Julia nodded and the screen went blank. She got up and started pacing around the ground floor of the house, from the den to the kitchen, then to Catherine's room, trying to calm the fear that gripped her like a cold clamp. A painful lump in her throat and stinging pressure behind her eyes finally gave way to a gush of tears and wrenching sobs. She stumbled into the bathroom and sat on the toilet lid, unraveling a streamer of toilet tissue. After wiping her eyes and blowing her nose, she dropped the tissue on the floor.

Chapter Twenty-one

Animal sports banned

A bill passed in Parliament today puts a ban on all gladiatorial contests involving animals. The penalties for violations of this law range from fines to prison terms. Foreign promoters of such games face deportation and permanent banishment from Canada.

"How can we call ourselves civilized if we allow such barbarous activities to continue?" stated deputy prime minister, Jack Kresge. "If men must fight—and the public seems to relish these battles—let them fight one another and leave innocent animals out of it."

Two well-publicized events last year brought this matter to a head: A contest in Calgary that left a bear fatally injured and allowed to die a slow painful death, and a tank event in Montreal in which a man lost his arm and a large shark was severely wounded.

171

Vicki Wootton

Vancouver Globe, September 2, 2073

After the Reverend Oregon's footsteps faded, Catherine tried to open the door, but there was no knob or handle on the inside, just a blank slab of fiber panel. The light from the small panel in the ceiling wasn't very bright. She looked around for a rheostat to turn it up, but couldn't find one so she tried voice command.

"Light, up," she said.

Nothing happened. It must be controlled from somewhere outside the room, she decided. She walked over to the window and pushed the button to raise the blind. She wasn't surprised to see the window was covered with bars; nowadays, most ground floor windows had them, but knowing that didn't make it any less like a prison. The window overlooked the back of the house. All she could see in the light from the kitchen window was a stretch of grass, a dark clump of trees and the edge of another building. She quickly closed the blind when Zach came into sight around the side of the building.

Catherine sighed and went over to the bed. She picked up the nightgown. It wasn't too bad: long sleeved, white cotton flannelette with a print of miniature pink roses. At least it smelled clean. It was cold in the room. So she removed her ski jacket and pants, and put the gown on over her other clothes.

She sat on the bed thinking. What were they going to do with her? They hadn't done anything so far, but they must have something in mind. Whatever it was, she was sure she wouldn't like it. All she wanted was to get away from them and go home to her mother. What was it they said about the Reverend wanting her in good condition?

That must mean there was another reverend. What were they, a bunch of religious nuts? They'd called her mother the whore of something. What was that supposed to mean? Catherine started to cry again. She lay down and curled up, clutching the nightgown. That stupid Zach had called her a virgin back in the van. She'd read about primitive religious cults sacrificing virgins, but that was in the olden days. Surely they didn't want her for some sort of sacrifice.

Don't think about that. Try to think of something nice, she told herself, but what? Her mother must be crazy with worry. She got under the covers and pulled them up over her head to stifle her sobs.

Catherine woke, shivering in the cold night air and found the house was completely silent.

It was daylight when a knock on the door woke her. At first, she wasn't sure where she was, but it soon came back to her when she opened her eyes and saw the dismal room.

"Your breakfast's ready," a quiet voice said. *That must be Tom,* she thought. "I've unlocked the door, you can come out when you're ready, but hurry, you have to leave soon."

Catherine sat up and stretched. She took off the nightgown and dropped it on the bed, and then she pulled on her pants and jacket. She bent down to put her boots on and went into the bathroom. After flushing the toilet, she washed her face and hands, and then examined the room. She had decided to try to find a way out from one of the other rooms, but needed something to distract the three men and gain a little time.

The bathroom had an old-fashioned combination bathtub and shower. Catherine turned on the shower and closed the sliding panel, then crept to the door and listened. She opened the door cautiously. The hallway was empty, but she could hear voices from the kitchen next door. She closed the bathroom door quietly and went along the hall to the door beyond the room she'd slept in. Peering through the opening, she saw it contained a bed with rumpled covers, a chest of drawers, and a window.

Catherine crept inside and closed the door, then went over to the window. It was one of those that slide along a horizontal track, and there were no bars. She tried to open it, but it wouldn't budge. Catherine had never seen this type of window before. She sighed. Examining the frame, she found a plastic catch on the inside edge. She worked the catch with her fingers until it moved upwards, and then tried to move the window again. This time it slid easily along the track.

She had to hurry; they wouldn't be fooled by the shower for long. Catherine hitched herself up onto the windowsill, then swung her legs over to the outside and dropped to the ground. The window was higher than she'd expected; she landed with a jolt on the hard-packed earth and she fell to her hands and knees. She stood up and brushed dirt off her clothes, then crouched low and crept along the outside of the house towards the back. And bumped into Zach Oregon who was just coming around the corner.

"Good morning. You'll have plenty of time to go for a walk later, when we get there. Right now we have to get going," he said with a snidely. He grasped her upper arm and led her around to the back door.

She pulled herself free, but knew it would be useless to try to run. "Where are you taking me?"

"You'll find out soon enough."

Reverend Oregon and Tom were sitting at the table, eating when Zach brought her in. They stared at her when she came through the door, but said nothing, although Reverend Oregon frowned and shook his head.

"Sit down, girl," Oregon said. "Get her a bowl of cereal, Zach."

He left the kitchen and a moment later, the shower in the bathroom stopped running.

She sat down, watched Zach ladle oatmeal into a bowl and bring it to the table.

Reverend Oregon returned. He poured himself a mug of coffee from a flask on the kitchen counter and sat down at the table.

"What do you want to drink? There's apple juice, coffee or milk," he asked Catherine.

"Juice," she replied.

Tom poured a glass of apple juice and handed it to her.

"Help yourself." He nodded towards a container of honey and dish of butter in the center of the table.

She hadn't had hot cereal since she was little, and then her mother had always put brown sugar and cream on it. She watched Zach put a big dab of butter on top of his cereal and a huge spoonful of honey, and then stir it in. She followed suit after taking a sip of juice. The cereal didn't taste too bad if you used enough butter, although it was too salty. She was hungry after the scanty dinner she'd eaten the night before.

"You'll have to learn to say grace, girl," Reverend Oregon said.

"What?" she said.

"Give thanks to the Lord for his bounty."

Seeing her puzzled look, Zach chipped in, "Before you eat."

She realized they were talking about the prayer they'd recited the previous night before dinner. Why should she have to learn that?

"I want to go home," she said flatly.

Oregon sighed and shook his head. "We can't let you go back to that den of iniquity." He looked at his watch. "Hurry up and eat your breakfast. We have to get moving."

Catherine put down her spoon and pushed the bowl away, her eyes filling with tears. "You've no right to take me anywhere. That's kidnapping. The police will be looking for me."

Zach snickered and his father gave him a sharp look. Tom was gazing down at his hands resting in his lap.

"It's the Lord's will, girl, and nothing can stop its inexorable advancement. You'll thank us when you learn about the blessings He reserves for those who are saved." With that, he stood up and pushed back his chair. "If you're not going to eat the rest of that, we might as well get going. Is the copter ready?" he asked Zach.

"Yes, dad. I rolled it out and fueled up."

"Right." Oregon looked meaningfully at Catherine.

Filled with despair and resignation, she stood up and followed him outside. The two younger men followed them.

The sky was gloomy and overcast, reflecting the way she felt. A small red helicopter stood outside the large, barn-like building behind the house. It was an older model than those she saw in the city, but looked clean and well maintained. She saw it would only hold two and understood why Tom had said *you'll* be leaving when he'd called her for breakfast.

Reverend Oregon turned to Tom and Zach. "Clean up here, then lock up and get moving. Don't waste a lot of time; I want you home by tomorrow morning."

"Yes, sir," Tom replied.

Zach merely scowled.

"Get in, girl," Oregon ordered her. He opened the door on the passenger side and held her elbow to help her climb up into the seat. When she was seated, he fastened her safety harness securely, and then closed the sliding door. He went around the other side and got into the pilot's seat. After switching on the motor and checking the dials, he turned to her. He was holding a cloth bag.

"I'm going to have to put this on you for the journey."

Catherine's heart fluttered in panic as he slipped the hood over her head. It didn't cut off all the light, but she couldn't see anything. The cloth smelled clean, at least, and there was a small slit level with her mouth, so she could breathe, but the claustrophobic feeling was still unpleasant. She felt him securing it to her jacket with clips, so she wouldn't be able to shake it off.

"Keep your hands down, or I'll have to strap them down," he added when he was finished.

Catherine took several deep breaths, trying not to panic. She felt the copter shift as Reverend Oregon settled in his seat, then the engine whine rose. The copter lifted smoothly from the ground and turned in a tight circle before straightening out and gradually gaining altitude. It would have been impossible for her to tell which direction they were traveling after the turns. She hadn't a clue where they were anyway.

Catherine sat still, trying to hold back the tears that continually threatened. She thought of various scenarios as she tried to guess what was going to happen to her, none of which was encouraging. All they had done so far was take her from her home and detain her against her will, but she was convinced they had something special planned for her. The most likely she could come up with was that they were going to sell her. That comment about her being a virgin might have something to do with it. She blinked rapidly, wondering if she would ever see her mother again, and reaffirmed her determination to take advantage of any opportunity to escape.

She had no idea how long they were in the air, but it seemed like hours. Reverend Oregon didn't speak to her, but he did occasionally talk into a radio, using in some sort of code she couldn't understand consisting mostly of strings of numbers and random words. At one point, he gave her a bottle of water and packet of cookies, which she had to feed into her mouth through the slit in the mask. Finally, when she felt she could wait no longer to go to the bathroom, the copter began to descend, its motor increasing to a high-pitched whine. They touched down gently and the engine was silenced.

The copter creaked as Reverend Oregon leaned towards her. "You can have this off now," he said, unclipping the hood and lifting it from her head. "Stay where you are until I come round to help you down."

Catherine blinked in the strong sunlight. Either the weather had cleared up, or they'd moved to a new region. She looked out the window beside her and saw they were in a large snow filled clearing in a forest. Some houses were visible nearby through the trees. A small group of people waited for them, prominent among them a tall middle-aged man in a black suit and hat. She also noticed two women, one a few years younger than the tall man, the other much older.

Reverend Oregon went over and said something to the tall man, who nodded in reply and came forward a few steps, followed closely by the old woman. The other woman and the two other men stayed back while Oregon opened the door and helped Catherine to the ground. It was even colder than the day before.

"This is Catherine, Reverend," Oregon said, pushing her forward slightly. "Catherine, say good day to Reverend Webster."

She squinted up at him. Webster's face was thin and bony with a hooked nose, and narrow lips. He had small dark eyes under thick brows and looked at her as if he could see right into her mind. "I need to use the bathroom," she said.

The old woman gasped. "I can see you need to learn some manners, girl," she said, stepping forward and grabbing Catherine's arm. "You show my son some respect, he's going to..."

"It's all right, mother," Webster interrupted in a rich melodious voice. "Take her to the house. She needs time to get used to things."

Catherine tried to pull away but the old woman's grip was too strong. "I don't want to get used to anything," Catherine said. "I want to go home."

The old woman slapped her face. Catherine froze from the shock. Nobody had ever struck her before. She put her hand up and touched her stinging cheek, unable to hold back the tears any longer.

The other woman came over. "I'll take her, mother," she said. She turned to Catherine. "Come with me, Catherine; I'll take you to the comfort room."

Relieved to get away from the mother, Catherine followed the other woman along a path where the snow had been cleared through the trees. They came out on a narrow street with small houses on each side. All the houses were neat and well maintained, built mostly of stone and wood, surrounded by unfenced yards. In some of the yards, crocuses were poking up through the snow. Farther down the street, she caught a glimpse of a large building constructed mostly of glass, which seemed somewhat incongruous against the rustic dwellings. Before she had a chance to think any more about it, the woman led her up a path to one of the larger houses.

"This is our house, where you'll be staying at first," the woman said.

Catherine saw several faces peering from the windows of the house. The people from the landing field were trailing behind and when the woman opened the door and ushered Catherine inside, they followed.

"My name's Martha," the woman said. "After you've freshened up, I'll introduce you to everyone else, and then we can have lunch."

She took Catherine's jacket and hung it on a hook in the hall then opened a door at the far end and gestured her to go in. "Use the yellow towel, and when you've finished, come back to the parlor."

The bathroom was large and spotlessly clean with two rows of towels of various colors hanging from hooks, one row above the other. Catherine dawdled in the bathroom, giving herself time to think. So far, nobody had been unfriendly, except the old woman. She made up her mind to avoid her, if she could. Martha was obviously the Reverend Webster's sister. They had the same dark hair and angular build. And the same stern look. Everyone looked stern, except possibly the little boys who had poured into the hall when she entered the house.

She looked at the window in the bathroom, but it was too narrow to climb through. Catherine folded the yellow towel and put it back on the counter where she'd found it. She straightened her hair as best she could without a comb, then, having nothing else to delay her return to the rest of the company; she opened the door and stepped quietly into the hall.

"There you are girl." The old woman was waiting in the shadows like a giant spider. "What took you so long?" Without waiting for Catherine to reply, she grabbed her arm and continued, "Hurry up, everyone's waiting in the parlor."

The men, including Reverend Oregon, were seated around the room on sofas and assorted chairs, straight-backed or padded. Four boys—ranging in age from around seven to sixteen—sat on the carpeted floor. Martha and another woman were passing around trays with glasses of pale liquid.

"Shall I introduce everybody?" Martha asked, looking at her brother for consent.

"Go ahead," he replied. He got up from the sofa and gave his seat to his mother, then pulled a straight-backed chair from the wall for himself.

"What's your surname, Catherine?" Martha asked.

"My what?"

"You have another name besides Catherine, don't you?"

"Oh, my family name. I use my mother's name until I come of age, then I get to choose my own. It's Finisterra."

She saw the Reverend scowl and his mother's lips tighten as she explained this. Now what had she said to annoy them?

"All right," Martha said. "This is my mother, Mrs. Webster, my brother, the Reverend Keaton Webster. He's the mayor of Blessings—that's what we call the community. He's also the pastor. You've met Reverend Jesse Oregon the first deacon of the church." She turned to the sandy-haired woman beside her. "This is Reverend Oregon's wife, Coral," she said, then pointed to a red-haired youngster sitting near Oregon, and that's her son, Devon." She pronounced it Dee-von.

Catherine nodded. She felt numb, paralyzed by the bizarreness of the situation—everyone acting as if things were perfectly normal and she was just a visitor. Did they expect her to stay here and live with these people?

Martha indicated a stocky man with reddish blond hair who was standing against the wall just inside the entrance. "This is my husband, Ben Carstairs. He's Coral's older brother, in case you noticed the resemblance."

Reverend Webster cleared his throat. Martha went on quickly, "Sorry. These are our sons, Timmy, Jacob, Wayne, and Christian." She waved her hand at three boys sitting on the floor and Christian, the eldest standing near his father. Christian and his father were the two other men who had met the helicopter.

Catherine glanced again at Christian. He was by far the best-looking person in the room, tall, slender, with blue eyes, and dark hair. His mouth twitched slightly before he dropped his eyes.

Martha looked at her brother who nodded. "Right, let's eat," she said. "Bring the chairs, boys," she added, addressing her sons.

Reverend Webster stood and went over to help his mother up, and then he took her arm and led the gathering into the next room, which was furnished with a massive table and several high-backed chairs. Martha's sons carried chairs from the parlor to fill in the gaps at the table.

Martha touched Catherine's arm. "Sit here," she said.

Catherine timidly pulled the chair away from the table and sat down, aware all the time of the penetrating gaze of Reverend Webster on her right at the head of the table. Making her even more nervous was old Mrs. Webster seated opposite. Catherine sat very still, looking down at her hands folded in her lap, wondering why the reverend and his mother watched her so intensely.

Once all the men and boys were seated, Martha and Coral brought in bowls and platters of food from the kitchen. Every dish was offered to the Reverend first. He helped himself to a portion before passing it on to his mother. Catherine waited patiently, her mouth watering from the savory aromas, until the food reached her. By the time they got to her, some of the platters and dishes were already empty, so she took small portions of what was left. She was keenly conscious of being the focus of everyone's attention and wished they would ignore her. She picked up a fork, wondering what everyone was waiting for.

The Reverend cleared his throat and stood up, his chair scraping noisily on the wood floor. She looked up to see what had disturbed him and saw he had his head bowed, eyes closed and fingertips resting on the table. Around the table, everyone followed suit. She waited very quietly, not sure what to do, until the Reverend cleared his throat sharply and started to proclaim in a solemn voice, "Oh, Heavenly Father, we thank Thee for Thy bountiful blessing..." He continued to enumerate the many blessing, which included the food they were about to eat and ended to her amazement, "... for bringing safely into our midst Thy blessed gift, our sister Catherine."

Everyone said "Amen!" and sat down again. They finally picked up their knives and forks and began to eat.

Feeling the old woman's eyes on her, Catherine began to pick at the chicken leg and salad on her plate. She hadn't had chicken before and wasn't sure what to do with it until she noticed the boy beside the old lady pick his up in his fingers and tear the meat off with his teeth. She found it a bit greasy and stringy, but the coating was tasty. She put the bones down and started on the salad. It was not a very filling meal, but there was some bread left, so she helped herself to a thick slice and buttered it. There was very little conversation, apart from compliments to the women who had prepared the meal and discussion among the men of some problem at the mill. The children were amazingly quiet, although they glanced at her from time to time, then looked at one another and grinned. Once, the youngest boy, whose name she had already forgotten, giggled, earning himself a glare from Reverend Webster. He bowed his head in shame and continued picking at his salad.

What the hell was going on here? They all seemed to know something she didn't, and were obviously intimidated by the stern figures of the Reverend Webster and his mother.

"I see you've got a good appetite, girl," Mrs. Webster said suddenly. Her eyes glittered like dark glass beads. "Put some meat on your bones."

She was saved from having to answer by Martha who stood up and began to pile up the empty plates.

"Help your sister," the old woman said, giving her a meaningful look.

"Excuse me?" Catherine responded.

"The dishes."

"It's all right, mother, we can manage," Martha said.

"She might as well start to get used to things," Mrs. Webster replied fiercely.

"Leave her be for now," Reverend Webster said. Obviously, his word was law.

Catherine flushed, unsure how to respond. She felt Martha's hand on her shoulder. "Sit still," she said. "We're only going to bring in the desert."

Catherine watched the Coral and Martha bring in bowls of ice cream and two large fruit pies, wondering why they didn't use bots instead of doing all the carrying themselves. This time, Coral, who was sitting on Catherine's left, intercepted one of the pies before it went down the table and made sure Catherine got some. It was made of some sort of red berry Catherine had never tasted before, but it was delicious. After everyone had eaten, they were served mugs of hot-spiced cider.

"Can you cook, girl?" Mrs. Webster asked her.

"No, ma'am. We buy everything prepared. We just have to heat it in the microwave. Except salad and stuff like that. I can make salad."

This was greeted by silence except for a snort from one of the boys.

"Just as I feared," Mrs. Webster replied in a disgusted tone. "Well, we'll soon fix that." She pushed back her chair and rose from the table.

This seemed to be a signal for everyone else to move.

"I'd better be getting back to the mill," Ben Carstairs announced. "Coming, Christian?" He beckoned to his eldest son. "You boys get to your chores," he told the other boys as he left the room.

"I'm going to take my nap," Mrs. Webster said.

She was followed from the house by the Oregon family, leaving Catherine alone with Martha and the Reverend Webster.

"You'll take care of her?" Webster said to his sister. It sounded more like a command than a question.

"Don't worry, Keaton, she'll be fine."

He turned to Catherine. "Have you been baptized, girl?"

"What do you mean?" she asked.

Webster frowned. "If you don't know, you obviously haven't. We'll have to see about that."

With a nod at Catherine, he left.

"What does he mean, baptized?" Catherine asked Martha after the door had closed.

"It's a symbol of purification, when you make a commitment to follow the Lord."

"What lord?"

Martha looked shocked. "Our Lord, Jesus Christ, of course. Heaven help us, you've got a lot to learn, my girl."

Oh I do, do I? Catherine thought. She couldn't understand any of it and didn't want to. She wasn't going to be around long enough to get into any of that nonsense, anyway. She'd find a way to escape, the first chance she got.

Martha went to clean up the remains of the meal. Catherine watched her pile dishes for a moment, then stood up and offered to help. "Don't you have any house bots?" she asked.

"My brother believes in using the hands God gave us," Martha replied. "But I'm certainly thankful for an extra hand now and then."

Catherine followed her into the kitchen, carrying a pile of dirty plates. "Don't the boys help you?" she asked, putting the plates down on a counter.

"This sort of thing is woman's work. They do have their own chores, though. You know the old saying, 'the devil finds work for idle hands'."

Catherine did not tell Martha she'd never heard it.

She was pleased to see that at least they had an old-fashioned dishwasher under one of the counters. She helped Martha clear the rest of the table and load the washer.

The question of why they had brought her here was pressing on her mind. The people she'd met so far seemed benign—if you didn't count Mrs. Webster—which in a way made it all the more confusing and not a little sinister.

"Now we can sit down for a while," Martha said." She glanced out the kitchen window and shook her head then she led Catherine back into the parlor.

Martha sat on an armchair and motioned for Catherine to sit near her on the sofa

"Why have they brought me here?" Catherine asked.

"Nobody's told you?" Martha responded.

"No. I was just getting ready to go out with my father when they grabbed me and shoved me into a van. It was my birthday," she sobbed. "They kidnapped me and I want to go home." Catherine's voice rose in indignation.

"Shush," Martha said, patting her shoulder. "Everything will work out. Your birthday? How old are you?"

"Fourteen." Catherine sniffed and rubbed her nose with the back of her hand.

"Here, use my handkerchief." Martha handed her a small square of white cotton trimmed with lace.

Catherine blew her nose and wiped her eyes. "I told you, I don't want to be here. I want to go home to my mother."

"You can't," Martha said gently. "It's the Lord's will. You'll get used to it and be grateful in the end that we rescued you from a life of sin."

"What lord? I don't know any lord," Catherine replied angrily. "It's your lord, not mine and I want to go home."

"God forgive you, child, you don't know what you're saying. You've been raised in ignorance of the wonders revealed in the scriptures, but we'll correct that. As I said before, you'll rejoice that we found you and brought you into the light."

"But why me?"

"The Lord led us to you. You are His chosen."

"What do you mean? I don't understand."

"Keaton had a dream, a vision sent by the Lord. He saw you, a lost soul, crying out in the wilderness, and sent his followers to rescue you and bring you here."

A sliver of icy fear went through Catherine. *Are they all crazy?*

"But it's against the law to kidnap people. You have to take me back. What do you want me for, anyway?"

"You're going to be Keaton's bride." Martha replied, as if she were offering a priceless gift.

"*No!*" Catherine screamed.

She jumped up and ran out into the hall. She grabbed her ski jacket from the hook and ran out the front door. She darted across the lawn onto the street and ran as fast as she could away from that hateful house, hoping to meet someone who wasn't part of this crazy bunch and would help her get away. She rounded a corner into a square lined with old-fashioned shops that looked as if they'd been transported from the set of a 20th century video. Surely one of them would have a phone she could use to call her mother. People on the street watched her curiously as she ran by, but did nothing to intervene. One thing that surprised Catherine was a number of women, walking around freely, without hindrance or protection.

The first shop in the square had a display of clothing in the window. She passed that and slowed down at the next, which looked like a combination of post office and bookstore. She pushed open the door and approached the counter where a man stood stamping a pile of documents.

"Can I use your phone?" Catherine asked breathlessly. She glanced over her shoulder; no one seemed to be coming after her.

The expression on the man's face seemed to be a mixture of pity and disapproval. He shook his head. "Sorry, it's not allowed."

"But why? I've been kidnapped and I want to call my mother." Seeing his look, which she interpreted as disbelief, she continued desperately, "It's true; you've got to believe me. Can you call the police then?"

"Just a minute." The man went to a com terminal at the end of the counter and pushed a few buttons. He said something in a low voice, glancing at her as he spoke. He ended up with a nod. "Right, I'll tell her." He came back to where she stood. "You wait here, somebody's coming."

Relieved, Catherine relaxed slightly. She looked out of the shop window, hoping none of the Reverend's people would spot her before she could be rescued. She wondered why Martha hadn't pursued her. That was strange, just letting her go.

Catherine heard men's voices coming from the back of the shop, where there were several racks of books, although she couldn't see anyone. The man went back and opened a door behind the books and to her horror, Reverend Webster and Reverend Oregon appeared.

"Thanks, Cody," Webster said. "We'll handle it now."

Catherine turned to run out the door and bumped into a man who was just coming in. He grabbed her arm and held on firmly until the two reverends came from behind the counter. They stood around her, emphasizing the hopelessness of her situation.

"It's no use trying to run away," Reverend Webster said sternly. "We're all the Faithful here, so there's nobody you can run to." He turned to Oregon. "Take her to your house, Jesse. I'll have a word with Martha." With that, he turned and left, followed by the man who had restrained her.

"Come on, Catherine. Let's go see what Coral's up to. I think you need a rest; you must be tired."

This last utterance filled her with foreboding. What were they going to do now? Drug her? Reverend Oregon paced beside her, his hand clasped lightly on her arm, greeting people as they passed. Catherine stared at the ground in front of her, feeling her face glowing red. They must all know about her.

Like an omen, the sky was clouding over and a chill breeze started to blow.

There was something about the town that made her think they were no longer in Canada. The houses in British Columbia were different somehow, usually built over ground-level basements and finished with synthetic coating. These houses were constructed with natural materials and sat low to the ground. Then she recalled that the mailbox outside the post office had been blue instead of red. If not in Canada, the only other place she could be was the United States—Washington or Oregon. The thought sent a shiver of renewed fear through her. She'd heard about some of the crazy religious cults whose members went around with guns all the time to protect their rights, confident of their superiority as God's chosen. At least she hadn't seen any guns so far.

Oregon's house was on the street behind the shops, so they didn't have far to walk. It was painted white with dark green trim around the windows and doors and looked quite old. It reminded her of the kind of houses people lived in a hundred years ago. The windows sparkled and the exterior appeared to be freshly painted.

Reverend Oregon opened the front door and led her into a hallway that had a clean waxy smell, sort of lemony. She noticed flowers growing in a bowl on a side table, and patterned rugs on the polished wood floor.

"Coral!" Oregon called. "Wait in there," he told Catherine, pushing her gently towards a sitting room on the right of the entrance.

She went in and perched on the edge of an old-fashioned sofa upholstered with a blue and yellow floral material.

"Coming." Coral's voice came from the back of the house, and then Catherine heard footsteps approaching. "Anything wrong?"

"Keaton wants us to keep Catherine here for a while." He and Coral came into the sitting room. "She tried to run away. I think she probably needs a rest; put her in the spare room. I've got to get back to work."

Coral's face filled with compassion. "Oh, Catherine." she came over and put her hand on Catherine's shoulder. "You shouldn't do that. It won't do any good. Come on, let me show you to the room, then you can lie down until supper time."

The tears she had been trying to hold back now flooded Catherine's eyes. "I'm not tired," she said, swiping at her wet cheek. She'd lost Martha's handkerchief in her rush to escape. "I just want to go home."

"It's no good, honey; we have to do what Reverend Webster says. Don't try to fight God's will; it will destroy you if you do." Coral sighed as if she knew from experience.

She led Catherine to a staircase around the corner behind the sitting room. They climbed the stairs, Coral with her arm across Catherine's shoulder. There was a small landing at the top with three doors opening off it.

"Do you need to go to the comfort room?" Coral asked.

Catherine shook her head.

"All right. Here we are." She opened one of the doors and guided Catherine into a small room with one tiny window framed by the inverted V of a sloping ceiling. It was a pleasant enough room, if a bit old fashioned. The furniture—a small bed, a dresser and high cupboard with a mirror in the door—was all made of polished brown wood. Probably genuine antiques, Catherine thought. The floor was wood planks with a striped rug beside the bed. There was mid-twentieth century lamp on the dresser, a glass base with a plastic shade and old style glass bulb.

"Lie down and try to rest," Coral said. She stood with her hand on the doorknob. "I'll look for some clothes that will fit you while you're resting. You'll need a change from those you're wearing. There's a bathrobe in the cupboard if you want to use it."

The door closed with a click followed by a scraping sound and a sharper click. Catherine stood in the center of the room for a moment, trying to sort out the turmoil in her mind. Slipping off her shoes, she went over to the door and stood listening for a moment, then tried the doorknob. It was locked. Reality. She was a prisoner. The room was as dark as twilight although it couldn't be more than two o'clock in the afternoon. It was cold too. She turned towards the window and saw the snow that had been threatening had arrived.

Before searching the room, she tried to figure out how to turn the lamp on. It did not respond when she said "light", so she looked around for some sort of mechanism. There was a cord attached to the back of it that led down behind the dresser. She followed it to an odd-looking panel on the wall. She wiggled it around then pulled it. The thing on the end of the cord came out of the hole in the panel, revealing two prongs. The light still didn't come on, so she shoved it back in and stood up. She finally found a little button on the neck of the lamp and pressed it. Light! The lamp glowed with a warm yellow radiance, not very bright, but enough to make the room seem cozier, warmer.

Catherine opened all the drawers in dresser, finding nothing very interesting, mostly old linens and a few faded pictures. The cupboard yielded some ancient dresses and jackets, and the bathrobe Coral had told her about. There were a few pairs of antique shoes in the bottom. Catherine wondered whose they were. Surely not Coral's. She took out the bathrobe, which was made of soft dark blue fabric. At least it would keep her warm. It smelled of some sort of chemical Catherine couldn't identify, but she put it on anyway, after removing her ski jacket. Then she turned to the bed. She'd seen one like it in a museum once, in a doll's house. It had four posts at the corners, about head height, with round pointed knobs on the top. The cover was quilted, made of rust, yellow, and turquoise paisley fabric. A weird combination, she thought, but somehow it worked. The window curtains matched the bed cover.

She pulled back the cover and lay down on the blanket underneath, wishing she had something to read, or better yet, her computer. Wishing she were home.

She sat up abruptly. That was another strange thing about this place: no com terminals. She was used to seeing them everywhere, in every room, but the only one she'd seen here was in the post office shop she'd gone to for help. If she had access to a terminal, she could call home. Catherine sighed. She clasped her arms around her shins and rested her cheek on her knees. It was like being taken back in time. God, she thought, then quickly amended—not *their* God.

After what seemed like hours, she heard the scraping and clicking of the lock, followed by a knock on the door. Coral had come to let her out

"How are you feeling?" she asked, pushing the door open. She carried some garments over her arm. "Here, I've found some things for you to wear."

Catherine sat up and rubbed her eyes. She must have fallen asleep after all. Probably from boredom.

Coral put the clothes down on the bottom of the bed. "Maybe you'd like to take a bath. The bathroom's next door. I'll be downstairs. Come down when you're ready."

As she turned to go, Catherine blurted, "Can I ask you something?"

Coral turned back. "Of course, honey. Ask away."

"Martha said they'd brought me here to marry Reverend Webster. It's not true, is it?"

"Yes, it is true," Coral replied.

Catherine watched Coral as she answered, hoping to discern how she felt about it, but Coral's face was neutral.

"But..." Catherine faltered. She sighed and looked at the ground. She couldn't expect any help here. Better to keep her feelings to herself.

Coral touched Catherine's upper arm. "When you're dressed, would you like to help me bake a cake?" she asked.

Reverend Webster had planned to keep Catherine at his sister Martha's home, but his mother thought living in close proximity to Martha's sons might prove too much of a temptation to her. The same applied to the Oregon's home, once Zach returned, so they finally moved her to the home of a childless couple, Joanne and Noah Ferguson.

Chapter Twenty-two

Population decline

The population of Vancouver has fallen to less than one third of its turn-of-the-century level. In the year 2000, approximately 600,000 people lived in the city; according to the 2072 census, the population is now 198,000. Of the 11,248 females, around 7,800 are of childbearing age.

Excerpt from report issued in July 2073

Joanne was in her late thirties. As Catherine later learned, she had conceived a number of times, but had never been able to carry a child to term. One of the aborted fetuses had been a girl. She was a tall gaunt woman with dark blond hair and large hands and feet, reminding Catherine of her grandmother.

Joanne was subject to episodes of depression, which, given her history, was not surprising. Sometimes, days went by without Catherine hearing her utter a single word. It wasn't that she resented Catherine or felt that she was intruding in her home; it seemed as if she just didn't have the energy or will to talk. In truth, Catherine was welcome; she could help take care of the house, which Joanne often felt too lethargic to handle. When someone is constantly depressed, there doesn't seem to be any point in tiresome day-to-day drudgery.

When Joanne was more communicative, she often derided Reverend Webster and his followers, calling them the Hallelujah Chorus. She reluctantly dressed up on Sundays and accompanied her devout husband and Catherine to service in the glass church—that was obligatory—but after a while, Catherine realized that Joanne always managed some little acts of rebellion to undermine the solemnity of the occasion. Nothing serious enough to warrant a reprimand, but effective nonetheless. She would sometimes sing off-key—she had a powerful voice—or drop her prayer book during silent meditation, have a coughing fit during the sermon. One time, she tried to depart for church wearing a pair of shoes that didn't match, with different heel-heights that made her walk with a drunken lurch. That time, Noah caught her and instructed her to put on some 'proper' shoes.

Catherine observed this activity with silent admiration and amusement, but felt it wouldn't be appropriate to remark on it. Given Joanne's attitude, Catherine would have expected more sympathy about her own situation, but whenever Catherine tried to bring it up, Joanne quickly changed the subject. It was not easy to talk to Joanne about anything, even when she wasn't buried deep within her mind. She seemed unable to keep a train of thought for more than a few seconds before she was off on a tangent.

Noah was a man of few words who took his religion more seriously than his wife. Every evening after the supper dishes were cleaned up, he would hold a bible reading at the dining table. He ran a nursery and garden supply business that provided the seedlings and fertilizers for the town's vegetable and flower gardens.

Joanne and Noah weren't unkind to Catherine; their attitude was closer to indifference. Noah's natural reticence and Joanne's frequent bouts of depressive withdrawal meant that she was left to her own resources much of the time. Nonetheless, from Catherine's point of view, they were still her jailers.

Joanne was supposed to teach her the finer points of homemaking, but the lessons were sporadic and piecemeal. Catherine did learn to prepare a few basic meals—roast chicken, beef stew, ham and peas, plus some deserts—using cookbooks and occasional instructions from Joanne. An unspoken conspiracy developed between the two: Catherine would cover for Joanne when she was 'unwell' and in return, she could spend her free time in whatever activity she liked, providing she didn't try to run away.

"But it's wrong to keep someone against her will," Catherine protested during an early conversation with Joanne. "I want to go home. Why won't you help me?"

Joanne sighed. "Cathy, honey," Joanne had called her Cathy from the start, saying that Catherine was too stuffy and reminded her of the old king of England's wife, who had been a terrible person, apparently. "It's a lot more complicated than you think. Don't you think my life is difficult enough? If I helped you get away—if it were possible for anyone to escape from this valley—my life wouldn't be worth living. Even I can't leave," she added cryptically.

"But nobody would have to know you'd helped me," Catherine persisted.

"Oh, they'd know. Do you think we aren't being watched every minute of the day?" Joanne put down the paring knife she'd been using to peel apples. "Pass me that cloth."

Catherine passed the dishtowel for Joanne to wipe her hands.

"If only I could get to a terminal and send my mother a message. Let her know I'm alive at least. Aren't there any terminals here at all?"

"Reverend Webster doesn't allow them, says the Net is a tool of Satan."

Catherine's heart sank. Her last hope of a link to the outside world dashed. Another thought occurred to her. "What did you mean, you can't leave?"

"Oh, it's nothing. Forget I said it." She stood up with a sigh and went to look out the kitchen window. She wasn't quick enough to prevent Catherine seeing the glitter of tears.

Of course, once it had been said, Catherine couldn't forget. Her attitude towards Joanne changed. She now saw her more as a fellow victim than jailer and wondered if maybe Joanne had been abducted too and brought here against her will. Noah Ferguson was about ten years older than his wife. Then she saw something that had been staring her in the face ever since she arrived: the number of women in the valley was way out of proportion to the ratio in the outside world. About three quarters of the adult males had wives.

Another time, when she and Joanne were alone, Catherine broached the subject of her impending marriage to the Reverend Webster.

"Will they really make me marry him?" she asked with a grimace of distaste.

"Oh, yes," Joanne replied bitterly. "God has spoken."

"But he's so old." She shuddered, remembering the ugly way the skin on his neck scrunched up when he swallowed. "The thought of.... Oh God!"

Joanne covered Catherine's fist with her own large hand. "Sh. I know. Try not to think about it. It won't happen until you are old enough, anyway. Anything could happen in the meantime."

"If only he would die." Catherine swiped angrily at the tears that that threatened to overflow.

Joanne stared at her, but didn't reply.

As the weeks passed, Catherine sank into a mood of despair. She knew she was being watched all the time. She was allowed to go outside for walks, but if she went too far away from home, someone would just happen to pop up, as if by chance, and lead her back to the Ferguson house.

While Joanne was shut in her room and Noah was at the nursery, Catherine snooped around the house, looking for a communications device. There was one room on the ground floor that was always kept locked, Noah's study, which was probably where they kept it. Every once in a while, she tried the door in case he had forgotten to lock it, but she was never able to get in. Once, she found a bunch of old keys in a drawer and tried them all as soon, as she got the opportunity, but none of them worked.

As far as she could tell, her schooling was over, apart from hours of mind-numbing bible study every week. The class was taught by a middle-aged man called Mr. Palmer who lacked the least suggestion of humor or imagination.

He was a stringy man with pale skin, thin mousy hair and bad breath, whose droning voice frequently lulled his students into a daze. When Mr. Palmer noticed the glazed eyes and drooping lids of a student, he would stop talking and bang his bible down on the table, pick up a short cane and approach the miscreant. The petrified child would watch, eyes wide like a deer caught in a headlight, until Mr. Palmer reached him and the cane whistled past his ear and landed on the desk, missing him by mere millimeters.

The class comprised eleven boys of various ages, including the two youngest Carstairs, but only one other girl—a frail little waif of around eleven called Emily who rarely spoke to anyone.

At first, Catherine questioned things that seemed illogical or contradictory to her, but Mr. Palmer would yell at her, "You dare to question the Word of the Lord?" He'd turn to the rest of the class. "See what comes of living in the Sodom and Gomorrahs of the world?" then turn back to her. "You must repent and put all that behind you or you'll burn in eternal hellfire along with that whore who bore you." This was enough to teach her not to voice her opinions. Following the lead of the other students, Catherine learned to parrot the required responses.

To her, what they were studying was virtually incomprehensible, and most of the time, downright boring. Admittedly, some parts were quite poetic and some of the characters almost likeable, but she couldn't get over the savagery of supposedly holy men. She liked reading about Jesus and thought most of what he said made a lot of sense, but there was little evidence that anyone paid much attention to his teachings. Unfortunately, Mr. Palmer seemed to prefer the Old Testament with its vengeful God, swift to punish the least infraction with ferocious cruelty. It was hard to believe that the compassionate, loving Jesus could be the Son of such an apparently vicious Father.

One day in late summer when Catherine was fifteen, Joanne took her into the hills to harvest blackberries. It was a hot day and Catherine wished she were allowed to wear shorts and a sleeveless top, but there was a strict dress code in the town. Women had to wear skirts and long sleeved shirts or dresses, except Catherine, who was allowed to wear loose cotton pants. She was sure this wasn't an act of kindness on the part of the powers. She suspected they didn't want to emphasize the fact that she was, for the time being, an unattached female, barely past puberty.

Catherine and Joanne picked the juicy ripe berries until their fingers were stained purple and their arms and legs covered in scratches from the prickly brambles. When they had gathered two pails full, Joanne flopped down on the ground in the shade of a pine tree and took the top off a water bottle. She drank a long draught then poured a little in her palm and used it to wash some of the juice off her hands. She wiped them on her already stained apron and lay back.

Catherine sat down near her and took a drink of water. She wet her kerchief, used it to wipe her face and hands, then she put the top back on the bottle, and closed her eyes. It was so hot, the sweat ran down her face and pooled under her eyes. The droning of bumblebees was like a lullaby, and before long, she dozed. She awoke with a start and looked around. The wind had picked up and was stirring the trees, cooling the air a little, but everything else seemed the same. She glanced over at Joanne and saw she was still sleeping.

Feeling urgent pressure in her bladder, Catherine rose slowly to her feet. She moved farther into the trees, looking for a place to relieve herself. There was a clump of non-prickly bushes a few meters in. As she stood up after voiding, she noticed a path leading into the trees, away from the town. *I wonder where it leads*, she thought, glancing behind her to make sure Joanne was still asleep.

"Sorry, Joanne," she murmured to herself and started walking. The path was narrow and stony, twisting up the hillside through the trees. Once she thought she heard Joanne's voice faintly calling her name, but she ignored it and kept on going, sweat pouring down her face and body. After a while, she started to feel thirsty and regretted not bringing her water bottle, but she hadn't planned this.

Catherine was a city girl, unfamiliar with the wilderness. The sounds of the forest made her nervous, especially the rustling of small animals in the bushes and the sudden flurry of birds taking off from trees. She tried to reassure herself with something she'd heard once: there are no dangerous animals in the world, apart from humans. *But what about snakes?* she thought, and bears and cougars? *Stop it, Catherine, there's no point in scaring yourself.* The secret is not to... The thought was interrupted by the sound of a helicopter. It had come silently over the hill and was above her almost before she heard it. She froze, hoping they wouldn't see her if she didn't move, wondering if they were searching for her. But how could they have known so fast that she had gone? Even Joanne had not had time to return to the town to report her missing. Knowing Joanne, she would probably leave it as long as possible before telling anyone.

Maybe it was someone else, someone who could help her get away. What to do? When there is insufficient information, do nothing unless it is really necessary, she recalled. In any case, the copter had already disappeared.

She was tired and her feet were getting sore, but she hiked on. The path just went on climbing, never reaching the top. Even if she did get to the summit, there would only be more walking on the other side. She couldn't expect suddenly to reach a settlement or even a lone house at the top of a mountain. Her feet were really hurting now, and her thirst was becoming intolerable. She'd have to take a rest soon. She turned a bend in the path and heard the burble of water trickling over rocks. She stood and listened for a moment, then veered off into the trees to her left.

A small stream flowed between shallow, fern-covered banks. She slid down the slope and sat on a rock to remove her boots. Water had never looked so inviting. It was so clear she could see every grain of sand at the bottom. When she dipped her foot in, the coldness of the water shocked her. She rolled up her pant legs and walked to the center of the stream. It only came up to mid-calf. She bent and scooped up a double handful and splashed it on her face. The next handful she drank. She continued to drink until she felt satisfied, then waded back to the bank and sat down with her feet dipping in the stream.

She closed her eyes and turned her face up to the sky. *This must be as what paradise was like,* she thought. Next to being back with her mother, she amended.

The rustle of vegetation startled her. She turned around and saw two of them standing at the top of the bank above her. She recognized them immediately; they were men from town and they carried rifles.

"Put your boots on, Catherine," the older man said. "It's over."

"Didn't they warn you it was no use trying to get away?" the other one added.

Tears filled Catherine's eyes. An oppressive blanket of impotence and hopelessness fell over her again.

While she was tying her bootlaces, the younger man descended to the stream and splashed some water on his face, and then he turned to her and said, "I hope you didn't drink any of this water, it might be contaminated."

"As if I care," she muttered, wiping her eyes with the back of her hand.

"Don't be like that," the man said. "Hurry, it'll be dark soon."

When Catherine stood up, he took her arm to help her climb the bank. They reached the path and turned in the uphill direction although Catherine expected them go the other way, towards town. A few meters up, they came out in a clearing with a small cabin, and a copter sitting on the scrubby grass.

"What is this place?" she asked.

"It's a hunting lodge," the younger man said. "And lookout post," he added.

"How did you know...?"

"Know you were coming up this way? Sensors. We've got them planted on the trees along the path. As soon as we got the signal, it was easy to spot you with the copter, and then all we had to do was land in the clearing and walk down..."

"Cut the chatter, Greg. Let's go," the older man interrupted impatiently.

When they landed in the town, Catherine was taken directly to Reverend Webster's house. His mother was with him. Her lips compressed when she saw Catherine, but there was a triumphant gleam in her eyes.

Chapter Twenty-three

Abortions surge

The number of abortions of male fetuses performed in Vancouver clinics has increased by twenty percent in the last twelve months. "Why should I give birth to sons who have no hopes of a real life?" said thirty-five-year-old Janette, who had just had her third termination.

"Pregnancy seems to have become a lottery in which every mother hopes to give birth to a girl, the prize," commented Reverend Arthur Stone of the of the United Church of Canada.

Vancouver Globe, August 2, 2074

Well, young lady, what have you got to say for yourself?" Before she could reply, the Reverend Webster continued, "I'm very disappointed in you, Catherine. You are being treated well, aren't you? It's not as if we are keeping you under lock and key. Look how we are rewarded."

Catherine glared at Webster and his mother. "I want to go home. I don't want to stay here. I hate this place."

Mrs. Webster was about to reply, but her son held up his hand to cut her off. He shook his head at Catherine. "You know that's impossible. The Lord has decreed that your place is here, and here is where you will stay." He walked over to the window and looked out, his hands clasped behind him. He turned to face her. "The reason I am being so lenient with you is that you are to be my wife. I was hoping at least that I could win some respect from you. I want ours to be a cordial relationship."

"Humph!" Mrs. Webster snorted.

"Mother, if you can't stay out of this, I will have to ask you to leave."

Mrs. Webster looked offended. "You're being too soft. A disobedient wife is a..."

"Mother!" He turned to Catherine. "Go and sit out in the hall for a moment while I talk to my mother."

She went out, leaving the door open a crack, and stood by the wall just outside.

"That woman is a bad influence on her. I warned you about putting her there."

"Joanne is a poor sad woman. It's not her fault this happened; she's doing her best."

"How do you know? Why did she take her up there, so far away from town?"

"Mother, everything is under control. Nothing happens in that house that I am not aware of, believe me."

A chill of horror went through Catherine. What did he mean? Did he have listening devices in the Ferguson house, or worse, hidden cameras?

"What are you going to do with her now?" Mrs. Webster said. "You can't send her back there."

"There's nowhere else for her to live, unless we have her here."

"It's tempting, but it wouldn't be proper, a young girl living under the same roof as a single man."

Thank God for that, Catherine thought with relief. Living in the same house as that old dragon would be the last straw.

"Maybe she'll be ready for the marriage soon," Reverend Webster said. "Some girls mature faster than others. In the meantime, she'll go back to the Fergusons'. I'll have a word with Noah."

Catherine heard movement in the room and swiftly moved away from the door. Reverend Webster peered out.

"You can come back in now." He held the door open for her. "I've decided that you are going back to live with Joanne and Noah. But you and I are going to be seeing more of each other from now on. It's time we got to know each other. You will come here for supper on Sunday evenings, and I will try to make time during the week to see you at least once. Maybe we can walk together. If there's any more of this nonsense, we may have to lock you in. Now, wait here while I make a call to tell them you're coming home."

Catherine stood under the baleful gaze of Mrs. Webster while Webster left the room to make the call. So he had a com, too. Catherine wondered where it was.

At least she wasn't going to be punished. Spending time with Reverend Webster would be punishment enough. She wondered what he had meant by her being 'ready' for marriage. She had reached puberty, but she knew she wasn't fully developed yet. Was there some sign she didn't know about that made a woman ready to marry? Catherine made up her mind to ask Joanna. She wrapped her arms over her chest and tried not to squirm at the thought of what would happen when they considered she was 'ready'. As far as she was concerned, she would never be ready. Why couldn't they at least marry her off to one of the younger men? Tom was nice, except that he had been one of the kidnappers, and Martha's son Christian was not bad. I wish something would happen to the horrible man, she thought.

He came back at that moment. "Everything's set. Before you go, I wanted to talk to you about your baptism."

"But I don't want to be baptized," she said stubbornly.

Mrs. Webster gasped and looked as if she were going to strike Catherine, but Webster held up his hand, warning her not to interfere.

"You have to be, Catherine. You have no choice. We'll talk about it later. Now run along home. Joanne has your supper ready."

Reverend Webster began calling unexpectedly at the Ferguson house, sometimes to sit and chat with them in their sitting room, other times he would ask Catherine to go for a walk with him. He never touched her, but her skin crawled when he got too close.

"I think you should start calling me Keaton when we are alone," he said to her one day. "You can't call me Reverend when we are married."

The dinners at the Webster house were a nightmare for Catherine with Mrs. Webster presiding at the table. She had a habit of interrogating Catherine rather than carrying on a conversation.

"Are you learning to cook, girl?" she would ask. "My son is used to good cooking and an orderly household."

"But aren't you...?" Catherine started to ask.

"I'll be here to keep an eye on you and make sure you're doing your duty, but don't expect me to do all the work. I'm not getting any younger."

"Mother, could we please change the subject." He turned to Catherine. "How do you like the lamb?"

The first time Mrs. Webster heard Catherine call her son Keaton, she scowled, but didn't say anything. She was getting the idea.

***

The next time she found Joanna receptive to conversation, Catherine asked her, "How can you tell when a girl is ready to be married?"

"There's no mysterious sign, or signal." Joanna replied, "In a rational world, you would feel desire for the man you want to marry."

"If that's the case, I will never be ready to marry Keaton."

Joanna sighed. "Unfortunately, Blessings is not part of the rational world."

"I don't know which will be worse," Catherine said. "Being married to Keaton, or living in the same house as Mother Webster."

"Tiffany? You haven't heard about her past, have you?"

"What is there to know?" Catherine responded. "She's a dried up, miserable old woman, that's all I need to know."

"Old Tiff was a lot different when she was younger. She's got quite a history."

"What? Tell me."

"This was back in the late twenties, early thirties." Joanne settled back in her chair. "She was a performer."

"What sort of performer?"

"I think it was nouveau cabaret. Dancing, singing. She may have been a stripper as well, from what I heard. She was quite beautiful, long golden hair and a lovely smile. Her stage name was Tiffany Leclare, or something like that. I saw an old video of her on the net once. She was quite good. You wouldn't believe it was the same person."

Catherine grinned at this new image of the old dragon. "What made her change?"

"A couple of things. She got pregnant with Keaton. She wasn't married, but she was expecting to marry the father. Instead, he disappeared with one of her colleagues—a female impersonator. You can imagine what that would do to a woman, her man preferring a pseudo-female to the real thing. After she had the baby, she became too depressed to work. It was around this time, she met one of those fundamentalist preachers. He was a charmer, treated her well. He convinced her of the sinfulness of her former life, and how the only way to be saved from eternal hell was to be reborn into his religion. She was ripe for the picking, as they say."

"So, did they get married?"

"He kept making excuses, putting her off, until one day she discovered he was already married." Joanne sighed and pushed her hair back. "God, they can be such hypocrites sometimes. She was already hooked on the religion, but she still didn't have a husband. She finally married another preacher—Elvis Webster. She always tried to pass Keaton off as his son. Martha is his daughter, though."

Since Joanne seemed to be in the mood for revelation, Catherine decided to ask her about something else that had been on her mind. "How did you meet your husband?"

Joanne's mood changed visibly. Her animation fell away, leaving a closed, bleak look. She got up and walked to the window. "I'd rather not talk about that right now." When she turned round to face Catherine, there was a trace of pity in her eyes. "We'll have to start getting ready for Christmas soon."

This put the final damper on Catherine's mood. Christmas already! Had she been here that long, almost two years?

***

Winter turned to spring and the snow was replaced by blossoms and new life. Lambs were born and birds' nests filled with twittering chicks. Ducks swam across the pond followed by processions of ducklings, and trees began to sprout delicate green shoots.

None of this cheered Catherine. It only served to remind her how much time had passed since she'd been taken from her home.

Chapter Twenty-four

Julia looked gloomily out of the window at the falling rain. It was March already, more than two years since Catherine disappeared. Catherine's sixteenth birthday had already passed.

"Catherine," she murmured with a sigh. "Where are you, baby?" A tear ran down her cheek. The feeling of emptiness was like a dull ache in her womb.

She turned away from the window and went to her terminal to see if any new messages had arrived since last night, but before she could turn it on, a musical chime alerted her to an incoming call. *Let the machine record it,* she thought. *I can't talk to anyone right now.*

She heard her father's voice saying, "It's me, honey. Call me as soon as you can. It's important."

With a sigh, Julia pushed the button to return the call. Raymond picked up immediately. He looked as bad as she felt.

"What is it, Daddy? Have you heard something about Catherine?"

Her father sighed. "No, I'm sorry, honey. It's Paul."

"What? Is he...?"

"Yes, he's gone."

Fresh tears pooled in her eyes and trickled down her face. "Oh, Daddy, I'm so sorry." She wiped her eyes. "How's Mother?"

"She's taking it badly. Robbie gave her a sedative and she's sleeping now."

"When did it happen?"

"Last night. There was a crisis and they called us to the hospital. I don't remember the technical terms, but the way they explained it, the center in his brain that controls his breathing and heartbeat had stopped functioning. They could still keep him alive with machines, if you could call it life. The medics wanted to know if they should continue." Raymond hesitated, rubbed his hands across his face, and then looked at Julia, his red-rimmed eyes filled with pain.

She noticed the grey stubble on his chin and the pallor of his skin. "And you said no?"

"Yes. What's the point in prolonging it? It wasn't as if Paul was there any more." He hesitated, and then went on. "It's just the ... finality of it..."

"I understand, Daddy. I think you did the right thing. I'm so sorry." What else could she say? "Do you want me to come over?"

He looked at her, almost pleading with his eyes. "I'd like that, if you're not..."

"I'll be there in an hour. I just have to get dressed."

God, what else can happen? she wondered after the call was terminated. Sighing, she went into her dressing room and picked out some clothes to wear. She found herself choosing the same drab colors she'd taken to wearing since Catherine had disappeared, the greys, dark blues and blacks she'd never have chosen before that happened. In truth, she hadn't even had such colors in her wardrobe until recently, much preferring cheerful hues and warm pastels.

Once Julia had resigned herself to the fact that the police weren't going to be able to find Catherine, she channeled her anger into activity. She started using the Net to create a support group for parents whose daughters had disappeared. Members of the group—fathers, mothers, and other relatives—shared information and sought to educate the public about how to identify females who might be kidnap victims. They also published information about the missing girls and women. They pressured politicians, local authorities and law enforcement to provide more protection for females, and allocate more funding to investigate disappearances.

After Paul's funeral, which was attended only by the family, they went back to the parents' home, but nobody could think of anything to say that wouldn't stir up heartbreaking memories of Paul or Catherine.

"How's the investigation going? Have they found anything?" Alda asked Julia.

Julia replied, "Nothing. Not a clue. The police didn't even manage to trace the vehicle."

"What are they doing?" David asked indignantly.

"Everything they can. Believe me David, the top guy in law enforcement is leading the investigation. He's a friend of Pascal."

"The commissioner?"

Julia realized she'd said something indiscreet. "Don't tell anyone, okay? I'm not supposed to reveal the identities of clients."

"What do you think's happened to her?" John asked.

"How would I know?" The question irritated Julia. "I'm sure she's alive though. I'm hoping my Net group will come up with something. I'm in touch with people all over the world. You wouldn't believe the number of girls that have gone missing. It's a growth industry in some of the poorer countries."

Noticing how exhausted her mother looked, Julia got up to leave. "I'll let you get some rest now," she said, bending down to kiss her. "Why don't you come over for tea tomorrow?"

"I don't know. I really don't feel like going out much."

"Think about it. It would do you good to get out and do something. I'll call you in the morning," Julia insisted, even though she knew it wouldn't do much good. Her mother seemed to have sunk even deeper into the perpetual state of depression she'd been in since Catherine disappeared.

She said goodbye to the rest of the family and called the elevator up to the rooftop helicopter pad. Just as it arrived, David darted out of the apartment carrying her clutch purse. "You forgot this. I see your memory isn't getting any better." He gave her a final hug and kissed her cheek.

As expected, when Julia called her mother the next day, she said she was too tired. Julia sighed. She didn't feel much better herself. It was as if the light had gone out of her life. She'd lost her reason for making an effort to keep going, but she had to. She couldn't give up; she had to keep a home together for when Catherine came back. It was an act of faith.

She stopped seeing all but a few clients, cutting her working time to four days a week in order to spend more time on the Net.

"I sometimes feel I'm wasting my time," she told Pascal during one of her visits. They still got together once a week. "She's not coming back."

"Don't say that. She might escape from whoever's got her. Lots of women do." Pascal replied. "Or someone might recognize her and report it."

"But she's only a little girl." Julia lapsed into tears, imagining her daughter growing into a young woman without her.

Chapter Twenty-five

Most of the time, Catherine found the life endurable. Nobody abused her, but the constant scrutiny—the feeling of always being watched—oppressed her spirit. Beyond everything else loomed the constant anxiety of what was in store for her. Not knowing when it would happen only served to increase her dread. They could spring it on her any day, without warning.

Whenever she was alone outside, Catherine noticed one or two of the young men in the community always seemed appear. She didn't mind once she realized they were not spying on her. It was as if they were in a conspiracy together and it gave her pleasure to defy those who were in charge. Not only that, she found she welcomed their attention, knowing they were interested in her as a girl. She especially liked Christian Carstairs. She smiled at him whenever they met, if no one else was around.

One day when Noah Ferguson was in town at a meeting and Joanne was in one of her dark moods, Catherine went to feed the animals in the barn before supper. There was a cow with a new calf, and five newborn lambs with their mothers, and a couple of horses. When she'd finished distributing their feed, she leaned on the rail around the sheep pen and watched the lambs.

"Cute, aren't they?"

Catherine jumped.

"Sorry, I didn't mean to scare you." It was Christian. He came over and leaned on the fence beside her.

Catherine suddenly felt breathless. She didn't know what she would say, even if she had been able to find her voice.

They stood side by side, silently watching the lambs for a few minutes, and then Christian's hand slid along the rail and settled on hers. She pulled away, afraid. "Don't..."

"Shh," he said. "I won't hurt you."

He moved closer and put an arm around her shoulder. "Catherine." He sounded as breathless as she felt. "Come over here." He gently urged her to a corner of the barn behind the door where it was darker.

With feigned reluctance, Catherine allowed herself to be guided into the shadows, barely willing to admit what her thudding heart testified to—it was desire, not fear, she felt. Christian maneuvered her until her back was against the wall facing him. He put both hands around her back and pulled her close. "Catherine," he murmured again. His breath was coming faster. She could feel his heart beating rapidly through their pullovers. He put his palms on the sides of her face and drew her towards him, then his lips were on hers, kissing her softly, tenderly.

Catherine gasped, gripping the hands holding her face. The heat inside her increased and she could barely breathe. Then he drew away and started to unbutton her shirt. One hand slipped inside and caressed her breast, causing the nipple to harden. God, it felt so wonderful.

They jumped apart suddenly, brought back by the sound of a motor laboring up the hill.

"Mr. Ferguson," she cried. "Hide. I'll distract him."

She buttoned her shirt and went out into the yard, hoping he wouldn't notice how flushed she was.

"I fed the animals," she said as Ferguson closed the truck door.

Christian and Catherine were only alone together three times the entire summer and barely progressed beyond the innocent fumbling of their first encounter. Although they both felt intense desire, Christian was always held back by his belief that what they were doing was a sin. Catherine had been brought up to believe there was nothing sinful about sex and she couldn't understand why the people in this community made such a big deal of it.

One evening in October, Joanne decided she wanted to do some baking and Catherine offered to help. It was less boring than reading the bible, which was the alternative. As they assembled the ingredients, Joanne noticed they only had one egg left.

"Would you run out and see if there are any in the nests?" she asked Catherine.

"Sure," Catherine replied.

She grabbed her sweater and went out the back door. On her way to the hen house, she heard one of the horses whinnying in the barn, so she detoured to see if anything was wrong. The horse was backed up in the corner of its stall snuffling and shaking, but she couldn't see anything that might have frightened him. Maybe it was a mouse or a rat, she thought. She checked the manger to see if there was enough food and threw in a handful of hay, then turned to leave.

A shadowy figure moved just inside the door. "Hey!" he whispered.

"Christian! You scared me," she murmured back. "What are you doing here? Was it you who scared the horse?"

"No. I was passing and saw you come in."

"Sure you were," she replied. "I can't imagine where you were coming from or going to." The Ferguson farm was at the end of a road with nothing but open woodland beyond.

"Come here."

She went over to where he was standing and put her arms around him. He kissed her gently.

"Mmm, it feels so good to hold you," he murmured.

Catherine moved until she was against a hay bale, then fell backwards and pulled him on top of her. They kissed again and Christian's hand moved down and brushed the hem of her skirt. She felt his hand moving up her leg. Don't stop, she begged silently.

"What the devil do you think you're doing?" a voice bellowed.

Mr. Ferguson! They jumped apart, Catherine smoothing her skirt and Christian shoving his hands in his pockets.

"N-nothing, sir," Christian stuttered.

"Get out of here," Noah Ferguson yelled. "Your father's going to hear about this."

"I'm sorry, sir. It's all my fault."

"Go."

When Christian had slunk away, Mr. Ferguson grabbed Catherine's wrist and dragged her to the house. "You wicked girl," he said. "How long has this been going on?"

"It hasn't," she replied meekly.

"Don't add lying to your other sins." He shoved her inside and slammed the kitchen door. "I don't know what the Reverend's going to say. It's true what they say, 'the fruit never falls far from the tree'. A whore for a mother..."

"Noah!" Joanne snapped. "What's going on?"

"I caught this whore in the barn with the Carstairs boy. Now she's infected him with her sinful ways. Who knows who else she's led on with her sneaky, seductive tricks?"

Catherine backed away from Noah until she reached the doorway to the dining room. "My mother's not a whore," she screamed, tears running down her face. "She's a person; I love her and I want to go back to her." She turned and ran upstairs to her room where she slammed the door and fell onto her bed, sobbing.

She could still hear Noah ranting downstairs and Joanne trying to calm him. Eventually the back door slammed and there was silence. A few minutes later, a board in the upstairs hall creaked, and then she heard a soft knock on the door.

"Can I come in Cathy?" It was Joanne.

"I don't care," Catherine replied sullenly.

Joanne opened the door and came over to where she was lying on the bed. She sat down on the edge beside Catherine and brushed her hair back from her face.

Joanne sighed. "I don't know what to say," she started. "I don't suppose anything I could say would make things any better."

Catherine burst into tears again and turned facedown. "I hate it here," she mumbled into the pillow. "I just want to go back to my mother."

"You know they won't let you go." Joanne put her hand on Catherine's back. "They've made up their minds and as far as they're concerned, it's settled. No doubts, no second thoughts. That would be like admitting they were wrong."

Joanne's tone and words surprised Catherine. She was talking as if she were not part of the community. Catherine turned over, wiping her eyes with her sleeve, and looked at the older woman.

"I wish there was some way I could get away."

"There isn't. They've made sure of that. Believe me, others have tried."

Catherine sat up and leaned against the headboard. "Who?"

Joanne shrugged. "What does it matter?" She turned away with a sigh and stared at the open door.

"It was you, wasn't it?"

Joanne's shoulders sagged. She turned back to look at Catherine again. Her eyes were brimming with tears.

"How old were you? Did they kidnap you too?"

Joanne shook her head. "I was eighteen," she said. "In my first year of college."

"What happened? Where did you live?"

"Medford."

"Where's that?"

"It's a small town in southern Oregon." Joanne sniffed and wiped her eyes.

"Is that where we are now? In Oregon?"

Joanne shook her head. "No. This is Idaho."

Catherine's heart sank. How would she ever find her way home from so far away? "So how did you get here?"

"This man came to visit my father. Dad was a minister." Joanne looked wistful. "Not fanatical the way they are here. He really believed in doing good and helping people." She fell silent for a moment. "Anyway, this guy was a student at some theological college in the area and Dad had invited him for supper. He was a bit older than you'd expect a student to be, almost thirty."

"What happened?" Catherine asked, half guessing who the theology student was.

"Noah was quite handsome in those days and a bit livelier than he is now," Joanne explained. "I took a liking to him and he seemed to like me. He visited a few more times, but we never went out anywhere together. One day he asked Dad if he could take me to visit his parents in Idaho. Dad was a bit worried about the idea, but he trusted both of us." Joanne huffed in disgust. "Poor Father. Anyway, once I met the people here and saw how they lived, I didn't want any part of it. It was so different from my father's brand of Christianity. This damned religion of theirs sucks the life out of people."

Catherine reached out and put her hand over Joanne's.

"After a few days, I realized that everyone was acting as if Noah and I were engaged. I asked him about it and he said, yes, of course we were. We were going to be married. Did I think I would have been allowed to travel alone with a man unless that was the case? I was stunned. When I said I didn't want to stay and marry him, he said he'd arranged it with my father and I couldn't go back."

"Did you believe that, about your father?

"No. That's not the sort of thing Daddy would do. He was too kind and honest. I told Noah that, but he insisted." Joanne shook her head. "I don't think he was lying. He really believed he had Dad's consent. Probably because he'd let me go on this trip."

"God, that's awful," Catherine replied. "Is that why you get depressed?"

"You have to watch what you say around here. You just blasphemed, taking God's name in vain," Joanne warned her with a wry grin.

Catherine shrugged. "Did you ever see you father again?"

Joanne shook her head. "Noah told me a couple of years later that they'd received news that my father had died."

"Weren't you even allowed to go to his funeral?"

"No. By the time they told me, it was already over."

"Don't they have any phones here or com links here?" Catherine asked.

"Only at the post office and in some of the more devout homes, but their use is restricted to the chosen," Joanne said bitterly. "They lock up the ones in people's houses."

"Didn't you try to run away?"

"Oh yes, several times. One time I stowed away in a delivery truck. I got almost as far as the next town sixty kilometers east of here, but the driver found me in the back of the truck and reported it. They sent someone to bring me back." Joanne gave a wry smile. "I think that's how I got pregnant the first time."

"How? You mean...?"

"Of course. He raped me, the driver. I don't know why he didn't just take me with him; I'm sure he didn't get to meet many women. I almost asked him to, but I didn't care much for him. I might have ended up even worse off."

"God." Catherine clapped her hand over here mouth. "Sorry. I mean, how awful. What did they say about that?"

"Here, you mean? Nothing. I didn't tell anyone. I guess in a way, it was a small revenge. I lost the baby anyway. Noah thought it was his."

"You seem to get on okay now," Catherine said.

"He's not a bad guy, behind all the religious sanctimony. It can't have been easy for him, being married to me, someone who rejected him at the start and couldn't give him children." She yawned and stood up. "You must be getting tired. Try to get some sleep. I'll see you in the morning. God bless!"

"What about the cake?"

"We can do it tomorrow."

Chapter Twenty-six

The following morning when Catherine came downstairs, she was met by a heavy scowling silence from Noah Ferguson. Joanne served her breakfast without comment, but the look in her eye warned Catherine not to say anything.

Noah's only comment was, "Aren't you going to say grace, girl?" when Catherine picked up her spoon.

She put down the spoon, closed her eyes and bowed her head to mumble a few words, then picked it up again and started to eat her oatmeal. She sneaked a sideways look at him as she spooned up the cereal, wondering what Joanne could have seen in him when they first met. He looked about fifty now and his dark hair was turning grey. He had a desiccated, stringy look about him, with his weathered skin and tall, lean body. His eyes were deep blue with dark lashes, but their impact was reduced by drooping eyelids. His eyes might have been beautiful when he was younger, if he'd ever smiled.

Later that day, after she and Joanne had finished their chores, Reverend Webster paid them a visit. Catherine expected him to be angry about her and Christian, but he looked sad more than anything else. He asked Catherine to sit with him in the living room while Joanne made them tea. Webster sat on one of the chairs and cleared his throat, gesturing for her to sit near him.

Here it comes, Catherine thought with a sinking feeling as she sat down.

"I don't have to tell you that I'm very disappointed by your behavior, Catherine. I had hoped that living among good Christians would have overcome the sinful influences you grew up under, but you seem determined to be willful and disobedient." He stopped speaking as Joanne came in with a tray of tea and some cookies. "Thank you, Joanne. We can manage now," he said, dismissing her.

"I have decided that you will have to move somewhere else until we can be married," he continued while Catherine poured the tea.

A hollow opened inside her. She stopped with the teapot in midair. "But..." What could she say? She had no power; they'd taken away her freedom.

Webster put up his hand to stop her saying anything. "I've spoken to my nephew and he assures me that things didn't go far."

Her eyes filling with tears, Catherine put the teapot down.

"I am disappointed in him, too, succumbing to temptation like that. I expected better from him, but he's young and these things..." He reached over for one of the cups Catherine had just filled. He took a spoonful of sugar and stirred it into the amber liquid. "I've sent him somewhere out of temptation's way."

Catherine gasped.

"I don't like doing it, but it's my duty. I have a higher purpose to fulfill, doing the Lord's work. I cannot let childish foolishness interfere." He took a few sips of tea, and then put the cup down. I'm sending Zach Oregon with him, so you can stay at Reverend Oregon's house until the wedding." He stood up, ready to go. "Pack your things. I'll have a word with Mrs. Ferguson while I'm waiting."

Knowing it was no use protesting, Catherine dragged herself upstairs to pack. She didn't have much, only a change of everyday clothes and one set for Sunday, a pair of boots, some flat shoes and her good shoes for going to church. She didn't even have any books, only a Bible.

Joanne was at the door to see her go. She hugged Catherine and gave her a regretful look.

"Thanks for everything," Catherine said. "I'm sorry."

Joanne nodded.

Catherine went outside with her little bundle and got into the passenger seat of Reverend Webster's car. He climbed in beside her and started the electric motor. He was silent all the way to the Oregon house.

When they reached the house, he parked the car in front and turned to her. "I was going to give you a couple more years to grow up a bit before we got married but, under the circumstances, I've changed my mind," Webster said in a voice as devoid of emotion as if he were talking about the harvest or something equally mundane. "You're almost seventeen now, not too young. The marriage will take place after your birthday in February. Until then, I want you to give your word that you will not misbehave again."

Catherine bowed her head, tears running down her face. This was it, her punishment. The sentence now had a date attached to it. She yearned hopelessly for her family.

"I don't want to," she mumbled.

"What did you say? Speak up, child."

"I said, I don't want to marry you," she blurted defiantly. "I don't love you and I never will." She jumped out of the car and ran up the path to the house.

Another gloomy Christmas passed. The valley was covered in a blanket of snow for about two months and people stayed indoors much of the time. Catherine missed Christian, but she was glad she didn't have to see Zach's leering face any more.

Sunk in a fog of depression and dread, she hardly spoke to anyone. Plans for the wedding were underway by the end of January, although she refused to participate. She had to submit to measuring and prodding from the woman who was making her wedding dress, but steadfastly declined to offer any opinions or comments. She felt as if she'd turned into a zombie with no volition of her own, only activated by others.

Coral Oregon tried to get her interested, asking if there was anything she would like to have at the wedding supper, but Catherine just shook her head and said, "I don't care." As far as she was concerned, it would be the *last* supper.

"Cheer up, Catherine. It won't be so bad."

"How do you know?" Catherine responded. "You don't have to marry the old creep. I hate him."

"Don't talk like that," Coral said sharply. "You must follow the higher purpose set out for you. This is God's purpose, His will for you. Everyone has to make sacrifices. You can't always have your own way."

"I don't believe in God."

"I think you'd better go to your room, young lady."

Coral decided to have a party to celebrate Catherine's sixteenth birthday. She invited all the young adults in the community. There was a birthday cake and dancing to recorded music, mostly country, with a few twentieth century ballads thrown in for variety.

Catherine sat glumly in a corner of the living room, dumbly accepting gifts from neighbors and setting them on the floor beside her, unopened. She didn't feel like eating anything. She smiled grimly to herself as she thought, the condemned woman did not eat a hearty meal. Eventually, a pall of gloom settled over the guests and they started to trickle away much earlier than they had expected.

The date set for Catherine's wedding was a week after her birthday. She stopped eating and slept badly at night, often waking in tears. Sometimes she had a nightmare in which a shadowy creature was pursuing her through dark streets. She knew that it would consume her if it ever caught her.

The night before the wedding, Coral came to her room and sat on the edge of the bed. "Catherine, you know what your duty is when you're married, don't you?"

Catherine shook her head. She wasn't going to make it easy for her.

"I mean the physical..." Coral went on, her face turning red.

"You mean I have to sleep with him."

"Yes, but you know what happens when a man and woman sleep together."

Catherine stared at her sullenly.

"You're making this very difficult, Catherine."

"I know what you're talking about and I don't care. My mother says sex is supposed to be something beautiful, shared by two people who love each other, by mutual consent. Well I don't consent to have him doing it to me. And I don't love him." *And as far as I'm concerned, it'll be rape.*

"You mustn't say such wicked things; it's your duty, as a wife."

Catherine turned to face the wall. She didn't want to be reminded of it anymore; it scared her too much.

The next morning, Coral, Martha and the dressmaker came to help Catherine get ready. To their dismay and Catherine's indifference, she'd lost so much weight, the dress hung loosely on her.

"Maybe I could take it in at the sides," the dressmaker said dubiously. "It was all right last fitting."

"There isn't time," Martha said, looking at her watch.

"Maybe we could stuff it a bit with tissues," Coral suggested. "What do you think, Catherine?"

"I don't care."

The dress made of eyelet-embroidered cotton with a high neck, long sleeves and deep flounce around the bottom, but it could have been a hospital gown for all the interest Catherine took in it. *A shroud would be more appropriate,* she thought. When she was ready, she was paraded down the street to the glass church in front of the whole village, wrapped in a warm cloak and feeling like a condemned prisoner on the way to the gallows.

The ceremony passed in a daze for Catherine, a fog of hopelessness, much as her baptism had two months earlier. She had to be prompted to make her responses, which she did in a whisper, crossing her fingers under her bouquet as she said them. After the ceremony, the congregation moved to the meeting hall for the wedding feast. She could see that people were trying to have a good time. To them it was a celebration, but Catherine's mood threw a pall on everyone.

Old Mrs. Webster, who sat next to her at the table, poked her in the side. "You want to smarten up, young lady, stop acting like a spoiled brat," she said in a low voice. "Don't you know what an honor it is to marry my son?" —*Your son the bastard,* Catherine thought— "Believe me, you'll soon change your ways. You'll be living in our house now, where I can keep an eye on you," she added triumphantly. "Eat something; you look like a refugee."

The threat and all it implied nauseated Catherine. She put her hand over her mouth and ran out to find the washroom, where she stayed until Coral came to find her. She refused to take any part in the celebration that followed the feast and numbly followed the Websters' home after it was over.

Later that evening, her husband said to her, "You go up now, girl, and get ready for bed. I'll be up shortly."

The hollow that had been growing inside her filled with ice. Having no choice, she dragged herself reluctantly up the stairs. Her mother-in-law had shown her where the bedroom was earlier when she'd wanted to change out of her wedding dress. The old woman had already gone up to bed—an unusual act of discretion—leaving the couple to sort things out for themselves. Someone had given Catherine a new nightgown, white cotton, trimmed with lace. She took off her outer clothes and put the gown on over her panties and bra. There was no way she was going to make it easy for him.

Catherine lay under the covers facing away from the door, as far from the center of the bed as she could get without falling off the edge. She didn't want to see him when he came in. She thought how wonderful it would be if it were Christian she was waiting for instead of a horrible old man. Her eyes filled with tears. Her body was rigid with tension and apprehension.

A little while later, she heard his tread on the stairs. Filled with dread, she pulled the covers up around her ears and curled up tight. He went into the bathroom and she heard the toilet flush and water running. Then the bathroom door closed and the bedroom door opened. He cleared his throat and moved around the room, rustling things, opening and closing drawers. Catherine felt pressure on the other side of the bed, but the covers didn't move. She held her breath, waiting then she heard him mumble a prayer. He finished with an *amen*, then the pressure on the bed was repeated. He must have been kneeling on the floor, she realized, and was using the bed for support. This time, he lifted the covers and slid in beside her.

The only light in the room came from a lamp on the other side of the bed. She'd deliberately chosen the side away from it so that she wouldn't have to turn it off. He moved around a bit then turned off the lamp. When he reached out to touch her shoulder, she flinched.

Her husband sighed. "Good night, Catherine. Sleep well." He turned over, away from her and settled down for the night.

Chapter Twenty-seven

Catherine's life as a drudge—that's how she classified it— began the day after the wedding with an early-morning wakeup call and an invitation to come and learn how Keaton liked his breakfast. It continued through house cleaning skills, from how to iron his shirts and cook his meals, to the proper way to make a bed. From the start, the old lady looked upon Catherine as her successor in the role of making her son's life comfortable and trouble-free.

In March, as soon as the snow had melted, she was started on the garden. At first, it was mainly cleaning up the winter litter and trimming some of the shrubs, but soon, she was planting vegetables and flowers, and pulling weeds. As summer advanced, she showed enough progress in her gardening skills to be allowed to work unsupervised.

Catherine had never thought of herself as an outdoor person, but she took to gardening with enthusiasm. The garden became her refuge. Old Mrs. Webster had taken care of it—with a little help from some neighborhood boys— until Catherine came to live at the house, but it was becoming too much for her with her worsening arthritis. Unwittingly, her mother-in-law had given her the thing she needed most, something of her own into which she could escape for a brief interlude every day and distance her from the constant misery and loneliness of her life.

She was gratified when her husband noticed how hard she worked in the garden and complimented her the good results she achieved with the vegetables and the flowerbeds.

Keaton asked her to call Mrs. Keaton 'Mother', but she couldn't bring herself to comply. She had a mother, someone worthy of the title, which this mean old woman certainly was not. Catherine compromised by addressing her as Ma'am, which in her own mind sounded a little derisive while seeming polite and respectful on the surface.

Their marriage continued to be unconsummated. Catherine thought about this constantly, wondering whether her husband was impotent, or just being considerate of her feelings and her fear. If it was the latter, she knew that it wouldn't last forever. The threat was always there, hanging over her like a cloud.

Catherine became accustomed to sleeping beside him and even started to feel a certain comfort in it. The fact that he did leave her alone, apart from the occasional pat on the shoulder, endeared him to her. She began to like the way he smelled, a clean soapy odor with a touch of peppermint and something she could only define as man. She wondered what it would be like to do it with a man. At first the idea of sex with Webster made her shudder with revulsion, but gradually, it began to seem less repellent, even though he was almost as old as her grandfather.

She often noticed her mother-in-law watching her, especially in the mornings, and one day the old woman came right out and commented, "You should be pregnant by now. I hope there's nothing wrong with you, girl." But Catherine was not going to reveal their secret.

Her husband was kind to her in other ways, especially when his mother wasn't around. He often praised her cooking or the way she looked, and inquired if she was feeling well or was tired, telling her she need not work so hard if it was too much for her. Not that Catherine had much choice about how much work she did, with Mother Webster watching her every moment and leaving more and more things for her to do, but she was determined not to complain to Keaton about it. She was wise enough not to try to cause bad feelings between mother and son, knowing she would be the one to bear the brunt of it if she did.

One evening in the summer after her seventeenth birthday, she went up to bed as usual, but Keaton came up before she started undressing. He cleared his throat, a sure indication that he was nervous, and approached her tentatively.

"Let me help you." he said.

Catherine couldn't speak. She felt a shiver of anticipation—not really fear and not really desire, but a bit of both, combined with curiosity. Was this it—the thing she had dreaded and wondered about for so long? She dropped her hands from the front of her shirt and allowed him to undo the buttons. As he slid the shirt down her arms, she became aware of his breathing. Before going on to remove her skirt, he ran his hands down her bare arms then kissed her on the forehead.

The realization came to her that he was shy. He was probably as frightened as she was. She reached up and started to unbutton his shirt.

Their first union was soon over. It was neither as bad as she had feared, nor as beautiful and exciting as she had been led to expect by her mother. After it was over, Keaton got out of bed and put his pajama trousers on, then went to the bathroom where she heard water running. She had turned to her usual position, curled up with her back to him, but when he came back, he lay closer, facing her with his arm resting protectively around her waist. He kissed her on the neck and murmured, "Thank you, my dear. I hope it wasn't too...."

Wasn't too what? she wondered. Awful? Painful? "No," she said. "I'm okay. Good night."

Maybe he's never done it before either, she thought. Two virgins! She coughed to cover an involuntary giggle.

Even after initiating their sexual relationship, Keaton still seemed to have a very low sex drive. He continued to make love to her, but not very frequently, maybe once or twice a month. To Catherine, it felt as if he was doing it more as a duty than for pleasure. He never became skillful enough to satisfy her, and she didn't know how to guide him to make it more exciting. She was always left with a feeling of emptiness and disappointment. Surely there was more to it than this. It was as if each of them were performing a necessary ritual. When she found she was pregnant, it stopped altogether.

Her son Brent was born a week after her eighteenth birthday.

The village didn't have its own doctor, so a physician came from a nearby town to hold a clinic every two weeks. Cases that were more serious would be flown by helicopter to the hospital in town. Catherine had hoped she would be able to speak to the doctor who attended her and get a message out to her mother, but the nurse was from Blessings and never left them alone together. Once, she tried to pass him a note, but he pretended not to notice. He must know what's going on, she thought.

Her hopes were raised when she overheard a conversation between the nurse and doctor after one of his prenatal examinations.

"She'll have to go into the hospital when the time comes," the doctor said. Doctor Salmon was a thin, grey-haired man with wire-rimmed eyeglasses and a perpetual frown. "You can tell by the depth of her pelvis that it will not be an easy birth. That and her age, of course. She's barely finished her own growth cycle," he added disapprovingly.

"We'll see when the time comes," the nurse replied.

If she went to the hospital, surely she would have an opportunity to talk to someone without anyone from the Blessings preventing her, although the thought of a difficult birth left her with a constant, gnawing anxiety.

When the time finally arrived, everything happened so fast, there was no time for her to be transported the sixty kilometers to town. Catherine's membranes ruptured while she was ironing some shirts in the kitchen. The sudden gush of warm liquid startled and scared her, but Mrs. Webster knew what it meant. She went for the nurse, Mrs. Brightwell, while Catherine went up to her room to change into dry clothes. When the nurse arrived, Catherine could hear the two women talking in low tones downstairs in the living room then they came upstairs.

"I think this girl could use a cup of tea, Mrs. Webster." Mrs. Brightwell said, effectively dismissing the old woman.

Thank you, Catherine said silently. She didn't need her mother-in-law breathing over her.

"You've got lots of time yet," Mrs. Brightwell told Catherine after examining her. "You can keep on doing whatever you have to do for a while, but nothing too strenuous. I think the garden can manage without you for today."

"But what about getting to the hospital? It's a long way, isn't it?" Catherine only had a vague idea where the town was.

"There's plenty of time," the nurse replied. "I'll come back in a couple of hours and check up on you." Then she left.

233

When Webster came home for lunch, Catherine's contractions were becoming quite frequent and strong. He looked at her in panic. "Get that nurse over here, right now," he ordered his mother. "Is there anything I can do?" he asked Catherine when she'd gone.

Catherine shook her head. "Shouldn't we be leaving now?" She was standing up holding the back of a chair while he hovered over her, flinching every time she bent over with a contraction.

"Wait 'til the nurse comes and takes a look at you." He put his hand on her lower back and massaged it.

Mrs. Brightwell took her upstairs and told her to get undressed and put on a clean nightgown, then helped her up onto the bed so that she could examine her. After the examination, the nurse straightened up and stripped off her gloves, shaking her head.

"What is it," Catherine asked, alarmed. "Is something wrong?"

"Everything's fine," Mrs. Brightwell replied with a brief smile. "I'll just go and have a word with your husband. You stay here."

She could hear the tone of the discussion downstairs, but not the words being said. The nurse's voice patient and reasonable, Mrs. Webster's sharp and angry, and her husband's raised in disagreement and concern.

Mrs. Brightwell returned with Keaton. "Do you want to stay here or come downstairs?" the nurse asked. "You've got a while yet."

"But shouldn't we be going to the hospital?"

"It's too late for that," her husband said with an angry look at Mrs. Brightwell. "We'd never make it in time and I'm not having you giving birth in the back of a car."

"But what about the copter? That could get us there in half an hour." Catherine gasped. She rolled onto her side and drew knees up, clenching her fists until the pain passed.

Keaton looked close to tears. He patted her shoulder and shook his head. "Reverend Oregon has taken it down to the coast to pick up some supplies. He won't be back until tomorrow."

"Come on, I'll help you up," Mrs. Brightwell said. "It's better if you move around. You can all go downstairs while I get the room ready."

Keaton and his mother spent the next three hours alternately praying and fussing around Catherine. Keaton tried to persuade her to pray with them, but she was in no mood. Mrs. Brightwell did join them in prayer, once she had everything set up to her satisfaction, in between checking Catherine and giving her advice on how to handle the painful contractions.

By the time their son was born, her husband looked as if he had just taken part in a marathon, even though he'd stayed out of the way for the actual birth. Catherine was surprised that he was such an emotional man. He'd always seemed so stiff and controlled.

Brent was not a particularly healthy baby. He was one of those infants that hardly ever smiles. He had a thin, whiney way of crying, except when he had a bout of colic; then he screamed, endlessly. It was hard to get him to nurse, and when he did, he fell asleep too soon. After a few weeks, Catherine was hardly producing any milk and they had to start feeding him with a bottle, which only made him more fretful.

Catherine was in despair. Not only did her son not thrive and seemed constantly sick, she had to endure her mother-in-law's accusing glances and constant interference.

One day, she handed the baby to Mrs. Webster. "Here, you take care of him if you think you can do it better." She burst into tears and ran out into the garden. Daffodils and tulips thrived under her care, so why was she such a failure with her own son? Overwhelmed with guilt, she realized that she felt nothing for the child. She knew it wasn't natural, but she couldn't help it. He was puny and weak, and not particularly attractive with his hairless head, pale face and tiny red-rimmed eyes.

So from that day on, Mrs. Webster took over the care of her grandson. She seemed to get great satisfaction from it, fussing over him, especially when Catherine was around. Even so, the boy's condition didn't change much. He still remained dull and listless, and developed more slowly than a normal healthy child would. Catherine wondered if he was retarded, but there was no one with whom she could talk about it, and no Net to look up answers.

Webster treated his son as if he were an exceptionally delicate and precious object at first, but gradually his interest turned to annoyance at the child's sickliness and constant crying.

A couple of months after Brent's first birthday, Catherine found she was pregnant again. The doctor came and did the tests, and then told her it was another boy. Oliver was born, also at home, in early November. Oliver was so different from Brent it was hard to believe they were brothers. He had dark hair and shining eyes. He fed robustly and gained weight steadily. Catherine was much happier with this active, laughing child and made it plain to her mother-in-law that she needed no help with his care. While Brent was relegated to the spare bedroom that had been turned into a nursery, Oliver's crib was placed in her and Keaton's room. He slept well at night and woke up happy and gurgling in the morning.

When Catherine was working in the garden, Oliver would be with her, lying in his basinet under a tree at first then crawling around on the lawn. He eventually took his first steps out in the sunny garden, giving his mother an exclusive performance of his new skill.

Chapter Twenty-eight

Gunfight at firearms show

Twelve men were killed and seventeen injured in a gunfight that broke at in the parking lot of BC Place Stadium where the annual Super-Power Gun Show was taking place. This is the third such fight in the Greater Vancouver area in the past month. On July 17, a similar altercation in a Surrey schoolyard left five dead and twelve wounded, and four men were left dead and three admitted to hospital in serious condition after a fight outside a Port Coquitlam bar two days earlier.

Vancouver Globe, July 28, 2083

Farida. What a lovely surprise!" Julia pushed her hair back, wishing she'd brushed it before starting work.

"How are you, Julia? Any news?"

Julia shook her head. "No. I've just about given up hope."

"I don't know what to say," Farida replied. "I can just barely imagine what you're going through and that's only because I've got kids of my own. I wish there were something I could do to help."

"It's all right, Farida. How's the baby?"

"He's doing great."

"You're so lucky, having two good husbands. If it's not a rude question, who's the father?"

Farida shrugged. "We decided not to make that distinction," she replied. "We don't want to start any

237

rivalry. As far as the children are concerned, they have two fathers."

Julia thought about this for a moment and concluded that it was probably the best way of handling it. "I think that's a good idea, actually," she said.

Farida brightened. "I've got some good news for you," she said, smiling. "That's why I'm calling."

"I could use with some of that for a change. What is it?"

"One of your eggs has been fertilized."

"God, you mean you've kept them all this time?" Then the implication hit her. A frisson of excitement went through her. "You mean...?"

"Yes. A girl." Farida beamed. "I called to ask you to come in for the implant."

"What?" Julia was speechless.

"You do want to carry it ... her, don't you?"

"I ... I'd never imagined ... I'm in shock. God!" Julia's mind raced. Another daughter? Did she want to...? Was she too old? It would be like writing-off Catherine. But would another daughter really be a replacement for Catherine? She had too many conflicting feelings to make an instant decision. "Can I have time to think about it?"

"Of course, but not too long. There's only a short period in which we can do the implant. And if you decide not to take it, we'll have to choose a surrogate mother. Not that that would be much of a problem."

"How long?"

"We have to know by this evening."

She turned from the screen and looked out the window. This would change everything. She turned back and looked at Farida. "How did it happen?"

"We've been working on a new technique. Taking half the chromosomes from an ovum during meiosis—as the cell is dividing—and replacing them with chromosomes from another. That way, you don't have a clone of the mother. It's been hard to get the ova to continue to divide and differentiate and not just continue to create identical cells, but it worked this time. I think we have a good chance."

"You mean she will have genetic material from two women?"

Farida nodded.

"God! Are you allowed to reveal who the other ... donor is?"

"We don't think that would be wise," Farida replied. "I should point out that this is still very new and we have no assurance that it will be a success. I mean, the implant may not take. Your body might reject the embryo. A thousand things could go wrong. But we have a contract, so we are giving you the first opportunity."

"What about the other woman, the one who provided the other egg."

Farida's smile faded. "She was killed in a copter crash."

But she'll live on in my daughter, if this works, Julia thought sadly.

"I see." She thought for a moment. The idea was beginning to sound more appealing, but did she want to set herself up for another loss? She was forty. Maybe she was too old. She needed to get some advice. "I'll call you back in a couple of hours. Thanks, Farida."

Robbie was semi-retired, but he was still at the clinic— it was his home—so Julia had no trouble reaching him. She told him what Farida had said.

"What do you think?"

Robbie scratched the bald spot on top of his head then stroked his beard. "When did you last have a checkup?"

"Six months ago."

"And was everything all right then?"

"I guess so. Nobody mentioned any problems."

"I can look it up. My chief concern is what this could do to you if it fails. You could be letting yourself in for another loss, Julia."

"I know. I've thought of that. But, Robbie, I'm not sure I could bear not knowing. You know what I mean. Having maybe two daughters out there somewhere and not knowing what is happening to them."

"I tell you what, let me look at your last checkup and call you back."

Julia got up and looked in the mirror. Something had changed. She looked more alive than she had in years. The pain was gone from her eyes. She put her hands on her cheeks. God, Catherine. I'm sorry, sweetheart, but I have to do this.

***

It was late August. Catherine had been married eight years. Brent, who clung constantly to his grandmother, was six and Oliver four. By now, she was trusted not to try to run away if she went out alone. Her husband and mother-in-law probably thought the children were enough to keep her from leaving. Not that she didn't think of it every time she left the house.

Oliver followed her up the steep path into the woods, stopping every few minutes to look at some bug, or pick a flower.

"How are we ever going to pick any berries if you keep stopping?" Catherine called over her shoulder. "Come on; it's not far now."

The little boy laughed and ran to catch up, swinging his empty plastic pail. "I bet I can pick more than you," he said.

"I hope you can."

They rounded a bend in the path and saw a large sprawl of blackberry brambles, the branches covered with glossy ripe berries. "This looks like a good place to start. Now show me what you can do," Catherine said.

It was a hot day, so Catherine, away from the snooping eyes of the villagers, tucked the hem of her skirt up into the waistband, leaving her legs bare. She unbuttoned her blouse and tied it in a knot at the front. The air was heavy with summer fragrances. Bees hummed drowsily among the flowers and birds chirped and twittered all around them.

They picked berries for a while, although Oliver was eating almost as many as he put in his bucket.

"Ouch, I've pricked my finger." He held out the injured digit for his mother to inspect.

She wiped the berry juice away and kissed it. "There, now it's better." Catherine smoothed his hair back from his sweaty face and added another kiss on his forehead.

Oliver's eyes had turned brown like hers, and his hair was dark, although it had lightened considerably when he was a baby. He looked like her father, she thought sadly. How wonderful it would be if her mother could see him. She wiped the corner of her eye with her knuckle. She missed her family so much. If only there were some way she could.... She sighed. What's the use?

"What's the matter, mommy?" her son asked, looking at her anxiously.

"Just a speck of dust in my eye," she replied.

"Did it make you sad?"

"No," she lifted him up in a hug and swung him around. "How could anything make me unhappy when I've got you?" she set him down again. "Now, let's fill these pails, and then I've got a surprise for you."

"What?"

"Not until we've picked enough berries."

When Catherine's pail was full, she helped Oliver fill his.

"I'm thirsty, mommy," he said. "What's the surprise?"

They sat down in a grassy glade and Catherine opened the canvas bag she carried by a strap on her shoulder. She took out a package wrapped in a table napkin and laid it on the ground, and then brought out two soft drink bottles. "It's a bit warm, I'm afraid." She unscrewed the top of one and handed it to her son.

"Wow, Coke! Did daddy say we could have it?" Keaton did not approve of children having soft drinks.

"It's a secret. Okay?"

Oliver nodded his head and took a sip. "It's good. Thanks, mommy; I won't tell."

Catherine opened the package to reveal two cheese-in-a-bun sandwiches, and four cookies. From the bag, she took two peaches. "A picnic," she said.

"Is that the surprise?"

"That's it. What do you think about it?"

"I like it." He picked up a sandwich then put it down again. "Aren't we going to say grace?"

"Do you want to?"

He shook his head, wrinkling his nose. "No."

"All right. Go ahead and eat."

Oliver laughed and pounced on one of the sandwiches.

After they had eaten, Catherine lay back and closed her eyes.

"I need to go pee," Oliver said.

"Go behind those bushes," Catherine told him. "But don't go away."

She heard a twig snap but was unconcerned; it was only Oliver returning. Then a shadow fell over her. Her eyes snapped open. A strange man was standing beside her, looking down at her bare legs. Another stood a meter away. They were dressed in jeans, plaid shirts and cowboy boots. One wore a black cowboy hat and the other a white one. At least, it had once been white; now it was so stained with sweat and dirt, it was a yellowish grey. Neither man looked very clean. They both had the seamed, ruddy faces of people who spent most of their time out of doors.

"Who are you?" Catherine asked, sitting up and pulling her skirt down over her legs. "What are you doing here?" She got to her feet and looked around for Oliver.

"Well, ma'am, we were looking for you," the closest man replied.

"I don't understand," Catherine said, backing away. She didn't like the way he was grinning at her. Then another thought struck her. "Did my mother send you?" she asked hopefully.

Black Hat looked at White Hat who shrugged. "Maybe," he replied, his grin turning cunning. "Come with us and find out."

"No," she shouted. "You don't know anything about my mother, do you?"

"Only way you'll know for sure is if you come with us," White hat said, moving closer. He had a stocky build, with blue eyes and light brown hair.

The two men moved quickly. One was on each side of her; they grasped her arms and tried to pull her forward. Catherine twisted, trying to free herself.

"Let me go," she shouted frantically.

"Leave my mommy alone." Oliver broke through the bushes and ran to her. He tugged on one man's sleeve. "Let *go* of her!"

"Run, Oliver. Go back home and tell your...."

243

But before Oliver could move, the man in the black hat grabbed him and tucked him under his arm. "Guess we'll have to take him along, too," he said to his partner.

"He won't be much use to us," the other replied.

Oliver was struggling to get free. He landed a kick on the man's knee, causing him to yell. The man responded by whacking him on the behind. "You do that again and I'll tie you up," he threatened.

"Don't you dare hurt him," Catherine yelled. "Are you all right, Oliver?"

The little boy twisted his head to look at her. He nodded, tears running down his face.

"Maybe we should tie both of them up," White Hat said from Catherine's other side.

"I don't think we'll need to do that, will we ma'am?" Black Hat said. He'd stopped smiling. "If you behave and do like we say, the boy won't get hurt."

"Let's get going, Cliff." White Hat urged. "We're wasting too much time. Somebody might come."

"Okay, we're on our way."

The two men guided the now docile mother and son towards the path and turned uphill. Catherine wondered what they intended to do with them. She wanted to get away from Blessings, but this might only be taking her into something worse. And what would they do to Oliver? If they hurt him.... She made up her mind that whatever happened, she would not be separated from her son. She'd rather die. Perhaps when they got out of this valley to wherever they were going, they might have a better chance of escaping, or at least contacting her mother.

They were climbing up the path that led to the hunting lodge. She thought about the sensors, but nobody could get up here in time to stop them. The Blessings helicopter was in the shop for repairs.

"Where are you taking us?" she asked.

"You'll soon find out," the man holding her arm said.

The other man, the one called Cliff, had set Oliver down and was now leading him by the hand.

A strange copter stood in the clearing by the lodge. It wasn't as clean and well maintained as the one belonging to the church. Its outer surface was crackled as if it had been exposed to high temperatures, and there were rust stains along the seams where the panels joined. She hoped it ran better than it looked; its appearance certainly didn't inspire confidence.

"Get in," White Hat ordered. "In the back, both of you. And fasten the harnesses."

Catherine knew there was no point in arguing. That's how vulnerable you are with a child. You'll do anything to keep him safe. She lifted her son up into the copter and climbed in beside him then she fastened the safety harnesses. When the front seats were adjusted so that the two men could get in, there was no way she and Oliver could get out.

The copter started up with a rough catching sound every few revolutions. Catherine sat tensely, her arm around Oliver, hoping the thing wouldn't crash.

The vehicle rose from the ground and swung around until they were facing away from the Blessings, towards the mountain ridge.

"Where are we going, Mommy?" Oliver asked, his eyes round as he looked past her at the sinking treetops.

The hum of the motor prevented her from hearing what the two men up front were saying. Catherine hoped it would also cover her conversation with her son.

"I don't know, sweetheart," she said close to his ear. She put her arm around his shoulders and drew him closer. "But I'll look after you, don't worry."

"Will they hurt us?"

"I don't think so," she replied. "Listen carefully; I want to tell you something very important, okay?"

Oliver looked up at her and said solemnly. "I will, Mommy. Is it a secret, like the Coke?"

Clever boy! "Yes, just between you and me." She put her hand on his shoulder. "If we get a chance to escape from these men, I want you to do exactly what I say without hesitation. Do you understand?"

Oliver nodded.

"It might be dangerous, so we'd have to be very quiet and not talk. Don't forget, you must do as I tell you and be very quick."

His little hand found hers and nestled in its warmth.

"Look out the window; we're going over the mountains." Catherine said. At least he was seeing something of the world outside the confines of Blessings, if that was any consolation.

"Look, Mommy. Snow."

Rocky hollows in the mountains below them were filled with pockets of snow, and in the distance to the north, they could see a perfectly conical peak capped in white.

They passed over several ridges before leaving the high mountains and coming out over forested foothills. Occasionally, Catherine spotted a clearing with a few houses, the glint of a stream, and before long, trails, and then roads. At least they were going west, closer to home. Now she wasn't separated from the coast by a mountain range. It would have been worse if they'd taken her farther east.

Chapter Twenty-nine

Vancouver woman has second daughter

A forty-one-year-old Vancouver (Canada) woman gave birth to her second daughter on July 27. The infant girl is the result of a new in-vitro fertilization technique first used at the University of British Columbia in which the genetic material from two ova are combined in one embryo.

"There was a lot of luck involved," stated Dr. Sarap Gurdwara Singh, one of the scientists working on the technique. "That we were able to induce cell differentiation in the ovum and then not have the embryo rejected once it was placed in the womb was extremely fortunate. Both of these stages have had a very low success rate so far."

The mother, who wishes to remain anonymous, revealed that her first daughter disappeared ten years ago when she was fourteen.

"This baby will not replace Catherine," the mother said. "No one could replace her. Francesca is a person in her own right."

Seattle Post, July 28, 2083

The copter set down in a clearing beside a cabin. As they were descending to land, Catherine took note of the surrounding terrain. There was a trail winding down to a road about half a kilometer away and a brook about ten meters from the building. There didn't appear to be any utility lines coming into the cabin. A vintage four-wheel drive vehicle, caked in mud, stood outside.

247

Vicki Wootton

"Get out," the man called Ryan said, putting the front seats forward. He lifted Oliver out and set him down on the ground, then turned to give Catherine a hand.

"You can go wherever you like while you're here, but keep in mind there's wild bears in these woods, and I even hear tell of wolves a few miles up that way," he said, pointing north.

"And cougars," the other man added.

Thanks a lot, Catherine replied silently. They were probably only telling her that to scare her, but she couldn't afford to take chances with her son. She took Oliver's hand and stood waiting to be told what to do.

White Hat had already disappeared inside the cabin. The building looked quite old. It had a distinct tilt to one side and the chinking between some of the logs had fallen out. One of the two small windows was cracked and both looked as if they hadn't been cleaned in this century. The door, loose on its hinges, had to be lifted to open it.

The interior was paneled in pine, darkened by years of wood smoke. The two men didn't object to Catherine's looking around. Although everything was dusty, the furnishings were not too bad. A pine table and four chairs, a sagging sofa covered in faded green material, and a couple of wooden chairs with padded seats completed the furniture of the main room, which took up about half the cabin. The other half was divided into a kitchen area and a bedroom with two narrow bunks

Ryan grinned at her when she'd finished her inspection. "As you can see, it needs a woman's touch. Problem is, they never stay long enough."

"Is that what you brought me here for, to be a servant?" she asked.

Ryan shook his head. "You're not going to be here long, either."

"Where's the bathroom?" Catherine asked.

"Oh, I beg your pardon," he replied. "Follow me." He led her outside and round the back of the cabin to a leaning outhouse.

Catherine opened the door and was greeted by a cloud of buzzing flies and a foul odor. Holding her breath, she let go of the door and turned back towards the cabin.

"It's all we've got," Ryan said. "You'll be glad of it when you need it badly enough."

Catherine gave him a cold look. "You could have left us where we were. We didn't ask you to bring us here."

"I notice you didn't put up too much of a fight."

Back inside, she sat down on the couch and drew Oliver down next to her. "How long are you going to keep us here?"

"We'll be moving on as soon as arrangements can be made."

"What sort of arrangements," she asked coldly.

"That's Jake's department," Ryan replied, nodding towards his partner. "Tell her, buddy."

"Highest bidder," Jake replied.

"What do you mean?"

"Whoever wants to pay for you."

Catherine got goose bumps. "You mean you're going to sell us?" she gasped.

"Not 'us', you."

She put her arm protectively around Oliver and drew him close. "I'm not going anywhere without my son. You'd have to kill me first."

"We'll see," Jake replied, leaving Catherine even more apprehensive.

Jake turned to Ryan and said, "I think I'd better go make a few calls before it gets dark." He went outside and started the four-wheel drive.

As the sound of the motor faded, Ryan said. "How about rustling up some food? You'll find everything you need in the kitchen."

"Why should I? I'm not your slave." She sat farther back on the couch and held Oliver close."

"If you want to eat, you'll have to cook it yourself. Even if you don't get hungry, the kid will." He went out and pushed the cabin door in a few centimeters, leaving an opening wide enough to pass through.

Catherine stood up and held out her hand for Oliver, then went to look around kitchen, which opened off the main room like a large alcove. She looked around to see what food was available and found some tins of soup, beans, and vegetables on the shelves attached to one wall, and a basket containing a few shriveled carrots, some potatoes, and onions on the floor. There was also a bag of dried beans next to a bag of rice and canisters of flour and coffee. No refrigerator and it appeared the cooking was done on a wood stove. She touched the top of the stove and found it was warm.

Ryan came into the kitchen while she was poking around. He'd taken off his hat and she saw his hair was cut so short it stuck out all over like bristles. He was both shorter and slimmer than his partner and had an ugly scar on his cheek.

"How do you light this thing?" she called.

"You don't need to light it," he said. "It's already lit. You just open this thingy and put some more wood in."

He took a small iron tool and lifted a round cover on top of the stove, then picked up a couple of small logs and dropped them in. "Like that."

"I don't like it here," Oliver said. "I want to go home."

"Be quiet, boy. If you give us any trouble, I'll lock you in the outhouse."

Oliver burst into tears and buried his head in Catherine's skirt.

"You don't have to talk to him like that. He's just a little boy. He's scared."

"You too, if you get out of line. Now get started with the cooking."

More to have something to do than because he ordered her to, Catherine decided to put a meal together. At least she and Oliver would get something to eat and she would have some control over how it was prepared. Ryan and his partner didn't look as if they had much respect for cleanliness. She brought a chair into the kitchen and sat Oliver on it so that she could keep him close

"Is this all there is?" she asked, pointing to the shelf.

"It's enough," he replied. "You can't keep meat and stuff without a fridge in this weather."

She pulled the bag of beans from the shelf and put it on the work top, brought over the basket of vegetables. Maybe she could make some kind of stew and have it with rice.

"I'll need some water." She'd noticed there was no running water at the sink.

"That pail in the corner." He pointed to a white plastic pail with a board over it.

Catherine put some dried beans into a large pot and filled it half full with water, then set it on top of the stove. "Where's the salt?" she asked.

He pointed out a small jar behind the tins.

While the beans were heating up, she chopped up a couple of onions, discarding the parts that had decayed, and added them to the beans then she peeled the carrots and potatoes and put them in another pot of water.

While she was working, Catherine thought about her mother's laborsaving kitchen. Preparing a meal was so effortless in that bright clean room, it was a pleasure to work there. Since she'd been abducted, she felt as if she'd gone back in time. First the Websters' twentieth century style kitchen, now this relic from, what? The nineteenth century, at the latest. She yearned so much to be back in her own time, with her own people. She'd take all the hazards of being a woman in a big city over this.

Catherine lifted the lid of the bean pot, sensing the man creeping up behind her. As she stirred the beans, he put his arms around her waist then slid his hands up to her breasts.

"Get away," she said softly, "Or you'll get this boiling pot all over you."

He jumped back. "Hey, there's no need to get mad." He said indignantly. "There's no law against sampling the merchandise."

"There is a law against kidnapping, though."

"Yeah, but who's going to find out?"

"Mommy, I need to go to the bathroom." Just in the nick of time.

"Do you have to do pee-pee?" The Websters preferred to use euphemisms for bodily functions.

"No, the other."

"Have you got any tissue?" Catherine asked the man.

"Here," he took a roll from a small cupboard by the sink. "Don't use too much, it's all we've got. Unless Jake remembers to pick some up."

That meant there was a store nearby, Catherine noted.

She took Oliver outside and looked around. She didn't want him to have to use the foul-smelling outhouse. "Go over there behind that tree," she said, handing him a bunch of tissue. "I'll stay here and wait for you."

He walked away, looking over his shoulder anxiously. It was all so strange and scary for him, poor little man. She must not let him see her fear.

When Jake came back two hours later, the bean stew was almost ready so Catherine put the rice on to cook.

Jake was carrying a plastic shopping bag, which he brought into the kitchen and set it on the worktop. "Dessert," he said.

Catherine looked inside the bag and found a box of cereal, some canned milk and a packet of cookies— chocolate covered marshmallows. That would be a treat for Oliver. He wasn't allowed sweets at home, only healthy homemade things. There was a can of frozen orange juice in the bottom of the bag. Jake had also brought a six-pack of beer. He pulled a couple from their plastic rings and offered her one. Catherine shook her head. She'd never tasted an alcoholic drink. Her mother wouldn't even drink wine, although she kept some for guests. In Blessings, it was out of the question.

Jake took the two cans into the living room and gave one to Ryan.

"Thanks." Ryan said. "Any luck?"

"Yeah, there's a guy in Portland, but we don't want to jump at the first offer. Elwood says there's a rich Jew from Seattle in the market. He said he'd find out what he would offer."

Catherine listened to this exchange, horrified. Then a thought struck her. "If you're taking bids for me, why don't you get in touch with my mother? I know she's pay anything to get me back."

The two men exchanged a look. "Is she rich, your old lady?" Ryan asked.

"Not very rich," Catherine replied. "But she makes good money, and there's my grandparents. I know she could raise it; she has lots of friends. Why don't you call her?"

"Where does she live?" Jake asked.

"In Vancouver. Canada, not Washington."

Ryan frowned. "If your ma lives in Vancouver, what were you doing living with those religious nuts in Idaho? Did she sell you to them or something?"

Tears stung Catherine's eyes. "No! She'd never do anything like that. They kidnapped me."

"How long is it since you saw your family?"

"Ten years."

"They probably think you're dead by now." Jake said. "Give us the number anyway. I might as well give her a call."

Catherine was elated, for the first time in ten years she felt a spark of hope. By this time next week, she could be at home in Vancouver. She hugged Oliver so tightly he started to struggle.

"You're holding me too tight. What's the matter, Mommy?"

"I love you so much." Catherine kissed him and set him down.

Before serving up the stew, Catherine took two bowls and some utensils down to the creek to wash them just to make sure they were really clean. She ladled rice and stew into the bowls for herself and Oliver, then sat down at the table with him to eat. She saw a look pass between the two men, but neither of them said anything. They helped themselves and sat in the two remaining chairs. They ate in silence.

After they'd finished eating, she took Oliver with her and went down to the creek to wash the dishes she and her son had used. She wasn't going to wait on the kidnappers;

they could clean up after themselves. While they were there, they washed their hands and faces then Catherine put Oliver to bed in the bedroom. Although the bunks themselves were ancient and had no sheets or pillows, they did have clean sleeping bags on top of the sagging mattresses. It didn't take long for him to fall asleep.

"Where's your friend?" she asked Jake when she returned to the main room and saw he was alone.

"Gone to get some water."

She looked around for a moment then said. "I think I'll go to bed as well."

"Just a minute," Jake said. He looked at her speculatively, with hunger in his eyes that had nothing to do with food. "How much is it worth to you for me to call your mother?"

Catherine suddenly felt deflated. *Here it comes, the payoff.* When she thought of the implications of the question, she realized she didn't really care. She'd had no freedom of choice for ten years, and she'd been forced into a relationship with a man she'd felt no desire for. What would one more matter, if it led to freedom?

"I haven't got any money now," she replied, pretending to misunderstand. "I could send you some when I get home."

"There's another way," he said, coming closer.

Catherine sighed. He wasn't a bad looking guy, a bit on the heavy side, and he needed a shave, but his features were pleasant enough, and he was young, maybe thirty or thirty-five.

Just as she was resigning herself, she heard footsteps outside and the door opened to admit Ryan, carrying two pails of water.

"How's it going, buddy?" he asked, setting the pails down in the kitchen. "Kid gone to sleep?"

Jake joined him in the kitchen where they held a whispered conversation then Ryan came back into the living room. "I think I'll go have a smoke in the truck," he said and left, pushing the door shut the door behind him.

Jake took Catherine's arm and drew her towards the bedroom.

"We can't do it in here. My son..."

"He's asleep, he won't hear anything."

"But he might wake up."

"All right, have it your own way. We'll have to do it on the couch."

The two small oil lamps they'd lit when the sun went down gave only a faint glimmer of light, leaving the room mostly in shadow. Catherine lay down on the couch.

"Aren't you going to take your clothes off?" Jake asked. He started to unbuckle his pants.

How much fuss could she make, and how much could she resist? She didn't want to scare Oliver by making a noise. With a sigh of resignation, Catherine sat up and started to unbutton her blouse.

It was over very quickly. The only difference from Keaton was that Jake was much more energetic and finished with a triumphant yell, before finally flopping down on top of her. He got up right away and put his pants back on.

Catherine started to get dressed, but Jake interrupted her. "Don't bother; my buddy's waiting for his turn."

After both men had finished taking their payment, Catherine went into the kitchen and poured some water into a bowl. She found a clean rag hanging by the sink and a piece of soap and dropped them into the water, then took them into the bedroom where she washed herself in the dark before getting into the sleeping bag. She wondered how many other women had spent the night here under similar circumstances. The last thing she thought of before falling asleep was that it had been a small price to pay if it meant being reunited with her family.

In the night, she was awoken by the chilling howl of a wild animal. *Maybe it was true about the wolves,* she thought. Or it could be coyotes; there'd been a few around Blessings and everyone had been warned not to go out unarmed at night.

***

Julia had just finished bathing Francesca and was sitting down to feed her when the com chimed. It was around ten fifteen on Saturday morning. Irritated by the interruption, she let her voicemail take it. Until one word—Catherine—electrified her. She leaned across and pressed the button to answer. The screen remained blank, so she couldn't see the caller.

"What did you say? Do you know something about my daughter?"

"Ah, Ms Finisterra, you are there." She didn't recognize the man's voice.

"Are you the police?"

He laughed. "No, Ms Finisterra. I'm calling to find out how much you'd pay to get her back?"

Julia's heart jumped and her throat constricted. "Do you know where she is? Is she all right?" *Catherine, alive!* It was almost too much to hope for … but still, she'd always kept on hoping.

"I've got her," the man replied. "She's safe enough, for now. You didn't answer my question. How much would you pay?"

"I don't believe you. You probably saw my notice on the Net and want to scam me for the reward."

"I don't know anything about any notice. I don't use the Net."

"How do I know you've got her? Prove it."

"Let me see now. She's got dark hair and brown eyes and she's about five feet four."

He was right, except for her height; she had been about 150 centimeters when she'd disappeared. She'd grown another five centimeters, if he was to be believed.

"Anyone could find out that from the Missing Person notices. You'll have to come up with something better than that if you want to convince me."

"Listen, lady, I don't care whether you believe me or not. I'm just trying to help you here. I've got other offers. She asked me to call you, so I'm giving you a chance. She thought you'd be glad to get her back."

His argument was compelling, but Julia still wasn't sure. She didn't want her emotions and hopes to overcome her common sense and lead her to do something foolish. She could ill afford to lose any money.

"Please," she said desperately. "Tell me something that will convince me."

"All right. She told me her Uncle Paul was hurt while he was serving with NAMA in South America."

"Anything else?"

"Jesus, lady, what does it take to convince you. Don't you want your daughter back? I think I'm wasting my time."

"No, don't hang up," Julia cried. "What do you want?"

"Well, the best offer we've got so far is two hundred and fifty. That's thousands—NA dollars. If you can beat that, she's all yours. We'll throw in the kid for nothing."

Kid? Oh, God. Julia clenched her fists, tears rolling down her cheeks. "You mean she has a child?"

"Cute little boy. But I haven't got time for that. What about the money?"

Julia thought fast. She'd have to borrow; her savings were severely depleted since she'd become pregnant and stopped seeing clients. The only people she might be able to count on were her father and Antoine, who were worse off than she was. There was Pascal, but she hated to ask her. God, she needed more time.

"I don't have that sort of money on hand," she said. "I'm sure I can get it in a few days. Can I call you back?"

He laughed again. "Oldest trick in the book. You should know better, Julia. No, I will not give you my number. I'll give you one more chance. Have an answer ready tomorrow morning, same time."

"I want..." she started, but it was too late. The speaker was silent.

Francesca, sensing her mother's stress, stopped nursing, stiffened her body and let out a cry. Julia stood up and put her on her shoulder, patting her back as she started to pace. She had to come up with a plan for getting the ransom money. Neal was useless. The last time she'd heard from him was when he had called her to beg for money. He'd looked like wreck, unshaven, his hair lank and oily, eyes sunk in grey sockets.

She'd have to start calling people at once. At least she didn't have a mortgage on the house. She could probably borrow fifty thousand on it, but that wasn't nearly enough.

Julia calmed Francesca and when she fell asleep, put her in her cradle, then flipped on her computer terminal and opened her accounting program. She opened the balance sheet and looked up her bank balances. Just under two thousand in her operating account and around sixteen thousand in savings. Where had all the money gone? She wrote down the figures on a piece of paper and added them up. It was hopeless. She couldn't even raise twenty thousand dollars. She'd have to swallow her pride and beg.

She dialed her father's number. Her mother had died three years earlier—of a broken heart, Raymond claimed. She had lost her will to live after Paul's death, but she had died of a heart attack. Antoine still lived with her father, and Edgar visited them frequently, but it was a sad, empty household without Aldina.

Antoine answered the call. He was working from home now. "Julia, what's the matter? You look as if something awful's happened."

"Awful and wonderful," she replied. "Is Dad there? I'd like to tell both of you at the same time."

"Right. Hold on a sec, I'll get him. He's outside on the terrace"

She heard Antoine yelling from another room, "Raymond, phone. Hurry."

Antoine returned and looked at her curiously then her father's face appeared beside him. He started to rub some sweat off his forehead and realized he was still wearing his gardening gloves.

"Julia, anything wrong?"

"I had a phone call this morning. Some guy claims he has Catherine. She's alive, Dad. Isn't that wonderful?" As she said this, tears started to roll down her face.

"It sure is, love. I'm..." Raymond beamed. "When's she coming home?"

Antoine nodded. "But? I take it there's a catch."

"Yes. He wants money for her. A lot of money."

"But where is she?" Raymond wanted to know. "Is she all right? I can hardly believe it. It's such a wonderful surprise." Then his face fell as he realized the full implications of what she said.

"I don't know where she is, Dad, he wouldn't tell me." she brightened up. "She's got a little boy, Daddy. You're a great grandpa." *And I'm a grandmother!*

Raymond wiped his forearm over his face to remove the sweat. "Wow. How old is he? What's his name?"

"I didn't get a chance to ask. He hung up too fast. Look, Dad, and Antoine, I need to get a lot of money together, by tomorrow. I don't have much and I was hoping you could help. I'm going to try to get a mortgage on my house, but it won't be enough."

Raymond banged his fist down on the console, shaking the camera. "Those bastards. They keep her all this time then have the nerve to ask us to pay to get her back, now they've had enough of her." He suddenly looked alarmed. "Maybe she's sick, something serious, and they don't want to pay for treatment."

"I don't think so, dad. He said he has another offer for her. They're trying to make some money, selling her to the highest bidder, by the sound of it. It's like a ransom." Julia glanced at the piece of paper on which she'd being writing the numbers. "About the money, Dad, Do you think you can...?"

"Off course we'll help." Antoine nodded agreement. "If it's the only way to get her back. You know I'd give my life, if it would help. How much do you need?"

Catherine steeled herself to deliver the bad news. "At least two hundred and fifty thousand. That's what he said the other offer was."

Antoine whistled.

Raymond looked startled. "That's a lot of money." He started to scratch his head, but the glove got in the way, so he shook his hand free and tried again. "I don't know how we could come up with anything near that." He looked at Antoine.

"I've got about thirty-five thousand in my retirement fund. You could have that. We could mortgage the condo, that might bring another fifteen," Antoine said

"Right. I've got, let me think now, I think my retirement is worth about fifty. What else? Your mother left some investment certificates, around twelve thousand."

"Oh, Dad, that's all you've got," Julia said. "I hate to have to ask you this."

"I told you, if it'll get my granddaughter back, it's worth anything. Is it enough though?"

"Almost," Julia replied. If.... If she could raise the rest. It would take some doing. "I'm going to make a few more calls now, there's not a lot of time."

"Do you want us to start liquidating?" her father asked.

"What do you think, Antoine?" Julia responded.

"We have to," he replied. "And, Julia, I think you should call the police and let them know about this."

"I will. Thanks, both of you."

"Hey, wait a minute," Antoine said. "I think I heard something about a special ransom fund set up by the government. I'll look into it and call you back if I get anything.

Even with her family's help, she could barely raise a hundred thousand and fifty thousand, unless she could get something from the fund Antoine mentioned. God, what was she going to do? Julia buried her face in her hands and wept. To have the return of her daughter so close, yet so out of reach. Julia stood up and gave herself a mental shake. *Now was not the time to sink into despair. I have to get some money somehow.*

She went into the kitchen and put some water on to heat, then took a mug from the cupboard and dropped in a tea capsule. Pacing the two meters between the den and the kitchen, she thought about the lucrative career she'd had to give up with Francesca's birth. She wasn't even sure she'd be able to start up again. At forty-one, she felt too old, and after having the baby, she'd have to get in shape again. It would be months.

Julia sighed. She poured the boiling water over the tea and took it back to her desk. She pressed the button to turn on the com equipment, and started making the calls.

Julia tossed restlessly all night, alternately imagining the joy of being reunited with Catherine and meeting her grandson, and the sinking fear that somehow it wouldn't work out; she couldn't raise the amount of money the man who'd called had asked for. And Antoine hadn't been able to find the department that administered the fund. Government offices were closed for the weekend, so they'd have to wait until Monday. The only hope she had left was that he would take less, or that by some miracle, she would find another source.

**

Catherine and Oliver were kept at the cabin for three days. Each morning, Jake disappeared for a couple of hours and returned to hold a private discussion with Ryan. Every day, she took Oliver for a walk down the trail, aware that Ryan was somewhere nearby, watching. Each night, as soon as Oliver was asleep, they exacted their payment from her.

She wasn't told anything about their negotiations. They just said, "We're working on it," if she inquired.

"But have you contacted my mother?" she asked, exasperated by their attitude.

"Like I said, we're working on it." Ryan replied.

**

Julia was up at six the next morning. Various scenarios ran through her mind: he'd reject her request for more time; he'd show some compassion; he wouldn't call...

The phone rang at eight. She darted to her desk and pressed the button. "Yes?" she said breathlessly, her heart pounding.

"Julia? How are you feeling?" It was Pascal.

"Oh, God, Pascal, I'm a complete basket case."

"You look as if you didn't get much sleep last night. Listen, I had a talk with one of my friends last night, and he said he could lend me thirty thousand dollars."

"But..." Julia started to say.

"Don't worry about it, he can afford it and I got the feeling he would be in no hurry to have it repaid. It'll help, won't it?"

"Oh, yes. You're an angel Pascal." Her shoulders slumped. She still didn't have enough, even with Pascal's generous offer.

Pascal looked back at her from the monitor, eyes filled with compassion. "You look as if you could use some company. I'm coming over." She looked at the tiny watch on her finger. "I'll be there in about half an hour, all right?"

Julia nodded.

When Pascal arrived, she made some coffee and placed the croissants she'd brought on a plate then she persuaded Julia to sit out on the patio with her. The south-facing patio was just starting to feel the heat of the sun, but a light ocean breeze made it comfortable. The two women sat silently, sipping their coffee and breaking off pieces of croissant spread with butter and strawberry jam.

"Where's the baby?" Pascal asked.

"I fed her early and put her back to bed. She'd so good, she sleeps all the time."

"Well, I hope she wakes up before I leave. I want to see her."

"Oh, she will, don't worry."

Julia was distracted, thinking about the coming phone call. She gazed absentmindedly at her garden, which was seriously in need of some work. All the bedding plants had died and were reduced to dried up brown sprigs in the parched soil. The only things that seemed to thrive were weeds. She just didn't have the energy to tackle it and she couldn't afford to hire someone. Maybe she could get her father to come over.

She looked at Pascal. In her early fifties now, she was still a beautiful woman, a little heavier maybe, but looking fresh and healthy. And she was still working; most of her friends and clients had remained loyal.

"It's like marriage," she'd told Julia one time. "With all the good attributes and few of the negative ones. They stay faithful, but I still have my freedom."

Julia believed her friend's attitude and temperament contributed greatly to her youthfulness. She was a confirmed optimist. Pascal believed if there was a problem, there was always a solution, so what's the point in letting yourself get in a state over it? It was just a matter of finding the right solution.

"What time is it?" Julia asked, brushing crumbs off her lap.

Pascal glanced at her watch. "Just coming up to nine-forty." She reached over and took Julia's hand. "Not long now. Just keep thinking positively."

Julia got up and started piling up the cups and plates.

Pascal stood up. "Let me give you a hand."

They took the dishes back in the house and put them in the cleaning appliance. Julia leaned against the counter and rubbed her forehead.

"I can't stand this waiting," she said, her voice betraying her anxiety.

Pascal put her arms around Julia and hugged her, patting her back. "I know. Come on, let's go back outside."

Julia released herself from Pascal's hold. "I should be doing something; I can't sit still." She looked around at her surroundings. "God, this place is a mess. It looks as if I haven't cleaned it in weeks." She went over to a cupboard between the den and the kitchen and opened the door. Pascal watched patiently as she took out the house bot and programmed it to pick up dust. Julia took it into the living room and set it on the floor.

"Come on," Pascal said, holding out her hand.

Julia took the proffered hand and allowed herself to be led back out to the patio, but before they could sit down, a cry from the nursery announced that Francesca needed attention. Julia rushed to pick her up.

"Can I hold her?" Pascal asked.

"She's wet. Let me change her first."

While she was attending to the baby, Julia said, "I forgot to ask you, how's Jessica?" Pascal's daughter had married the son of one of Pascal's clients four years earlier. The last Julia had heard Jessica was pregnant.

Pascal's eyes reflected sorrow. "She lost the baby."

"I'm so sorry, Pascal," Julia said. "How far along was she?"

"Four months." Pascal sat on the nursery chair, her fingers interlaced over her knee. "This is the second time."

"I didn't know that. Poor Jessica. She must be heartbroken."

Before Pascal could answer, the phone chimed.

Julia jumped. She handed Francesca to Pascal, and darted into the den. "Yes?" she answered.

"How did you make out with the money?"

"I can only get a hundred and ninety-five thousand right now, but I might be able to get more in a few days,"

Julia said, trying to make her voice sound as if she wasn't pleading. "It's the weekend; nothing's open."

Pascal came to stand beside her with the baby, resting her free hand on Julia's shoulder as she listened.

"That's not enough, Julia. Sorry. It was nice talking to you."

"Wait," Julia begged. "How can you be so inhuman? This is my daughter."

"Like I told you yesterday, it's business. We put a lot of work and expense into this. We have to recover our costs and make a profit."

"What kind of monsters are you?" Julia shrieked, tears filling her eyes.

Pascal moved to where Julia could see her and shook her head.

The man at the other end remained silent, but she knew he was still there; she could hear atmospheric noise.

"Please tell me how she is?" Julia pleaded.

"She's fine," he replied.

"What about her little boy. How old is he? What's his name?"

The man sighed. "He looks around four or five. Name's Oliver."

Julia choked back a sob. "Please let them go."

"Can't do that, ma'am."

"At least tell me where they are."

She was answered by silence. This time it was complete, no atmosphere.

Francesca started to howl.

***

On the morning of the fourth day, Catherine sensed a change in the air.

"Wash up and make yourself pretty," Ryan said after a breakfast of cereal and tinned milk diluted with water. "Today, we're rolling."

Catherine's heart missed a beat. "You mean...?"

"Yup, we've found a buyer."

A hopeless emptiness descended on Catherine. "But what about my mother? Didn't you call her? You said if I ... paid you...."

"Honey, you'd have paid us anyway," Jake said.

"But did you call her?"

Jake nodded. "She's a cagey lady, your ma."

Tears of frustration and disappointment filled Catherine eyes. "What did she say?"

"At first, she didn't believe we had you, but I managed to convince her. She kept saying she didn't have that sort of money, but she could raise it if we gave her some time." he shoved his hands in his pockets and walked out the door.

Catherine grabbed Oliver's hand and went after him. "So?"

He opened the door of the vehicle and turned to look at her. "Honey, we don't have time to mess around. Anyway we got a better offer." He spat on the ground and climbed in behind the wheel. "Come on. Get in; we've got an appointment to keep."

Catherine looked back and saw Ryan standing behind her, a blank look on his face. Reluctantly, she helped Oliver climb into the vehicle, and got in beside him.

"I don't know how you can do something like this," she said, intent on keeping tears at bay. "We're not animals to be bought and sold."

"It's business, honey. You have to understand the market forces at work here. Supply and demand. The merchandise goes to the one who can pay the price, and you're luxury goods, baby," Ryan replied through the window.

Jake started up the four-wheel-drive and put it in gear. "Catch you later, buddy," he called out to Ryan as they started to move.

"Did you tell my mother I'm all right," Catherine asked. "And that I have a son?"

"Course I did."

Catherine sighed. At least she knows I'm still alive, she thought. If only I could get away. She put her arm around Oliver's shoulder and hugged him. She felt a rage building up inside her at her impotence, her helplessness and lack of control over her own destiny. She was so close to her family and yet could do nothing to bring them together. She willed herself not to cry and frighten Oliver.

The vehicle jolted and bumped over the rough track, throwing them about in their seats and making Catherine feel sick.

"Where are we going, Mommy?" he asked.

"I don't know, sweetheart, just for a ride."

"When can we go home to my Daddy and Granny?"

What could she say? She couldn't lie to him, yet the truth would hurt him too much.

"We may not see them for a long time, Oliver," she said. "We're going to a new house."

"But why? I want to go home." He rubbed his eye with his knuckle.

"Remember our secret?" she replied.

Oliver nodded. "You mean..."

Catherine put her finger to her lips and looked at Jake at the wheel in front of them.

"Where are you taking us?" she said a little louder, so she would be heard over the noise of the fan.

"I guess there's no harm telling you. Seattle. Remember the rich Jew?"

Catherine screwed her eyes shut. Oh God, not again. She envisioned an old man dressed in black, a skullcap atop his grey hair, or maybe he would be bald and fat. The only positive thing she could think of about the situation was that it was a lot closer to Vancouver. If she could get away, she wouldn't have so far to go.

"What about my son?"

"That depends on you," Jake replied ominously.

They reached the road at the end of the trail and turned right. A few meters down the road, they stopped behind a van that was parked on the shoulder. The van was windowless except for the driver's compartment. By its glossy green finish and unfamiliar design, Catherine guessed it was new.

After waiting for a truck to go by and disappear down the highway, Jake told them to get out. The driver of the van stepped down and came around to meet them. He was an African American dressed in a high-necked navy blue business jacket and matching fitted trousers. The man looked about forty and was clean-shaven with close-cropped hair and caramel-colored skin. When he came closer, she could smell the clean tea-like scent of his cologne.

"Hey, Jake my man, right on time." He shook hands with the kidnapper then turned and looked at Catherine. "Nice," he said, smiling at her.

"Yeah, this is Catherine," Jake replied. "And this is her son, Oliver."

"How was it?" the new man asked.

"Easy," Jake replied. "Piece of cake. They're much more docile when they've got a kid to worry about."

"Hmm, never thought of that. Maybe we should make that a feature, young mothers." He went over to the van and slid a side door open, then turned to her. "Get in, please."

As she started towards the van, Jake squeezed her shoulder. "Bye, honey. It was nice knowing you," he said with a wink.

Catherine scowled and shook him off. She lifted her son in first and then stepped up behind him. The interior was a surprise. It had high-backed padded seats covered in soft grey suede-like fabric, or maybe real suede. The floor and walls were covered in plush fabric matching the seats. The compartment also contained a small refrigerator, a music system and a small flat-screen monitor embedded in the wall behind the driver, and a small slit of a window behind the driver's compartment.

"Make yourselves comfortable," the man said. "There drinks in the cooler." As he slid the door shut, lights came on inside, small spots sunk in the ceiling that gave soft, even illumination. Catherine noticed there was no handle inside the door.

The van started to move, its electric motor humming faintly. The ride was pleasantly smooth; a welcome change after the four-wheel drive and unpaved road. After strapping Oliver into one of the chairs, Catherine opened the refrigerator and saw it was filled with soft drinks and bottles of juice. There was also a small container of cheese spread, some cherry tomatoes and a jar of olives. She wondered if there was anything to go with them and looked in the tiny cupboard next to the fridge. It contained some packets of crackers, potato and corn chips as well as a box of cookies. At least they wouldn't go hungry. In a drawer above the cupboard, she found some knives and forks, a pile of disposable plates and a tube of plastic cups. He seemed to have thought of everything.

"Would you like some juice, sweetheart?"

"What kind?"

"Well there's apple, orange and cranberry." Cranberry? It had some significance for her, but she couldn't put her finger on what it was. The only thing she could associate with it was a time when she'd felt happy and safe.

"Apple, please."

She unscrewed the top and poured some apple juice into a paper cup for him. Then she remembered. Pascal, her mother's friend. She always drank cranberry juice. She fought back tears at the memory of her happy childhood as she took out a can of tonic water and opened it, then sat back in one of the comfortable chairs.

"I wish we could see outside, Mommy."

"I know, so do I. I'm sorry, Oliver."

"Try the TV." They were both startled by the disembodied voice.

Catherine looked up to see where it was coming from, but there was no sign of any speakers. Obviously, he could hear everything they were saying, in addition to being able to speak to them.

She looked around for a remote control to turn the set on, but found nothing. "How do we turn it on," she asked the front panel.

"The arms of the chairs; just lift up the flap."

Catherine was overcome by a feeling of unreality. This was so different from her experiences over the past ten years; it was almost as if she was dreaming. Never in her wildest imagining had she ever envisioned herself in such a situation. Her original abduction had been mundane compared with this.

She found the lip of the panel on the arm and pried it up to reveal a standard remote control setup. All she had to do was press the On button. She searched around the channels until she found the children's spiritual network that Oliver liked. It was the only channel Keaton would allow the children to watch. He put a block on the other channels so that neither she nor the children were able to tune into anything else, although in the evenings, they sometimes watched a gospel program for adults.

After they'd been on the road for about three hours, the van stopped. Catherine heard the driver's door close with a clunk then the door panel on the side slid open and he reached inside. She watched apprehensively as he opened the fridge and took out a can of Pepsi then he went and sat on the doorsill with his back to her. Through the open door, she could see a weed-filled roadside ditch backed up by a two-meter hedge. There didn't seem to be any traffic on the road apart from their vehicle.

She stood up and stretched. "Can we go out and stretch our legs?" she asked, longing as much for fresh air and natural light as exercise.

"Sorry," the man said. "You have to stay inside 'til we get there."

"How long will it take?"

"About three more hours."

Julia looked at the man's back. How could he be so trusting? It would be easy for her to attack him from behind—if she could find something to hit him with; a bottle of juice, maybe? That was the heaviest thing she could think of. She opened the fridge door and touched one of the bottles. It clinked against the one next to it.

"Careful," the man said, as if he could read her mind. He stood up and moved away from the door.

"Mommy, I need to go to the comfort room," Oliver said. He was starting to get restless.

"All right, sweetheart." Catherine unbuckled his seat belt and led him to the doorway. "Can I take him outside to go to the toilet?" she asked.

The man looked at her and shook his head. "Inside at the back," he said.

Catherine looked over her shoulder at what she had taken for another cupboard. It jutted out in the rear corner of the van, reaching from floor to ceiling and was about the width of a man's shoulders. She turned Oliver round and squeezed between two of the chairs. When she opened the door of the cubicle, she was greeted by the clean fragrance of lavender air freshener that reminded her of the soap her mother used to buy. The cubicle contained a small chemical toilet and a tissue dispenser. They'd thought of everything.

"Here you go, sweetheart," she said squeezing into the other corner behind the chairs to let him pass. "Don't forget to put the seat up."

While Oliver was in the bathroom, Catherine stood in the doorway and spoke to the driver. "I don't understand why you go to the trouble of making us so comfortable after..."

"The customers might be disappointed if we turned up in an old wreck. We're trading in a quality product and packaging makes all the difference. We want to make the right impression; it's good business."

He stood up, opened the passenger door of the van and pulled out a zippered nylon bag. "Take this. It's some clean clothes. When we are moving again, you can get changed."

Catherine gave him a withering look as she took the bag then turned her back on him. It was obviously no good talking to him if that was the way he thought. A few minutes later, the driver closed the side door and then climbed into the front and drove on.

Nevertheless, she was thankful to change out of the clothes she'd been wearing for the last four days. Even though there were no facilities for bathing, she felt measurably better. They were simple, but obviously quality clothes: underwear, a pair of beige linen trousers and matching shirt, both a little on the loose side, but a welcome change from what she had been wearing. In addition, there were a pair of shorts and a shirt for Oliver, but no shoes for either of them. She rubbed their sandals with Oliver's cast-off t-shirt to remove some of the accumulated dust.

After another hour, Catherine became aware of more traffic on the road with them, and the van was going much faster. It slowed down once, caught in heavy traffic, and then sped up again as soon as it was free. An hour later, they slowed down again, but this time the slow-moving traffic was continuous. Once, she heard the screaming jets of heavy aircraft coming in low overhead. Finally, the van turned right off the highway and started to climb a steep hill. They continued for another fifteen minutes, going up and down hills, twisting and turning through the streets. Outside, they could hear the sounds of a large city all round them.

Seattle, Catherine thought. If they had told her the truth, they were only a little over two hundred kilometers from home. She'd never been to Seattle, but she knew from films and video that it was very hilly, so she was fairly sure that's where they were.

The van slowed down again, then stopped. She heard a tinny voice outside to which the driver replied, then a gate rolled back and the van started moving again. It drove a slow sinuous course for a few meters and stopped again.

A child's voice yelled, "Aaron, they're here."

The driver got down from the van and came around to open the side door. "You can get out now; we're there."

Chapter Thirty

Catherine lifted Oliver out of the van and set him on the ground, then looked around. Her heart was thumping so furiously; she was sure it must be visible. Her throat tightened, making her struggle for breath.

They were in a large garden in front of a wide stucco building. A boy of about eight came running around the van.

"Hi," he said. "What's his name?" he asked pointing to Oliver.

"Oliver," her son replied.

"That's a funny name. My name's Jonathan, but you can call me Jon. Are you going to live here as well?"

"What are you doing, Jon? Interrogating them already?"

The man who spoke had come through an archway in the middle of the building. He looked about thirty and was startlingly handsome with a wiry build. His black curly hair was cut about ear-length framing his face in a dark halo. He had blue eyes, the irises ringed with a darker blue, which made them very striking. He was about five centimeters taller than Catherine.

He came forward, smiling and holding out his hand to shake. "Hi, you must be Catherine. I'm Aaron. Welcome."

Catherine was stunned. Like an automaton, she proffered her hand and felt him clasp it in a warm dry grip.

She nodded and looked at the ground, conscious of her face turning red.

"And this must be Oliver." He crouched so that he was level with Oliver. "What do they call you? Ollie?"

"Oh, no," Catherine stammered. "Just Oliver."

Aaron stood up again. "I think you're going to like it here, Oliver."

Oliver took his mother's hand and leaned against her leg.

"Well, I expect you'd like to freshen up. Just let me have a word with Mr. Moscrop and I'll show you to your rooms."

He went around the other side of the van where he and the driver held a muffled conversation then Moscrop climbed into the van and started the motor.

"Right," Aaron said, brushing her back with his fingers. "Let's get you settled."

His touch sent a current through Catherine. She could barely keep herself from shivering. Could this be the 'rich Jew'? He was so far from what she had expected, and feared, she felt as if she was dreaming. And he wasn't wearing a black suit. On the contrary, he was wearing khaki shorts, a short-sleeved gold shirt, and brown sandals. His legs and arms were tanned and covered with black hair.

"I'll let you get settled in before introducing you to the rest of the family," he said.

He led them through the archway into a courtyard, which had tiled paving surrounding a lawn with big shady tree in the middle and flower borders. The courtyard was surrounded on all four sides by buildings, beautiful structures. Two had glass walls between slender columns of warm pink stucco. The remaining two had smaller multi-paned windows and regular doors. Several people watched through the window wall on the right—two young men and

277

some teenage boys, also a striking older woman with dark hair tied back from her face.

Rather than go to the building where the people were waiting, Aaron took them around the back of the house opposite. They came to another garden with tree-shaded lawns and a small pond, surrounded by flowerbeds and shrubbery. A smaller structure stood on the far side of the garden, backed by a three-meter-high brick wall. Catherine noticed the wall continued around all three sides of the garden, closing it off from the outside world.

"This is your house," he said, pushing open the French doors. "I hope you like it."

My own house? Surely he can't be serious, but she decided to go along with it until someone saw fit to clarify the situation. The little house was unlike the modern structures of rest of the compound, more like an English country cottage, built of pale orange bricks with two sets of French windows facing the garden. The windows opened into a sitting room furnished with a sofa and several armchairs upholstered in yellow with white piping. Two floral patterned rugs sat atop the gleaming parquet floor. The room also contained two tall, glass-fronted bookcases filled with real books, and there was also an entertainment center with disk player, monitor and video player. No computer or any sort of com equipment, she noticed.

"It's beautiful," she said.

"It used to be a guest cottage," Aaron explained. "Let me show you around."

First, he showed her the modern kitchen and dining room then went through an opening that led into a short hallway where he opened a door close to the sitting room.

"This is your bedroom. There's your bathroom," he pointed to a door on the left side. "Now, let's show this young man his room."

He took Oliver's hand and led them down the hallway towards the back of the cottage. Catherine followed numbly. "We haven't had a chance to set it up for a child; we didn't know he was coming until yesterday," Aaron apologized. "You'll be able to help with that."

The bedroom, decorated in taupe and white, contained a queen-size bed with a turquoise duvet, built-in wardrobe and drawers finished in a beautiful blond wood, an entertainment monitor on one of the cabinets, and a couple of comfortable chairs with turquoise and taupe covers. Another door led into a bathroom.

"I don't know what to say," Catherine stammered. "I mean, this is so ... amazing."

Aaron smiled. "You'll get used to it. Oh, by the way, the door in the kitchen opens onto a private patio. You can eat outside when you feel like it." He stopped and looked around as if he was making sure he'd explained everything. "I'll leave you both to get settled, then." He turned to go, then came back. "I almost forgot, you'll find some clothes in the wardrobe and drawers in your room. Mother ordered a few things in several sizes, so you'd have something that fits until we can order more. I'll check and see if there's anything Oliver's size at the house. There's sure to be something of Jonathan's that he's outgrown. I'll be right back."

"Are we going to live here?" Oliver asked after Aaron had left.

"I suppose so," Catherine replied. "Do you like it?"

"I'd rather be at home with my father."

She gathered him in her arms and snuggled him. "I know, sweetheart, but sometimes, you don't get to choose." She kissed the top of his head, noticing the smoky odor of his hair then set him down. "How would you like to take a bath and wash your hair?"

"Can I have a shower?"

"I think a bath would be better," she replied. "Then you can sit and soak while mommy takes a shower." There was no point in having him sit around waiting until he had something to put on.

After shampooing Oliver's hair, Catherine went to her own room. It really was amazing, the taupe carpet extending into the bathroom and the colorful abstract paintings on the walls of both rooms. She pulled aside the sheer curtains and found Venetian blinds covering the multi-paned window that overlooked the side garden. She went over to the built-in closet and opened one of the doors. Three simple cotton dresses hung on the hangers, one with vertical white and dark blue stripes, one a multi-color floral design, and the third plain green with white piping around the neck and armholes. She took them all out and held them up in front of her, looking in the mirror that covered the bathroom door. She wouldn't know which one would fit until she tried them on, and she wasn't going to do that until she had showered and washed her hair.

She was just about to open one of the drawers when she heard a soft knock on the door and Aaron poked his head around. He held out a bundle of boy's clothes to her.

"Here's a few things. They may be a little large for him, but they'll be all right until tomorrow."

Catherine took the clothes from him. "Thank you," she said shyly. "He's taking a bath. I'd better go and see if he's ready to come out."

Aaron smiled at her again, the warmth extending to his beautiful eyes. "There's some food in the kitchen, if you're hungry," he said. "But don't eat too much. Save some space for dinner. You'll be eating with the family tonight so that you can be introduced to everyone. I'll come back for you at eighteen-thirty."

Catherine took the clothes into Oliver's bathroom and got him out of the bath. She dressed him a pair of shorts that reached his knees and a t-shirt that was almost as long then they went into the kitchen. She made him a peanut butter sandwich and poured a glass of orange juice, and then she left him to eat his snack while she took a shower.

When Aaron came for them at eighteen-thirty, they were both asleep on her bed; Catherine in a white toweling bathrobe with Oliver curled up in her lap. She woke up when Aaron cleared his throat in the bedroom doorway, momentarily uncertain of her whereabouts. Then it all flooded back into her awareness with a mixture of apprehension and something lighter. It had been such a long time since she'd been really happy, apart from the joy she got from Oliver, that she wasn't sure how it felt any more.

"Sorry, I fell asleep," she said superfluously as she pulled her arm out from under her son and sat up. "It won't take me long to finish getting dressed."

She looked at Aaron, wondering if he was going to stand there and watch her, but he seemed to take the hint. "I'll wait in the sitting room."

She tried on the blue and white striped dress first and it seemed to fit all right, so she kept it on. All she needed to do was brush her hair and she was ready. There had been no cosmetics in Blessings, so she had never been concerned about them and it didn't occur to her to use those sitting on a crystal tray in the bathroom, along with several flasks of expensive-looking perfume.

She woke Oliver and brushed his hair, then took him into the sitting room. "We're ready," she said meekly.

Aaron stood up and looked at her appreciatively. "You look very nice," he said.

They crossed the garden to the house from which the people had been watching when they arrived. On the way, Aaron explained a little about his home.

"This is the Goldman family compound. That's the main house," he said, pointing to their destination, "And the one adjacent to it is what we call 'the cousins house'. My father is now the head of the family. It used to be Uncle Benjamin, but he and his wife were killed in a plane crash five years ago. Now his four sons, my cousins, live there." He steered Catherine to a garden seat shaded by a tree with delicate fern-like leaves. She later found out it was a mimosa. "Let's sit here for a few minutes."

Oliver spotted a swing hanging from the branch of a nearby maple. He looked at his mother hopefully and when she nodded permission, he ran over to the swing and lay forward over the seat then began to kick himself back and forth.

"He seems like a very well-behaved child," Aaron commented. "Not like my rambunctious little brother, Jon; he's a complete savage. Anyway, to continue: My mother's name is Yosefina Costa and my father is David. My other two brothers are Yefrem—he's eighteen—and Yitzak, who is sixteen. As you may have guessed, my mother goes in for traditional names. She grew up in Israel."

"Will they all be there tonight?" Catherine asked, wondering how she would keep track of everyone. She was dreading the coming meeting, feeling like a new slave being offered up for approval.

"All except my cousin, Jack. He's off on a business trip."

"What do you all do?" Catherine asked.

"We run the family business, mostly. Actually, I work on my own project." He nodded towards the building opposite the main house. "That's my lab. My cousin Freddie and I are working on a new process for sound recording. You may hear some weird noises coming from there sometimes, but don't be alarmed."

A light went on in the cousins' house and Catherine noticed a woman sitting in a chair by the window. Catherine's eyes rested on her, not really paying attention, until she realized that the woman sat like a statue, never moving, not even a twitch. Then part of the glass wall of the main house slid open and the dark haired woman she'd seen earlier leaned out.

"We're ready to eat now," she said in a beautifully modulated voice with a slight accent.

"Come on Oliver," Aaron said, holding his hand out to the boy. "Dinner's ready."

Oliver straightened up from the swing and trotted over to Aaron to take the proffered hand. Catherine was amazed by her son's easy manner with this man he'd only met a few hours ago. He'd certainly not been so relaxed with Ryan and Jake, always staying well clear of them when they were around. Maybe he was a good judge of character. She hoped so.

The dining room in the Goldman house held a table large enough to seat twenty people. It was made of a material that looked and felt to Catherine like opaque black glass, but it could have been some kind of highly polished stone. The chairs were black wood with high, slatted backs and yellow-green seat cushions. A long buffet along the wall held a number of hot and cold dished and piles of various sized plates.

"Catherine," Aaron's mother said as they entered. "Welcome. I'm Yosefina, but you can call me Yosi. Everyone does, even my impudent sons." She gave Catherine a warm smile and held out a slender tanned hand with impeccably manicured nails.

As she tentatively shook hands with Aaron's mother, Catherine became conscious of her own work-roughened hands with their short-clipped fingernails.

"The dress is very becoming on you," Yosi continued.

Catherine was not convinced. She felt like a hick next to Aaron's elegant mother in her floor-length yellow silk sheath. Her olive skin and makeup were flawless and her dark, grey-streaked hair was fastened up in an elaborate cascade of curls that must have taken her, or her stylist, hours to arrange. She gave off a glorious floral fragrance.

Next, Catherine endured inspection by and introduction to each of Aaron's brothers and three of his cousins. While this was going on, Oliver had sidled over to the buffet and was walking its length, studying the dishes of food.

"Help yourselves," Yosi said. "I should warn you, Catherine, this is a vegetarian household, but I think you will find the food tasty enough. We have an excellent chef."

Without waiting for further encouragement, the younger boys rushed to grab plates and started to pile them with the contents of various dishes.

Aaron and Catherine followed more sedately and picked up plates. "Mother believes that by not eating meat, we can make a small contribution to restoring the environment," Aaron said.

"I don't understand," Catherine said.

"Raising animals for food is incredibly damaging to land," Aaron explained. "Not to mention the pollution of rivers and streams. It is much more economical and productive to use the land for the cultivation of food crops. Not only that, vegetarianism is much healthier. You avoid all that fat and cholesterol and chemicals that come with meat." He picked up a serving spoon and loaded his plate with something colorful and spicy from one of the bowls. "Try some of this, it's delicious."

"What is it?" she asked.

"Mexican salad. It goes great with these *chilis rellenos—*stuffed peppers."

They reached the end of the buffet, then carried their plates over to the table and sat down. Catherine lifted Oliver onto a chair next to her. She had put some of the less exotic food on a small plate for him.

"Are we going to say grace, Mommy?" he asked, speaking for the first time. He seemed to be as overwhelmed as she was by everything.

Catherine was aware that everyone had stopped eating and was waiting for her response. Conscious of her son's need for something familiar he could relate to, she replied. "Do you want to?"

He nodded, then closed his eyes and put his hands together in front of his chin. Together they softly recited the simple, familiar words. "Oh, Lord, bless this house and all who dwell in it, and thank you for Thy bountiful gifts and the food we are about eat. Amen."

To her astonishment, Catherine heard several voices echo the Amen, including Aaron's.

Just as they were starting to eat, a middle-aged man hurried into the room. He was about Aaron's height, but a little heavier around the middle. His hair was cropped short and stood around his head in a cap of black curls peppered in grey. He had a grey beard and Aaron's remarkable eyes. After kissing his wife, he came around the table to where Catherine was sitting.

"Sorry I'm late. The ferry broke down again." He held out his hand. "David Goldman. Don't get up." Catherine had to twist around in her chair to shake his hand. "And who's this young man?" he asked, patting Oliver on the head.

Oliver twisted his neck and looked up at the stranger. "Oliver Webster," he said.

David Goldman laughed and rubbed his hands together. "Good. Welcome to our house."

"Is that your last name, Webster?" one of Aaron's teenage brothers asked.

"It's my married name," Catherine said.

There was an uncomfortable silence as the implications of this statement sank in. Even though these people were charming and kind to her, Catherine saw no reason for pretending that she was here by choice. The fact that they had bought her was humiliating and she didn't intend to make it easy for them.

The silence was broken by Aaron's other brother, Yefrem, asking, "What's your real last name?"

"Finisterra," she said.

After they'd finished eating, the family gathered in the living room, all except the two older cousins who were going out. Jonathan, at his mother's suggestion, took Oliver off somewhere to show him his games.

When they entered the living room, Catherine noticed a woman sitting in a chair in the corner. She was quite attractive, with perfect skin and blonde hair cut stylishly short. Her voluptuous figure was encased in a short silvery sheath. Catherine couldn't understand why she hadn't joined the rest of the family for dinner. She looked at the woman, waiting for her to move or say something to acknowledge their entrance, but the woman remained perfectly still.

Seeing her bewilderment, one of Aaron's brothers burst out laughing. "Say hello to Catherine, Sofia."

The woman jerked as if she had been woken up, then she smiled and turned her head towards the brother. "Good evening. How are you?" she said in a rather mechanical although attractively musical voice.

Catherine was about to reply when she caught the expression on Aaron's face. It warned her that things may not be quite as they seemed. "It's all right, Catherine," he said. "She's not real. Her response is voice-activated when you say her name."

"But what is she?" Catherine asked.

David Goldman put his arm around her shoulder. "She's the goose that lays the Goldmans' golden eggs." Seeing she was still puzzled, he continued, "She's the original prototype of the Ladylove."

"The...?" Catherine still didn't know what he was talking about.

Aaron took pity on her. "Haven't you heard of Ladyloves?" Catherine shook her head. "They were invented by my grandfather. Sort of a substitute woman for men who don't have wives. They're what made our family fortune. This one is a bit primitive; they're much more lifelike now."

"They respond to verbal cues," one of the cousins added. "Watch this. Sofia, I'm home, honey," he said a little louder.

The pseudo-woman stood up and walked towards him, smiling. "Did you have a good day, dear?" she inquired, putting her arms around him and kissing him.

Her movements were a bit jerky and the kiss missed his mouth and landed beside his nose, but she was still realistic enough to amaze Catherine.

The cousin grinned and said, "She has lots of other skills, too, and I don't mean cooking and cleaning."

Catherine felt her face redden.

"She gets the picture, Freddie," Aaron said, guiding Catherine to one of the sofas.

Freddie, Jack, Charlie. Obviously, the cousins' mother had preferred more commonplace, old-fashioned names for her children.

David Goldman put some music on—haunting, plaintive melodies played on a violin.

"Tomorrow, we'll get you both measured for some new clothes," Aaron's mother said, looking Catherine up and down. "I'll get the hairdresser to have a look at you too."

"Don't be offended," Aaron said. "Mother's a designer. All she thinks about is clothes and style."

"My mother's a designer too," Catherine blurted thoughtlessly.

This aroused Yosi's interest. "What a coincidence. Do you want to tell us about her. What field is she in? Where does she live?"

I don't believe these people, Catherine thought. Here they've just purchased me like a slave from a bunch of criminals, and now they want me to pretend I'm a guest and chat with them as if there were nothing unusual about the situation.

Seeing Catherine's expression, Aaron said. "Maybe she doesn't want to talk about it, mother."

Yosi had the grace to look embarrassed. "I'm sorry, Catherine, I didn't think."

This endeared the woman slightly to Catherine, but not completely. "I haven't seen my mother in ten years," she said. "When I was kidnapped the first time, she designed fabric and gift wrap."

This brought silence for a few minutes as everyone contemplated the implications of Catherine's statement.

Aaron broke the silence. "Catherine is a beautiful name but it's a bit of a mouthful; is there something shorter we could call you?"

Catherine thought about this. The only person who had ever used a diminutive of her name was Joanne, and she didn't fancy being called Cathy. It would remind her too much of her life in Idaho. "I guess you could call me Kate," she replied.

"Good, Kate it is, then."

New person, new name, she thought.

A repetitive chime sounded from somewhere in the house. David Goldman got up from his seat. "Excuse me, that must be the call I've been waiting for," he said, hurrying from the room.

A com. Of course they'd have a com, she thought. *They probably have several if they run a business from here. If only I could find out where they were kept and get to one without anyone seeing me.*

Catherine yawned, covering her mouth with her hand.

"You must be tired," Aaron said, standing up. "Would you like to go back now?"

Catherine looked at the digital clock on the entertainment console. It was ten-thirty. She couldn't believe the time had gone so fast. She nodded and stood up. "Where's Oliver?" she asked.

"I'll find him," Aaron said. He went out into the hall and yelled, "*Jonathan!*"

They seemed to be a family of shouters. In Blessings, children were trained not to yell, but to use decorum at all times. It caused a noticeable lack of spontaneity, especially when they were playing. Catherine thought she preferred the Goldman's way.

"By the way, what size shoes do you wear, Kate?" Yosi Costa, asked while they were waiting for Oliver. "We can have some samples brought over for you tomorrow."

289

Hearing her new name for the first time gave Catherine an unexpected feeling of sophistication. It really did make her feel like a different person. She liked it.

"Six and a half," she replied. Yosi was certainly an improvement over Mrs. Webster. She believed she could be happy here, if only she could see her family again. If only she wasn't a prisoner. Maybe, after he had a little time to get used to her, she could persuade Aaron...

She realized Yosi was looking at her and blushed. "Thank you for everything," she said. "The food was delicious."

Oliver ran into the room and grabbed her hand. "Mommy!" he grinned up at her. Catherine was moved to realize he was already relaxing some of the self-control he had been forced to practice at home.

When they got back to the cottage, Aaron went in first to turn on the lights. He waited while she put Oliver to bed. Catherine's heart thudded as she closed the door to his room and saw Aaron standing in the hallway near her bedroom, looking at her speculatively. She stood outside her son's door, afraid to move, not quite sure of what she wanted to happen. She was his now to do with as he wished. He had bought her; he owned her.

She looked down at the floor and waited.

"Come here," he said, holding out his arms.

She went to him and he enfolded her in an embrace. His heart was beating fast through his shirt and she could smell the faint man odor under the clean detergent scent of clothes. It felt good to have his arms around her and she relaxed, wondering what would happen next.

"I think you've had enough for one day." He held her away from him and kissed her on the forehead. "Get some sleep. I'll see you in the morning. Goodnight, Kate." He pushed open the bedroom door and turned to leave.

Another surprise and she had to admit, something of a disappointment. Catherine was even more confused as she got ready for bed. It was hard to believe she'd woken up in a primitive shack that same morning and was now going to bed in the most luxurious home she had ever seen from the inside.

Chapter Thirty-one

Fem-traders

Despite an increase in government funding, federal and local law enforcement agencies have failed to curb the trade in women and girls. In North America, the price paid for a healthy woman of childbearing age can be as much as $300,000 and a young woman with a female child can fetch as much as $750,000.

Excerpt from Blog on World Net

What may have been an explanation for Aaron's apparent lack of physical interest in her came the following morning. She and Oliver were eating their breakfast of cereal, fruit and pineapple juice when Aaron arrived.

"Good morning. Did you sleep well?" he asked, plopping himself down in an empty chair.

"Yes, thank you," Catherine replied.

"Mother's waiting for you. She wants to measure you and Oliver for some new clothes." He helped himself to a peach and started to peel it with a fruit knife. "A doctor is coming later this morning to give you both a checkup."

"Why?" she asked. "There's nothing wrong with us."

"I know. You certainly look healthy enough, but just to make sure..."

When the doctor told her he was going to take a vaginal swab, Catherine realized that was probably the point of the whole checkup. They wanted to make sure she had no STDs before Aaron slept with her. If she were honest, she had to admit she wasn't sure herself. She could have been infected by the two men who had abducted her from Blessings.

After the doctor's examination was finished, Yosi took Catherine to see the schoolroom and meet the tutor. Earlier, while taking Catherine's measurements in her studio, Yosi had advised her that Oliver would be welcome to join the other boys in their lessons. A tutor came every morning to teach Jonathan until he was old enough to go to prep school.

The schoolroom was in the building at the front of the quadrangle. It was on the ground level, a bright room with windows facing both directions, looking out on the driveway and the courtyard. There were six workstations as well as shelves of real and electronic books. The walls were hung with maps and posters of animals and plants, famous people: artists, explorers, and scientists.

"Gordon, I'd like you to meet Kate," Yosi said to a slim red-haired man of about thirty-five. "She's going to be living with us. And this is her son, Oliver." She turned to Catherine. "How old is Oliver?"

"He'll be five in November," Catherine replied.

"Pleased to meet you," Gordon said. He had a slight Scottish accent. "And you too, Oliver."

Oliver looked at him with solemn eyes.

"How do you feel about starting school, Oliver?"

Oliver's eyes lit up. He looked up at Catherine. "Can I, Mommy?" When she nodded, he turned to Gordon and said, "I'd like to."

"I think you'll get along fine," the tutor said. "You're a smart boy, I can see that." He turned back to Catherine. "If you'd like to bring him over tomorrow at eight-thirty, we'll get him started."

"Do you have any questions?" Yosi asked.

Catherine rubbed her hands together, unable to think of a way to say what she had in mind. She wanted to go to school as well. Seeing the computer terminals not only made her homesick, they reminded her of her interrupted education. She looked longingly at the workstations then shook her head.

"Right. Let's go and have lunch."

Catherine took Oliver's hand. "Thank you, Gordon," she said shyly. "We'll be here in the morning."

"We'll start him out with a couple of hours, if that's all right with you, Ms Costa." Yosi nodded. "Kids his age have trouble keeping still any longer than that, but he'll get used to it in time."

They left the schoolroom by the courtyard door and crossed over to the main house.

"I do have a question," Catherine said timidly.

"What is it?" Yosi asked.

"What am I going to do all day? I mean ... well ... I'm used to working."

"What sort of work?" Yosi inquired, pushing open the sliding glass door.

"Taking care of the house, cleaning, cooking."

"Well you certainly won't have to do anything like that here, unless you want to in your own place, of course. We've got plenty of help for that sort of thing." Yosi led them into an eating area off the kitchen where Aaron and his brothers were already having their lunch.

"Sit down, both of you. Eric will bring your food."

Catherine found places for herself and Oliver at the massive oval table, which had room enough for at least ten people. It stood in a bow window facing the vegetable garden at the side of the house. The kitchen was huge, all white and burnished steel with terra cotta tiles on the floor. Oliver was sitting next to Jonathan who immediately began plying him with questions, in response to which her son became more and more animated. Glancing up from under her brows, Catherine found Aaron watching her with a slight smile on his lips.

She leaned back in her chair while an Asian man in a white cotton shirt and shorts set a glass bowl of milky pale green liquid in front of her. Taking her cue from Yosi, she picked up a spoon and dipped into it. When she put it into her mouth, she was surprised that it was cold. She savored the taste for a moment before swallowing it, not sure if she liked it. It had a creamy, slightly sour taste and something that seemed familiar that she was at a loss to identify.

"How do you like it?" Yosi asked. "It's iced cucumber soup. It's made with yogurt and a few other things. Perfect for this hot weather."

She took another taste and nodded. "It's different," she replied. "I think I could get used to it, though."

"Mommy, I don't like it," Oliver said, putting his spoon down in the bowl.

Catherine reddened with embarrassment, surprised at his outspokenness. He would never have dared to say such a thing in front of his grandmother. In a way, she was pleased at the change in him. She didn't want him to turn into one of those dull, docile children in Blessings who cringe at the least confrontation.

"It's all right," Aaron said. "He can have something else. I used to hate it myself when I was his age, but it grows on you." He turned round in his chair. "Hey, Eric, got anything else Oliver might like?"

Eric came over and took Oliver's bowl away. "What sort of things does he like?" he asked Catherine.

She looked at her son, then at the dishes in the center of the table. There were bread rolls, fresh fruit, salads and several varieties of cheese. "It's all right," she said. "I can make him a cheese sandwich and he can have some salad. I'm sorry to be such a bother."

Their soup finished, everyone else started piling salad onto plates and cutting pieces of cheese.

"I'll walk you back," Aaron said when they'd finished eating.

He took her arm as they sauntered across the lawn behind the cousins' house towards her cottage. "How was your morning?"

Catherine shrugged. "All right, I guess." She had not really enjoyed it, but it seemed churlish to complain.

An elderly man came around the side of her cottage carrying an edge trimmer. Catherine's eyes lit up. "Is that the gardener?" she asked in a low voice.

"Yes. That's Elijah." He stopped walking. "Elijah, I'd like you to meet somebody. She's going to be living in the cottage with her son here."

The old man put the trimmer on the ground and came towards them, wiping his hands on his olive trousers.

"This is Ms Finisterra and Oliver."

Catherine wasn't sure whether she should shake his hand or not. He didn't seem to expect her to, so she just smiled.

"Pleased to meet you, ma'am."

"Me too," she replied.

Elijah picked up the trimmer and went back to work.

Seeing her yearning look, Aaron asked, "What is it?"

"I was talking to your mother before lunch about what I'm going to do," she said.

They went in through the French doors into the cool sitting room.

"Can I go play with Jon?" Oliver asked.

Catherine looked quizzically to Aaron.

"Sure, go ahead, if you can find him," Aaron said. As Oliver trotted off across the lawn, he added. "I hope Oliver's not in for a disappointment. Jon is a lot older than he is; he might get tired of Oliver once the novelty wears off."

"He's going to be starting school tomorrow," Catherine said. "But I'm afraid he'll miss being able to play with boys his own age. He'll miss his brother too."

Aaron looked at her sharply. "I didn't realize you had another son."

She wondered why he hadn't asked her anything about her life before she came here. He probably can't handle the idea that she had a life, which because of him, she would never return to. Not that she was keen to go back to Blessings. "My mother-in-law looks after him. He's not as robust as Oliver, that's why he wasn't with me when I was kidnapped." *Let him deal with that!*

"I'm sorry," he said.

Isn't he curious about my husband or my home or anything else?

Aaron went into the kitchen and poured himself a glass of water, then leaned back against the counter while he drank it. "You were saying something about what you're going to do. What did you mean?"

Catherine sat down on one of the chairs by the table. She looked down at her folded hands. "Everybody seems to have some sort of work to do," she said. "I mean, I want to do something useful, not just sit around. I'm used working all day."

"Doing what?" he asked.

"Housework, cooking," she looked longingly out the window at the flowerbeds against the rear wall of the compound. "Gardening."

"Well you don't have to do housework. What do you like doing?"

"Gardening."

"We've got Elijah to do that."

"If I could help him sometimes..."

Aaron frowned and shook his head. "You can't do that; he's one of the staff, you're...."

She looked at him steadily, waiting for him to define what she was expected to be.

"Family," he said, as if he'd only just defined her place to himself. "Isn't there anything else you're interested in?"

Catherine twitched her foot nervously. "I'd really like to finish my education."

Aaron's eyebrows rose. "That sounds like a worthwhile ambition," he said pompously. "How far did you get?"

"I was barely fourteen when I was kidnapped the first time, and after that, all I got was forced bible study."

He looked taken aback by that, but still resisted asking for details. "I'll have a word with Gordon and see if he can come up with a study plan. I take it you're familiar with computers?"

"Yes. I got most of my education by home-study."

"Right. We can move a terminal in here and get Gordon to bring in some education disks. The two of you decide what subjects you'll study."

"But can't I get the courses online?" she asked.

"No," he replied without further explanation, making it clear to her that she would have no contact with the outside world.

He put the glass down on the counter. "I have to get back to the lab," he said. "I'll see you around six."

"Can I...?"

He turned halfway out the door. "What?"

"Do you think I could look around?" She didn't feel like being cooped up again after the confinement of the past five days.

Aaron smiled. "Of course. You can go wherever you like as long as you respect people's private spaces."

She frowned, puzzled.

"Their living quarters, bedrooms and so on," Aaron explained.

After Aaron left, Catherine snooped around the cottage for a while, but didn't find anything particularly interesting, so she went outside. From behind one of the buildings, she could hear the children shrieking with laughter, so she made her way over, curious to see what was causing Oliver to be so boisterous. Behind the main house, she discovered a tiled patio with a small wading pool and some children's playground equipment. Oliver and Jon were both in the pool, completely naked, throwing pails of water at each other. While Jon's water found its mark more frequently than Oliver's, this in no way diminished the enjoyment her son was getting from the game.

"Mommy, look at me," he shouted joyfully when he spotted her.

The moment Oliver's attention was sidetracked, Jon doused him with another bucketful. Taken by surprise, her son fell back on his bottom in the water. Unperturbed, he jumped up, rubbing his eyes and spurting water out of his mouth. He stepped out of the pool and ran towards her, eyes shining, and then stopped in front of her looking down at himself.

"I haven't got any clothes on," he said mischievously.

"So I see," she said with a smile. She was happy to see this new Oliver, freed from all the inhibitions imposed on him by the fundamentalist mores of Blessings.

Jon came over to join them. He looked pointedly at Oliver and said, "Why isn't he circumcised?"

Oh boy. "Where we come from, they don't do that."

"Why not? I thought all Jews had to be circumcised."

"Maybe because we're not Jewish," Catherine replied, hoping she wasn't revealing more about herself and Oliver than she was supposed to. *To hell with it,* she thought, grinning at the forbidden expression, *we didn't ask to be brought here.*

"Oh," Jon said to this revelation. "Duncan isn't Jewish. I bet he's not circumcised, either. I'm going to ask him. Come on, Oliver."

The two naked little boys ran off around the corner towards the schoolroom, leaving Catherine smiling.

Divided from the patio by a low wood fence was the vegetable garden. She could see the gardener bending over some plants at the other side and made her way across. He was picking green beans and putting them in a basket on the ground.

"Hi, Elijah. Need any help?"

The old man straightened up, groaning as he unbent his legs.

"I can manage fine, miss," he replied.

"But I'd like to do something. I love working in the garden. I had my own garden in ... where I come from, and I miss it."

"Well, I suppose it wouldn't do any harm, as long as Aaron doesn't object."

"We'll let it be our secret, shall we? Now what can I do?"

"You could pick some of those tomatoes if you like."

He lifted his basket and revealed another underneath it. He handed the empty one to Catherine and she went to the staked tomato plants and started to fill it with the ripe fruit. She pressed one of the freshly picked tomatoes to her nose and breathed deeply, savoring its tangy aroma.

As she moved along the row of vines, she paused occasionally to pull out a weed, not that there were many. The garden, even this late in the summer, was immaculate. If only Aaron would let her have a little patch of ground of her own to work on.

There was a fresh explosion of giggling as the two boys returned. She went over to the fence. Oliver's shoulders and buttocks, unaccustomed to being exposed to the sun, were getting red. She ought to get him some sunscreen, but from where?

"How would you like to come over to the cottage and get a cold drink?" she invited the boys.

Catherine set the basket of tomatoes on the ground near Elijah and thanked him.

She found a bottle of sunscreen in her bathroom cupboard. The Goldmans really had thought of everything. While Oliver was drinking his iced tea, she rubbed on some lotion. The two boys rushed back outside as soon as they'd finished their drinks.

Catherine decided to take a look at the front of the compound, by the main entrance. She went through the archway in the school building and casually strolled down the meandering driveway, pausing occasionally to admire some flowers or a tree. Around the bend, out of sight of the buildings, she walked a bit faster until she reached the gate. It was about two and a half meters high and made of solid wood. She could discover no way to open it. Catherine sighed. Maybe there was another gate somewhere she could try.

She turned to her left and started to trace the wall. In some places, she had to squeeze through thickets of shrubs, but she persevered until she came to a barrier running from the main house to the outer wall. It was low enough to see over, but effectively blocked her path and she certainly wasn't going to try climbing over. The children's play yard was on the other side.

She turned back and began to follow the wall to the right of the front gate. This time she was rewarded by the discovery of a small door to the outside. The door was also solid wood and was set in an archway in the wall. Like the front gate, it was locked but the means of release was obvious—a card slot on the gatepost. That was something. The front gate didn't even have that. At least with a card slot, there was a chance of getting hold of the keycard. From its situation behind Aaron's lab, Catherine assumed it was a tradesmen's entrance for the delivery of supplies.

As she turned away from the gate to continue along the wall, she noticed a stranger watching her from a window of the lab. The gate was probably an employee entrance as well, she realized.

The following day, Yosi invited Catherine to have her hair and nails done by her hairdresser. She submitted, feeling humiliated by the amateur way her hair had been cut in Blessings, and nails that had never had a professional manicure. Looking at her reflection when the stylist had finished, she saw it had been worth it. To her surprise, the face she saw looking back at her was quite pretty now that her dark hair was brushed off her forehead. He'd got rid of the unflattering bangs and uneven ends. The woman who cut hair in Blessings had one style that she used on everyone: shaggy ends and bangs. Maybe she thought that good Christian women didn't need to look attractive.

Catherine liked her new, more attractive self, and Aaron's expression when he saw her confirmed that he did too.

The first of her and Oliver's new clothes were delivered a couple of days later. She laid them out on the bed where she could examine them. There were trousers, dresses and blouses made from soft fabrics in gorgeous colors—pale green, orange, sapphire, light turquoise and violet—and underclothes and nightwear in ivory silk trimmed with lace. She had forgotten what it was like to wear fine things. Everything they wore in Blessings had been made from durable synthetics and utility-grade cottons.

She and Oliver settled in and became comfortable with the new home. Oliver was happy with his new friend who was a far livelier companion than his brother had been, and he loved school. As Aaron had promised, Catherine got her terminal and began to study again. After talking to Gordon, she settled on an arts program that included literature and art history.

But she was far from content. Knowing how close she was to Vancouver and still being unable to reach her mother filled her with grief and frustration. It was all very well to be pampered and treated like a family member, but she still wasn't free. She lay awake many nights, thinking about how she could get out of the compound or at least find a communications link she could use to contact her family. If she could just get hold of a keycard.

Chapter Thirty-two

The com chimed just as Julia was getting out of the shower. She wrapped a towel around herself and stepped into the bedroom to answer it, switching off the video camera before pushing the respond button.

"Julia? Hope I haven't caught you at a bad time."

She was surprised to see the Provincial Superintendent of the RCMP. She couldn't tell by his expression whether he had good news or bad. Her old friend and former client had honed the art of hiding his feelings to perfection. Her pulse quickened; it might be news of Catherine.

"Carlton. I just got out of the shower. I hope you've got some good news."

Carlton Bannerman allowed a touch of glumness to show through. "Good and not so good." He looked down at something on his desk, then back at the camera. "We've heard something from the Idaho State Police. It seems a doctor in a small town in western Idaho reported a woman answering to your daughter's description living in a nearby community. The whole area is full of religious fundamentalist groups and this one—it's called Blessings—has a suspiciously large ratio of women. The State Police went to investigate and found that several of the women had been brought there against their will."

Get to the point, she thought, but Julia knew from experience that he couldn't be rushed. "Was Catherine one of them?"

"Yes. They talked to a fellow who was perhaps less zealous than the rest. Could have been sour grapes because he didn't have a woman, but he told them she was brought there about ten years ago. Said the Reverend—their leader, Reverend Webster—had a vision. God had called him to rescue this girl and bring her to Blessings to be his bride."

A stab of anguish shot through Julia. "Rescue her from what? Was she there?"

"Julia, I'm sorry. You know what these fundamentalist nuts are like. Anyway, it was just an elaborate excuse for kidnapping her."

"But did they find her?"

He shook his head. "They claim she disappeared about six weeks ago. She and her youngest son."

"That ties in with the phone call I got a few weeks ago, but I didn't know she had more than one child."

Bannerman looked at her sharply. "What phone call? Why didn't you report it?"

"Can you hold on a minute?" Julia asked, playing for time to think.

She went back into the bathroom and put on a thick robe, then returned to the com unit. This time, she turned on the video.

"There was a call from a man offering to sell her to me if I could come up with..."

"Why didn't you report it?"

"It was a weekend and ... by Monday, it was too late. Carlton, can we meet and talk about it?"

"Would you like me to come over?"

"Do you have time?"

"I'll make time. You know I'm fond of you, Julia. I wish you hadn't given up your ... occupation."

Julia sighed. "I know. When can you be here?"

"Give me a couple of hours."

"Carlton, did they tell you anything about the place, Blessings, and this reverend guy. What was he like?" She pictured a raw-boned elderly man, humorless and rigid. Tears welled as she thought of her young daughter being forced into marriage to some dried up old man.

"They sent me a video of the investigation. I'll bring it."

***

It rained for a week. Instead of going to the main house for dinner, Catherine stayed in her cottage and cooked simple meals for herself and Oliver. Aaron dropped in a few times to find out if she was all right, but she was cool and distant, uncommunicative, and he didn't stay long.

Finally, the rain stopped and she was able to go out and walk in the garden. She met Aaron on the way from the house to his lab. He stopped and looked at her, obviously unsure of her mood and how she would respond if he spoke to her.

"Aaron," she said. "I was wondering if you would like to come for supper this evening."

He looked surprised. His eyes lit up. "I'd like that," he replied, touching her arm. "Any special time?"

"Around eight?"

"Great. I'll see you at eight."

There was a spring in his step as he continued to the lab.

***

"Where's Oliver?" Aaron asked as he sat down on the sofa in Catherine's sitting room that evening.

"I fed him earlier. He was tired from all the running around, so I let him go to bed."

Now that her plan was in motion, Catherine was unsure of herself. She stood awkwardly in a long lavender silk sheath dress, hands clasped in front of her. When Aaron looked at her, such warmth and raw hunger in his eyes, she felt as if she would melt.

"Would you like some wine?" she stammered, feeling her face flush. *Get a grip, Catherine. What's wrong with you?*

"That would be nice." He stood up. "Let me help you."

Before she could protest, he put his hand on her back and steered her towards the dining room. The table was set for two with a bowl of flowers from the garden in the center and candles waiting to be lit.

"The wine's in the...."

"I know," Aaron said going through to the pantry. "Red or white?"

"You choose."

Catherine had found some recipe books in one of the cupboards and from them she'd chosen a recipe for feta cheese and spinach lasagna that looked fairly easy and foolproof. She'd also baked some rolls—bread making was one of the skills she'd learnt at Blessings. As she set the dishes on the table, she wondered if maybe the meal was too simple for someone as sophisticated as Aaron. She herself didn't like to eat a heavy meal in the evening.

"This is perfect Kate. It smells wonderful," Aaron said, helping himself to the salad. "More wine?" he filled her glass without waiting for a reply.

After eating, they went back to the sitting room.

"Would you like some coffee?" Catherine asked.

"Not really," he replied. "How about some Grand Marnier?"

Catherine was already feeling the effects of two glasses of wine, but it might make what she had in mind a little easier. "All right. Where is it?"

"I'll get it." He was already on his way back to the dining room. "It's in the buffet."

Aaron returned with a tray containing a stubby brown bottle and two small stemmed glasses. He poured a small amount of the Grand Marnier in a glass and handed it to her, then poured himself some of the golden liquid and sat in the adjacent chair.

Catherine put the glass to her lips and sipped a small amount. She rolled the liqueur around in her mouth, savoring its tangy sweetness, and then swallowed it. Her body was suffused with a flush of warmth.

Aaron was watching her, a smile on his lips. "Like it?"

"Mm." She nodded. "It tastes like oranges."

She finished the liqueur in small sips, following Aaron's example, and put the glass on the tray, then leaned back on the sofa, trying to suppress a yawn.

Aaron stood up. "I think I should be going; you're tired."

"Do you have to leave?" Her heart thumped at her own audacity. She was afraid to look at him.

He moved over to the sofa where she was sitting and put his arm around her, pulling her against his chest. "Not if you want me to stay." He smoothed back her hair and kissed her forehead, and then he stood up and held out his hand.

Catherine took it and allowed him to pull her to her feet and lead her into the bedroom.

"Turn round," he said.

She turned her back to him and he pulled down the zipper of her dress then eased it off her shoulders, allowing it to fall to the floor. She crossed her arms and rubbed her biceps.

"Cold?" he asked, turning her to face him.

She was trembling, more from nervousness than cold. She shook her head.

"I won't be a minute," she said and darted into the bathroom, closing the door behind her.

She went to the toilet and then washed her hands, studying herself in the mirror. Would he find her attractive? Would the marks of childbearing put him off? She noticed how flushed her skin was. Catherine sighed. It had to happen sometime. She removed her undergarments and put on a light robe, feeling the burning of unaccustomed sexual excitement in her groin. Catherine brushed her hair back and took a deep breath, then opened the bathroom door.

Aaron was on the bed, covered with a sheet, his clothes neatly hung over a chair. He held the cover up, revealing that he was naked.

"Come here," he said. "And take that robe off."

As Aaron gently caressed her, touching her in places she hadn't realized could elicit such arousal. She felt something building up inside her like a volcano. The feeling was almost unbearable, but she was terrified it would stop before she was able to discover where it led. She was not disappointed. Catherine cried out when the climax finally came, her eyes filled with tears.

So that's what it felt like, what she had been missing all this time, what her mother had meant when she talked about men and women together. She held Aaron's head between her palms and kissed him over and over, tears streaming down her face.

"Thank you," she whispered, pulling him close and holding him tightly in her arms. "Thank you."

"Why the tears, little one? I didn't hurt you did I?"

"No. It was just so wonderful. It's never happened like that before."

"Was this the first time you reached a climax?"

She buried her face in the curly hair on his chest. "Yes," she mumbled.

His arms tightened around her.

Catherine woke to the sound of rain pattering on the roof. It was still dark. She put out her hand to make sure he was still there. At her touch, he moaned and reached out for her, enfolding her in his arms and pulling her close. She sighed contentedly and went back to sleep.

A small hand was patting her face persistently.

"Mommy, wake up, I'm cold.

She opened her eyes and saw Oliver, shivering, dressed only in his underpants. "Where's your nightshirt?"

"It's wet. Can I come in your bed?"

At that moment, Catherine realized two things: one, she was alone in the bed, and two, she was naked. She felt a pang of disappointment. Aaron had slipped away without waking her. "Bring me my robe, please. It's on the chair," she said to Oliver.

When Oliver handed her the robe, she wrapped it around her, then lifted the covers so that he could climb in beside her. "How did your shirt get wet?" she asked, cuddling him.

"I spilled some juice on it. Aaron gave it to me."

"Oh."

"Why was Aaron sleeping in your room, Mommy?"

"He ... well..." How to explain it?

"Is he my new daddy?" Oliver asked, looking at her with wide, innocent eyes.

"Would you like it if he was?"

Oliver frowned, working this out in his mind. "Can I have two daddies?"

Catherine blew a puff of air. How do you tell a child he may never see his real father again?

She didn't see Aaron again until the next evening. Thinking about how to broach the subject of contacting her mother distracted her throughout the day, when she wasn't reliving the previous night. Surely he would agree. She would hate to have to go to plan B, which was stealing his keycard.

***

Francesca had woken up in a cranky mood. After her bath, Julia sat down to feed her, but the child wouldn't nurse. Clenching her tiny fists, her face darkening, she screamed. Julia lifted her onto her shoulder and rubbed her back.

"What is it, Francesca? Got a tummy ache?"

The baby let out a big burp and stopped crying, but when Julia put her back to the breast, she took a couple of sucks and turned away, whimpering and waving her arms and feet.

Julia didn't know what to do. The baby was dry; she was warm and clean, but she just didn't want to eat. She stood up and rested Francesca on her shoulder, then began to pace around the apartment, patting her back and murmuring soothing words. She felt her daughter relax and when she looked down, the infant was asleep.

"I guess you were just tired," she said, putting Francesca in the cradle that had been Catherine's. She sighed and stroked the baby's cheek with her finger. "I'm getting too old for this."

She had about an hour to clean up and be ready for Carlton's arrival.

Before she could start, the com chimed. She pushed the button, brushing her hair back. "Julia," her father said. "How's my new granddaughter?"

"She's a bit cranky. I just got her to sleep. How are you?"

"Not too bad, considering. I thought I'd take you out for lunch and then take a look at your garden."

"Dad, I'd love to, but I've got someone coming to talk about Catherine—he'll be here in about an hour."

"What about Catherine?"

"I was going to call you when I had more information. The American police have found out where she's been the past ten years. Some small town in Idaho. She's not there now, though. They claim she disappeared. But my friend has a video of the investigation and he's bringing it over to show me."

Raymond stroked his beard. "So they've caught the bastards who kidnapped her? What's going to happen to them?"

"I don't know," Julia replied. "I'll find out when Carlton gets here. Listen Dad, I'm in a bit of a mess here, so I should start to clean up. I'll call you later."

When Carlton Bannerman arrived, he hugged Julia and kissed her cheek then held her away from him and looked at her. "You haven't changed much; you're just as lovely as ever. I've missed you, you know. I wish you hadn't given up your ... business."

"Thank you. You're looking good yourself."

Carlton Bannerman wasn't a conventionally handsome man; he was short and a little too thin, with a hawk nose and thick black eyebrows, but there was something magnetic about him that drew people to him. Perhaps it was his warm hazel eyes and his beautifully shaped mouth.

Julia showed him into the sitting room and offered him a drink. He sat down on the sofa and got up again, pulling a toy kitten from under him.

"What's this?" he asked, holding it out to her.

"I'm sorry; my daughter's toys pop up everywhere."

"I didn't know ... Oh, it's you ... you're the woman who had two daughters. I had no idea. Congratulations."

Julia nodded. "I couldn't face all the publicity, so I asked them not to mention my name," she said.

She handed him a glass of mineral water and sat down in a chair next to the sofa. "What have you got to show me?"

"Do you mind?" he stood up and went over to her com center, holding up a video disk. He slipped it into the slot and picked up the remote control, then sat back down.

"Let's talk before I show you the video."

"All right," Julia replied.

"Now, tell me about the phone call."

When she had finished, he said, "I still don't understand why you didn't call the authorities."

"You can't imagine the turmoil I was in. I was so close to getting her back. I didn't want to take any chances on things going wrong. Then, when I realized it wasn't going through, I...." Julia shrugged. "What was the point? It wouldn't have done any good."

"Julia." Bannerman shook his head and sighed. "Well, it's too late now. What can you tell me about the man? Did he have an accent? Was he young?"

"I assumed he lives in the country, not the city. He sounded like ... I don't know how ... you know how country people sound in videos? He sounded young, probably between twenty-five and forty."

"American?"

"Yes, I'd say so." She took a sip of her mineral water. "Can we get to the video?"

"In a moment. As I told you on the phone, several people have been arrested in Blessings, Idaho, and are currently awaiting trial. These include several members of the church, including the minister's mother."

"You say Catherine was married to this minister?"

"That's right. And they had two sons."

"Can I see...?"

The first scene was shot from a vehicle entering the town of Blessings. It showed neat houses lining the road and a few men dressed in work clothes watching the approach. The vehicle went past a row of shops and stopped in front of a store with a blue mailbox outside. Two men in uniform got out and went into the shop. The camera followed them.

"Good day, can I help you gentlemen?" the man at the counter said. He was middle-aged with short grey hair, neatly dressed in a blue shirt and pressed pants.

"Can you tell us where we can find the Reverend Webster?"

"Nothing wrong, I hope?" the man replied.

"Nothing that need concern you," the lawman replied. "We just need to talk to the Reverend."

"At this time of day, he should be in his office at the town hall. He's the mayor as well, you know."

"Thank you, sir. Now if you could just point the way."

"Turn right at the next corner and go about half a block," the man replied. He kept darting anxious glances at the communications equipment on the counter beside him. "It's the big red building."

The camera followed them back to the car and on to the town hall. After speaking to a man in the lobby of the old building, the lawmen continued up a flight of stairs and into an office with a glass-paneled door.

A gaunt middle-aged man sat behind a large wooden desk his hands on a pile of papers. He looked tired.

"Is that him?" Julia cried. "Oh, my God, he's so old. Poor Catherine, how awful."

"That's the reverend Keaton Webster." He clicked the video pause button. "Do you want to skip to the interview?"

"Did they get a picture of her son?"

"Yes, but that comes later, near the end of the recording."

"All right, let's see what he has to say for himself."

Julia watched the interview of Keaton Webster intently. This was the person responsible for her losing her daughter and for stealing Catherine's youth. She wanted to hate him, but he came across as pathetic and sad.

"So you admit that you had this girl abducted and brought here against her will to be your wife?" one of the interrogators asked.

"Yes, sir. It was God's will. He sent his angel to bring her to me."

"I thought it was your followers who brought her here."

"I mean before they went to get her. I received a message from the Almighty."

"That may be what you believe, sir, but what you did was a serious violation of the law—I'm sure you know that—with serious penalties. You robbed this young woman of her freedom and her family."

"She was a good wife and mother," Webster replied. "I...." he wiped his eyes. "I cared for her. I thought she was happy here, once she adjusted."

"God!" Julia exclaimed. "The damned hypocrite."

The interviews with Webster and some other members of the church were followed by a shot of three men and an old woman being led out of a house in handcuffs. One of the men was the Reverend Webster. The others were a stocky middle-aged man with a beard and a surly-looking younger man who resembled him. The other was a pleasant-looking man of around thirty. The old woman was the one who caught Julia's attention. She looked about eighty and had a grim, sour expression that looked as if it had been in place for half a century.

"Is that Webster's mother?"

"Yes. A bit forbidding, isn't she?"

"Poor Catherine. Imagine having to live with that."

Then she noticed a thin woman with dark hair holding the hand of a little boy. "That's him, isn't it?"

"Yes. That's Catherine's son, Brent."

The boy was pale and thin. He was watching the lawmen take his grandmother and father away with tears streaming unheeded down his face. He wiped mucous from his nose with the back of his hand and tried to pull away from the woman, but she held tight.

"Granny!" he called in a thin quivery voice.

"Who's the woman?" Julia asked

"Webster's sister, Martha."

"She looks a bit grim, too," Julia said.

"She's looking after Brent while they're away. She's got four sons of her own, but they're all grown up now."

"What do you think will happen to them?"

"Webster and Oregon will probably go to prison. They're out on bail now, awaiting trial."

"Oregon?"

"The other guy. He's the Reverend Jesse Oregon. He's the one who led the kidnapping team. The other two were young at the time, so they'll probably get off with community service. They were influenced by their elders. One of them is Oregon's son. The old lady will probably get off."

"Not much for stealing someone's life."

***

Aaron arrived just as she was starting to prepare dinner. He walked up behind her and put his arms around her, resting his chin on her head.

"How are you feeling?" he asked.

Catherine was flustered and felt herself blushing. "Fine. Good."

He turned her to face him, lifted her chin with his fingers and kissed her. "I enjoyed last night and I know you did. I was wondering..." he glanced out of the window. "How would you feel if we made it permanent?"

"What do you mean?" Catherine's heart beat faster.

"I could move in here with you."

"You could do that any time you want. You own this place, and me," she blurted.

Aaron sighed. A flush spread over his face and neck. "I was hoping you would ... want to be with me. I can understand that you would feel resentful about the way we met, but ... I'm not saying this very well. How about we talk about it some other time?" He rubbed the back of his neck and walked over to the door.

Catherine's heart sank. She knew that if she were free to choose, she probably wouldn't find anyone more attractive than Aaron, but, damn it, she wanted that freedom of choice.

"Aaron, you're welcome to move in here with us, but I have a son to consider. He's lost his father and everyone he knew and, although he may not show it, I know he's hurt. He needs a man in his life. Would you be able to ... not take his father's place, but...?"

"Sure. I like the little guy. I'm sure we can be friends." He looked down at his feet for a moment, then at her. "I came to invite you to come over to the house for dinner."

"Do they know...?

"What? That I stayed over? I don't know. Nobody said anything."

"I'll have to find Oliver and clean him up then we'll be over." All Catherine had done so far was put some potatoes on to boil, so she didn't mind abandoning the dinner she'd planned. She turned off the burner under the potatoes.

"He's probably somewhere with Jon. I'll go and find him while you get ready."

Aaron walked them back to the cottage after dinner. Once Oliver was in bed, they sat down in the sitting room. Aaron put his arm around Catherine and drew her close. She felt the same excitement she'd felt the night before, but pulled away, determined not to be sidetracked.

"Aaron, can we talk?"

"Go ahead." He looked at her anxiously, as if fearing she would say something he didn't want to hear.

"It's about our relationship. How can we form any kind of bond without honesty and trust?" He started to reply, but she hurried on, "You have to admit that the circumstances that brought me here are not ... you know what I mean."

"Aren't you happy here? We gave you your own house to live in and we can get you anything you need. Everyone's been friendly and...."

"That's not what I mean," Catherine replied, frustrated by his refusal to face reality. "You have to face certain facts about me. We need to have everything out in the open. I'm sure if we had met under normal circumstances, I would have been happy to marry you. But as things stand, I feel like a prisoner here."

"What do you want me to do? Marry you?"

"It's not that, Aaron." Catherine sighed. "I already have a husband." He frowned at that. "I want you to face what has happened to me. I want you to know about my life. If you can't face that, I don't see much chance of our having anything but a master-slave relationship."

Aaron flinched. He stood up and began to pace, then sat down again, this time in the armchair next to the sofa. He sighed. "All right, tell me what you want me to know."

"I have been a prisoner for more than ten years," Catherine began. "I was taken away from a loving family when I was fourteen and never allowed to speak to them again or hear any news of them. My mother didn't even know I was alive until a few weeks ago. I love my mother; she's beautiful and kind. I miss her so much." She paused to wipe her eyes.

Aaron moved over to sit beside her on the sofa and took her hand.

By the time she had finished telling him about the last ten years of her life, she felt emotionally drained, wrung out.

Aaron went to the kitchen and returned with two glasses of water and some paper towels. He put the glasses on the table and gave her the towels to wipe her eyes.

"What can I do to make you feel less ... confined?"

Catherine put the crumpled paper towel in her lap and took a drink of water. She might only have this one chance, so she had to word it right.

"I want to talk to my mother."

Chapter Thirty-three

Aaron shook his head. "I don't see how that's possible."

Catherine looked down, her eyes stinging. "If you're afraid of getting into trouble," she said, "we could promise not to tell anyone. It would be worth it to us just to see each other again."

"It's too much of a risk." Aaron folded his arms. "You can't speak for your mother. How do we know she wouldn't go to the police once she found out where you are?"

"She's not like that."

Catherine wasn't really sure her mother wouldn't inform the police out of sheer anger once she knew where her daughter was.

"I can't take that chance." Aaron sighed and sat back in his chair. "Look. Kate, I was hoping, after last night, that you would ... could come to be happy here."

"I could, but only if I was reunited with my family. How could I be happy if I'm a prisoner? I could sign something, promising not to go to the police."

"Can we talk about this some other time? I'll have to think about all the ramifications and talk to the family."

"Does that mean you'll consider it?"

"Yes, but don't get your hopes up. I can't see any safe way right now." He looked at Catherine. "I know we met under unusual circumstances but was hoping you would get to like me."

Catherine didn't answer. She was afraid to. She realized she was falling in love with Aaron in spite of everything. He had given her the sexual satisfaction she'd never experienced before and it would be hard for her to resist him from now on.

"Do you want me to leave?" Aaron asked.

No, don't go, Catherine's body cried out. In spite of their relative positions, she was hooked by her own desire. If only he weren't so attractive. She shrugged, wishing her will were stronger. She'd leave the decision to him.

Aaron stood up. "Maybe I should go." He moved over to where she was sitting and kissed her on the forehead. "I'll see you tomorrow." His voice sounded cool and indifferent.

As soon as he was gone, Catherine rushed into her bedroom. "Damn!" She clenched her fists as tears slid down her cheeks.

The next time Catherine saw Aaron, she asked if she could see his work.

"I could show you around this evening," he replied.

"Why not now?" she asked.

"I'm too busy right now with an experiment. I'll pick you up around six."

Catherine didn't learn much from her tour of the lab. In one large room, lined with workbenches filled with electronics equipment and monitors, she asked, "How many people work here?"

"Apart from me and Freddie, there are five techs and two engineers."

She had been hoping someone might have left a keycard lying around that she could commandeer, but she saw none apart from the one Aaron kept attached to a thin chain in his pocket.

Aaron put his arm around her shoulder as they left the lab. "Not mad at me, are you?"

"What do you think?" she replied. "How would you feel if you were me?"

He sighed. "I'm sorry, Kate. We have no other choice. There's too much at stake. My family has too much to lose. You could be a lot worse off, you know."

"I'm surprised you didn't think of that before you bought me."

He stopped walking and put his hands on her shoulders, turning her to face him. "I didn't expect to feel this way about you."

Her heart thumped. She looked into his eyes. They were so warm and sincere, her heart almost melted. What if he hadn't liked her? Or if she had not been attracted to him?

She forced herself to harden her heart. He had complete control over her life and was keeping her against her will, even if the prison was luxurious. She was denied nothing except what she really wanted: to see her family.

She shook her head and turned away. What could she do to persuade him? She could deny him sexual favors, but she would only be depriving herself of pleasure. And it was possible that if she did refuse, he would take her anyway. She had a better chance of winning him over by keeping him happy. The thought made her feel cheap. It would turn what could have been a loving relationship into something tawdry.

She sensed him looking at her, waiting for her response.

"Can't we be friends?" he asked. "Things will work out."

"All right," Catherine said. "But don't forget."

After confronting Aaron with her desire to contact her family, Catherine's feelings for his family cooled. She didn't exactly go out of her way to avoid them, but she kept out of their way and turned down their occasional invitations, concentrating on her studies and Oliver.

"You might as well move in," Catherine told Aaron one morning as he was leaving.

His eyes lit up. "Do you really mean that?"

"Why not? You sleep here most of the time anyway. There's plenty of room in the closet for your clothes."

***

Aaron was sleeping soundly when she awoke. She looked at the clock. Four twenty. He would sleep for hours yet and, as she had soon discovered, once Aaron was asleep, it would take an earthquake to wake him.

She slipped out of bed and dressed in pants and a warm sweater then she went over to where Aaron's clothes lay on a chair. His key card was there, attached to his trousers. She unclipped it and slipped it in her pocket, then crept out of the room, closing the door behind her. She'd left some shoes near the French windows in the sitting room.

She went into Oliver's room and gently woke him.

"Shh, don't make a noise," she said, touching his lips with her finger.

"What's the matter, Mommy? It's dark outside."

"I know. Remember our secret?"

The little boy looked puzzled for a moment, then nodded, rubbing his eyes with a fist. "You mean now?" he whispered.

"Yes. Hurry up and get dressed." Catherine handed him some jeans and a sweater.

When he had them on, she put some warm socks on his feet and helped him fasten his shoes. When he was ready to go, she took him to the kitchen and took out a pack of food she'd stowed in a cupboard the previous evening. She put it in a backpack, and carried it to the French windows where she stopped to put on her own shoes.

"Ready?" she whispered.

"Mommy, where...?"

"Shh, don't forget," she replied in a low voice.

Catherine closed the French windows with a soft click and took Oliver's hand, leading him towards the back of Aaron's lab. When they reached the gate to the outside, she took the keycard from her pocket and slipped it into the slot. There was a click and the gate swung open.

"Where are we going, Mommy?"

Catherine closed the gate behind them before answering. "I don't know yet."

She looked around. They were in a wide paved alley between the Goldman compound and a high fence lined with trees on the other side. There were several cars parked in the alley outside the gate. "This way," she said, turning left towards the street in front of the compound.

Catherine stood undecided about which way to go. The street was a wide curving slope lined with trees. Walls bordered both sides of the street with high gates at intervals. Many of the walls were draped with trailing vines. Amber streetlights about thirty meters apart provided enough illumination for them to see by. There was no sign of life, no vehicles, no people, and no animals.

"This way," she said at last, taking Oliver's hand and turning downhill. She remembered they had driven uphill when she arrived, so the city center must be down that way.

As they walked, Catherine was alert for the sounds of voices or vehicles that might indicate their departure had been discovered. She was also looking out for possible hiding places in case they did encounter someone. Most of the walls and fences lining the street were featureless, apart from the gates, but a few had shrubberies planted in front of the walls. They were the only possible places to hide.

Catherine had no plan. She had no idea what she would find outside the compound, or what the security situation was now. She knew it would still be dangerous for women to be out alone. As she walked, she was thinking furiously. They couldn't stay on the streets for long, that was certain. The best thing she could think of was to go to the police. The only alternative, which was much more risky, was to stow away in some transport vehicle going north.

They reached the corner. Catherine read the street sign embedded in the edge of the sidewalk: Dogwood Crescent. The intersecting street was Parkfield Road. She could see the lights of a commercial center to the left. After a moment's thought, she turned onto Parkfield and headed in the direction of the lights.

Suddenly approaching headlights flashed on the wall across the street. She looked around in a panic and saw a small shrubbery about a meter away.

"Hurry, hide," she said, urging Oliver towards the bushes.

They crouched together behind the bushes against the fence and watched through the leaves as the vehicle rounded the bend and came in their direction. It was a utility van, moving very slowly, its spotlights scanning from left to right. It went right past them and disappeared down the hill.

Chapter Thirty-four

She was just about to leave the hiding place when the another set of lights appeared coming up the hill. Catherine held Oliver close, barely breathing as the lights came closer. It was the same van. It must have turned round at the bottom of the hill. The van stopped when it reached their hiding place and Aaron got out.

"Catherine. Come on out."

She stood up, defeated, tears in her eyes. She took Oliver's hand and walked him out of the bushes.

"What did you hope to accomplish by running away?" he said gently.

"Don't you understand how much I want to go home?" She allowed him to lift Oliver into the van. "How did you find us so quickly?" she asked resignedly.

"Alarms." He thumbed the goggles hanging from a strap around his neck. "Infrared glasses. I saw where you were hiding by your body heat. Come on, Catherine, get in."

When she was secured in the passenger seat, Aaron closed the door and went around to the driver's side. He started the vehicle and silently drove them back to the compound.

When they got back to the cottage, he gave Oliver a glass of milk and took him to his bedroom.

"I've put him back to bed," he said when he returned. He held his hand out to Catherine. "Can I have my key back?"

Catherine took it out of her pocket and gave it to him, then burst into tears and rushed into her bedroom, slamming the door behind her.

Aaron left on a business trip the next day. Since her escape attempt, he was cool towards her, although he hadn't moved back to his parents' house. It was just as well he would be away for a week. It would give them both time to cool off and reassess their relationship.

***

It was twenty-one thirty and Catherine had just finished putting Oliver to bed. She was trying to complete an art history assignment when someone knocked at the window. She jumped. Maybe Aaron had come back early ... but he wouldn't knock. She went to the window and looked through the slats of the blind. It was Jack, one of the cousins. What could he want at this hour?

She opened the French door.

"Kate, thought you might like a little company," he said in a slurred voice.

"No," she replied as she started to close the door.

Vicki Wootton

But he was too fast for her and elbowed his way in before she could get it shut. "Don't be like that, Kate. I know you're lonely with Aaron away.

"You're drunk, Jack. What do you want?"

He giggled and pushed her towards the sofa. "What do you think?" He pressed her down on the seat. "Do you think it's fair for old Aaron to be the only one getting any...? Don't you think we have feelings? How do you think the rest of us feel, seeing him with a woman? He should share with the rest of us," he rambled, tears of self-pity filling his eyes. "It's not fair."

Catherine struggled from his grasp and stood up, "I want you to go, right now."

Jack stood up and lurched towards her, grabbing her arm before she could escape. "I'll tell you what it's like. Feel this." He forced her hand down to his crotch.

She snatched her hand away and pushed him. He fell backwards, sprawling half on the sofa, half on the floor. She rushed to the bedroom, but he was on his feet and after her before she could get the door closed. He put his arm around her, pinning her arms, and pressed his mouth on hers.

"I want you, Kate."

"No. Get out of here. I'll scream!"

"No you won't. You don't want to scare the kid, do you?"

Catherine knew he was right. She struggled with him, heart thumping, tears of rage flooding her eyes. She managed to get an arm free and raked her fingernails down his face.

He let go with one hand and touched his face, then he swung his fist hard against her ear. "Want to play rough, do you? I'll show you rough."

He tore at her tunic top until it ripped at the neck. He dragged it over her head and threw it on the floor then he pushed her down on the bed and yanked her trousers off. Catherine sobbed and tried to scramble off the bed, but he held her fast by the ankle. "Stay still or I'll tie you."

Holding her leg with one hand, he used the other to undo his pants. He fell on top of her and held her down with his body while he dragged her panties off.

Suddenly, Catherine felt calm. "What do you think will happen when your family finds out?" she said. "Do you think they'll let you stay here after you do something like this?"

He looked as if he had abruptly come to his senses. His erection collapsed and he moved off her. He wiped his eyes with his sleeve and fastened his pants, then slunk out of the room without looking at her or saying a word. Catherine heard the door click shut. She pulled up her panties and rushed into the sitting room to lock the window; she locked the one in the dining room as well.

Aaron returned on Monday morning. He entered the cottage smiling, dropped his bag on the floor and hugged Catherine then he noticed her expression and lack of response.

"You're not still mad, are you?"

Catherine shook her head and gazed down at the floor.

"What, then? Has something happened?"

"I'm fine. It's just ... this rain gets me down."

"Well, cheer up, I've got some good news for you." He took her hand and led her to the sofa.

Catherine couldn't imagine anything he might have to say that would cheer her up. She just wanted to get away from here. She sat waiting, hands folded in her lap while he rummaged in his travel bag. He straightened up holding a folder filled with documents and sat down beside her.

"I thought about what you said and talked it over with Epstein, our lawyer."

Catherine's interest perked up a little.

"I want you to know that I wouldn't be doing this if I didn't care for you." He put his hand over hers. "How would you like us to be married?"

She turned and looked at him, heartbeat accelerating. "How can ...?"

"We've got it all worked out. First, you're going to divorce your husband."

"But..."

"Sorry, Kate, I guess I'm taking a lot for granted. Do you want to marry me?"

"Will I be able to see my mother if I do?"

"Of course. That's what all this is about ... I mean, I do want to marry you, but I can't bear to see you suffering over your family."

"How can I divorce Keaton? He'd know where..."

"He's in no position to complain, is he? He'll go along with it, don't worry."

Catherine put her hands on her cheeks. Her eyes glistened. "Oh, my." She turned and put her arms around Aaron, pulling him closer and kissing him. "Thank you. This is wonderful news. I can hardly believe it."

Aaron dropped the documents and took her in his arms. "I love you, Kate."

Feeling herself becoming aroused Catherine pulled away and pushed her hair back. "How long will all this take?"

Aaron picked up the documents. "We can get it rolling right away. We need you to sign these."

"What are they?"

"One is a statement saying that you came to live here of your own free will."

She nodded, wondering if it was the right thing to do. Could it be a scheme to get them off the hook? She looked at Aaron. No. The way he was looking at her, there was little doubt how he felt.

"What are the others?"

"They're the divorce papers. Once they're signed, they'll be served on your ... on Webster."

"Can I see them?"

Aaron handed them to her. Catherine waded through the legalese in the documents. She couldn't see anything to object to, but she realized she felt sorry for Keaton. Apart from abducting her from her home and keeping her a prisoner, he'd been kind, and he was Oliver's father. She was asking for custody of their son.

She stood up and went over to the desk. "I'll get a pen and sign them now."

"We have to have your signatures witnessed, so you can't do it now. An associate is coming over this afternoon so you can sign them in his presence, then he'll take them back to the office to be processed."

"When do you think I'll be able to contact my mother?" Catherine asked that night when they were getting ready for bed.

"It won't be long, honey. Epstein will contact her first and make arrangements."

"But why can't I just call her?"

Aaron cleared his throat. "We have to be sure first. We have your statement, but we have to be sure your mother will go along with it."

"She will, I know she will."

"You are probably right, honey. It's just a precaution. You don't want your future husband to go to jail, do you?" He pulled back the covers and got into bed. "Come here."

Catherine went through the next few days in a state of euphoria. Even Oliver noticed how happy she was. She forgot about Jack's nocturnal visit until she saw him crossing the compound one morning.

He blushed when he saw her and stopped. "I'm sorry about what happened the other night, Kate. I made a complete fool of myself. I feel really bad about it. What can I say? I was drunk. Thanks for not ... for keeping quiet." He turned abruptly and continued on his way.

Catherine shivered, remembering how scared she'd been that night, but it didn't pay to make enemies in her future husband's family.

One evening, just after she and Aaron had gone to bed, Catherine heard a strange noise. It sounded like a series of loud tones running down the scale. Aaron jumped out of bed and pulled on his trousers, looking panicky.

"What is it?" she asked.

"Get dressed quickly, we've got to go."

"But what ...?"

"Don't ask questions, just hurry. It's the alarm."

She got out of bed and put on some trousers and a sweater, not bothering about underwear. Aaron grabbed her arms and pulled her along as he rushed from the room

"What's that noise, Mommy?"

Oliver was walking down the hall, rubbing his eyes.

"Come on Oliver, we have to hurry." Aaron scooped him up in his arms and continued out the French door.

Catherine followed him numbly, a cold hollow feeling opened under her diaphragm—dread. They went across the lawn to Aaron's lab. The interior of the building was illuminated by dim nightlights set at intervals along the baseboards. Without turning on any more lighting, Aaron took them down the ground floor hall and through a door into a storeroom. He closed the door and locked it from the inside, then went over to a rack of shelves. She couldn't see what he was doing, but she heard a click and the shelves moved sideways, revealing an opening.

"Inside, quick."

He urged Catherine forward through the opening. She found herself at the top of a flight of wooden stairs, illuminated by a light panel in the ceiling at the bottom. She looked questioningly at Aaron.

"Go on down." He put Oliver down on the top step then turned to push a button on the wall. The shelves rolled back into place over the opening.

The room at the bottom of the stairs was furnished like a comfortable apartment with carpeted floor, beds, chairs and table, a small kitchen and bathroom.

"What is this place?" Catherine asked.

"It was built when the riots started as a bolt hole in case we were attacked."

"But why do we need it now?"

"I don't know, but the alarm means danger. We may be here for a while, so we might as well get comfortable."

"What about your family?"

"There's a bigger one under the office block. They must have gone there; it's closer to the house." The office block was the school building, the second floor of which housed the business offices of Goldman Brothers, Inc.

Catherine rubbed her upper arms. This was a situation of which she had no experience. "Should I put Oliver to bed?"

"I think that would be a good idea. And we might as well settle down ourselves."

"I'm thirsty," Oliver said.

"You get into bed," Aaron said. "And I'll bring you some water."

When they were all settled, Aaron lowered the lights.

They were woken up by another signal; this time the tones went up the scale.

"All clear," Aaron said. He looked at his timepiece. "Four hours; that's a long time. It must have been something serious."

"Can we go back now?" Catherine asked.

"Yes. It's over, whatever it was."

But, as Aaron soon discovered, it wasn't quite over.

Chapter Thirty-five

Aaron accompanied Catherine back to the cottage then went over to the main house to find out about the alarm. He was met by Joseph Epstein, the family lawyer, his father, and two men in dark suits.

The men in suits moved in and bracketed him between them, each holding one of his arms. One of them flashed an identification disk at Aaron, too fast for him to read, and began to speak. "Aaron Goldman, we have a federal warrant for your arrest on a charge of unlawful detention of Catherine Finisterra and accessory to kidnapping the same Catherine Finisterra and her son, Oliver Benjamin Webster. You have the right to remain silent..." when they had finished reading him his rights, one of them took out a pair of handcuffs.

Aaron was stunned. The blood drained from his face and his shoulders slumped. How did this happen? Could Catherine have had anything to do with it? He clenched his fist, trying to control his anger and fear and looked from his father to Epstein.

Epstein came closer and spoke to the two men. "I don't think he needs to be cuffed, do you? He's not going anywhere."

The man with the cuffs looked at his partner and shrugged, but didn't let go of Aaron's arm.

"I'd like to speak to my client in private before you take him away. You can wait outside the door. There's no other way out of the room, Check for yourselves." He moved towards David Goldman's office.

As soon as the door closed, Aaron asked his father. "How the hell did they find out?"

"Apparently, they've been investigating the group that abducted her for some weeks. One of them must have given the feds your name."

"Why were they here so long?"

"They searched the whole place, the cottage ... everywhere," Epstein said. He leaned forward in his chair, facing Aaron, and rested his forearms on his knees.

Aaron went pale. "Did you tell them where we were?"

"What choice did we have? The bed had been slept in. Women's things all over and the kid's toys."

"They threatened to charge us with obstructing justice," David Goldman said.

Epstein lifted his hand, palm down. "I managed to get them to back off a bit and let me talk to you before they take you in. I'll go with you downtown to the Federal Building."

"Will I be kept in jail?"

Epstein nodded. "We may be able to get bail. This is a serious crime and I'm afraid they have no doubt about your role."

"Aaron rubbed his face with both hands. "Oh, God. What are we going to do? Will I go to prison?"

"We may be able to bargain it down, if you agree to cooperate."

"What about the paper Kate signed? That should help."

"If she stands by it."

Aaron stood up and paced to the window. Dawn was painting the sky with pink streaks. A bad sign, he thought. He put his hands in his pockets and turned to face the two older men. "What about Kate? What will happen to her?"

"She'll probably be shipped back to Vancouver immediately. They may ask her to come back and testify at your trial, if it goes to trial."

***

Someone was knocking on the French doors. Catherine peeked through the slats and saw two strangers, a man and a woman in formal business suits. She opened the door a crack. "Who is it?"

The woman held up a round identification tag. Catherine examined it. The disk had an eagle engraved on it and the name, B. J. Fulman, Federal Investigator, and some numbers. She also read United States Department of Justice in small letters around the edge. She shivered and rubbed her upper arms. A feeling of dread burrowed through her, leaving an icy wake.

"What's happened?" she asked.

"Can we come in and talk, ma'am?"

Catherine opened the door wider and let them in.

"Are you Catherine Aldina Webster, née Finisterra?" The man asked her.

Catherine nodded. She rubbed her hands together then buried them under her arms.

The female officer came closer to her and touched her arm. "We've come to take you home, Catherine."

"You mean ...?"

"Yes. Back to Vancouver and your family." The woman smiled warmly.

Tears filled Catherine's eyes. "Excuse me," she said rushing out of the room. She went into her bathroom and grabbed a hand towel, then sat down on the stool and wept. All the pain and misery of the last ten years poured out of her in the flood of tears.

She sensed a movement in the doorway and looked up to see officer Fulman standing there. With a shudder and a couple of heaves, Catherine stopped crying and wiped her face with the towel.

"I know this is a shock to you, Catherine, but it will be over soon and you can go home to your family. Can I get you anything?"

Catherine shook her head. "What happens now?"

"I suggest you get dressed and then we'll take you downtown. We need to ask you some questions before we take you back to Canada."

"My son ..." Catherine tried to put her thoughts in order. Everything was becoming so confusing.

"He'll come with you, of course."

"I think I'll take a shower," Catherine said, "Then I'll wake him up and get him ready."

"Would you like me to make some coffee while you're getting dressed?"

"No, thank you. You can make some for yourselves if you like. I usually have tea." She got up and closed the bathroom door.

"Do you want to pack a bag to take with you?" Fulman asked when they were ready to leave.

"How can I? They provided everything; it all belongs to them." Catherine looked down at the silk trouser suit she was wearing, wondering if she should return it when she got some new clothes, and whether she would be able to

335

afford anything as good. "I have nothing of my own, except my son."

She left the cottage and closed the French doors, realizing this might be the last time she would ever see it. *If only things could have been worked out … not like this*, she thought sadly. She took Oliver's hand and followed the two agents between the buildings into the courtyard. Several people were watching from the cousin's house and the main house, but Catherine kept her eyes on the ground until Jonathan came racing around the side.

"Oliver. Where you going?" he yelled as he ran towards them.

"I don't know," Oliver replied, hunching his shoulders.

"Will you be coming back?"

Oliver looked up at his mother.

"Maybe," she said.

"The police came and took Aaron away," Jonathan said.

"Is he going to jail?" Oliver asked.

Jonathan shrugged and kicked some gravel on the ground.

"I like Aaron," Oliver said. "I hope he doesn't go to jail. He's going to be my other daddy."

Nobody spoke again until the four of them were in the car.

"What's going to happen to Aaron?" Catherine asked as they drove out of the gate into the road.

Dogwood Crescent. She'd remember that. They turned into Parkfield Road and continued down the hill to the city center.

"We can't tell you that, ma'am," the male agent, who was driving, replied.

"Does that mean you don't know, or you aren't allowed to tell me."

"We don't know," Fulman replied.

"We were going to be married," Catherine said.

"I thought you were already married."

"I filed for divorce from Keaton ... my husband. I was married against my will. I love Aaron." Her eyes filled again. "I hope he doesn't go to prison."

Chapter Thirty-six

Interstate abduction ring caught

The FBI announced today that a kidnapping gang operating in several northwestern states has been captured. This gang is alleged to be responsible for the kidnapping and sale of at least fifteen young women over the past five years in Oregon, Idaho, and Washington.

"Although we have been investigating this case for two and a half years, it was a tip from Canada's Royal Canadian Mounted Police (RCMP) that led to the ultimate resolution," announced US Attorney Kennedy Westlake at a news conference in Seattle. "The most rewarding outcome of this is being able to restore these young women to their families.

Seattle Examiner, September 2, 2084

Julia had just put Francesca down for a nap when the com rang.

"Carlton!"

This time he didn't try to hide the fact that was bringing good news. "You'd better sit down, Julia."

"Carlton, don't play with me. What is it?"

"We've found her."

"What?" She clapped her hands over her mouth and jumped up. She spun round in a circle then returned to the com, eyes glistening. "God, I can't believe it. Where is she? Is she all right?"

"Seattle, and yes, she's fine." Carlton grinned.

"Oh, my God." Julia sat down again. "I don't know what to say. I'm so happy. How ...?" She stood up again. "Is she coming home?"

"Yes, they're flying her up here after she's given a statement to the U.S. federal attorneys."

***

"I'll take Oliver for some ice cream and a soda," Agent Fulman said as they entered the Federal Building. "Would you like that, Oliver?"

Oliver nodded and looked anxiously at his mother. "It's all right, honey, go with the lady. Mommy has to talk to some men for a while."

"Then can we go home?"

Catherine looked at the two agents. "I'm not sure what we'll be doing afterwards. We'll see." She wasn't sure to which home he was referring; he probably didn't know himself, poor little guy.

The male agent took her up in an elevator to the eighteenth floor. They entered a room lined with bookshelves and a window wall overlooking Puget Sound and the mountains of the Olympic Peninsula beyond. A long table surrounded by padded chairs almost filled the middle of the room.

"This is US Federal Attorney, Kennedy Westlake," the agent introduced an African American man of around fifty. "And this is his assistant, Bordan Briggs."

The assistant looked very young, around twenty-two, Catherine estimated.

"Please take a seat," Westlake said after shaking Catherine's hand. "Help yourself to some coffee and muffins."

Catherine realized she was starving. All she'd had that morning was a cup of tea. She put a muffin on a plate and poured herself a glass of water, then sat down and began to break the muffin apart with her fingers.

Westlake sat facing her at the end of the table with his assistant by his side. The agent sat adjacent to them, facing down the table. Briggs pushed a button on the edge of the table and a microphone popped up in front of each of them.

"Just to let you know, we'll be recording the interview," Briggs informed her. "You'll get a copy of the transcript to go over when we've finished."

Catherine nodded. Sounds as if we'll be here for a while, she thought.

"First let me say how happy we are to be able to restore you to your family, Ms ... what name do you use?" Westlake said.

"Finisterra. Catherine Finisterra," she replied.

"Could you spell that, please?" When she'd finished, he continued, "Thank you. Regrettably, these cases don't always have such a happy outcome. It's unfortunate that it took so long to find you. Before we continue, do you have any questions?"

"What happens after I've made the statement?"

"We're sending you home." Westlake beamed. "To Vancouver. If we get through in time, you could be home this evening."

"Does my mother know?"

"Yes, we've informed the Canadian RCMP of our progress and they will contact her.

Vicki Wootton

"Now, we'll get to the business at hand." Westlake looked at a notebook in front of him on the table. "What we'd like you to do is state your name, date of birth and birthplace for the record then tell us everything you can remember since you were abducted from Blessings with particular emphasis on descriptions of people, places, and vehicles used."

"But what about when I was first kidnapped in 2074?"

"We'll cover that in another interview. That's a different case in another jurisdiction. For now, we want to concentrate on the latest abduction."

Catherine was exhausted when they broke for lunch at eleven-thirty. She'd been up since dawn and was emotionally drained with everything happening so fast, but the thought of seeing her mother kept her going. She would get through this and would probably sleep around the clock when it was over. Then maybe she would be able to sort out how she felt—about Aaron, about her future and her son's future.

The interview wound up at around 14:30 after some questions from Westlake and Briggs once she'd finished her narrative account. They broke for coffee and cookies while the transcript was being printed—this time they also provided soft drinks and tea. The agent must have told them she didn't drink coffee. Briggs came back with several copies of the transcript and handed them out.

"I can see you're getting tired," Westlake said. "It won't be long now. If you wouldn't mind reading through the transcript, then if you've nothing to add, you can sign it and be on your way."

Catherine's mind was in too much turmoil for her to be able to concentrate on the lengthy document. She skimmed through it while the other three were reading their copies, then closed it and looked at Westlake.

"It seems all right," she said. "Can I contact you if I think of anything else later?"

"Of course. We are liaising with the RCMP, so you can contact them and they'll relay the information to us. I expect they'll be dealing with the other case as well—the first abduction, which took place in their jurisdiction." He stood up, smiling. "Thank you for coming in, Ms Finisterra. You've been very helpful. Agent Hibbings will take you down to pick up your son, then he'll drive you to the airport and put you on a plane for Vancouver." He came around the table and shook her hand. "Good luck!"

**

Francesca had been in a better mood when she woke up from her nap and had nursed enthusiastically. She was now sleeping again in the car safety capsule behind Julia in the back seat. Carlton Bannerman was driving an official car and she was sitting in the passenger seat next to him.

Julia was keyed up to such a level of anticipation that she barely noticed the passing scenery. Bannerman's few attempts at conversation had met with blank looks or vague, irrelevant responses.

Her heartbeat accelerated as they crossed the bridge over the Fraser River and the airport came into view. She tried to imagine what Catherine would look like, but all she could bring to mind was the quiet little girl she'd lost at the age of fourteen. Only minutes now, she thought.

Because of his official status, Bannerman was able to drive into a secured area of the airport, circumventing the arrivals terminal altogether. He parked by the wall of the terminal and got out while Julia was freeing Francesca from the capsule. He opened her door and took the baby while she stepped out onto the pavement.

"I'll take her," she said, holding out her hands for Francesca. "Do I look all right?" She glanced at her reflection in the car window.

"You look wonderful. Stop fretting."

He put his hand on the back of her shoulder and led her to a door marked 'No Admittance to Unauthorized Personnel' in both English and French. He pushed a button beside the door and was answered by a disembodied voice. "Name and authorization, please."

Bannerman gave the information and the door clicked open, admitting them to a featureless corridor. They went down the corridor and turned a corner where they came face-to-face with an elevator. It ascended two stories, bringing them to a similar hallway. Bannerman led the way to a door that opened into a large room with windows overlooking the inside of the arrivals terminal. Catherine noticed a monitor on one wall displayed a view of a hallway decorated with Native art along which several people were walking purposefully, most pulling luggage or carrying shoulder bags.

"Sit here," Bannerman said, directing Julia to a row of upholstered chairs facing the window. "I'll see what time they're due to arrive."

Julia sat and watched the people, mostly men, flow by below. They seemed to come in spurts as different flights arrived and disgorged their passengers, with short interludes of inactivity in between. Francesca woke up and yawned. She smiled up at her mother, tiny fists waving energetically, feet peddling the air.

"You're in a good mood," Julia said, lifting the baby and kissing her on the nose. "You're a very lucky girl; your big sister's coming home." She looked around. "I wonder what's taking Carlton so long."

Catherine

Catherine was surprised when Agents Hibbings and Fulman boarded the commuter plane with her and took seats across the aisle.

"We're going with you to make sure of your safety, until we hand you over. There'll be a representative of the RCMP at the airport to meet you."

In spite of this being Oliver's first flight in a fixed-wing aircraft, he fell asleep almost as soon as they were airborne. The flight only took about twenty minutes, so they were coming in to land almost as soon as they'd settled in their seats. As they descended over the ocean, coming in from the west, Catherine gazed at the city laid out on her left with its dramatic backdrop of mountains and felt a lump in her throat. She was really home.

"Wake up, honey, we have to get off now," she said, patting Oliver's cheek. "We're nearly home, and then you'll be able to go to bed and get a good sleep.

Oliver valiantly tried to rally, rubbing his eyes, but he was still drowsy.

"Let me carry him," Agent Hibbings offered and picked Oliver up.

When they reached the end of the walkway from the plane, Catherine saw a man who looked vaguely familiar waiting. He took out an ID plaque and showed it to her escorts who had gone ahead, then he turned to her and held out his hand.

"You probably don't remember me, Catherine, Carlton Bannerman of the RCMP. I'm a friend of your mother."

Catherine shook his hand. "Is she here?" she asked.

"Yes, she's waiting in the security lounge. I'll take you to her. Follow me," he said, addressing all of them.

Bannerman led them along a blue-carpeted hallway to an elevator, which required a keycard to open the doors.

They went up one floor and exited into a similar corridor. Bannerman pushed open the door across from the elevator and allowed Catherine to precede him into the room.

She saw a woman holding a baby, sitting on a chair by a big window. Her breath caught in her throat ... It couldn't be. She suddenly felt dizzy. Then the woman stood up and started across the room towards them.

Her mind churned out random almost irrelevant thoughts. My mother. It's really her. She looks so small. A baby. Whose is it? Did she get married again?

"Catherine?" A question, as if the woman wasn't sure who she was.

Hearing her mother's voice, sounding just as she'd remembered it all these years, brought tears to Catherine's eyes. She saw Julia's eyes were glistening too.

Then Julia handed the baby to the RCMP officer. She ran the rest of the way and they embraced each other. Catherine realized she was almost the same height as her mother.

Julia

A few minutes later, the door at the end of the room opened and Carlton came in behind a slender young woman and a little boy, and two other people she hardly noticed. Julia stood up. Her throat tightened and her eyes filled with tears.

"Catherine?"

She hoisted Francesca onto her shoulder and moved slowly towards her other daughter, taking in the changes, trying to reconcile this mature young woman with the little girl she'd lost. She handed the baby to Carlton and ran the rest of the way to take Catherine in her arms.

"Oh, my God, you're really here." She pulled away and held Catherine's face between her palms. "Look at you.

You're all grown up. I can't believe..." Julia hugged Catherine again.

Finally, Catherine pulled away. "Mother," she said shyly, wiping away tears with the back of her hand. She turned to the little boy who was looking on, puzzled. "This is your grandson, Oliver."

Chapter Thirty-seven

On the ride downtown, Julia sat in the back with the baby in her capsule on one side and Oliver strapped in on the other. After a short conference and some paper signing between Bannerman and the two agents, the American team had left to return to Seattle and Bannerman had taken them out of the security entrance to his car. Catherine took the front passenger seat. She was torn between seeing where they were going and swiveling the seat so that she could face her mother, as if letting her out of her sight would cause her to vanish. She settled on holding Julia's hand over her the seat back while watching the view unfold before her.

She was not aware of how the city had changed in the past ten years as she hadn't seen much of it before she had been kidnapped, just the areas around her homes, both of which had been in the same general neighborhood. The skyline hadn't changed; the mountains still stood like majestic sentinels over the city. The lights were going on in the buildings and the setting sun painted the sky every shade of pink and lilac imaginable.

"I can't believe it," Catherine said, turning to look at the sleeping infant. "A baby sister. How old is she?"

"She was born on July 27; that makes her just over three months."

"When I first saw you with the baby, I thought maybe you'd married again."

Bannerman turned his head and looked at her, then refocused on the road ahead.

When they reached the house at False Creek, it seemed both grander than Catherine remembered it, and a bit shabbier. The garden was weedy, but someone had obviously started to clean it up. She got out of the car and went around to the other side where she unfastened Oliver's harness while her mother unbuckled the baby's capsule.

"Let me help you with the baby," Bannerman offered.

Julia handed him the capsule and felt in her pockets.

"Oh, my God," Julia said at the door. "I've forgotten my key."

"Where did you leave it?" Bannerman asked.

"It must be inside," Julia replied. "Try the door."

Catherine pressed the catch and the door opened. She smiled at her mother. "I see you're still losing things."

They all crowded into the entry hall and Julia took the baby capsule from Bannerman.

Bannerman shook Catherine's hand and kissed Julia on the cheek. "I'll leave you to it, then. I'll pick you up in the morning, Catherine, if that's all right with you. We'll need you to come and make a statement about the first abduction." He left, closing the door behind him.

That was the moment Francesca chose to wake up. She yawned and started to cry. Julia took her out of the capsule and held her against her shoulder.

"She's hungry. Could you find something for you and Oliver to eat while I feed her?"

"I'm thirsty," Oliver said in a whiny voice.

"I know, love. Mommy'll get you something to drink."

Julia took the baby upstairs to change and feed her, while Catherine went to explore the kitchen. It wasn't the same as she remembered it, having been renovated and was equipped with even more modern appliances than the ones she recalled. Catherine sighed; she had missed so much.

She gave Oliver a glass of milk and some cheese puffs then she cut up an apple for him. She made herself a tomato-cheese sandwich and poured herself a glass of grapefruit juice. Oliver managed to down half the milk and a couple of cheese puffs before his eyelids began to droop.

Julia came into the kitchen carrying Francesca.

"He's exhausted. Where do you want him to sleep, Mom?"

"You can put him on the divan in the den if you like," Julia replied, "Or he can sleep with you in your old room.

"I think he'd be better off with me. He might be scared if he wakes up alone in another unfamiliar place."

Catherine felt an almost physical shock when she saw her old room. It was exactly as she had left it on her birthday ten years ago, right down to the book and music disks she'd been using at the time. She had dreamed about this room countless times with deep yearning, never believing she would ever see it again.

She carried Oliver to the bed and sat down beside him to remove his clothes. Then she went across to her old clothes cabinet and opened the drawer where she used to keep her underwear. It was all there still, looking much too small. She pulled out an undershirt and eased it over her son's head, then pulled his limp arms through the armholes. He was already asleep, so she pulled back the covers and rolled him over to the side so that she could cover him.

Once Oliver was tucked away for the night, Julia brought the white cradle out of her bedroom and put Francesca in it then she turned to Catherine with glistening eyes and opened her arms. The two women embraced.

"Welcome home, darling. I can hardly believe you're here. I've missed you so much." Julia held her daughter at arm's length and looked at her. "You're tired, aren't you? Do you want to go to bed now?"

"In a little while. Before I go to bed, let's do some catching up. How are Grandma and Grandpa?"

Julia led her to the sofa and sat beside her, holding her hand. "I'm afraid your Grandma passed away a few years ago, just after Paul died." She went on to fill Catherine in on family news until she realized her daughter was falling asleep sitting.

The following morning, Carlton Bannerman came to take Catherine to RCMP headquarters. Two members of the American FBI were present, gathering evidence for their case against the Reverends Webster and Oregon.

"Can I ask something before we start?" Catherine asked in a soft voice.

"Go ahead," Bannerman replied.

"How did you find out where I was?"

"It was the phone call they made to your mother. They slipped up there. As soon as Julia told us about receiving a call from the kidnappers, we got a printout of her phone records. We traced the two calls to a pay phone in eastern Oregon and gave the information to our American counterparts." He nodded towards the two Federal agents. "It could have been a lot more difficult if the phone had been in a more populated area, but as it was, there were very few people living in the area, so there weren't many to investigate.

"So you caught Jake and Ryan?" Catherine felt a twinge of satisfaction.

"That's right. Their whole setup was suspicious, especially the copter. They claimed it was a hunting camp, but there was no hunting equipment, and besides, it wasn't hunting season."

Catherine nodded. "But how did that lead you to Aaron ... I mean Mr. Goldman?"

"Those two were only too happy to give up the others involved in exchange for leniency. That sort always do."

"What'll happen to Mr. Goldman? He wasn't a member of the gang." This was her chief concern.

One of the FBI agents replied, "It depends on several factors. Buying and selling people comes under the anti-slavery act. It's a very serious charge. A lot depends on you."

"How?"

"You are the victim. How he is sentenced depends on your testimony."

Catherine twisted her hands in her lap. "But what if I don't want to testify against him?"

"Is there a reason why you wouldn't?" the agent asked.

She didn't want to answer the question, but felt nervous about refusing. The agents represented authority and she felt intimidated by them. "I think I'd like to talk to a lawyer before answering."

Bannerman looked at her sympathetically. "That's all right, Catherine. We'll get on with your statement now."

During the drive back to Julia's, Catherine asked Bannerman about her husband, Webster.

"What's happening to him? Is he in jail?"

They'd told her about how the authorities had found out about her being in Blessings. She was surprised when she heard it had been the doctor who'd first alerted the authorities. She'd always believed he was deliberately turning a blind eye to the situation in Blessings.

"No," Bannerman replied. "Webster was charged and released to await trial."

Catherine was glad Keaton was not in prison. It would be very hard on Brent to lose his father as well as his mother, not that she had had much influence with her elder son. "Will I have to testify against him?"

"They can't make you, but you will be asked. How do you feel about it?"

Catherine looked out of the car window while she thought about it. They were coming down Oak Street towards the city center. Keaton was responsible for the loss of ten years of her life. She tried to imagine what her life would have been like if she hadn't been kidnapped. She would probably have been married and had some children. She had that now, although she hadn't been happily married. But was there any guarantee that she would have been any happier married to someone else? Look at her mother. She was beautiful and loving, but her marriage had been such a disaster, she'd shied away from the institution altogether. What it boiled down to in the end was the freedom to choose. She might have made wrong choices, but they would have been her choices.

Another thought occurred to her: If she hadn't been married to Keaton, she wouldn't have Oliver, and she couldn't imagine being without her son. Catherine felt a twinge of shame that she didn't feel the same way about her other son, Brent.

She wouldn't have met Aaron, either, although she could hardly credit Keaton with that. And Keaton had been kind to her during the time she'd lived with him. She sighed.

"I'll do it, of course, but it won't be all negative, my testimony."

"That's fine. All you need to do is tell the truth," Bannerman said.

"Do you think he'll go to prison?"

"Yes. He probably will."

"You know one thing that puzzles me." Bannerman nodded. "How did they find me in the first place? They seemed to know all about my mother and me. I mean, I lived so far away from them. Why did they pick me?"

"Those people—fundamentalist religious sects—have networks all over the U.S. and Canada. They look out for suitable targets and advise the network. They usually want to take the target a good distance from her home so that she won't know where she is, and so that nobody recognizes her. Why you? Who knows what goes on in their twisted minds?"

"They told me I was being rescued from a life of sin. They even said Keaton had a dream with an angel telling him about me."

Bannerman sighed. "I guess that's a motive. It sounds very hypocritical, or they do a good job of fooling themselves."

"Is this sort of thing still happening?"

"We are keeping these groups under much closer observation now, so it has died down a bit."

There was a message waiting for her from Joseph Epstein when she returned to Julia's.

Eager for news of Aaron, she called the Seattle lawyer.

"Hello, Catherine. How are you?" the lawyer greeted her.

"Fine," she replied. "Is Aaron all right?"

"He's a bit shaken up, but otherwise, he's fine." Joseph Epstein gave her a piercing look. "The reason I called is to ask if you would be willing to testify on his behalf."

Catherine looked down at her hands while she thought about the request. Would he still want to marry her now? Had they heard anything from Keaton's lawyers about the divorce?

"Do you think I could talk to Aaron?" she asked, looking directly into the camera.

"I don't see why not." He looked down at something on his desk. "I should warn you that the prosecution will ask you to appear as their witness. I understand you've already given them a statement?"

"Yes. What will happen if they do ask me? I mean, will I still be able to testify for Aaron?"

"Indirectly. If you were a prosecution witness, we would have an opportunity to cross-examine you. That would be your chance to speak on his behalf, if you wanted to, of course."

"I see." Although she wasn't sure if she really understood what he was telling her, not being familiar with legal proceedings. "When could I talk to him? Is he still in jail?"

"No, he's been released on bail. You could call him at home, if you like."

"I don't have his number." Something else occurred to her. "He doesn't think I had anything to do with this, does he?"

Epstein shook his head. "No. We've seen the prosecution case and it looks as if the kidnappers tripped themselves up."

***

"Are you sure that's what you want to do?" Julia asked.

Catherine considered her mother's question. There was a certain ambivalence in her feelings about Aaron now. She resented the fact that he had bought her like a slave and kept her confined, although he had begun to take steps that would lead to her having more freedom. And he had said he loved her and wanted them to be married. Then. But that had been as much for his protection as anything. Maybe now that he's been found out, he might change his mind about that. She wasn't sure whether she was really in love with Aaron, or just addicted to the incredible sex. It had been so good, so new to her, she felt reluctant to give it up.

"Yes, if he still wants to marry me. He's really nice, mom, you'd like him."

"He may have changed after what's happened," Julia replied, not realizing she was voicing Catherine's own thoughts. "Did he tell you he loves you?"

"Yes, and the way he acted ... I could tell he really did. That's why I want to talk to him, to find out if anything's changed."

"Sweetheart, I hope it does work out. I just don't want you to be hurt again." Julia put her glass down and stood up. She kissed Catherine on the forehead. "Go ahead. You can use the com in the den."

When she got through to Aaron's number, a man she didn't recognize answered. "Goldman Sound Lab."

"Can I speak to Aaron, please?"

"May I tell him who's calling?"

"Catherine."

His face disappeared from the screen, leaving a view of an empty chair with shelves of equipment behind it, then a hand pulled out the chair and Aaron's face appeared. Her heart lurched. She yearned to touch him.

"Kate. How are you?"

353

"Fine." Now that she was face to face with him, she was tongue-tied.

"Happy to be back in Vancouver?"

"Yes, but..."

"I miss you."

"That's what I was just going to say." She looked in his eyes. "I really miss you."

"Did Epstein call you?"

"Yes. I spoke to him this morning."

"And ...?"

"You mean, will I testify for you? Yes, of course. What's going to happen, Aaron?"

"I expect I'll have to pay a huge fine, but I doubt I'll have to spend time in prison."

"I mean ... with us. Do you still want to marry me?"

A look flashed across his face so fast, she wasn't sure she'd seen it, but she felt a momentary twinge of fear. It might have been irritation. But it was gone and he was smiling at her again. "Of course."

Chapter Thirty-eight

The Girls are Returning!

Yes, it's true! Although scientists have been cautious about announcing the good news, there's no denying the statistics. Last year, the number of female births in Vancouver increased by 1.5%. The worldwide the numbers are less promising, but encouraging nonetheless, with an increase of 1.1%.

"The virus has probably run its course," stated Dr. Gurdwara Singh of the UBC Department of Life Sciences. "It was inevitable that this would happen eventually, given the tendency of viruses to mutate.

Tests show that the X-virus has undergone some
changes that render it less virulent."
Vancouver Globe, September 18, 2084

The letter had traveled by a circuitous route, forwarded on to Catherine via the Grangeville Sheriff's Department, through two different lawyers until it finally reached the desk of Carlton Bannerman at RCMP headquarters. Bannerman brought it over personally and gave it to Catherine.

Catherine tore open the envelope and immediately recognized Keaton's handwriting. In spite of the cramped nature of the letters, the writing was neat and easy to read, although when Catherine read the contents, she wished it hadn't been so easy.

Dear Catherine:

I trust you are well. I felt I should inform you that our son Brent is seriously ill. They tell me he has leukemia. He is in the Grangeville Hospital and the doctors say he may not be with us much longer.

It is in God's hands and I would not presume to question His purpose. I pray continuously for relief of the boy's suffering. My mother is beside herself with grief and has become quite frail since Brent was taken ill.

If you wish to see your son before it is too late, I suggest you contact Grangeville Hospital directly. This is the number to call...

Catherine crumpled the letter in her lap and wiped an angry tear from her eye.

"What's the matter, Mommy?" Oliver asked.

"It's a letter from your father. Brent is not feeling well."

Oliver's eyes lit up. "Can we go and see them?"

Catherine sighed. "I don't know. I'll have to think about it."

She smoothed out the notepaper and read the rest. Not a word about the divorce or his trial. What an infuriating man.

Then she was overcome with grief and remorse. That poor little boy. He was her son, her firstborn, although it seemed as if they had been alienated from each other right from his birth. She recalled his pale little face and bruised eyes, his listlessness and clinging to his grandmother. It seemed the only time he'd been happy was when he was playing with his little brother, Oliver. And now even that had been taken away from him.

Maybe she'd instinctively known he was doomed and had protected herself by not allowing herself to become too close to him. If she had anything to thank Mrs. Webster for, it was the love she'd given to Brent.

Catherine got up and went into her bedroom. She looked out of the window and saw her mother and Carlton Bannerman sitting at a garden table, sipping coffee from ceramic mugs. Her mother leaned forward and touched Bannerman's hand to emphasize what she was saying. He put down his mug and covered her hand with his.

Catherine turned away. She had to think about what she was going to do. She had to go—she had no doubts about that. Her main problem was she had no money. Should she take Oliver? Of course she should. She'd seen the look in his eyes when she'd told him the letter was from his father. It would be cruel to deprive him of the opportunity to see Keaton, and Brent.

The first thing she had to do was call the hospital and confirm the information in Keaton's letter. Maybe he was exaggerating, or they'd made a mistake with the diagnosis. She dialed the hospital number.

"Grangeville Memorial Hospital," said a mechanical voice, which then went on to list a number of options for reaching a real person.

Catherine had no idea who could give her the information she wanted, so she pressed the number for inquiries.

"Good afternoon. How may I help you?" a chirpy male voice answered.

"I'm Brent Webster's mother. I've been away..." Why did she feel the need to make excuses? "I'd like to find out how he is."

"One moment please, I'll find someone to talk to you." The line went dead and irritating, insipid music came on.

The music was replaced by a new voice. "Mrs. Webster? Sorry to keep you waiting. Just for confirmation, can you tell me your son's date of birth?"

Puzzled, Catherine relayed the information.

"Sorry about that, just wanted to be sure. I'm afraid I don't have very good news, Mrs. Webster. In spite of everything we've tried, Brent won't last much longer."

"How long?" Catherine asked, her eyes filling with tears. "I want to come and see him."

"Well I suggest you get here as soon as you can."

***

Catherine entered the small hospital, Oliver clinging to her hand. A security guard greeted her and scanned them both with a detector wand.

"I'm here to visit a patient," Catherine said as she showed him her ID.

"Over there, Ma'am," he replied, nodding towards a booth by the far wall.

She followed the directions to the children's ward given her by the receptionist in the booth. Leaving the elevator at the second floor, the first person she saw was Keaton's mother. The old lady looked much older than the last time Catherine had seen her three months earlier. She was sitting on a chair in the hallway looking shrunken and stoop-shouldered, dabbing her eyes with a tissue clutched in a claw-like hand. She looked up at the sound of their footsteps and rose slowly from the chair.

Her red-rimmed eyes gleamed maliciously. "You're too late."

Catherine gasped and clapped her hand over her mouth. "You mean he's..."

"Yes," Mrs. Webster replied. "A few minutes ago. My son is in there with him, praying."

Ignoring her mother-in-law's malice, Catherine said, "I'd like to see him. Could you watch Oliver while I go in?" She let go of Oliver's hand and nudged him towards his grandmother. "Stay with Granny Webster, Oliver. I won't be long."

"But I want to see Brent," Oliver objected.

"Let me go in first, then I'll come for you. All right?"

Mrs. Webster took Oliver's hand. "Let's go and look at the playroom," she said in a much friendlier voice than she'd used with Catherine.

Surely she can't blame me for this, Catherine thought as she pushed open the door to Brent's room.

Catherine stopped short on the threshold, startled at the sight of Keaton. She had known he was there before entering the room, but she wasn't prepared for the image he presented. He was sitting beside the bed, leaning forward, elbows on knees, hands clasped. His hair—now almost completely grey—fell over his brow, but it did not hide the tears that ran unheeded down his face. Like his mother, he seemed to have shrunk since she had last seen him.

Her glance strayed reluctantly to the figure on the bed—her firstborn son. His eyes were closed and he looked as if he was sleeping. The pallor of his skin had taken on a blue undertone; otherwise, he seemed unchanged. A tremendous feeling of regret and sorrow overcame her, if only she'd paid more attention to him, if only she could have loved him as she loved Oliver. She took the two steps from the door that brought her to the bedside opposite Keaton. Aware of her at last, he looked up, eyes clouded with pain then he rubbed his forearm across his face.

"Catherine," he said in a strangled voice. He looked at the boy on the bed. "I'm afraid you got here too late."

"Yes. I'm sorry, Keaton." Tears welled in her eyes. "When did ... it happen?"

"He passed on about fifteen minutes ago," he replied after consulting his watch. "Will you pray with me, Catherine?"

A wave of pity for Keaton overcame the annoyance she felt at this request. She still did not feel comfortable with overt displays of piety, even though she did not entirely reject the theology behind it. "I've brought Oliver. I told him I'd let him see Brent," she explained. "He's excited about seeing you, as well," she added hastily. "Shall I bring him in now?"

Keaton sat up a little straighter and some of the lines on his face relaxed. He nodded and stood up. "I'll come with you."

Oliver's eyes lit up when he saw his father. "Daddy!" he shouted and ran towards them, smiling. Suddenly, he realized where he was—not in a hospital, he had no experience of such places, but in his father's presence. He slowed to a walk, and the smile disappeared. "Sorry, I forgot," he said, eyes on the floor.

"Son," Keaton said with a catch in his voice. "It's all right. Come here."

He crouched in front of Oliver who came forward cautiously. "Son," Keaton repeated. He took Oliver in his arms and stood up, clasping him to his chest. His eyes glittered with unshed tears.

Mrs. Webster looked at her son and grandson, an expression on her face that was neither censorious nor affectionate, but held a touch of sadness and a touch of satisfaction. Then she turned and gave Catherine a triumphant look.

What's going on? Catherine wondered. Is she planning something? But Catherine was stronger and more determined now that she had her freedom. No one was going to take that away from her, nor was she going to lose Oliver.

Oliver pulled away from his father and said, "Can I see Brent now?"

***

Catherine went to Blessings for Brent's funeral, but she chose to stay with Joanne and Noah, rather than at the Websters'. Blessings had no hotel. She had brought some books for Joanne in her luggage and gave them to her the first time they were alone.

She had several unprofitable discussions with Keaton about the divorce and his coming trial. If he had shown any trace of contrition for what he had done to her, she might have felt some sympathy for him, but all she felt was pity for a broken man who had lost everything, even the respect of his community. When he asked if Oliver could stay with him, she refused, but told him their lawyers might work something out so that Oliver could visit. It would not be fair to deprive the boy of access to the father he obviously loved.

On the evening before they left, Catherine and Oliver had dinner with Keaton and his mother. Martha and her husband Ben were there also.

"How's Christian?" Catherine asked after the greetings were over. Christian had become a missionary and had been married three years to a girl he'd met while he was attending theology college.

Ben Carstairs scowled at her, but Martha replied, "He's in Central America, doing mission work. He'll be home for a visit at Christmas."

"Any children yet?"

"Not yet," Martha said, shaking her head. "We're praying for them."

Why, was there some problem? she wondered. "Give him my regards," Catherine said, ignoring a dirty look from Mrs. Webster.

Mrs. Webster had been far more restrained and less malicious on this visit than on previous occasions. Maybe she was losing her strength. But the old woman couldn't resist a dig when Catherine spoke about her mother.

"Is she still whoring?"

"Mother!" Keaton said sharply. "Let him who is without sin cast the first stone," he quoted

Mrs. Keaton bowed her head. Catherine could swear she was blushing.

"Are you going to marry this man?" Keaton asked.

"I don't know," Catherine replied. "I'm still trying to decide."

"Why would you want marry someone who had bought you like a slave?" Martha asked.

"We were lucky he did," Catherine replied. "He was good to us, gave us a home and everything. It could have been much worse." What was the use? They would never understand how she had felt with Aaron even if she could have explained. "And he was going to let me see my mother again, if those ... the kidnappers hadn't been caught."

"Why did you have to report Keaton if you were so happy?" Mrs. Webster asked spitefully.

Catherine looked surprised. "I didn't. It was someone here in Idaho who turned you in." She did not want to put the blame on the doctor; he'd done her a big favor by reporting her presence in Blessings.

"I don't suppose there's anything I could say that would make you change your mind and come back," Keaton said as he walked her back to the Fergusons' after dinner. He cleared his throat and gave a little cough, then continued, "I have grown very fond of you, Catherine," which was as close as he could come, she supposed, to telling her he loved her.

"I'm sorry, Keaton. We just didn't get off to a very good start, the way I was brought here. I can't forget all those lost years, but I think we got along pretty well in the end. You were kind to me and I appreciate that, but I can't live here." She turned and gave him a brief hug, then continued walking. She didn't want to bring her son into the discussion—that would be like rubbing salt in Keaton's wounds—although without Keaton, there would be no Oliver.

"I wanted to thank your mother for taking such good care of Brent, but she didn't give me an opportunity." Catherine thought for a moment then added, "Will you tell her I'm grateful? I know she really cared for him."

Chapter Thirty-nine

Have you thought about what you're going to do now?"
Julia asked when Catherine returned from Idaho.

"I think of nothing else," Catherine replied. "I don't seem to have much choice, do I? I'm not trained for anything apart from being a wife and mother. Oh, I'm a pretty good gardener, but I don't see how I could make a living doing that. The only thing I can think of is to marry Aaron, if he still wants to."

"Do you want to marry him?"

"It would be wonderful, for me *and* Oliver."

"But ...?"

"I'm not sure. I feel everything is tainted by..." she hesitated.

"You mean the way you met?"

"I guess so. I don't know.... It might come up in the future if we have a disagreement or something. It'll always be there like a shadow. I'm not sure his family would respect me because of what's happened. Do you know what I mean?"

"It wasn't your fault. You were the victim. Surely they can't blame you. Were there any signs...?

"No. Except one of his cousins tried to ... he came over when Aaron was away. He was drunk. It felt as if they owned me and could do anything they wanted with me. They chose to be kind and make me welcome, gave us a lovely home to live in and anything we wanted, but ... the feeling was always there, underneath."

"Were you happy with Aaron? Do you love him?"

"Yes, but I'm not sure if he loves me." She was recalling the odd expression that had come and gone in his eyes the last time she'd spoken to him.

"Well I suggest you just relax until the trial's over. It will give you time to think about everything. And there's nothing wrong with being a gardener. Maybe you and Grandpa could go into a partnership. And we should see about getting Oliver into school."

Talking it over with her mother had clarified a few things for Catherine. She wandered out into the garden and started to break off some dead flowers. She yearned for Aaron, but still wondered if he wanted her, if they could overcome the circumstances of their introduction and make a life together. Maybe if they could live somewhere away from his family.... She dumped the deadheads into a trash barrel and stood gazing at the mountains across the water. It was so beautiful here in this peaceful enclave.

Catherine realized this was the first time in her life she had been a free adult, able to make her own choices and decisions. It gave her a heady feeling, but it was also confusing with so many possibilities and opportunities, some of which she hadn't even thought of yet.

END